# MICHAEL BISHOP

In 1973, the novella "Death and Designation Among the Asadi," a haunting evocation of the *alienness* that is central to the best science fiction, was a Nebula Award finalist.

Now Michael Bishop has expanded his story, amplified the *alienness*, and crafted the whole into a powerful, compelling novel of humankind confronting its own origins on the frontiers of space . . .

# TRANSFIGURATIONS

A SCIENCE FICTION BOOK CLUB SELECTION

# TRANSFIGURATIONS

## MICHAEL BISHOP

BERKLEY BOOKS, NEW YORK

A portion of this book, under the title "Death and Designation Among the Asadi" copyright 1973 by UPD Publishing Corporation, originally appeared in *Worlds of If*.

TRANSFIGURATIONS

A Berkley Book / published by arrangement with the author

PRINTING HISTORY
Berkley–Putnam edition / October 1979
Berkley edition / December 1980

ISBN: 0–425–04696–6

A BERKLEY BOOK® TM 757,375

PRINTED IN THE UNITED STATES OF AMERICA

*For Ian Watson*

# CONTENTS

# PROLOGUE

Well over six years ago Egan Chaney disappeared into the mute and steamy depths of the Calyptran Wilderness on the planet BoskVeld. "Don't come after me," he wrote before leaving us, "I won't let you bring me back." Nevertheless, despite what many people persisted in believing in the interval between his disappearance and my recent return to Earth, we made repeated attempts to rescue Chaney from the Wild and to discover what had happened to him.

None of those attempts was successful, and the last such endeavor before Elegy Cather's arrival took place only about a year ago: a privately financed expedition led by the Bhutanese explorer Geoffrey Sankosh, who once made a solitary descent into the major caldera of Nix Olympica on Mars. Sankosh managed to shoot a stunning holographic film of an Asadi female giving birth to twin infants in her arboreal nest, but he found no trace of either Chaney or the huge winged pagoda that Chaney had described so meticulously in his journals and in-the-field tapes.

*

On the night before young Cather was due to take the shuttle bringing her out of probeship orbit to the surface of Bosk-Veld, I took a long walk around the perimeters of Frasierville. As I walked, I carried on a one-sided conversation with Chaney's ghost.

*Egan*, I thought, *you must be dead.*

1

I had supposed as much six years ago—only weeks after he had left us—but I had always believed that one day we would stumble upon his glowing bones and so establish my supposition as fact. No such luck. Chaney continued to elude us, and there were nights when nearly inaudible trillings from the jungle reminded me of his rueful and laconic laughter.

*Are you still out there?* I asked his ghost.

The base camp from which Chaney and the rest of us had worked we now called Frasierville, and plasma lamps on tall vanadium-steel poles made an eerie presidio of what had once been a jumble of quonset huts and storage sheds on the boundary between the rain forest and the twilight desolation of the veldts. The infirmary in which Chaney recuperated after Eisen and I answered the summons of his flares had become a hospital, albeit a rather small one. Wood-frame dwellings had taken the place of our prefabricated dormitories, and a dozen of our most senior scientific personnel had imported their families to share with them the backbreaking joys and the poignant midnight nostalgias of the pioneer. I was an exception because I had had no family to import, and I lived alone in one of the dilapidated quonsets from base-camp days.

As I was walking that evening, I heard a baby cry.

*Think of that, Egan,* I addressed my old friend's ghost: *BoskVeld remains a mystery to us, but we are actually bringing children here. An overeager colonial authority has approved the immigration of five thousand families during the coming fiscal year, and a policy of computer-directed homesteading will soon determine the fate of the grasslands, steppes, and savannahs that give this planet half its name. Such changes in only six years! A baby!*

*Are you happy you're safely dead, Egan?*

Chaney would never know the ambivalent pleasure of tasting a breakfast cereal made from a grain hybridized for BoskVeld's soil and climate. The human palate might suffer, but our human pride told us that the accomplishment was sweet. *Whilais.* That's what our agrogeneticists called that grain, and already I could envision children running through fields of its delicate reedlike stalks and devouring breadsticks baked from its coarse pinkish meal.

I couldn't escape the topic of children. This was probably because the following morning Egan Chaney's daughter would set foot on BoskVeld for the first time in her life and it seemed imperative to me that I anticipate and prepare for her arrival. Seven years ago I had had no idea that Chaney had once had a family, had presumed him a bachelor like myself. Tomorrow morning, though, I would come face to face with a young woman whose existence shamed his failure to acknowledge her and whose purpose was to succeed where Chaney's most stalwart colleagues, not to mention the famous Geoffrey Sankosh, had met only frustration and defeat.

That night, then, I sought amid the lacework of stars that so reminded Chaney of "flaming cobwebs" the orbiting star of his daughter's probeship. I think I saw it. It was hard to be certain.

In any case, there came together briefly in a glittering arc of sky Balthasar, Caspar, and Melchior, the trio of moons whose winelike bouquets of light had intoxicated him so cruelly during his field work among the Asadi. In memory of Chaney I tried to feel drunk with homesickness for Earth. But all I managed to feel was a nagging anticipation of the dawn.

\*

Six years ago I compiled from Egan Chaney's notes, letters, and random recordings an unorthodox monograph about the hominoid Asadi.

Over a period of weeks, as the priority scheduling of light-probe transmissions from our base-camp radio room allowed, I sent the manuscript home piecemeal. Eventually the fragments were gathered, proofread, and published by The Press of the National University of Kenya in Nairobi, the same institution from which I had taken my graduate degrees in paleoanthropology and extraterrestrial ecological theory. The monograph was released as *Death and Designation Among the Asadi*, and it went through nine printings in a year's time, focusing an inordinate degree of public attention on the work of the Third Denebolan Expedition here on Bosk-Veld and incidentally apprising me of the fact that Chaney had once had a domestic relationship with a woman who was still alive. Thenceforward, royalties from the monograph were divided between the National University's research foundation and the surviving members of Chaney's unacknowledged but contractually lawful family. This arrangement persists.

Because our monograph has since appeared in nearly a hundred additional printings in sixteen languages, few people on Earth and the Glaktik Komm colony worlds have not heard of BoskVeld and the Asadi. Moreover, although the monograph deals exclusively with Chaney's field work in the rain forests, it has given the entire planet—officially, GK-World Leo/ Denebola IV—an aura of romance.

Colonists arrived on BoskVeld with the name of the Asadi on their lips, even though their first priority after planetfall was to homestead the veldts. They came into Frasierville from the Egan Chaney Shuttle Field (for so we had eventually named it), spent a week or so listening to orientation lectures and outfitting themselves for the hard times ahead, and then departed in helicraft or veldt-rover caravans for the territories preassigned them by Colonial Administration. Only a few of these venturesome people took time out from their in-doctrination for a look-see into the rain forests, and those who did stuck close to beaten paths, tempting the sirens of romance no further than seemed politic. They knew that the real business of their lives lay elsewhere, even if the legend of Egan Chaney and the mystery of the Asadi had played no small part in enticing them to BoskVeld.

The trouble, of course, was that people didn't regard *Death and Designation Among the Asadi* as anything but a clever and compelling fiction.

Stay-at-home experts continued to dismiss the monograph as my own exploitative work of the imagination, meanwhile self-righteously damning me for plundering the private and professional scholarship of a dead colleague for my own wealth and fame. The two accusations seemed to me mutually exclusive: Either I had composed a fiction to which I had put Chaney's name, or else I had unconscionably appropriated Chaney's legitimate field work for my own, but surely not both together. No matter. Most of the academic reviewers of *Death and Designation Among the Asadi* made both charges at once.

In fact, the furor created by Chaney's and my collaborative monograph seemed to substantiate his belief that unswayable pygmies of the intellect abound and prosper. They had been using the ineffectual blowguns of their wits against me for more than five years. Because I didn't return from BoskVeld to face them, many surmised that they had stung me to the heart. What use to Thomas Benedict on the fourth planet of the Denebolan system, they wondered, are the wealth and fame he's filched from Egan Chaney's suffering? And not realizing that I didn't give a damn about either riches or celebrity, they concluded I was afraid to come home and face them.

The truth?

The only thing I was really afraid of was something I also anticipated with high hopefulness: the arrival of Chaney's daughter, a twenty-two-year-old woman who signed her light-probe communications *Elegy Cather*. My apprehension derived from the fact that young Cather put implicit faith in even the most credulity-straining portions of her father's in-the-field tapes and journals.

Even I didn't go that far. I knew that Chaney had *subjectively* experienced everything that appears in our monograph—but having spent so much time in the Wild searching for demonstrable proof, I found it difficult to credit the objective reality of the ornate pagoda at which the Asadi had supposedly concluded their ritual of death and designation. The hard plastic *eyebooks*, or spectrum-displaying cassettes, that Chaney had brought out of the Wild with him were indeed tangible evidence that he had found *something* indicative of advanced technology in there, but not necessarily a towering building that cunningly eluded our discovery. I had to believe that Chaney had erected his imaginary pagoda on the ruins of a genuine structure about which he had read in an early monograph of Oliver Oliphant Frasier's.

Elegy Cather believed otherwise. Nearly eight months before this little history of mine opens, I had checked my box in Frasierville's radio room and found this unexpected communication:

Dear Dr. Benedict,

The residuals from the American edition of my father's book on the Asadi have put me through the Goodall-Fossey College of Primate Ethology here in East Africa. I have done field work with both chimps and baboons in the Gombe Stream Reserve in Tanzania. You must know that I am grateful to you for making this possible. By editing and seeing to the publication of my father's work, you have given me both the financial support and the incentive to obtain my degree as a primate ethologist.

But for my initial fear that I might not succeed here, I

would have written to thank you long ago.

Maybe I am over that hurdle now. The Nyerere Foundation of Dar es Salaam has just provided me with a grant to study the Asadi on BoskVeld. In addition, the colonial authority of Glaktik Komm and Kommthor itself have approved my application for an interstellar visa. I will arrive aboard the probeship *Wasserläufer IX* before the end of the year.

You should know, Dr. Benedict, that it is my intention not only to study the Asadi but to determine without doubt the fate of my father. I also wish to vindicate the reliability of his final in-the-field reports, even those that seem most suspect. In fact, as soon as I had learned of the failure of the Sankosh expedition to find either my father or his notorious pagoda, I put in for my grant.

Although skeptics describe the pagoda as an architectural Yeti or Sasquatch, I believe in its existence and think we can demonstrate its reality to our own and others' satisfaction. (I say "we," Dr. Benedict, because I have hopes of enlisting you in my cause.) All that is necessary is a new approach to the problem, one that Sankosh didn't know to attempt and that even your people in Frasierville have never thought to try. The time remaining to me here in the Reserve I intend to spend preparing for my arrival on BoskVeld.

Heinrich Schliemann took Homer literally and so managed to discover and excavate the ruins of Troy. *The Iliad* was Schliemann's guidebook.

I believe in the literal truth of my father's final tape, which you have published in his ethnography as "Chaney's Monologue." I also proclaim the accuracy of all his previous field work and reportage. Why shouldn't I? Schliemann wasn't related by blood to Homer, as I am to Egan Chaney, and yet Schliemann's faith in the historicity of an ancient poem led him to great discoveries. I would be a traitor to my heritage if I didn't invest my father's words with at least as much authority as Schliemann found in Homer's *Iliad*.

I'm looking forward to meeting you.

Cordially yours,
Elegy Cather

\*      \*      \*

After this first communication, Elegy Cather relayed to me via light-probe transmission four or five additional messages, none of which went very far toward explaining how she hoped to succeed where dedicated, intelligent, and experienced adults had met only tangled jungle and the palpable mockery of their own rank sweat.

That's why I was looking forward to meeting her, too, and that's why I was a little frightened as well. How long would it take Elegy Cather to discover that she was on a fool's errand, thus dashing her youthful hopes along with my grey and haggard ones?

\*

And I? My name is Thomas Douglas Benedict, but call me Ben. I originally went to BoskVeld as the Third Denebolan Expedition's junior paleoxenologist, in the wake of Oliver Oliphant Frasier's discoveries near the Great Calyptran Sea and the disaster of the Second Expedition. For a good while, though, I was merely a general flunky to those with more formidable scientific credentials than mine.

I was in my late thirties. My most marketable skill was not my university training but my ability to pilot that all-purpose variety of Komm-service helicraft known familiarly as the Dragonfly. I had learned to fly them during the closing years of the African Armageddon, which threatened to end humanity's tenure on Earth in approximately the same general area where it may have begun.

At an age when most literate adults are settling into positions of executive responsibility or at least securing the career gains of their youth, I had been languidly finishing up my graduate work in Nairobi. By rights, I ought to have been further along. It's impossible to grab at the hostilities in Africa as an excuse, because I had frittered away a decade of my life before landing in Luanda with a contingent of foreign mercenaries, and immediately after the conflict I took my sweet time "recuperating." When I finally reached Nairobi and used my status as a Pan-African veteran to enroll in school there, I caroused as often as I studied, and only my late acquaintance with a woman older than I who had found several promising protohominid fossil sites in Ethiopia near Lake Shamo returned my interest and my attention to paleoanthropology.

Then I began to do well in school, but not exceptionally well. Just well enough not to be totally ashamed of myself when, my degrees newly in hand, I summoned the courage, or the brassiness, to apply for an auxiliary scientific post with the Third Denebolan Expedition then making ready at Kommthor Headquarters in Dar es Salaam.

Surprisingly, I was selected. I owed my selection, I knew, to my presence on the continent, an overgenerous letter of recommendation from a professor at the National University who had once met Moses Eisen in London, and, finally, the personal intervention of the woman who had turned me around in my studies. She visited Kommthor Headquarters on my behalf and pled my case with one of Captain Eisen's personnel officers. She did this, I somewhat belatedly came to realize, because she loved me and because my devil-may-care indifference to her love demanded not only an admonitory generosity on her part but a real effort to remove me from her life. Two birds with one stone. Off went Thomas Douglas Benedict to BoskVeld.

Once we had established our base camp, I began to hope for a chance to examine and date several specimens of pre-Asadi statuary discovered by Oliver Oliphant Frasier in the ruins of a temple near the Calyptran Sea. But my immediate superior, a woman named Chiyoko Yoshiba, took this duty right out of my hands by virtue of her greater experience. I might have helped her in the appraisal of these artifacts, I suppose, but my attitude, even at thirty-nine, was that of a know-it-all joove; and I alienated Yoshiba with my clumsy self-confidence, my intellectual jokes, and my unauthorized absences from base camp in the Dragonfly belonging to the paleoxenological cadre of which she was the head. Many, many times I went off flying over the veldt country or the jungle simply to get away from people more in control of their lives than I was of mine, usually in the vain hope of purging the loneliness in my soul by getting better acquainted with myself. In retrospect, I can't say that I blame Yoshiba for disliking me. After Chaney's disappearance, though, we patched up our differences and eventually made friends. . . .

Yoshiba soon discovered that every specimen of Asadi artwork or technology dug up from Frasier's ruins defied accurate dating. Techniques employing the carbon-14 method, potassium-argon comparisons, geomagnetic determinations, fission-track readings, and measurements of thermoluminescence all proved equally useless because they gave her contradictory results. It was impossible to find out how long ago the Asadi's ancestors—we'd begun calling them the Ur'sadi to distinguish them from their living but uncommunicative evolutionary spawn—had built their temples or what had brought about their swift and mysterious demise. I was of no help to Yoshiba or the other two paleoxenologists because my own theories about Asadi prehistory were so obviously either cynical or facetious constructs meant to provoke laughter rather than to cast light. Also, I was frequently absent when the others had need of an additional pair of hands or a different perspective. The result was that Yoshiba, in disgust, finally asked Moses Eisen to reassign me, to get me out of her and her colleagues' hair.

Since it was impossible to send me home, Eisen transferred me to the personal bailiwick of Egan Chaney, the cultural-xenology unit. Chaney, interestingly, *was* the cultural-xenology unit. Eisen made me his pilot. I could not have been happier with the transfer.

Chaney was a cultural xenologist trained in Africa before the hostilities there disrupted most scientific endeavors on the continent for better than a decade. Even better, to my parochial way of thinking, he was a man with few friends on BoskVeld and no apparent ties to the home world. We were brethren, I felt. This was a delusion I didn't see through until several months after his disappearance—when I was compiling and annotating the monograph that made Chaney, me, and BoskVeld famous.

Although he kept copious written records and often used a tape recorder to supplement the materials in his journals, Chaney seldom talked just to be talking. I did. Once we began sharing a dormitory section in the Third Expedition's base camp, I spent a lot of time detailing my personal history for him. I told him about growing up during the sixties and early seventies in the Dakota Territories of the Rural American Union. Chaney listened. I told him about the women who had loved or pretended to love me, and whom I had invariably found cause to bid farewell. Chaney listened. I talked about my desire to write a popular account of all three expeditions to BoskVeld, the successes and failures, the hopes and the heartbreaks, the trials and the tribulations, and so on *ad nauseam*, and Chaney merely listened. He listened with such intentness that it was not until he had disappeared that I realized I knew absolutely nothing about him.

The only thing I ever understood in those days was that both of us, Egan Chaney and Thomas Benedict alike, were lost and at sea. That made us brothers, and so what if he held his tongue while I talked?

\*

After my walk around Frasierville on the night before Elegy Cather's arrival, I returned to my quarters and took a small book off my shelf. . . .

# Death
# and Designation
# Among
# the Asadi

Sundry Notes for an Abortive
Ethnography
of the Asadi of BoskVeld,
Fourth Planet of the Denebolan System,
as Compiled from the Journals
(Both Private and Professional),
Official Reports, Private
Correspondence, and Tapes
of
Egan Chaney,
Cultural Xenologist,
by his Friend and Associate,
Thomas Benedict

The Press of the
National University of Kenya, Nairobi

# PART ONE

## PRELIMINARIES:
## REVERIE AND DEPARTURE

*From the private journals of Egan Chaney:* There are no more pygmies. Intellectual pygmies perhaps, but no more of those small, alert, swaybacked black people, of necessarily amenable disposition, who lived in the dead-and-gone Ituri rain forests; a people, by the way, whom I do not wish to sentimentalize (though perhaps I may). Pygmies no longer exist; they have been dead or dying for decades.

But on the evening before the evening when Benedict dropped me into the singing fronds of the Synesthesia Wild* under three bitter moons, they lived again for me. I spent that last evening in base camp rereading Turnbull's *The Forest People*. Dreaming, I lived again with the people of the Ituri. I underwent *nkumbi*, the ordeal of circumcision. I dashed beneath the belly of an elephant and jabbed that monstrous creature's flesh with my spear. Finally, I took part in the festival of the *molimo* with the ancient and clever BaMbuti.

All in all, I suppose, my reading was a sentimental exercise. Turnbull's book had been the first and most vivid eth-

---

*This was Chaney's private and idiosyncratic term for the rain forest the rest of us called either the Calyptran Wilderness or the Wild. *T.B.*

13

nography I had encountered in my undergraduate career; and even on that last night in base camp, on the hostile world of BoskVeld, a planet circling the star Denebola, his book sang in my head like the forbidden lyrics of the pygmies' *molimo*, like the poignant melodies of BoskVeld's moons.

A sentimental exercise.

What good my reading would do me among the inhabitants of the Synesthesia Wild I had no idea. Probably none. But I was going out there; and on the evening before my departure, the day before my submersion, I lost myself in the forests of another time, knowing that for the next several months I would be the waking and wakeful prisoner of the hominoids who were my subjects. We have killed off most of the "primitive" peoples of Earth, but on paradoxical BoskVeld I still had a job.

And when Benedict turned the copter under those three antique-gold moons and flew it back to base camp like a crepitating dragonfly, I knew I had to pursue that job. But the jungle was bleak, and strange, and nightmarishly real; and all I could think was *There are no more pygmies, there are no more pygmies, there are no*

# METHODS: A DIALOGUE

*From the professional notebooks of Egan Chaney:* I was not the first Earthling to go among the Asadi, but I was the first to live with them for an extended period. The first of us to encounter the Asadi was Oliver Oliphant Frasier, the man who gave these hominoids their name—perhaps on analogy with the word *Ashanti*, the name of an African people who still exist, but more likely from the old Arabic word meaning lion, *asad*.

Oliver Oliphant Frasier had reported that the Asadi of BoskVeld had no speech as we understood this concept, but that at one time they had possessed a "written language." He used both these words loosely, I'm sure, and the anomaly of writing without speech was one that I hoped to throw some light on. In addition, Frasier had said that an intrepid ethnographer might hope to gain acceptance among the Asadi by a singularly unorthodox stratagem. I will describe this stratagem by setting down here a conversation I had with my pilot and research assistant, Thomas Benedict. In actual fact, this conversation never took place—but my resorting to dialogue may be helpful at this point. Benedict, no doubt, will forgive me.

BENEDICT: Listen, Chaney, what do you plan on doing after I drop you all by your lonesome into the Wild? You aren't thinking of using the standard anthropological ploy, are you? You know, marching right into the Asadi hamlet and exclaiming, "I am the Great White God of whom your legends foretell"?

CHANEY: Not exactly. As a matter of fact, I'm not going into the Asadi clearing until morning.

BENEDICT: Then why the hell do I have to copter you into the Wild in the middle of the goddamn night?

CHANEY: To humor a lovable eccentric. No, no, Ben. Don't revile me. The matter is fairly simple. Frasier said that the Asadi community clearing is absolutely vacant during the night; not a soul remains there between dusk and sunrise. The community members return to the clearing only when Denebola has grown fat and coppery on the eastern horizon.

BENEDICT: And you want to be dropped at night?

CHANEY: Yes, to give the noise of the Dragonfly a chance to fade and be forgotten, and to afford me the opportunity of walking into the Asadi clearing with the first morning arrivals. Just as if I belonged there.

BENEDICT: Oh, indeed yes. You'll be very inconspicuous, Chaney. You'll be accepted immediately—even though the Asadi are naked, have eyes that look like the murky glass in the bottoms of old bottles, and boast great natural collars of silver or tawny fur. Oh, indeed yes.

CHANEY: No, Ben, not immediately accepted.

BENEDICT: But almost?

CHANEY: Yes, I think so.

BENEDICT: How do you plan on accomplishing this miracle?

CHANEY: Well, Frasier called the stratagem I hope to employ "acceptance through social invisibility." The principle is again a simple one. I must feign the role of an Asadi pariah. This tactic gains me a kind of acceptance because Asadi mores demand that the pariah's presence be totally ignored; he's outcast not in a physical sense, but in a psychological one. Consequently, my presence in the clearing will be a negative one, an admission I'll readily make—but in some ways this negative existence will permit me more latitude of movement and observation than if I were an Asadi in good standing.

BENEDICT: Complicated, Chaney, very complicated. It leaves me with two burning questions. How does one go about achieving pariahhood, and what happens to the anthropologist's crucial role as a gatherer of folk material: songs, cosmologies, ritual incantations? I mean, won't your "invisibility" deprive you of your cherished one-to-one relationships with those Asadi members who might be most informative?

CHANEY: I'll take your last question first. Frasier told us that the Asadi don't communicate through speech. That in itself pretty much limits me to observation. No need to worry about songs or incantations. Their cosmologies I'll have to infer from what I see. As for their methods of interpersonal communication, even should I discover what there are, I may not be physically equipped to use them. The Asadi aren't human, Ben.

BENEDICT: I'm aware. Frequently, listening to you, I begin to think speechlessness might be a genetically desirable condition. All right. Enough. What about attaining to pariahhood?

CHANEY: We still don't know very much about which offenses warrant this extreme punishment. However, we do know how the Asadi distinguish the outcast from the other members of the community.

BENEDICT: How?

CHANEY: They shave the offender's collar of fur. Since all adult Asadi have these manes, regardless of sex, this method of distinguishing the pariah is universal and certain.

BENEDICT: Then you're already a pariah?

CHANEY: I hope so. I just have to remember to shave every day. Frasier believed that his hairlessness—he was nearly bald—was what allowed him to make those few discoveries about the Asadi we now possess. But he arrived among them during a period of strange inactivity and had to content himself with studying the artifacts of an older Asadi culture, the remains of a temple or a pagoda between the jungle and the sea. I've also heard that Frasier didn't really have the kind of patience that's essential for field work.

BENEDICT: Just a minute. Back up a little. Couldn't one of the Asadi be shorn of his mane accidentally? He'd be an outcast through no fault of his own, wouldn't he? An artificial pariah?

CHANEY: It's not very likely. Frasier reported that the Asadi have no natural enemies; that, in fact, the Synesthesia Wild seems to be almost completely devoid of any life beyond the Asadi themselves, discounting plants and insects and various microscopic forms. In any case, the loss of one's collar through whatever means is considered grounds for punishment. That's the only offense that Frasier pretty well confirmed. What the others are, as I said, we don't really know.

BENEDICT: If the jungles are devoid of living prey, what do the poor Asadi live on?

CHANEY: We don't really know that, either.

BENEDICT: Well, listen, Chaney, what do *you* plan to live on? I mean, even Malinowski condescended to eat now and again.

CHANEY: That's where you come in, Ben. I'm going to carry in sufficient rations to see me through a week. But each week for several months you'll have to make a food-and-supply drop in the place you first set me down. I've already picked the spot. I know its distance and direction from the Asadi clearing. It'll be expensive, but the people in base camp—Eisen, in particular—have agreed that my work is necessary. You won't be forced to defend the drops.

BENEDICT: But why so often? Why once a week?

CHANEY: That's Eisen's idea, not mine. Since I told him I was going to refuse any sort of contact at all during my stay with the Asadi—any contact with you people, that is—he decided the weekly drop would be the best way to make certain, occasionally, I'm still alive.

BENEDICT: A weapon, Chaney?

CHANEY: No, no weapons. Besides food, I'll take in nothing but my notebooks, a recorder, some reading material, a medical kit, and maybe a little something to get me over the inevitable periods of depression.

BENEDICT: A radio? In case you need immediate help?

CHANEY: No. I may get ill once or twice, but I'll always have the flares if things get really bad. Placenol, lorqual, and bourbon, too. But I insist on complete separation from any of the affairs of base camp until my stay among the Asadi is over.

BENEDICT: Why are you doing this? I don't mean why did Eisen decide we ought to study the Asadi so minutely. I mean, why are you, Egan Chaney, committing yourself to this ritual sojourn among an alien people? There are one or two others at base camp who might have gone if they'd had the chance.

CHANEY: Because, Ben, *there are no more pygmies*. . . .
—End of simulated dialogue on initial methods.

I suppose that I've made Benedict out to be a much more inquisitive fellow than he really is. All those well-informed questions! In truth, Ben is amazingly voluble about his background and his past without being especially informative. In that, he is a great deal like me, I'm afraid. . . . But when you read the notes for this ethnography, Ben, remember that I let you get in one or two unanswered hits at me. Can the mentor-pupil relationship go deeper than that? Can friendship? As a man whose life's work involves accepting a multitude of perspectives, I believe I've played you fair, Ben.

Forgive me my trespass.


# CONTACT AND ASSIMILATION

*From the private journals of Egan Chaney:* Thinking *There are no more pygmies, there are no more pygmies, there are no* . . . I lay down beneath a tree resembling an outsized rubber plant and I slept. I slept without dreaming, or else I had a grotesque nightmare that, upon waking, I suppressed. A wrist alarm woke me.

The light from Denebola had begun to copper-coat the edges of the leaves in the Synesthesia Wild. Still, dawn had not quite come. The world was silent. I refused to let the Wild distort my senses. I did not wish to cut myself on the crimsons, the yellows, the orchid blues. Nor did I have any desire to taste the first slight treacherous breeze, nor to hear the dawn detonate behind my retinas.

Therefore, I shook myself awake and began walking. Beyond the brutal fact of direction, I paid no attention to my surroundings. The clearing where the Asadi would soon congregate compelled me toward it. That fateful place drew me on. Everything else slipped out of my consciousness: blazing sky, moist earth, singing fronds. Would the Asadi accept me among them as they negatively accept their outcasts? Upon this hope I had founded nearly five months of future activity. Everything, I realized, floundering through the tropical undergrowth, derived from my hope in an *external* sign of pariahhood; not a whit of my master strategy had I based on the genuine *substance* of this condition.

It was too late to reverse either my aims or the direction of my footsteps. You must let the doubt die. You must pattern the sound of your footfalls after the pattern of falling feet—those falling feet converging with you upon the clearing where the foliage parts and the naked Asadi assemble together like a convention of unabashed mutes. And so I patterned the sounds of my footfalls after theirs.

Glimpsed through rents in the fretworkings of leaves, an Asadi's flashing arm.

. Seen as a shadow among other shadows on the dappled ground, the forward-moving image of an Asadi's maned head.

The Wild trembled with morning movement. I was surrounded by unseen and half-seen communicants, all of us converging.

And then the foliage parted and we were together on the open jungle floor, the Asadi clearing, the holy ground perhaps, the unadorned territory of their gregariousness and communion, the focal point of Asadi life. The awesome odor of this life—so much milling life—assailed me.

No matter. I adjusted.

Great grey-fleshed creatures, their heads heavy with violent drapings of fur, milled about me, turned about one another, came back to me, sought some confirmation of my essential *whatness*. I could do nothing but wait. I waited. My temples pulsed. Denebola shot poniards of light through the trees. Hovering, then moving away, averting their murky eyes, the Asadi—individual by individual, I noticed—made their decision and that first indispensable victory was in my grasp: *I was ignored!*

## XENOLOGY: IN-THE-FIELD REPORT

*From the professional tapes of the library of the Third Denebolan Expedition:* I have been here two weeks. Last night I picked up the second of Benedict's food drops. It's fortunate they come on time, arriving on the precise coordinates where Ben first set me down. The Asadi do not eat as we do, and the Synesthesia Wild provides me with foodstuffs neither in the way of edible vegetation nor in that of small game animals. I cannot tolerate the plants. As our biochemists in base camp predicted, most of them induce almost immediate vomiting. Or their furry bitterness dissuades me from swallowing them.

A few may be edible, or a few may have juices pleasing to the palate—Frasier, after all, discovered the tree from which we have distilled the intoxicant called lorqual—but I'm no expert at plant identification. Far from it. As for animals, there simply are none. The jungle is stagnant with writhing fronds. With the heat, the steam, the infrasonic vibrancy of continual photosynthesis. Rainwater I can drink. Thank God for that, even though I boil it before considering it truly potable.

I have reached a few purely speculative conclusions about the Asadi.

With them nothing is certain. Their behavior, though it must necessarily have a deep-seated social/biological function, does not make sense to me. At this stage—I keep telling myself—that's to be expected. But I persist. I ask myself, "If you can't subsist on what BoskVeld gives you, how do the Asadi?" My observations in this area have given me the intellectual nourishment to combat despair. Nothing else on BoskVeld has offered a morsel of consolation. In answer to the question, "What do the Asadi eat?" I can respond quite truthfully, "Everything I do not."

They appear to be herbivorous. In fact, they eat wood. Yes, wood. I have seen them strip bark from the rubber trees, the rainthorn, the alien mangroves, the lattice-sail trees, and ingest it without difficulty or qualm. I have watched them eat pieces of the very hearts of young saplings, wood of what we would consider prohibitive hardness even for creatures equipped to process it internally.

Three days ago I boiled down several pieces of bark, the sort I've seen so many of the young Asadi consume. I boiled it until the pieces were limply pliable. I managed to chew the bark for several minutes and finally to swallow it. Checking my stool nearly a day later, I found that this "meal" had gone right through me. Bark consists of cellulose, after all. Indigestible cellulose. And yet the Asadi eat wood and digest it. How?

Again, I have to speculate. I believe the Asadi digest wood in the same manner as earthly termites; that is, through the aid of bacteria in their intestines, protozoa that break down the cellulose. A symbiosis, Benedict might say, being versed, as he is, in biological and ecological theory . . .

This is later. Tonight I have to talk, even if it's only to a microphone. With the coming of darkness the Asadi have disappeared again into the jungle, and I'm alone.

For the first three nights I was here, I too returned to the Wild when Denebola set. I returned to the place where Benedict had dropped me, curled up beneath the overhanging palm and lattice-sail leaves, slept through the night, and then joined the dawn's inevitable pilgrimage back to this clearing. Now I remain here through the night. I sleep on the clearing's edge, just deep enough into the foliage to find shelter. I go back into the jungle only to retrieve my food drops.

Although the Asadi disapprove of my behavior, because I'm an outcast they can do nothing to discipline me without violating their own injunction against acknowledging a pariah's existence. As they depart each evening, a few of the older Asadi—those with streaks of white in their mangy collars—halt momentarily beside me and breathe with exaggerated heaviness. They don't look at me because that's apparently taboo. But I don't look at them, either. Ignoring them as if *they* were pariahs, I've been able to dispense with those senseless and wearying treks in and out of the clearing that so exhausted me in my first three days here.

To absolve myself of what may seem a lack of thoroughness, I suppose I ought to mention that on my fourth and fifth nights here I attempted to follow two different Asadi specimens into the jungle—in order to determine where they slept, how they slept, and what occupies their waking time when they are away from the clearing. I wasn't successful, however.

When evening comes, the Asadi disperse. This dispersal is complete: No two individuals remain together, not even the young with their parents. Each Asadi—I believe—finds a place of his or her own, one completely removed from that of any other member of the species. This practice runs counter to my experience with almost every other social group I've ever studied—although it's somewhat analogous to the solitary nest building of chimpanzees, as observed frequently in the Gombe Stream Reserve in East Africa. Female chimps, however, *do* sleep with their young. Perhaps, now that I think of it, Asadi females do, too. . . . In any case, I was humiliatingly outdistanced by the objects of my pursuit. Nor can I suppose I'd have any greater success with different specimens, since I purposely chose to follow an aged and decrepit-seeming Asadi on the first evening and a small, scarcely pubescent creature on the second. Both ran with convincing strength, flashed into the trees as if still arboreal by nature, and then flickered from my vision and my grasp. . . .

Two moons are up, burnt-gold and unreal. I'm netted in by shadows and my growing loneliness. Field conditions, to be frank, have seldom been so austere for me, and I've begun to wonder if the Asadi were *ever* intelligent creatures. Maybe I'm studying a variety of Denebolan baboon. Ole Oliver Oliphant Frasier, though, reported that the Asadi once had both a written language and a distinctive system of architecture. He wasn't very forthcoming about how he reached these conclusions—but the Synesthesia Wild, I'm certain, contains many secrets. Later I'll be more venturesome. But for the present I've got to try to understand those Asadi who are alive today. They're the key to their own and the distant Ur'sadi past.

One or two final things before I attempt to sleep.

First, the eyes of the Asadi: These are somewhat as Benedict described them in the imaginary dialogue I composed two weeks ago. That is, like the bottoms of thick-glassed bottles. Except that I've noticed the eye really consists of two parts: a thin transparent covering, which is apparently hard, like plastic, and the complex, membranous organ of sight that this covering protects. It's as if each Asadi is born wearing a built-in pair of safety glasses.

Frasier's impression of their eyes as "murky" is one not wholly supported by continued observation. What he saw as murkiness probably resulted from the fact that the eyes of the Asadi—behind the outer lens or cap—are almost constantly changing colors. Sometimes the speed with which a yellow replaces an indigo, and then a green the yellow, and so on, makes it difficult for a mere human being to see any particular color at all. Maybe this is the explanation for Frasier's perception of their eyes as "murky." I don't know. I'm certain, though, that this chameleonic quality of the Asadi's eyes has social significance.

A second thing: Despite the complete absence of a discernible social order among the Asadi, today I may have witnessed an event of the first importance to my unsuccessful, so far, efforts to chart their group relationships. Maybe. Maybe not. Previously, no real order at all existed. Dispersal at night, congregation in the morning—if you choose to call that order. But nothing else. Random milling about during the day, with no set times for eating, sex, or their habitual bloodless feuds. Random plunges into the jungle at night.

What's a humble Earthling to make of all this? A society held together by institutionalized antisocialness? What happened today leads me irrevocably away from that conclusion.

Maybe.

This afternoon an aged Asadi whom I'd never seen before stumbled into the clearing. His mane was grizzled, his face wizened, his hands shriveled, his grey body bleached to a filthy cream. But so agile was he in the Wild that no one detected his presence until his strangely clumsy entry into the clearing. Then, everyone fled from him. Unconcerned, he sat down in the center of the Asadi gathering place and folded his long, sparsely haired legs. By this time, all his conspecifics were in the jungle staring back at him from the edge of the clearing. Only at sunset had I ever before seen the Asadi desert the clearing *en masse*.

But I haven't yet exhausted the strangeness of this old man's visit. You see, he came *accompanied*.

He came with a small, purplish-black creature perched on his shoulder. It resembled a winged lizard, a bat, and a deformed homunculus all at once. But whereas the old man had great round eyes that changed color extremely slowly, if at all, the creature on his shoulder had not even a pair of empty sockets. It was blind, blind by virtue of its lack of any organs of sight. It sat on the aged Asadi's shoulder and manipulated its tiny hands compulsively, tugging at the old man's mane, then opening and closing them on empty air, then tugging once again at its protector's grizzled collar.

Both the old man and his beastlike/manlike familiar had a furious unreality. They existed at a spiritual as well as a physical distance. I noted that the rest of the Asadi—those who surrounded and ignored me on the edge of the communion ground—behaved not as if they feared these sudden visitors, but rather as if they felt a loathsome kinship with them. This is difficult to express. Bear with me. Maybe another analogy will help. Let me say that the Asadi behaved toward their visitors as a fastidious child might behave toward a parent who has contracted a venereal disease. Love and loathing, shame and respect together.

The episode concluded abruptly when the old man rose from the ground, oblivious to the slow swelling and sedate flapping of his *huri*, and stalked back into the Wild, scattering a number of Asadi in his wake. (*Huri*, by the way, is a portmanteau word for *fury* and *harpy* that I've just coined.)

Then everything went back to normal. The clearing filled again, and the ceaseless and senseless milling about resumed.

God, it's amazing how lonely loneliness can be when the sky contains a pair of jagged, nuggetlike moons and the human being inside you has surrendered to the essence of that which should command only your outward life. That's a mouthful, isn't it? What I mean is that there's a small struggle going on between Egan Chaney, cultural xenologist, and Egan Chaney, the quintessential man. No doubt it's the result more of environmental pressure than of my genetic heritage.

That's a little anthropological allusion, Moses. Don't worry about it. You aren't supposed to understand it.

But enough. Today's atypical occurrence has sharpened my appetite for observation, temporarily calmed my internal struggle. I'm ready to stay here a year, if need be, even though the original plan was only for six months. Dear, dear God, *look* at those moons!

# THE ASADI CLEARING: A CLARIFICATION

*From the professional notebooks of Egan Chaney:* My greatest collegiate failing was an inability to organize. I'm pursued by the specter of that failing even today. Consequently, a digression of sorts.

In looking over these quirkish notes for my formal ethnography, I see I may have given the reader the completely false idea that the Asadi clearing is a small area of ground, say fifteen by fifteen meters. Not so. As best I'm able to determine, there are approximately five hundred Asadi individuals. This figure includes mature adults, the young, and those intermediate between age and youth, although there are no "children" or "infants," surprisingly enough. By most demographic and anthropological estimates, five hundred is optimum tribal size.

Of course, during all my time in the Wild, I've never been completely sure that the same individuals return to the clearing each morning. It may be that some sort of monumental shift takes place in the jungle, one group of Asadi replacing another each day. But I doubt it. The Wild encompasses a finite (though large) area, after all, and I have learned to recognize a few of the more distinctive Asadi by sight. Therefore, five hundred seems about right to me: five hundred grey-fleshed creatures strolling, halting, bending at the waist and glaring at one another, eating, participating in loveless sex, grappling like wrestlers, obeying no time clock but the sun, their activities devoid of any apprehensible sequence or rationale. Such activity requires a little space, though, and their clearing provides it.

The reader may not cheerfully assume that the Asadi communion ground is a five-by-eight mud flat between a Bosk-Veld cypress and a malodorous sump hole. Not at all. Their communion ground has both size and symmetry, and the Asadi maintain it discrete from the encroaching jungle by their unremitting daily activity. I won't quote you dimensions, however, I'll merely say that the clearing has the rectangular shape, the characteristic slope, and the practical roominess of a twentieth-century football or soccer field. This is pure coincidence, I'm sure. Astroturf and lime-rendered hash marks are conspicuously absent.

# A DIALOGUE OF SELF AND SOUL

*From the private correspondence of Egan Chaney:* The title of this exercise is from Yeats, dear Ben. The substance of the dialogue, however, has almost nothing to do with the Old Master's poem of the same name.

I wrote this imaginary exchange in one of my notebooks while waiting out a particularly long night on the edge of the Asadi clearing (just off the imaginary thirty-yard line on the south end of the field, western sideline), and I intend for no one to read it, Ben, but you. Its lack of objectivity and the conclusions drawn by the participants make it unsuitable for any sort of appearance in the formal ethnography I've yet to write.*

But you, Ben, will understand that a scientist is also a human being and may perhaps forgive me. Because I've withheld my self from you in our many one-sided conversations (you dominate them, I realize, because my silence is a spur to others' volubility; they speak to fill the void), here I

---

*Even though we shared a dormitory room for a time, Chaney "mailed" me the letter containing this dialogue. We never discussed his "letter." *T.B.*

mean to show you the mind these silences conceal.

But since you can't tell the players without a program, I herewith provide a program. The numbers on the backs of the players' metaphysical jerseys are Self and Soul.

PROGRAM

Self = The Cultural Xenologist

Soul = The Quintessential Man

Manager(s): Egan Chaney

SELF: This is my eighteenth night in the Synesthesia Wild.

SOUL: I've been here forever. But let that go. What have you learned?

SELF: Most of my observations lead me to state emphatically that the Asadi are not fit subjects for "anthropological" study. They manifest no purposeful social activity. They do not use tools. They have less social organization than did most of the extinct earthly primates and hominids, and not much more than chimpanzees and baboons. Only the visit, three days ago, of the "old man" and his frightening companion indicates even a remote possibility I'm dealing with intelligence. How can I continue?

SOUL: You'll continue out of contempt for the revulsion daily growing in you. Because the Asadi are, in fact, intelligent—just as Oliver Oliphant Frasier said they were.

SELF: But how do I know that, damn it? How do I know what you insist is true is *really* true? Blind acceptance of Frasier's word?

SOUL: There are signs, Chaney. The eyes, for instance. But even if there weren't any signs, you'd admit that the Asadi are as intelligent, in their own way, as you or I. Wouldn't you, Egan?

SELF: I admit it. Their elusive intelligence haunts me.

SOUL: No, now you've misstated the facts—you've twisted things around horribly.

SELF: How? What do you mean?

SOUL: You are not the one who is haunted, Egan Chaney, for you're too rational a creature to be the prey of poltergeist. *I* am the haunted one, the bedeviled one, the one ridden by every insidious spirit of doubt and revulsion.

SELF: Revulsion? You've used that word twice. Why do you insist upon it? What does it mean?

SOUL: That I hate the Asadi. I despise their every culturally significant—or insignificant—act. They curdle my essence with their very alienness. And because they do, you, too, Egan Chaney, hate them—for you're simply the civilized veneer on my primordial responses to the world. You're haunted not by the Asadi, friend, but by me.

SELF: While you, in turn, are haunted by them. Is that it?

SOUL: That's how it is. But although you're aware of my hatred for the Asadi, you pretend that that portion of my hatred which seeps into you is only a kind of professional resentment. You believe you resent the Asadi for destroying your objectivity, your scientific detachment. In truth, this detachment doesn't exist. You feel the same powerful revulsion for their alienness that works in me like a disease, the same abiding and deep-seated hatred. I haunt you.

SELF: With hatred for the Asadi?

SOUL: Yes. I admit it, Egan. Admit that even as a scientist you hate them.

SELF: No. No, damn you, I won't. Because we killed the pygmies, every one of them. How can I say, "I hate the Asadi, I hate the Asadi," when we killed every pygmy?— Even though, my God, I do. . . .

# PART TWO

## DAILY LIFE: IN-THE-FIELD REPORT

*From the professional tapes of the library of the Third Denebolan Expedition:* Once again, it's evening. I've a lean-to now, and it protects me from the rain much better than did the porous roof of the forest. I've been here twenty-two days now. Beneath this mildewed flesh my muscles crawl like the evil snakes BoskVeld doesn't possess. I'm saturated with Denebola's garish light. I'm Gulliver among the Yahoos.

This, however, isn't what you want to hear.

You want facts, my conclusions about the behavior of the Asadi, evidence that we're studying a life form capable of at least elementary reasoning and ratiocination. The Asadi have this ability, I swear it—but only slowly has the evidence for intelligence begun to accumulate.

Okay, base-camp huggers. Let me deliver myself of an in-the-field report as an objective scientist, forgetting the hunches of my mortal self. The rest of this tape will deal with the daily life of the Asadi.

A day in the life of. A typical day in the life of.

Except that I'm going to cap my reporting of mundane occurrences with the account of an extraordinary event that took place just this afternoon. Also, I'm going to compress time to suit my own artistic/scientific purposes.

At dawn the Asadi return to their football fields. For approximately twelve hours they mill about in the clearing doing whatever they care to do. Sexual activity and quirkish staring matches are the only sort of behavior that can in any way be called "social"—unless you believe milling about in a crowd qualifies. Their daylight way of life I call Indifferent Togetherness.

But when the Asadi engage in coitus, their indifference dissolves and gives way to a brutal hostility. Both partners behave as if they desire to kill each other, and frequently this is nearly the result. (Births, in case you're wondering, must take place in the Wild, the female self-exiled and unattended.) As for the staring matches, they're of brief duration and involve fierce gesticulation and mane shaking. The eyes change color with astonishing rapidity, flashing through the entire visible spectrum, and maybe beyond, in a matter of seconds.

I'm now prepared to say these instantaneous changes of eye color are the Asadi equivalent of human speech. Three weeks of observation have finally convinced me that the adversaries in these staring matches control the internal chemical changes that trigger the changes in the succeeding hues of their eyes. In other words, patterns exist. The minds that control these chemical changes cannot be primitive ones. The alterations are willed, and they're infinitely complex.

Ole Oliver Oliphant was right. The Asadi have a "language."

Still, for all the good it does me, they might as well have none. One day's agonizingly like another. And I can't blame my pariahhood, for the only things even a well-adjusted Asadi may participate in are sex and staring. It doesn't pain me overmuch to be outcast from participation in these. To some extent, I'm not much more of a pariah than any of these creatures. We're all, so to speak, outcast from life's feast. . . .

Unlike every other society I've ever read about or seen, the Asadi don't even have any meaningful communal gatherings, any festivals of solidarity, any unique rituals of group consciousness. They don't even have families. The individual is the basic unit of their "society." What they have done, in fact, is to institutionalize the processes of alienation. Their dispersal at dusk simply translates into physical distance the incohesiveness by which they live during the day. How do the Asadi continue to live as a people? For that matter, *why* do they do so?

Enough questions. As I mentioned earlier, something extraordinary took place today. It happened this afternoon, and, I suppose, it's *still* happening. As before, this strange event involves the old man who appeared in the clearing over a week ago. It also involves the huri, his blind reptilian companion.

Until today I'd never seen two Asadi eat together. As an Earthman from a Western background, I find the practice of eating alone a disturbing one. After all, I've been eating alone for over three weeks now, and I long to sit down in the communal mess with Benedict and Eisen, Morrell and Yoshiba, and everyone else at base camp. My training in strange folkways and alien cultural patterns hasn't weaned me away from this longing. As a result, I've watched with interest, and a complete lack of comprehension, the Asadi sitting apart from their fellows and privately feeding—as if, again, they were merely an alien variety of chimpanzee or baboon.

Today this changed. An hour before the fall of dusk, the old man staggered into the clearing under the burden of something damnably heavy. I was aware of the commotion at once. Like last time, every one of the Asadi fled to the edge of the jungle. I observed from my lean-to. My heart, dear Ben, thumped like a toad in a jar. The huri on the old man's shoulder scarcely moved; it appeared bloated and insentient, a rubber doll. During the whole of the old man's visit it remained in this virtually comatose state, upright but unmoving. Meanwhile, the aged Asadi—whom I've begun to regard as some sort of aloof and mysterious chieftain—paused in the center of the clearing, looked about, and then struggled to remove the burden from his back. It was slung over his shoulders by means of two narrow straps.

Straps, Eisen: S-T-R-A-P-S. Made of vines.

Can you understand how I felt? Nor did the nature of the old man's burden cause my wonder to fade. He was lowering to the ground the rich, brownish-red carcass of an animal. The meat glistened with the failing light of Denebola and its own internal vibrancy. The meat had been dressed, Eisen, and the old man was bringing it to the Asadi clearing as an offering to his people.

He set the carcass on the dusty assembly floor and withdrew the straps from the incisions he'd made in the meat. Then, his hands and shoulders bloodstained, he stepped back five or six steps.

Slowly, a few of the adult males began to stalk into the clearing. They approached the old man's offering with diffident steps, like thieves in darkened rooms. Their eyes were furiously changing colors. All but those of the old man himself. I could see him standing away from the meat, and his eyes—like unpainted china saucers—were the color of dull clay. They didn't alter even when several of the Asadi males fell upon the meat and began ripping away beautifully veined hunks. Then more and more of the Asadi males descended upon the carcass, and all about the fringes of the clearing the females and the young made tentative movements to claim their shares. I had to leave my lean-to to see what was going on. Ultimately, I couldn't see anything but bodies and manes and animated discord.

Before most of the Asadi were aware, Denebola set.

Awareness grew, beginning with the females and the young on the edges of the clearing and then burning inward like a grass fire. A few individuals flashed into the Wild. Others followed. Eventually, in a matter of only seconds, even the males contesting for the meat raised their bloody snouts and scented their predicament. In response, they bounded toward the trees, disappearing in innumerable directions, glimmering away like the dying light itself.

And here is the strange part, the truly *strange* part. The old man didn't follow his people back into the Synesthesia Wild. *He's sitting out there in the clearing right now!*

When all of the Asadi had fled, he found the precise spot where he'd placed his offering, hunkered down, lowered his buttocks, crossed his legs, and assumed sole ownership of that sacred piece of stained ground. The moons of BoskVeld throw his shadow in three different directions, and the huri on his shoulder has begun to move a little. This is the first night since I came out here that I haven't been alone, base-camp huggers, and I don't like it. I don't like it at all. . . .

# PERSONAL INVOLVEMENT: THE BACHELOR

*From the private journals of Egan Chaney:* My meeting of the The Bachelor, as I called him almost from the beginning, represented an unprecedented breakthrough. It came on my 29th day in the field—although, actually, I had noticed him for the first time three days prior to his resolute approach and shy touching of my face. As far removed from a threat as a woman's kiss, that touch frightened me more than the first appearance of the old chieftain, more than the nightmare shape of the huri, more even than the chaos of rending and eating that followed the old man's gift of the flame-bright carcass. I'd been alone for weeks. Now, without much preamble, one of the Asadi had chosen to acknowledge my presence by . . . by *touching me!*

I must back up a bit—to the night the Asadi chieftain, against all custom, stayed in the clearing. My first realization that he intended to stay was a moment of minor terror, I'll confess, but the implications of his remaining overrode my fear. Wakeful and attentive, I sat up to study his every movement and to record whatever seemed significant.

The old man didn't move. The huri grew restive as the night progressed, but it didn't leave the old man's shoulder. To be painfully brief, they stayed in the clearing all that night and all the following day, sitting on the stained ground, guarding the spot. Then, when twilight fell on that second day, they departed with all the rest.

I despaired. How many days would I have to suffer through before something else unusual occurred?

Not long, apparently. On my 26th day on the clearing's edge I saw The Bachelor. If I'd ever seen him before, I'd certainly never paid him any real attention, for The Bachelor was a completely unprepossessing specimen whom I judged to be three or four years beyond Asadi adolescence.

Grey-fleshed and gaunt, he had a patchy silver-blue mane of so little length the others must surely consider him a virtual outcast. In fact, in all the time I knew him he never once took part in either coitus or the ritualized staring matches of the full-maned Asadi. When I first felt his eyes upon me, The Bachelor was on my imaginary twenty-yard line looking toward my lean-to from a pocket of his ceaselessly moving brethren. He had chosen me to stare at. That he didn't receive a cuffing for violating the one heretofore inviolable Asadi taboo confirmed for me the negligibility of his tribal status. It was he and I who were brethren, not he and the other Asadi.

In one extremely salient particular The Bachelor didn't resemble the vast majority of Asadi at all: his eyes. These were exactly like the old man's—translucent but empty, enameled but colorless, fired in the oven of his mother's womb but as brittle-seeming as sun-baked clay. Never did The Bachelor's eyes flash through the rainbow spectrum as did the prismatic eyes of his conspecifics. They were always clayey and cold, a shade or two lighter than his flesh.

And it was with these eyes, on my 26th day in the field, that The Bachelor took my measure. The noonday heat held us in a shimmering mirage, our gazes enigmatically locked.

"Don't just stand there making google faces," I shouted, beckoning at him. "Come over here where we can talk."

My voice had little effect on either The Bachelor or the teeming Asadi. Although a movement of the head indicated that he had heard my invitation, The Bachelor regarded me with no more, and no less, interest than before. Of course, he couldn't "talk" with me. My eyes don't have even the limited virtuosity of traffic lights, and since The Bachelor's never changed colors, he couldn't even "talk" with his own kind. He was, for all intents and purposes, a mute.

When I called out to him, though, I believed his dead, grey eyes indicated a complete lack of intelligence. It didn't then occur to me that they might signal a physical handicap, just as dumbness in human beings may be the result of diseased or paralyzed vocal cords. . . .

"Come on over here," I urged him again.

The Bachelor, still staring, didn't approach. He stared at me for the remainder of the afternoon. I tried to occupy myself with note-taking, then with a lunch of some of the rations Benedict had dropped, and finally with cursory observations of other Asadi. Anything to avoid that implacable gaze. It was almost a relief when dusk fell.

But that evening my excitement grew as I realized that something truly monumental had happened: *I had been acknowledged.*

The next day The Bachelor paid me little heed. He wandered forlornly in and out of the slow, aimless files of his aimless kindred, and I was sorely disappointed he didn't demonstrate the same interest in me that he had the day before.

On the 28th day he resumed his shameless staring. I was gratified, too, even though he now pursued a strategy different from that of the previous day: He moved tirelessly about the clearing, weaving in and out of the clusters of Asadi, but always staying close enough to the western side-line to be able to see me. His eyes remained as dead as the insides of two oyster shells. I was fighting stomach cramps and bouts of diarrhea, and by late afternoon his stare had grown annoying again.

I felt better the following morning, my 29th day. The light from glowering Denebola seemed softer, the tropical heat less debilitating. I left my lean-to and went out on the assembly ground.

Bathed in the pastel emptiness of dawn, the Asadi came flying through the lianas and fronds of the Synesthesia Wild to begin another day of Indifferent Togetherness. Soon I was surrounded. Surrounded but ignored. Great ugly heads with silver, or blue, or clay-white, or tawny manes bobbed around me, graceless and unsynchronized.

At last I found The Bachelor.

Undoubtedly, he had had me in his sight all that morning—but, moving with circumspection among his fellows, he had not permitted me to see him. And I had fretted over his apparent absence.

Then Denebola was directly overhead. Our shadows were small dark pools around our feet, like fallen trousers. The Bachelor threaded his way through a dissolving clump of bodies and stopped not five meters from me, atremble with his own daring. I, too, trembled. Would The Bachelor fall upon and devour me as the Asadi males had fallen upon and devoured the old chieftain's gift of meat?

Instead, The Bachelor steeled himself to the task he had set and began his approach. My shadow wrinkled a little under my feet. The grey head, the patchy silver-blue mane, the twin carapaces of his eyes—all moved toward me. Then the long grey arm rose toward my face and the perfectly humanoid hand touched the depression under my bottom lip, touched the most recent of my shaving cuts, touched me without clumsiness or malice.

And I winced.


# A RUNNING CHRONOLOGY: WEEKS PASS

*From the professional notebooks of Egan Chaney:*
*Day 29:* After this unusual one-to-one contact with the Asadi (hereinafter referred to as The Bachelor), I did my best

to find some method of meaningful communication. Words failed. So did signs in the dirt. Hand signals attracted and held his attention, but I have no training in the systematic use of American Sign Language or any of its several variants and so eventually gave this method up, too. I don't really believe it's a likely solution to our communication problems.

Nevertheless, The Bachelor couldn't be dissuaded from following me about. On one occasion, when I left the clearing for lunch, he very nearly followed me into my lean-to. I was almost surprised when at dusk he left with the others, he had been so doggedly faithful all day. Despite this desertion, I'm excited about my work again. Tomorrow seems a hundred years off. . . .

*Day 35:* Nothing. The Bachelor continues to follow me around, never any more than eight or nine paces away. His devotion is such that I can't take a pee without his standing guard at my back. He must think he's found an ally against the indifference of the others, who blithely ignore us. I've begun to weary of his attentions.

*Day 40:* I'm ill again. The medicine Benedict dropped during an earlier bout of diarrhea is almost gone. It's raining. As I write this, lying on my pallet in my lean-to, the odor of the Asadi's morose, grey dampness assaults me like a poison, intensifying my nausea. In and out they go, back and forth. . . .

I have formulated the interesting notion that their entire way of life, in which I've had to struggle to see even one or two significant patterns, is itself the one significant and ongoing ritual of their species. Formerly, I had been looking for several minor rituals to help me explain this people. It may be that *they are the ritual.* As the poet said, "How tell the dancer from the dance?" But having formulated this new and brilliant hypothesis about the Asadi, I'm still left with the question, *What is the significance of the ritual the Asadi themselves are?* An existential query, of course.

The Bachelor sits cross-legged in the dripping, steam-silvered foliage about five meters from my lean-to. His mane clings to his skull and shoulders like so many tufts of matted, cottony mold. Even though he's been dogging my footsteps for eleven days now, I can't get him to enter my shelter. He always sits outside and stares at me from beneath an umbrella of leaves. Even when it's raining. His reluctance to come under a manufactured roof may be significant. If only I could make the same sort of breakthrough with two or three others I've made with The Bachelor.

*Day 50:* After the Asadi fled into the jungle last night, I trudged toward the supply pickup point where Benedict leaves my rations and medicine each week. The doses of Placenol I've been giving myself lately, shooting up the stuff like a junkie, have gotten bigger and bigger—but Eisen, at the outset of this farcical expedition, assured me that P-nol, in any quantity, is absolutely nonaddictive. What amazes me beyond this sufficiently amazing attribute of the drug, though, is the fact that Benedict's been dropping more and more of it each week, providing me with a supply almost exactly in tune with my increasing consumption.

Or do I use more because he drops more?

No, of course not. Everything goes into a computer at base camp. A program they ran weeks ago probably predicted this completely predictable upsurge in my "emotional" dependency on P-nol. At any rate, I'm feeling better; I've begun to function again.

Trudging toward the pickup point, I felt a haunting uneasiness seeping into me from the fluid shadows of the rainthorn trees. I heard noises. The noises persisted all the way to the drop point: faint, unidentifiable, and frightening. I believe, however, that The Bachelor lurked somewhere beyond the wide leaves and trailing vines where those noises originated. Once, in fact, I think I saw his dull eyes reflect a little of the sheen of the evening's first moon. I don't know.

A typed note on the supply bundle: "Look, Dr. Chaney, you don't have to insist on 100% nonassociation with us base campers. You've been gone almost two months. Let us drop you a radio. A little conversation with genuine human beings won't destroy your precious ethnography, sir. You can use it in the evenings. If you want it, send up a flare tomorrow night before Balthazar has risen and I'll copter it out the next day."

The note was signed by Benedict. But of course I don't want a radio. Part of this business is the suffering. I knew that before I came out here. I won't quit until things have begun to make a little sense.

*Day 57 (Predawn):* I haven't been asleep all night. Yesterday, just six or seven hours ago, I went into the jungle to retrieve Benedict's eighth supply drop. Another typed note on the bundle: "Dr. Chaney, Eisen says you're a pigheaded ninny. That you don't even know how to conjugate your own first name. It should have been *Ego*, he says, and not *Egan*. Have you started preaching neo-Pentecostal sermons to the trees? What a picture. Send up a flare if you want anything. Ben."

On the way back to the clearing I heard noises again. The Synesthesia Wild echoed with the plunging greyness of an indistinct form—The Bachelor, spying on me, retreating clumsily before my pursuit. Even with a backpack of new supplies weighing me down, I determined to follow these suspicious tickings of leaf and twig. Although I never overtook my prey, I was able to keep up! It had to be The Bachelor. None of his fellows would have given me so much as a glimpse of the disturbed foliage in the wake of their disappearance. I went deeper and deeper into the Wild, farther away from the supply drop and the assembly ground. Two hours. Three.

At last, panting with the sheer momentum of my pursuit, I broke into an opening among the trees. All at once I realized that the noises drawing me on had ceased. I was alone, and lost, and confused.

Filling the clearing, rising against the sky like an Oriental pagoda, there loomed over me the broad and impervious mass of something *built*. The resonances of Time dwarfed me. Thunderstruck, I felt panic climbing hand over hand up the membranous ladder in my throat. Oliver Oliphant Frasier had studied the *ruins* of one of these structures, learning only that the Asadi may once have had a civilization of some consequence. I was staring at a huge, intact relic of that civilization. Amethyst windows. Stone carvings above the entablature. A dome. A series of successively smaller roofs as the eye went up the face of the structure. At last I turned, plunged back into the jungle, and raced wildly away, my backpack thumping.

Where was I going? Back to the assembly ground, I hoped. Which way to run? I didn't know, but I didn't have to answer this question. Blindly, I moved in the direction of the suspicious tickings of leaf and twig that had resumed shortly after I fled the pagoda. The Bachelor again? I don't know. I saw nothing. But in three hours' time I had regained the safety of my lean-to. . . . Now I'm waiting for the dawn, for the tidal influx of Asadi. I'm exhilarated, and I haven't even touched my new supply of P-nol.

*Day 57 (Evening):* They're gone again. But I've witnessed something important and unsettling. The Bachelor didn't arrive this morning with the others. Could he have injured himself in our midnight chase through the Wild? By noon I was both exhausted and puzzled—exhausted by my search for him and my lack of sleep, puzzled by his apparent defection. I came to my lean-to and lay down. In a little while I was sleeping, though not soundly. Tickings of twig and leaf made my eyelids flicker. I dreamed that a grey shape came and squatted on the edge of the clearing about five meters from where I lay. Like a mute familiar, the shape watched over me. . . .

*Kyur-AAACCCCK!*

Groans and thrashings about. Thrashings and hackings. The underbrush beside my lean-to crackled beneath the invasion of several heavy feet. Bludgeoned out of my dream by these sounds, I sat up and attempted to reorient myself to the world. I saw The Bachelor. I saw three of the larger and more agile males bearing him to the ground and pinioning him there. They appeared to be *cooperating* in the task of subduing him!

Ignoring me with all the contemptuous élan of aristocrats, the three males picked up The Bachelor and bore him to the center of the clearing. I followed this party onto the assembly ground. As they had during the old chieftain's two unexpected visits, the Asadi crowded to the sidelines—but without disappearing into the jungle. They remained on the field, buffeting one another like rabid spectators at a World Cup event. I was the only individual other than the four struggling males in the center of the assembly floor, however, and I looked down at The Bachelor. His eyes came very close to changing colors, from their usual clay-white to a thin, thin yellow. But I couldn't help him, couldn't interfere.

They shaved his mane. A female carrying two flat, beveled stones came out of the crowd on the eastern perimeter of the field. She gave these to the males. With these stones the males scraped away the last sad mangy tufts of The Bachelor's silver-blue collar. Just as they were about to finish, he gave a perfunctory kick that momentarily dislodged one of his tormentors, then acquiesced in his shame and lay on his back staring at the sky. The entire operation took only about ten minutes. The three males sauntered off from their victim, and the satisfied spectators, aware that the barbering was over, filtered back into the clearing with all their former randomness. But now, of course, they ignored The Bachelor with a frigidity they had once reserved for me. I stood in the center of the clearing waiting for him to get to his feet, but for a long time he didn't move. His narrow head, completely shorn, scarred by their barbering stones, looked unnaturally fragile. I leaned down and offered him my hand. A passing Asadi jostled me. Accidentally, I think. The Bachelor rolled to his stomach, rolled again to avoid being stepped on, curled into the fetal position—then unexpectedly sprang out of the dust and dodged through a broken file of his uncaring kin.

Did he wish to attain the edge of the Wild? Intervening bodies blocked my view, but I suppose that The Bachelor disappeared into the trees and kept on running.

What does all this signify? My hypothesis is that the Asadi have punished The Bachelor for leading me last night, whether purposely or inadvertently, to the ancient pagoda in the Synesthesia Wild. His late arrival in the clearing may have been an ingenuous attempt to forestall this punishment. Why else, I ask myself, would the Asadi have moved to make The Bachelor even more of an outcast than he already was?

Patience, dear God, is nine-tenths of cultural xenology. Mystified, I pray for patience.

*Day 61:* The Bachelor has not returned. Knowing that he's now officially a pariah, he chooses to be one on his own terms.

During The Bachelor's absence, I've been thinking about two things: 1) If the Asadi did in fact punish him because he led me to the pagoda, then they fully realize I'm not simply a maneless outcast. They know I'm genetically different, a creature from elsewhere, and they consciously wish me to remain ignorant of their past. 2) I would like to make an expedition to the pagoda. With a little perseverance it shouldn't be exceedingly difficult to find, especially since I plan to go during the day. Unusual things happen so rarely in the Asadi clearing that I can afford to be gone from it a little while. One day's absence should not leave any irreparable gaps in my ethnography. If all goes well, that absence may provide some heady insights into the ritual of Asadi life.

I wish only that The Bachelor would return.

*Day 63:* Since today was the day of Benedict's ninth scheduled drop, I decided to make my expedition into the Wild early this morning. Two birds with one stone, as Ben himself might put it. First, I would search for the lost pagoda. Second, even failing to find it, I would salvage some part of the day by picking up my new supplies. I left before dawn.

The directional instincts of human beings must have died millennia ago: I got lost. The Wild stirred with an inhuman and gothic calm that tattered the thin fabric of my resourcefulness.

Late in the afternoon Benedict's Dragonfly saved me. It made a series of stuttering circles over the roof of the jungle. Once I looked up and saw its undercarriage hanging so close to the treetops that a sprightly monkey might have been able to leap aboard. I followed the noise of the helicopter to our drop point. From there I had no trouble getting back to the clearing. Today, then, marks the first day since I've been in the Wild that I've not seen a single member of the Asadi, and I continue to miss The Bachelor. . . .

*Day 68:* I went looking for the pagoda again. Very foolish, I confess. But the last four days have been informational zeroes, and I had to take some kind of positive action. I got lost again, terrifyingly so. Green creepers coiled about me. The sky disappeared. How, then, did I get home, especially since Benedict's helicopter isn't due for two more days? Once again, the suspicious tickings of leaf and twig: I followed them, simply followed them, confident again that The Bachelor is still out there and steadfast in my decision to make no more expeditions until I have help.

*Day 71:* The Bachelor is back!

*Day 72:* The Bachelor still has very little mane to speak of, and the Asadi treat him as a total outcast. Another thing: The Bachelor, these last two days, has demonstrated a considerable degree of independence in his relations with me. He follows me less often. He no longer hunkers beside my lean-to at all. Does a *made* structure remind him of the pagoda to which he led me and for whose discovery to an outsider he was publicly humiliated? I find this new arrangement a felicitous one, however. A little privacy is good for the soul.

*Day 85:* The note on yesterday's supply bundle: "Send up a flare tomorrow night if you wish to remain in the Wild. Eisen is seriously considering hauling you out of there. Only a flare will save you. My personal suggestion, sir, is that you just sit tight and wait for us. Your good friend and subordinate, Ben." I've just sent up *two* goddamn flares. Day 85 will go down in cultural-xenological history as Egan Chaney's personal Fourth of July.

*Day 98:* I'm holding my own again. I've survived an entire month without venturing away from the assembly ground. Most of my time has been devoted to noting the individual differences among the Asadi. Since their behavior, for the most part, manifests a bewildering uniformity, I've turned to the observation of their physical characteristics. Even in this area, though, most differences are more apparent than real; beyond the principles of sex and the quality of the mane (length, color, thickness, and so on), I've found few useful discriminators. Size has some importance, certainly—but no matter how tall the Asadi, his or her body usually conforms to an ectomorphic configuration.

The ability of the eyes to flash through the spectrum is another discriminator. Of sorts. The only Asadi who don't possess this ability in a complete degree are the old chieftain and The Bachelor.

Still, I can recognize on sight several Asadi other than these prominent two. I've tried to give descriptive names to these recognizable individuals. The smallest adult male in the clearing I call Turnbull because his stature puts me in mind of Colin Turnbull's account of the pygmies of the Ituri and of my own work among that admirable people, now gone and unrecoverable. . . . A nervous fellow with active hands I call Benjy, after Benedict. . . . The old chieftain continues to exert a powerful influence on my thinking. His name I derived by simple analogy: Him I call Eisen Zwei.

The Bachelor now seems intent on retaining his anonymity. His mane has grown very little since the shaving. I would almost swear he plucks it at night, keeping it short on purpose. These last few days, after ascertaining my whereabouts in the morning and then again before sunset, he's completely avoided me. Good. We're both more comfortable.

Today was another drop day. I didn't go out to retrieve my parcels—too weary. But I've sworn off Placenol, and the psychological lift attendant on this minor victory has made my physical weakness bearable. As I've tapered off the "nonaddictive" drug, the amount of P-nol in each drop has correspondingly decreased. To hell with the base-camp computer. I refuse to let the predictability of my victory detract from its beneficial effects on my mental health.

Tonight I'm going to read Odegaard's official report on the Shamblers of Misery. And then I'm going to sleep. Sleep, sleep, sleep.

*Day 106:* Eisen Zwei, the old chieftain, came back today! I first saw him enter this clearing ninety days ago. Has a pattern begun to emerge? I can't interpret its periodicity. I don't even know what sort of life span the Asadi have. . . . But to come back to the issue at hand, Eisen Zwei entered the clearing with the huri on his shoulder, sat down, remained perhaps an hour, then stalked back into the Wild. The Asadi, of course, fled from him—motivated, it seemed, more by loathing than fear . . . . How long will I have to wait until ole E.Z. returns?

*Day 110:* The behavior of the Asadi has undergone a very subtle change, one I can't account for.

For the last two days every member of this insane species has taken great pains to avoid stepping into a rather large area in the center of the clearing. As a result, the Asadi have crowded themselves into two arbitrary groups at opposite ends of the field. These "teams"—if I may only half facetiously call them that—do not comport themselves in exactly the same way as did the formerly continuous group. Individuals on both sides of the silently agreed-upon no-man's land exude an air of heightened nervousness. They sway. They clutch their arms across their chests. They suffer near epileptic paroxysms as they weave in and out, in and out, among their fellows. I sometimes believe they writhe to the music of an eerie flute played deep in the recesses of the jungle.

Sometimes staring matches take place between individuals

on opposite sides of the imaginary chasm. But neither participant puts a foot inside the crucial ring of separation, which is about thirty meters long and almost the entire width of the clearing. Not quite, mind you—because there's a very narrow strip of ground on each sideline through which the two "teams" may exchange members, one member at a time. These exchanges occur infrequently, with a lone Asadi darting nervously out of his own group, down one of these unmarked causeways, and into the "enemy" camp. Do they avoid the center of the clearing because that is where Eisen Zwei once made his bloody offering of flesh? I really don't know.

The Bachelor has reacted to all this by climbing into the branches of a thick-boled tree not ten meters from my lean-to. From dawn to sunset he sits high above his inscrutable people, watching, sleeping, maybe even attempting to assess the general mood. Occasionally he looks in my direction to see what I make of these new developments. But I'm only good for a shrug. . . .

*Day 112:* It continues, this strange bipartite waltz. The dancers have grown even more frantic in their movements. Anxiety pulses in the air like electricity. The Bachelor climbs higher into his tree, wedging himself in place. The nonexistent flute that plays in my head has grown shrill, stingingly shrill, and I cannot guess what the end of this madness must be.

*Day 114:* Events culminated today in a series of bizarre developments that pose me a conundrum of the first order. It began early. Eisen Zwei came into the clearing an hour after the arrival of the Asadi. He bore on his back the carcass of a dressed-out animal. His huri, though upright on his shoulder, looked like the work of an inept taxidermist, awkwardly posed and inanimate. The people in the clearing deserted their two identically restive groups, fleeing to the jungle around the assembly ground.

The Bachelor, half hidden by great lacquered leaves, unsteady in the fragile upper branches, leaned out over the clearing's edge and gazed down with his clay-white eyes. Surrounded now by the curious, loathing-filled Asadi who had crowded into the jungle, I clutched the bole of the tree in which The Bachelor resided, and all of us watched.

Eisen Zwei lowered the burden from his back. But now, instead of stepping away and permitting a few of the braver males to advance, he took the huri from his shoulder and set it upon the bleeding lump of meat. The huri's blind head did not move, but even from where I stood I could see its tiny fingers rippling with slow but well-orchestrated malice. Then this hypnotic rippling ceased, and the huri sat there looking bloated and dead, a scabrous plaything.

Without a farewell of any sort, Eisen Zwei turned and stalked back into the Synesthesia Wild. Foliage clattered from the efforts of several Asadi to get out of his way. No one else moved.

Denebola, fat and mocking, crossed a small arc of sky and made haloes dance in a hundred inaccessible grottos of the Wild. An hour had passed, and Eisen Zwei returned! He had simply left the huri to guard his first offering. Yes, first. For the old chieftain had come back with still another carcass slung across his bony shoulders. He set it down beside the first. The huri animated itself just long enough to shift its weight and straddle the two contiguous pieces of meat. Then the old Asadi departed again.

An hour later he returned with a third piece of meat—but this time he entered the clearing from the west, about twenty meters up from my lean-to. I realized that he had first entered from the east, then from the south. *A pattern is developing*, I told myself. *Now he'll depart once more and reenter from the north.* Many peoples on Earth ascribe mystical characteristics to the four points of the compass, and I was excited by the possibility of drawing a meaningful analogy.

But Eisen Zwei remained on the assembly floor, shattering my hopes. (In fact, as on my 22nd night in the Wild, he still has not left. Under the copper-green glow of Melchior the old chieftain and his huri squat on the blood-dampened ground waiting for the dawn's first spiderwebbings of light.) Instead, he made one complete circuit around the clearing, walking counterclockwise from his point of entrance. The huri did not move.

This done, Eisen Zwei rejoined his familiar at midfield.

Here, the second stage of this new and puzzling ritual commenced. Without unloosening the third carcass from his back, E.Z. bent and picked up the huri and put it on his shoulder. Kneeling, he tied straps through the two pieces of meat over which the huri had kept watch. Next, he began to drag these marbled chunks of brown and red through the dirt. He dragged the first into the southern half of the clearing, unslipped the strap by which he had pulled it, and set the huri down once more as his guardian. This procedure he duplicated in the northern half of the clearing, except that here he necessarily stood guard over the second offering himself. The final carcass he still bore on his back.

Eisen Zwei stepped away from the second offering. Deep in his throat he made a noise that sounded like a human being trying to fight down a sob. This noise, I suppose I should add, is the first and so far the only example of *voiced* communication, discounting vague growls and involuntary moans, I've heard among the Asadi. The huri responded to Eisen Zwei's plaintive "sobs"—undoubtedly a signal—by hopping off the object of its guardianship and then scrabbling miserably through the dust toward the old man, its rubbery wings dipping and twisting. (I've almost decided the huri is incapable of flight. Perhaps its wings represent an anatomical holdover from an earlier stage of its evolution.) When both E.Z. and his wretched huri had reached their sacred patch of ground at midfield, the old man picked up the beast and let it close its tiny hands over his discolored mane.

Then the wizened old chieftain extended his arms, tilted his head back, and, staring directly at the sun, made a shuddering inhalation of such piteous depth it seemed either his lungs would burst or his heart break. The clearing echoed with his sob.

At once, the Asadi poured out of their hiding places onto the assembly ground—not simply the adult males, but individuals of every sex and age. Even now, however, in the midst of this lunging riot, the population of the clearing divided into two groups, each one scrimmaging furiously, intramurally, in its own cramped plot of earth. Manes tossed, and eyes pinwheeled with inarticulate color. The hunger of the Asadi made low sad music over the Wild, like summer thunder.

Slashing at and sometimes half maiming one another, the Asadi quickly devoured the two carcasses. *Like piranhas*, I thought.

Then E.Z., inhaling mightily, moaned again, and the confusion ceased. Every lean grey snout turned toward him. The dying went off to die alone, if any were in fact at the point of death. I saw no one depart, but neither did I see anyone lying helplessly injured in the dirt. The Asadi waited. The Bachelor and I waited.

The third and final act of today's baroque ritual: Eisen Zwei lowered the last carcass from his back, sat down beside it, and, in full view of his bemused tribespeople, ate the monstrous thing piece by piece. He gave the huri nothing, and the huri, inert but clinging, did not protest this selfish oversight. Meanwhile, terribly slowly, Eisen Zwei ate.

Eventually I retired to the shade of my lean-to, emerging at fairly frequent intervals to check the goings-on in the clearing. By the second hour the Asadi had begun to move about within their separate territories. By the third hour these territories had merged, making it impossible to distinguish the two distinct "teams" of previous days. The old pattern of Indifferent Togetherness had reasserted itself, except that now the Asadi moved with incredible sluggishness, suspiciously eyeing their chieftain and refusing to encroach on the unmarked circle containing him.

I noticed that The Bachelor had come down out of his tree, but I was unable to find him in the clearing. All I saw was E.Z., isolated by a revolving barricade of legs, peeling away the last oily strips of meat from his dinner and chewing them with an expression of stupid pensiveness. The huri flapped once or twice, but the old man still did not feed it.

Finally, sunset.

The Asadi fled, but Eisen Zwei—no doubt as surfeited as a python that has just unhinged its lower jaw to admit a fawn—slumped in his place and did not move.

Now a single alien moon dances in the sky, and I'm left with a question whose answer is so stark and self-evident I'm almost afraid to ask it: *From what sort of creature did the old man obtain and dress out his ritual offerings?* Huddled beneath the most insubstantial of roofs, I am unable to fend off the frightening ramifications of the Asadi way of death. . . .

# SPECULATIONS ON CANNIBALISM: AN EXTEMPORANEOUS ESSAY

*From the unedited in-the-field tapes of Egan Chaney:* It's a beautiful day, and if I hold my microphone out—I'm holding it out now, extending it toward the Asadi—all you'll be able to hear is five hundred pairs of feet slogging back and forth through a centimeter of hot dust. There. Hear that? Perhaps you don't. Nevertheless, Eisen, it's a beautiful day.

It's four days since your counterpart, Eisen Zwei, stirred things up with his disorderly three-course banquet. Since then, nothing.

I'm walking. I'm walking among the Asadi. They fail to see me even though I'm just as solid, just as *real*, as they are. Even the ones I've given names to—Campy, Werner, Gus, Oliver, and the others—refuse to grant me the simple fact of my existence. This is hard, Ben. This is difficult to accept. Nonetheless, I continue to feel a paternal tenderness toward these few Asadi—Jane, Thelma, Dianne, Celestine, and the others—I've been able to recognize and name. . . .

I've just walked by Celestine. The configuration of her features gives her a gentle look, like a Quaker woman wearing a parka. Her seeming gentleness leads me to the topic of this commentary: How could a creature of Celestine's mien and disposition actually eat the flesh of one of her own kind? God help me if these aliens are intelligent and self-aware, base-camp huggers, because I'm walking among cannibals!

They encircle me. They ensorcel me. They fill me with a sudden dread, an awe such as the awe of one's parents that consumes the child who has just learned the secrets of conception and birth. Exactly thus, my dread of the Asadi, my awe of their intimate lives. . . .

Turnbull is missing. Do you remember him? I named him Turnbull because he was small, like the pygmies the first Turnbull wrote about, like the pygmies I worked among. . . . Now I can't find Turnbull. Little Turnbull, squat and sly, is nowhere among these indifferent, uncouth people. I'd have found him by now, I know I would. He was my pygmy, my little pygmy, and now these aloof bastards—these Asadi of greater height than Turnbull—have eaten him! Eaten him as though he were an animal! a creature of inferior status! a zero in a chain of zeroes as long as the diameter of time! May God damn them for their impious rapacity!

*[A lengthy pause during which only the shuffling of the Asadi can be heard.]*

I think my shout unsettled some of them. A few of them flinched! But they don't look at me, these cannibals, and I don't know whether to be outraged or gratified. A cannibal may never go too far toward acknowledging the existence of another of his kind, so uncertain is his opinion of himself. A cannibal's always afraid he'll ascribe more importance to himself than he deserves. In doing so, he discovers—in a moment of hideous revelation—where his next meal is coming from. He always knows where it's coming from, and he's therefore nearly always afraid.

Cannibals—the civilized sort—are the most inwardly warring schizophrenics in all of Nature. On the one hand, Eisen, it requires a colossal arrogance to think oneself enough better than another member of one's own species to eat him. On the other, this same act demonstrates the abject self-abasement of the cannibal in his readiness to convert the flesh of his own kind into . . . well, let's be blunt about this, into *shit*. Grandiose haughtiness versus the worst sort of voluntary self-degradation. Have the Asadi incorporated these polar attitudes into the structure of their daily life? Does their indifference to one another result from the individual's esteem for himself? Could it be that the individual's lack of regard for his kind precipitates the practices of pariahhood and public humiliation? A schizophrenic society? Does the pattern of indifferent association during the day and compulsive scattering at night mirror the innate dichotomy of their souls? After all, who's more deluded than the cannibal? His every attempt to achieve union with his kind results in a heightened alienation from himself.

*[Chaney's microphone picks up the incessant shuffling of Asadi feet and the low sighing of a breeze in the rain forest.]*

Yes, yes, I know. This is all very bad anthropology, But I'm not really speaking anthropologically. I'm speaking metaphorically, and maybe I'm not talking about the Asadi at all. I realize full well, gang, that among human populations there are two types of cannibalism: exocannibalism and endocannibalism. I haven't forgotten *all* my training.

Exocannibalism, Ben, usually occurs in a context of continuing warfare between tribes that are dependent to some extent on agriculture for their livelihoods. They war, you see, to protect their sedentary way of life or to expand their holdings into areas where the soil hasn't been depleted by overuse. Enemies eat one another to steal their adversaries' strength and to gain power over them. In such a context, cannibalism is patriotic, and human flesh is invariably kosher.

The Asadi, not being agriculturists, and having no natural

enemies here in the Synesthesia Wild, are not adherents of exocannibalism. Instead, Ben, they practice endocannibalism. Is that clear?

What this means, in short, is that the Asadi regularly eat members of their own tribal unit, the only tribal unit on Bosk-Veld. Usually, this form of cannibalism signifies an attempt on the part of the deceased's relatives and friends to incorporate the dead one's memories and spirit by a ritual ingestion of his flesh. Eating the dead under such circumstances, then, is an act of homage and a visible expression of the community's desire to insure the continuity of its lifestyle and its membership. Christians, by the way, participate in symbolic endocannibalism every time they celebrate Holy Communion. *Eat this—drink this—in remembrance of Me.*

Why, you may wonder, does the endocannibalism of the Asadi so offend and demoralize me? Because, God help me, I've begun regarding them as alien projections of my own consciousness, and, expecting better of myself, I expected better of them. Does that make sense? I'm afraid you'll think it doesn't. But, damn it, just when I'd begun to see glimmerings of something lofty in their makeups, old E.Z.—like some nineteenth-century Indian headman putting on a potlatch—comes dragging three carcasses into the clearing and unleashes the ravenous animal in every one of his goggle-eyed subjects! It's more than I can stand.

The Asadi ignore me. It's hot out here, and they ignore me. They go by, they go by, revolving about me like so many motorized pasteboard cutouts. And Turnbull's not among them, he doesn't revolve anymore, he's been butchered and consumed. *Butchered and consumed*, do you hear? With the same wanton self-centeredness that we used to poison the Ituri and rout out the people who lived there. Turnbull's dead, base-camp huggers, and *There are no more pygmies, there are no more pygmies, there are no*

# PART THREE

## THE RITUAL OF DEATH
## AND DESIGNATION

*From the final draft of the one complete section of Egan Chaney's otherwise unfinished ethnography:*

### DEATH

On Day 120 the old chieftain, whom I called Eisen Zwei, took ill. Because it had been several days since he had gorged himself during the general "feast," I then supposed that his sickness was unrelated to his earlier intemperance. I am still of this mind. For five days he had eaten nothing, although the other Asadi refused to observe his fast and began eating whatever herbs, roots, flowers, bark, and heartwood they came across. They ignored the old man, and the old man's huri, much in the way they ignored The Bachelor and me.

Eisen Zwei's sickness altered this pattern. On the afternoon of the first day of his illness, he abruptly rose and made the horribly glottal, in-sucking noises he had used to summon his people to the meat six days before. I came running from my lean-to. The Asadi moved away from their old chieftain, stopped their shuffling and shambling, and stared with great platterlike eyes whose pinwheeling irises had stalled on a single color. A spastic rumbling replaced the old man's in-sucking noises, and he bent over at the waist, his arms

51

above his head, to heave and heave again—until it seemed he would soon be vomiting into the dust the very lining of his bowels. Out of his mouth came the half-digested crimson oddments of his spectacular, six-day-old meal. Abashed by the sight, stung by the odor, I turned away. The heaving continued, and since the Asadi stared on, I turned back to observe their culture in action. Duty is a harsh mistress.

The chieftain's huri flew up from his shoulder and flapped in the air like a small, wind-collapsed umbrella. I had never seen it fly before, and was surprised that it was capable of flight. Its ungainly flapping excited the already well-aroused population of the clearing, and together we watched the huri rise above tree level, circle back, and dip threateningly toward the branches of the trees on the western perimeter. The old man continued to vomit, but now every pair of color-stalled eyes followed the uncertain aerial progress of the huri, which, at one point, plummeted toward the perch where The Bachelor sometimes sequestered himself.

But The Bachelor wasn't there, and I had no idea where he could be.

Crashing downward through the branches, the huri caught itself up and returned with blind devotion to the airspace over its master. An ugly joke, it sardonically defied gravity.

I thought that at last the huri was going to feed, that its sole diet might well consist of Eisen Zwei's vomitings. I expected the starved creature to fall to earth upon these—but it did not. Somehow it kept itself aloft, flapping, flapping, waiting for the old man to finish.

Finally, it was not the huri that waded into the vile pool of vomit, but the old man's shameless conspecifics. My curiosity overcame my revulsion, and I watched the Asadi carry away their portions of the half-digested mess as if each semisolid piece were an invaluable relic. No fighting, no elbowing, no eye-searing abuse. Each individual simply picked out his relic, took it a short distance into the jungle, and deposited it in some hidden place for temporary safekeeping.

During the solemn recessional, the huri quickened the air with its wing beats and an anonymous Asadi supported Eisen Zwei by clutching—tenderly clutching—his mane. When everyone had taken away a chunk of regurgitated flesh, the chieftain's attendant laid him down in a dry place, and the huri descended to squat by its master's head.

I should mention that The Bachelor was one of those who appeared in the mourning throng to select and depart with some memento of Eisen Zwei's illness. He came last, took only a palm-sized morsel, and retreated to the clearing's edge. Here he climbed into the tree above which the huri had flown its nearly disastrous mission only minutes before. Until sunset The Bachelor remained here, observing and waiting.

On Days 121, 122, and 123, Eisen Zwei continued in his illness, and the Asadi paid him scant attention. They brought him water twice a day and considerately refrained from stepping on him. The huri sat by the old man's head. It seemed to be waiting for him to die. It never ate.

At night the Asadi deserted their dying leader without a glance, and I was afraid he would die while they were gone. Several times, looking out at his inert silhouette, moonlight dripping through the fronds, I thought he *had* died, and a mild panic assailed me. Did I have a responsibility to the corpse?

But the old man did not die, and on Day 124 another change occurred. Eisen Zwei sat up and stared at Denebola as it crossed the sky—but he stared at the angry sun through spread fingers, hands crooked into claws, and he tore impotently through the blur of light that Denebola must have seemed to him. The huri sat smug and blindly knowing, as always. But the Asadi noticed the change in the old man and reacted to it. As if his writhing dissatisfaction with the sun were a clue, they divided into two groups again and formed attentive semicircles to the north and south of Eisen Zwei. They watched him wrestling with the sun's livid corona, tearing at its indistinct streamers of gas with gnarled hands.

At noon the old man rose to his feet, stretched out his arms, sobbed, clawed at the sky, and suddenly sank back to his knees. A pair of Asadi from each group went to his aid. They lifted him from the ground. Others on the clearing's edge selected large, lacquered palm leaves and passed these over the heads of their comrades to the place where the old man had collapsed. The Asadi supporting Eisen Zwei took these leaves, arranged them in the shape of a pallet, and then placed the old man's fragile body on the bed they had made.

The second cooperative endeavor I had witnessed among the Asadi, the first having been the shaving of The Bachelor's mane. It was short-lived, though, for aimless shambling replaced chieftain-watching as the primary activity within the two groups on either side of his pallet. Denebola, finally free of the old man's gaze, fell toward the horizon.

I walked unimpeded through the clearing and bent down over the dying chieftain, careful to avoid the huri that eyed me with its uncanny, eyeless face. I looked down into the genuine eyes of its master.

And experienced a shock, a physical jolt.

The old man's eyes were burnt-out, blackened holes in a hominoid mask. Utterly dead they were, two char-smoked lenses waiting for the old man's body to catch up with their lifelessness.

And then the diffused red light that signaled sunset in the Wild came pouring through the foliage, and the clearing emptied.

Alone with Eisen Zwei and his huri, I knew that it would be during this night that the old man died. I tried to find some intimation of life in his eyes, saw none, and withdrew to the cover of the Wild and the security of my lean-to. I did not sleep. But my worst premonitions betrayed me, and in the morning I looked out to see Eisen Zwei sitting cross-legged on his pallet, the huri once again perched on his shoulder.

And then, filtering through the jungle, the tenuous, copper-colored light signaling sunrise and rejuvenation on BoskVeld. The Asadi returned, once again taking up their positions to the north and the south of their dying chieftain. Day 125 had begun.

I call the events of Day 125, taken as a cumulative whole, the Ritual of Death and Designation. I believe that we will never fully understand the narrowly "political" life of the Asadi until we can interpret, with precision, every aspect of this Ritual.

The color of the eyes of every Asadi in the clearing—only The Bachelor's excepted—declined into a deep and melancholy indigo. And stalled there. Profound indigo and absolute silence. So deeply absorbent were the eyes of the Asadi that Denebola, rising, could throw out scarcely a single dancing, shimmering ray. Or so it seemed. The morning was an impressionist painting rendered in flat pastels and dull primaries. A paradox.

And then the Asadi's heads began to rock from side to side, the chin of each individual inscribing a small figure eight in the air. The heads moved in unison. This went on for an hour or more as the old chieftain sat nodding in the monumental morning stillness.

At last, as if they had inscribed figure eights for the requisite period, the Asadi broke out of their groups and formed several concentric rings around the old man. The members of each ring began to sway. The inaudible flute I had once believed to be in the Wild had now certainly been exchanged for an inaudible bassoon. Ponderously, the Asadi swayed, their great manes undulating with a slow and beautifully orchestrated grief. And The Bachelor—all by himself, beyond the outermost ring—swayed also, swayed in lugubrious cadence with the others. The rhythmic swaying lasted through the remaining hours of the forenoon and on toward the approach of evening.

I retired to my lean-to, but thought better of just sitting there and climbed the tree in which The Bachelor had often perched. I forgot about everything but the weird ceremony in the clearing. I gave myself up completely to the hypnotic movements of the grey, shaggy-headed creatures that a bewildering universe had given me to study. . . .

I nodded but I did not sleep.

Suddenly Eisen Zwei gave a final sob, maniacal and heartrending, and grabbed the beast clinging with evil tenacity to his mane. He grabbed it with both palsied hands. He exerted himself to what seemed his last reserve of strength and, strangling the huri, lurched out of the dust to his feet. The huri flapped, twisted, and freed one wing. The old man squeezed his hands together and attempted to grind the life out of the creature who had imprisoned him even as it did his bidding. He was not successful. The huri used its tiny hands to scour fine crimson wounds in Eisen Zwei's withered cheeks and buckled forehead. Then it flapped out of the old man's grasp and rose to tree level.

I feared it would dive upon me in my borrowed perch, but it skirted the perimeter of the clearing, dipping, banking, silently cawing. Its imaginary screams curdled my blood. Meanwhile, Eisen Zwei fell sideways across his pallet and died.

The Asadi chieftain was dead. He died just at sunset.

I waited for his people to flee into the Wild, to leave his brittle corpse for an Earthman's astonished scrutiny. They did not flee. Even though the lethal twilight was gathering about them, they stayed. The attraction of the old man's death outweighed their fear of exposing themselves in an open place to the mysteries of darkness.

In my arboreal lookout I realized I had witnessed two things I had never before seen among the Asadi: Death and a universal failure to repair.

## DESIGNATION

The Ritual of Death and Designation had passed into its second stage before I truly comprehended that stages existed. I ignored my hunger and put away the thought of sleep.

The Asadi converged upon the old man's corpse. Those of smallest size were permitted to crowd into the center of the clearing and lift the dead chieftain above their heads. The young, the deformed, the weak, and the congenitally slight of stature formed a double column beneath the old man's outstretched body and began moving with him toward the northern end zone.

Arranged in this fashion, they forced a new revelation upon me. These were Asadi whose manes were a similar texture and color: a stringy, detergent-scum brown. They bore the corpse of Eisen Zwei with uncomplaining acquiescence. The larger, sleeker specimens of Asadi—those with luxuriant silver, silver-blue, or golden manes—formed single columns on each side of their lackluster counterparts; and together these two units, like water inside a moving pipe, flowed toward the north—

The one direction that Eisen Zwei had not entered from on the day he brought those three dressed-out carcasses into the clearing.

Driver ants in Africa use just this sort of tubular alignment when they wish to move great distances as a group: the workers inside the column, the warriors without. And nothing on that immense dark continent is more feared than driver ants on the march. With, of course, the singular and note-worthy exception of Humankind.

Almost too late I realized that the Asadi would be out of the clearing and beyond my reach unless I got out of The Bachelor's tree. Nearly falling, I scrambled down. As if viewed through a photographer's filter, the foliage through which the mourners marched gave off a soft gauzy glow. I ran. I found that I could keep up with very little effort, so cadenced and funereal was the step of their procession. I slowed to a walk behind it.

Trudging in the wake of the mourners, incorrigibly hangdog in his pariahhood, was The Bachelor. Meanwhile, the twilight reverberated with the footfalls and leaf nudgings of a host of single-minded communicants.

I saw the huri flying above the part of the procession where its master was being borne forward on the shoulders of the smaller Asadi. Avoiding branches, the huri turned an inadvertent cartwheel in the air, righted itself, and landed on Eisen Zwei's bony chest. Here it did a little preening dance, for all the world like an oil-coated rooster wooing a hen. Then the column snaked to the left, the Wild closed off my view of the marchers, and darkness began drifting in like black confetti.

How long we trudged, I have no idea. An eternity of infinitesimal moments. I won't attempt to estimate. Say only, quite a long time. Finally our procession flowed into another clearing.

There in the clearing, rising against the sky like an Oriental pagoda, loomed the broad and impervious mass of something *built*, something *made*. All three moons were up, and the solid black bulk of this structure was spotlighted in the antique-gold claret shed by the three moons together. Even before those of us at the end of the procession were out of the jungle, we could see the lofty, winglike roofs of this sudden artifact and its high, deep-violet windows. Was I the only one whose first inclination was to plunge back into the nightmare forest? I don't believe so.

As we approached, members of both the inner and the outer columns began to sway from side to side, marching and swaying at once. The Bachelor's head, in fact, moved in wide arcs; his whole marching body trembled as if from the paroxysms of ague. If he had been punished for once leading me to this place, perhaps he trembled now from fear. On the other hand, if the Asadi wished this temple kept inviolate, wouldn't they somehow punish me if they discovered my presence?

I almost bolted back the way the Asadi had led me, but the pagoda had captured my imagination and I resisted the impulse to run. However, I did have the good sense to climb a tree on the edge of the clearing fronting the pagoda. From this vantage I watched the proceedings in relative safety.

Grey shadows moved in the deep shadow cast by the Asadi temple. And suddenly two violently green flames burned in the iron flambeaux on either side of the top step of the immense tier of stone steps leading to the temple's ornate doorway! The torchlighters—formerly the moving grey shadows—came back down the steps. Once again I was stunned with wonder and disbelief. This sophisticated use of both flambeaux and a starting agent I couldn't even guess at destroyed a multitude of my previous conclusions about the Asadi. Fire! They understood fire!

By this time the four columns of Asadi had ranged themselves in parallel files before the stairway of the ancient pagoda, and six slightly built menials bore the corpse of Eisen Zwei—now an uncanny apple green in the torchlight—up the broad stone steps to the stone catafalque before the door. Here they set the corpse down and lined up behind him, staring out over their waiting kinspeople, facing the cruel ambivalence of the Wild, three on each side of the old man. Unaccustomed to such tawdry grandeur, I began to think that Placenol, or something more sinister, was flowing through my veins. Surely this was all hallucination!

The moons cried out with their silent mouths. The flambeaux uttered bright screamings of unsteady light.

But the ritual did not conclude. The night drew on, the moons rolled, and the four files of Asadi tribesmen shuffled in their places. Some stretched out their hands and fought with the tumbling moons just as Eisen Zwei had wrestled with Denebola, the sun. None left the clearing, though I felt that many would have liked to. Wrestling with their own fears, they waited. The pagoda and the corpse of their chieftain commanded them. I, in turn, was commanded by their awesome patience. Wedged like a spike into my tree, I watched as Melchior drifted down the sky toward the jungle. The Bachelor fidgeted, and the two iron torches began to gutter like spent candles.

Dawn delayed.

Two vacuums existed: the vacuum in Nature between the end of night and the beginning of day, and the vacuum in the peculiar hierarchy of the Asadi tribal structure. Night and death. Two vacuums in search of compensatory substance. When would dawn break? How would the Asadi designate their dead chieftain's successor?

A commotion in the clearing! Looking down, I saw that the

four neat files of Asadi had dissolved into a single disorganized mass of milling bodies. A chaos, an anarchy—as on their original assembly ground. How could a vacuum of "leadership" exist in such an arbitrary mélange of unrelated parts? Only the pagoda had solidity, only the pagoda did not move.

Then, looking up, I saw the old man's huri floating high above this disorder, floating rather than flailing: a gyrfalcon rather than a pelican. It rode the prismatic, predawn breezes with uncommon grace, flew off so effortlessly that in a moment it had dwindled to a scrap of light far beyond the temple's central spire.

Then the huri folded its wings behind it and plummeted dizzyingly down the roseate sky. I almost fell. My feet slipped through the fork that had supported me, and I was left dangling, arms above my head, over one edge of the pagoda's front yard. The anxiety-torn communicants were too caught up in their panic to notice me.

Meanwhile, the huri rocketed earthward. It dived into the helpless crowd of Asadi and skimmed along their heads and shoulders with its cruel, serrated wings. Dipping in and out, it flapped, once again, like a torn window shade, all its ephemeral grace turned to crass exhibitionism (I don't know what else to call it) and unwieldy flutterings. But the creature did what it sought to do—it scarred the faces of several of the Asadi. A few tried desperately to capture the huri. Others, more reasonably, ducked out of its way or threw up their arms to ward it off. The huri didn't discriminate. It scarred all those who got in the way of its bladed wings, whether they attempted to catch it or to flee. The eyes of the harassed Asadi flashed through their individual spectral displays, and the heat from so many changes made the clearing phosphorescent with shed energy.

The fact that The Bachelor's eyes remained cool and colorless subtracted very little from the heat of those thousand burning eyes. The Bachelor. I had nearly forgotten him. He stood apart from his panicked comrades and observed, neither grappling for nor fleeing from the huri. His eyes were clay white, mute, devoid of all intellect or passion. As for the huri, it flew up, flew down, performed a wobbly banking movement, and slashed with its murderous pinions at everything. Finally, it shot up through the shadow of the pagoda, wildly flapping, then pitched over and dived upon

The Bachelor. It flew into his face. It bore him to the ground and battered him with countless malicious thrashings.

To the last individual, the Asadi quieted, queued up randomly, and watched this penultimate act in their day-long ritual. It took me a moment to understand. Then I realized:

The Bachelor was the designee, the chosen one, the chieftain elect. Somehow it seemed an inevitable choice.

My arms aching, I dropped from the tree onto the floor of the clearing. In front of me were the narrow backs of twenty or thirty Asadi. I couldn't see The Bachelor at all, though I could still hear the churning of the huri's wings and the altered breathing of the tribespeople.

Suddenly a figure, insanely rampant, disrupted the smooth surface of the crowd and darted through a quickly closing gap of bodies to my right. The Bachelor had regained his feet, was trying to fight the huri off. The two of them thrashed their way up the tier of steps in front of the temple. Soon they were on the paving beside the catafalque where Eisen Zwei still lay. There on that sacred, high place The Bachelor surrendered to the inevitable.

He went down on his knees, lowered his head, and ceased to resist. The huri, sensing its victory, made an air-pummeling circuit over the body of the dead chieftain, sawing devilishly at the faces of the corpsebearers and rippling like dry brown paper. At last it settled on The Bachelor's head. Beating its wings for balance, it faced the onlooking multitude, and me, with blind triumph.

No one breathed. No one acknowledged the dawn as it revealed the caustic verdigris coating the pagoda like an evil frost.

Slowly, painfully slowly, The Bachelor got to his feet. He was draped in his own resignation, in the invisible garb of an isolation even more pronounced than that he had suffered as an outcast. He was the designee, the chosen one, the chieftain elect.

The huri dropped from The Bachelor's head to his shoulder, entwined its tiny fingers in the tufts of his butchered mane. Once again inanimate and scabrous, there it clung.

Now the Ritual of Death and Designation was nearly over. Two of the six corpsebearers on the temple's highest tier moved to complete that ritual. They touched the head and feet of Eisen Zwei with the tips of the two great flambeaux, and instantly the old man's body raged with green fire and the raging flame leaped up the face of the temple as if to abet the verdigris in its more patient efforts to eat the building away.

The Bachelor stood almost in the very blast of this configuration. I feared that he, too, would be consumed. But he was not. Nor was the huri. The fire died, Eisen Zwei had utterly disappeared, and the corpsebearers came back down the steps and joined the shaggy anonymity of their revitalized people.

The Ritual of Death and Designation had ended.

For the purposes of this ethnography I will minimize the significance of what then occurred and report it as briefly as I am able.

Several of the Asadi turned and saw me in the pagoda's clearing. They actually *looked* at me. After having been ignored for over four months, I didn't know how to react to the signal honor of abrupt visibleness. Out of monumental surprise, I returned their stares. They began advancing upon me, hostility evident in the rapid blurring of colors that took place in their eyes. Behind me, the Synesthesia Wild. I turned to escape into it. Another small group of Asadi had insinuated themselves into the path of my intended escape, blocking my way.

Among this group I recognized the individual whom I had given the name Benjy. Cognizant of nothing but a vague paternal feeling toward him, I sought to offer him my hand. His own nervous hand shot out and cuffed me on the ear. I fell. Dirt in my mouth, grey faces descending toward me, I understood that I ought to be terrified. But I spat out the dirt, the manes and faces retreated as quickly as they had come, and my incipient terror evaporated like alcohol in a shallow dish.

Overhead, a familiar flapping.

I looked up and saw the huri returning to The Bachelor's outstretched arm. He had released the creature upon his fellows in order to save me. An action illustrating the mind-boggling complexity of the relationship between the Asadi chieftain and the huri. Which of them rules? Which submits to command?

At that moment I didn't very much care. Denebola had risen, and the Asadi had dispersed into the Wild, leaving me dwarfed and humbled in the presence of their self-sustaining pagoda and the reluctant chieftain who stared down from its uppermost tier. Although he remained aloof, before the day was out The Bachelor had led me back to the original assembly ground. Without his help, I ought to add, I never would have found it. I would be out there still today. . . .

# PART FOUR

## AN INTRODUCTION TO "CHANEY'S MONOLOGUE"

*Thomas Benedict speaking:* I have put this paper together out of a complicated sense of duty. As one of the few people who had any substantial contact with Egan Chaney before his defection, I am perhaps also the only man who could have undertaken this task—despite my limited qualifications in the area of cultural xenology. But this is not really the place to discuss the strange *fait accompli* of our collaborative monograph. Suffice it to say that I owed Chaney my dedication to this project.

The section you have just read—"The Ritual of Death and Designation"—Chaney wrote in our base-camp infirmary while recuperating from exposure and a general inability to reorient himself to the society of human beings. In one of our conversations, as well as here in the monograph itself, he compared himself to Gulliver after his return from the land of the Houyhnhnms. At any rate, beyond Part Three of this monograph Chaney never wrote anything about the Asadi for publication, although immediately after his release from the infirmary I believe he intended to write a book about them. This monograph is the ghost of that unwritten book.

After returning to the original assembly ground of the Asadi, Chaney stayed two more weeks in the Calyptran Wild. On Days 126 and 133 I made supply drops, but, just as

63

Chaney had requested, I did not fly over the clearing in the vain hope of spotting him and thereby determining the state of his health. It was enough to verify his robustness, he told me, from the fact that each week when I coptered in his supplies I could note that he had dutifully picked them up and carried them off. The argument that he was not the only creature in the Wild capable of hauling away the goods intended for him impressed Chaney not at all.

"I might as well be," he wrote on one of his infrequent notes left in a canister at the drop point. "The Asadi have all the initiative of malaria victims. More horrible than this, friend Ben, is the face-slapping truth that there is no one else out here. *No one else at all.*"

I am now the sole owner of the personal effects of Egan Chaney. These include his private journals and professional notebooks, a number of unfiled "official" reports, a series of in-the-field tapes, and a small bit of correspondence. Those records concerning the Asadi that I don't own myself I have access to as a result of my affiliation with the Third Denebolan Expedition as Chaney's pilot and aide. I tell you this only because I know for an incontrovertible fact that during his last fourteen days in the Wild, either Chaney did not make a single entry in any of his journals or notebooks, or he so completely effaced these dubious entries that they may as well never have existed.

We have only one complete report of any kind dealing with this final phase of Chaney's field work. It is a tape, a remarkable tape, and I believe Chaney would have destroyed it, too, had we not taken his recorder from him the instant we picked him out of the jungle.

I have listened to this tape many times—in its entirety, I should add, since doing so is a feat requiring almost supernatural patience. On the one occasion I tried to discuss its contents with Chaney (several days after his release from the infirmary, when I believed he could handle the terror of the experience with a degree of objectivity), he protested that I had imagined those contents. He told me he had never recorded the least word in the tape's running account of The Bachelor's . . . "*Metamorphosis?*" he asked. "Is that the word you used?"

I promptly played the tape for him. He listened to ten minutes of it, then got up and shut it off. His face had gone unaccountably lean and bewildered, and his hands trembled.

"Ah," he said, not looking at me. "An elaborate practical joke, Ben. I made it up because there was nothing better to do."

"The sound effects, too?" I asked incredulously.

Still not looking at me, he nodded his head—even though the circumstance of his rescue belied this clumsy explanation, exploded it, in fact, into untenable shrapnel. Chaney remained mute on the subject. In all of his writings and conversations in those last three months among us, he never mentioned or even alluded to the sordid adventure of his final two nights. I present here a transcript, somewhat edited, of the tape in question.

# CHANEY'S MONOLOGUE: TWO NIGHTS IN THE SYNESTHESIA WILD

## PRELIMINARIES

CHANEY *[enthusiastically]*: Hello all! What day is it? A day like any other day, except that you happen to be along for the ride. I'm going to be leading you on an expedition, you see. How often do I lead you on expeditions?

It's Day 138, I think, and yesterday The Bachelor returned to the clearing—the first time he's been back since the huri anointed him, so to speak, with the fecal salve of chieftainship. I'd almost given him up. But he came back into the clearing yesterday afternoon, the huri on his shoulder, and squatted in the center of the assembly ground just as old Eisen Zwei used to do. The reaction among his Asadi brethren was identical to the one they always reserved for E.Z. . . . Everybody *out* of the clearing! Everybody *out!* . . . It was old times again, gang, except that now the actor holding down center stage was a personal friend of mine. Hadn't he saved my life several times? Certainly he had.

After the heat, the boredom, and the rainfalls, my lean-to leaking like a colander, I couldn't have been more gratified.

Following the pattern Eisen Zwei established on one of his visits, The Bachelor spent the entire afternoon in the clearing, all of last night, and maybe an hour or so this morning. Then he got up to leave.

I've been following him ever since. Denebola hovering overhead, I'd judge it to be about noon. The Bachelor permits me to follow him. Moreover, it's easy. I'm not even breathing hard. *[Simulated heavy breathing.]* I'm recording as we walk. If this were a terrestrial wood, you could hear birdsong and the chitterings of insects. As it is, you'll have to content your-selves with the sounds of my footfalls and the rustlings of leaf and twig. . . . Here's a little rustle for you now.

*[The sound of a branch or heavy leaf slapping back. General background noises of wind and, far less audibly, distant running water.]*

The Bachelor is several meters ahead of me. You may not be able to hear him—he walks like one of James Fenimore's stealthy Indians. *Pad, pad, pad.* Like that, only softer. I don't care to be any closer than I am because the huri's riding The Bachelor's shoulder, clinging to his mane. It is *not* a winsome creature, base-camp huggers; no, indeed it's not. Since it hasn't any eyes, you can't tell whether it's sleeping—or awake and plotting a thousand villainies.

That's why, jes' strollin' along, I'm happy back here.

Let me impress you with my cleverness. *[A heavy thump.]* That's my backpack. I've brought provisions for three or four days. You see, I don't know how long we're going to be out here. I don't know where we're going. But in The Bachelor I trust. Up to a point, at least. This backpack also houses my recorder—Morrell's miniaturized affair, the one that has a capacity of two hundred forty hours. Or, as Benedict might phrase it if he knew me better, ten solid days of Chaney's uninterrupted blathering.

I've rigged it so my voice will trigger the recording mechanism whenever I speak. The absence of my voice for a ten-minute period automatically shuts it off. That's to con-serve recording time—not that I plan on talking for ten straight days—and to keep me from fiddling with buttons when there might be other things to do. I can always go manual if I have to, of course, countermanding the exclusive lock on my own voice, but so far none of the Asadi have been particularly voluble. Only Eisen Zwei. And his voice would not be apt to woo the ladies. . . .

I've been thinking. And what I wouldn't give for a copy of one of those centuries-old works no one reads anymore. *The Brothers Karamazov*, say. Surely The Bachelor is none other than the Asadi equivalent of Pavel Smerdyakov, the illegitimate son who destroys himself out of his innate inability to reconcile the spiritual and the intellectual in his nature. Such passionate despondency! He cannot escape—nor can he accept—the dictum that the individual is responsible for the sins of all. . . .*

## THE FIRST NIGHT

I. CHANEY *[whispering]*: It's quiet in here, as still as the void. And though you probably can't believe it, I've held my peace for the entire afternoon. Maybe I said, "Damn!" two or three times after scraping my shin or tripping over a root gnarl—but that's all. In here I scarcely feel it's appropriate to talk, to raise my voice above even this hoarse whisper.

*[Chaney clears his throat. There is an echo, a hollow sound that rings and fades.]*

We—the three of us—are inside the pagoda in front of which The Bachelor became the designated "leader" of his people. I feel free to talk only because he and the huri have gone up a narrow iron stairway inside the temple's central vault. They're climbing toward the small convex interior of the onionlike dome from which the outside spire rises. I can see them from here. The stairway makes a tremendously wide spiral up toward that dome, and The Bachelor is trudging upward toward it. The huri, meanwhile, is flying in languid circles inside the spiral of the stairway, staying even with The Bachelor's head. The strange thing here is that I can barely hear its wings flapping.

It's preternaturally cold in here, too. Cold and dead. Like the interior of no other building ever erected in a tropical rain forest. My whispers echo, but the huri's flapping is silent.

Outside, it's nearly dark. At least it was nearly dark twenty minutes ago when we came through the heavy doors that the Asadi, twelve days ago, didn't even open. Now at least one of the moons must be up. Maybe a little moonlight falls through the dome overhead. . . . No, no, Chaney. The light in here comes from those three massive globes in the metal ring suspended several meters below the dome like a spartan chandelier. The Bachelor's climbing toward that huge ring, the

---

*There follows a totally irrelevant analysis of the ways in which The Bachelor resembles the character of Smerdyakov in Dostoevski's novel. This remarkable analysis, delivered extemporaneously while Chaney follows the Asadi chieftain through the Wild, lasts better than an hour. To spare the reader, I've deleted it. I believe that the passage which follows was recorded almost six hours later. *T.B.*

spiraling stairway mounts toward it. . . . Light also seeps into this place from the amethyst windows set high in all the walls. Listen. Listen to the light seep through. . . .

*[There is no sound for several minutes, perhaps a slight amplification of Chaney's breathing. Then his voice descends conspiratorially.]*

Nevertheless, Eisen, I think—I don't know, mind you, but I think—I think that both the chill and the luminosity in here originate in those globes up there. Just a feeling I have. Winter sunlight. The *texture* of the light reminds me of the glow around probeship ALERT and EVACUATE signs, a cold but hellish sheen.

All right. Let's move to where we can see.

*[Silence. Rhythmic breathing. Footfalls echoing hollowly off polished stone.]*

I'm looking straight up the well of the stairway. *[An echo: "Way way way way. . . ."]* Come on, Egan, keep it down, keep it down. . . . Better, much better. . . . I can see the huri flapping up there, noiselessly, and The Bachelor's legs ascending the spiral. The staircase seems to terminate in a glass platform off to one side of and just a little below the suspended ring of the "chandelier." I'm looking up through the axis of the dome, right up through the chandelier ring hanging beneath it.

Outside, above the dome, there's a spire pointing at Bosk-Veld's sky. Inside the dome, depending from its apex, there's a sort of plumb line—of what looks like braided gold—dropping down the central shaft of the pagoda to a point . . . well, about half a meter above the suspended ring. I can't tell for certain, my depth perception's not that good. Been in the jungle too long. Just as the pygmies of the Ituri used to have trouble adjusting their vision to open savannah.

I apologize for the complicated description of the upper recesses of this temple, but the *arrangement* is intricate. Also, that's where The Bachelor's going. I can make sense neither of the architecture nor of his intentions. And, my head tilted back like this, my neck's getting sore. I need a rest, base-camp huggers. 'Deed I do. . . .

II. CHANEY *[Conversationally, but still in something of a whisper]:* Me again. About an hour ago The Bachelor *reached* the glass platform beneath the chandelier ring. He's been standing up there like a Pan-Olympic diver ever since. Insofar

as I can tell, he appears to be looking at the braided gold
plumb line dangling slightly above him, its far end attached to
a hook or threaded through some invisible grommet high in
the dome. He can't quite reach the plumb line from his platform, though clearly he would like to. . . . He seems to be hypnotized by it.

Let me leave him there for a moment and take a walk about
the interior of this pagoda. I'll be your tour guide, base
campers. Follow me.

*[The sound of footfalls as, apparently, Chaney walks.]* This
pagoda seems to be a museum. Or, perhaps, a mausoleum. At
any rate, a monument to a dead culture. I'm reminded of the
Palace of Green Porcelain in Wells's *The Time Machine*. . . .
The walls around three sides of the bottom of this place are
lined with tall spindly cabinets, glass display cases of a wildly
improbable design. Each one consists of fan-shaped shelves
that fold out from a central axis and lock into place on different levels from one another. *[Chaney blows.]* Dust. Dust
on everything. But not particularly thick. And on these
shelves—which have the fragile warmth of mother-of-
pearl—there are specimens of various kinds of implements
and artwork.

*[A click, like stone on stone.]* I'm holding a statue that's
about as tall as my forearm is long. It represents an Asadi
male, full-maned and virile. . . . But the statue depicts him
with a kind of cape around his shoulders. A garment, if you
can imagine that. Very strange. . . . Here's an iron knife, with
a wooden handle carved so that the top resembles the skull of
an early terrestrial hominid. An Asadi skull, no doubt. . . .
The statue's definitely an anomaly here; everything else in the
cabinet looks like a weapon or a heavy tool.

I'm going across the chamber, past an open corridor
leading off down the pagoda's western wing and into
darkness. *[Footfalls. Echoes.]* I'm going toward the one wall
in here without any of these spindly cabinets against it. . . .
The Flying Asadi Brothers are still up there, more rigid than
the statue I just picked up. I'm passing directly beneath them
now, beneath the iron ring and its energy globes. There's a
huge circular pattern on the polished flagstones I'm walking
upon. Inside this circle I feel I'm trespassing on sacred
territory. . . . Ah, I'm out of the circle and heading toward the
horn-colored wall beyond the helical stairway. There are no
cabinets on the wall. Instead. . .

Damn this light! this hollowness! Let me get closer. . . . On the wall are what appear to be rows upon rows of tiny plastic wafers. Rows of wafers hung from a couple thousand silver rods protruding for several centimeters at right angles to the wall. . . . The wall's just one big, elegant pegboard glowing like a monstrous fingernail with a bonfire behind it. The rows of these wafers—cassettes, cigarette cases, matchboxes— whatever you want to call 'em—begin at about waist level and go up two or three hands higher than I can reach. Asadi height, I suppose.

*[For three or four minutes only Chaney's breathing can be heard. Then, slowly]*: Interesting. I think I've figured this out, Eisen. I want you to pay attention. . . . I've just unfastened this intricate, ah, *wingnut*, say, from the end of one of these protruding rods and removed the first of several tiny cassettes hanging from it. . . . *Wafer* was a serendipitous word choice, because these little boxes are as thin as two or three transistor templates welded together. The faces of the things are about seven centimeters square. . . . I've counted fifty of them hanging from this one rod, and, as I said, they're probably three thousand rods on this wall. That's about 150,000 cassettes altogether, and this section of the pagoda, more than likely, is just a display area.

But I want to describe the one I've got in my hand, tell you how it works. Maybe, if I can restrain myself, I'll let you draw your own conclusions. Okay, then. In the center of this wafer—which, by the way, does seem to be made of plastic— there's an inset circle of glass with a diameter of about a centimeter, maybe a little more. A bulb or an eye, call it. Beneath this eye there's a rectangular tab that's flush with the surface of the cassette. Above the bulb, directly under the hole through which the wall rod passes, there's a band containing a series of different-colored dots. Some of the dots touch each other, some don't. The spacing or lack of it between dots probably has signficance.

And here's how this little crackerbox works. *[Chaney chuckles.]* Oh, Eisen, don't you wish Morrell were here instead of me? I do, too—I really do. . . . It's purposely simple, though. Even a cultural xenologist can figure it out. . . . All you do is hold your thumb over the right half of the tab at the bottom of the cassette. Then the fireworks begin.

*[A pleased laugh, and its subsequent echo.]* Ah, yes. Right now the eye in the center of the wafer is flashing through an

indecipherable program of colors. Reds, violets, greens. Sapphires, yellows, pinks. All premeditatedly interlaced with pauses. Pregnant pauses, no doubt. . . . In this dimness my hands are alternately lit and shadowed by the changing colors. Beautiful, beautiful. That's just it, in fact. The entire system probably sacrifices a degree of practicality on the altar of beauty.

There. I've shut it off. All you do is cover the *left* half of the control rectangle with your thumb. . . . It may be possible to reverse the program—rewind it to a desired point, so to speak—but I haven't stumbled on the method yet. At least I don't think I have. It's impossible for me to remember the sequences of colors—though it probably wasn't a bit difficult for the Asadi, or Ur'sadi, who composed, manufactured, and used these things, however long ago that may have been.

They're *books*, or the Ur'sadi equivalent, as I'm sure you've already guessed. *[A thumping noise.]* I'm pocketing six of them, putting them in my backpack. For the greater glory of Science. To set the shirttails of ole Oliver Oliphant aflame with envy, may his ghost go angrily blazing across the heavens. Not to mention the fact that they'll be just one more thing for Morrell to put his screwdriver to.

*[Musingly]*: Look at that wall. Can you imagine the information on hand here? Or the level of technology necessary to devise a storage-and-retrieval system for a "language" that consists of complicated spectral patterns? One fifteen-minute program in one of these cassettes probably represents the equivalent of a three hundred-page book. . . . By the way, what do you suppose I was "reading"? I'd guess that the band of colored dots above the eye is the description of the contents. The title, so to speak. Maybe I was scanning a sex-and-sadism tract by the late Marquis de Asadi—my hands had begun to sweat while the program was running.

*[Sober again]*: No, no, the eyebook—let's call 'em eyebooks—was the first one on that particular rod. Maybe it's their *Iliad*, their *Divine Comedy*, their *Origin of the Species*, their *Brothers Karamazov*. And what the hell have they done with it? Stuck it in a forgotten, godforsaken temple in the middle of the Synesthesia Wild and left it to commemorate their fall! What colossal waste! What colossal arrogance!

*[Shouting]*: Where the hell do you creatures get off neglecting the accumulated knowledge of millennia? You're animals! *ANIMALS!*

*[A cacophony of echoes. A prolonged, painful ringing.]*

Forgive me, Eisen, Benedict, all of you. Forgive me. *[Chaney's voice drops to a whisper, scarcely audible.]* And you, you Asadi aerialists, that's right, pretend I don't exist, pretend you can't hear me, ignore the voices of your ancestors whispering to you from their deaths. *[Venomously]*: And may God damn you both to hell!

III. CHANEY *[in a lifeless monotone]*: I think I slept for a while. Under the rows upon rows of eyebooks. Maybe an hour. Then a noise woke me, a ringing of iron.

Now I'm on the helical stairway high above the museum floor. I'm in a curve of the stairway a little below and opposite the glass platform where The Bachelor was standing. He's no longer there. A moment ago he chinned himself up to the cold ring of the chandelier, gained his feet, and balanced on the ring, quite precariously. Then he reached out and grabbed the plumb line that drops down from the dome.

The huri, meanwhile, squats on the foremost globe in the triangle of globes set in the great iron ring. He's been there awhile.

The Bachelor, after grabbing the gold braid, fashioned a noose and slipped his neck into it. Then he swung himself out over the floor so that his feet are hanging a little below the ring of the chandelier. I'm watching him hang there, his feet inscribing an invisible circle inside the larger circle of the globe-set energy fixture.

But he isn't dead, not a bit dead. The noose is canted so that it catches him under the throat in the plush of his mane. In the two weeks since his designation his mane has thickened considerably, especially along his jaw and under his throat, and the new fur cushions the steadily constricting braid. So now he's just hanging there. The dangling man.

*[Listlessly]*: A pretty damn interesting development, I suppose. At least the huri acts as if it's interesting. The huri's watching all this—should I say *watching*, considering its eyelessness?—with either excitement or agitation, beating its wings sporadically and skittering to stay atop the globe it's perched on. See if you can hear it. I'll hold the microphone out for you. *[A vaguely static-filled silence, followed by a distant scratching sound.]* That's it, the huri's claws scrabbling on the globe. And the sound of The Bachelor's feet turning north, northeast, east, southeast, south, south-southwest. . . .

*[After almost ten minutes of static-filled silence]*: The huri's been joined by two of its fellows. They flew up silently out of the lower darkness of the pagoda, I don't know precisely from where, and settled like miniature brood hens on the other two energy globes. As soon as they had arrived, the original huri—The Bachelor's huri—fluttered to the Asadi's head, grabbed his mane with its claws, and began crabwalking around his shoulders and upper body like a steeplejack. After a couple of minutes had passed, I noticed that a kind of milky cobwebbing had begun to net in The Bachelor's head and that the huri was paying out this glistening fiber from a pair of axillary spinnerets beneath its half-open wings. The huri's tiny hands pulled out the thread, stretched it around the dangling Asadi's shoulders, and looped the stuff so expertly and with such gentle speed that the beastie appeared to be spinning cotton candy out of its armpits. Wingpits, make that. In any case, this is still going on, base-camp huggers, although the other two huri have spelled The Bachelor's huri a couple of times apiece already and The Bachelor has begun to resemble a huge, nylon-pile-lined sleeping bag turned inside out and made strangely translucent. I no longer know which huri is which, they've alternated their spinning chores so many times. . . .

*[Unawed]*: Beautiful. Beautiful and grotesque at once. I'll bet you think I'm drunk or drugged. Making silk out of a souse's fears, so to speak. Not so. I've imbibed no bourbon, played with no Placenol, and I wish it was you, Eisen, or you, Morrell, who was sitting up here on this cramped stairway watching this ritual unraveling of three huri's innards. Is it silk cable or a kind of solid, filamentous milk payed out through these creatures' axillary mammaries? Who knows? The show is beautiful and grotesque, grotesque and beautiful, but at this stage my principal reaction seems to be one of . . . well, of disgust. *[Unemotionally]*: God, but my patience has been tried. . . .

*[Several more minutes pass. A faint flapping commences, continues for a time, ceases, and commences again.]*

One of the three huri—don't ask me which—let a strand of silk drop down The Bachelor's body and through the axis of the dome until it damn near reached the floor. Another of the huri flew off its globe and caught up a section of the strand in its claws. Then, with both its claws and hands, flapping in higgledy-ziggledy circles, it covered The Bachelor's feet, his ankles, and his shins. After that, it settled on the old boy's wrapped feet. Now, its wings outspread and its spinnerets, I'd imagine, virtually exhausted, the huri's hanging up there like a bat and still bravely mummy-wrapping its master. It's got help, though. The other two huri are also single-mindedly crawling his body, getting The Bachelor ready for Christmas. And all three of them, mind you, are blind, as blind as . . . as a besotted cultural xenologist. Good boy, Chaney, no more clichés than the experience itself calls for.

I don't know how long it'll take—not much longer, apparently—but in a while The Bachelor will be completely encased in a murky chrysalis, a sheath which the huri look as if they would like to finish and tie off as soon as they can. Already they're binding in the Asadi's hands, tightening thread around his thighs, thickening and padding the glowing gauze of his enormous sleeping bag. Soon The Bachelor will be nothing but a lopsided pupa hanging from a golden cord inside the eerie loft of his ancestors' rickety barn. I guess. So to speak.

*[Chaney grunts. Shuffling sounds. Perhaps the weary shifting of a burden.]*

I guess. Don't ask me. I won't watch any more of this foolishness. I'm dizzy. I'm fed up with this nonsense. . . . If I can make it down these steps in the half-light, the hell-glow, I'm going to lie down beside the wall of eyebooks, where I was before, and go to sleep. Directly to sleep. Before the worm turns. . . .

*[Footfalls on the iron steps. Unintelligible mumblings]*

## INTERLUDE: EARLY AFTERNOON OF DAY 139*

CHANEY *[Speaking conversationally]*: Hello. I'm talking to Benedict alone now. Ben? Ben, you're supposed to make a drop tomorrow. Your twentieth. Can you believe that? No, I can't either. It doesn't seem like more than ten or twelve years that I've been out here. Twenty drops. Well I may not pick up this latest one. Not for a while, anyway. God knows when The

---

*From the end of the previous section to the beginning of this one Chaney engaged in a great deal of irrelevant "blathering." I have deleted it. Altogether, about twelve or fourteen hours of real time passed, time during which Chaney also slept and ate. In this "Interlude" I have taken the liberty of borrowing small sections from the deleted passages in order to provide a continuity which would not otherwise exist. *T.B.*

Bachelor will choose to lead me out of here and back to the clearing. At the moment he's occupied. Let me tell you how.

First, let me tell you what's going on. I'm standing here by one of the dusty display cases. All its shelves are folded up against the central axis, like the petals of a flower at night. But it's early afternoon, Ben, there's dull light seeping through the swirling violet windows between the separate stories of the pagoda's exterior column. Even so, every cabinet in the place is shut up like a new rose. Every one of them. It happened, I guess, while I was sleeping. The fires have gone out of the three globes overhead—they're as dead and as mutely mottled as dinosaur eggs. I don't know exactly when that happened, either. The eyebooks still work, but everything else in here is dead.

The pagoda's dead. That's all there is to it. And I have the feeling it won't come alive again until Denebola has set and BoskVeld's moons climb the sky. Moonlight is reflected light, indirect light, and this place seems to function best when the light comes at you cockeyed and filtered. Don't ask me why. . . .

But The Bachelor. You want to know what happened to him. Again, I don't know exactly. During the night the plumb line from which he fashioned the noose and then hung out over the pagoda's floor while a trio of huri wrapped him in silk—that golden line, I tell you, has lengthened and dropped through the ring of the chandelier so that it's now only a meter or so from the floor. It descended, I suppose, of its own accord. *[A chuckle.]* Now the ungainly pupa hangs in the daylight gloom of this chamber and turns slowly, slowly, first to the right, then to the left, like the gone-awry pendulum in a grandfather clock. . . . That's it, Ben, my somber Big Ben, this whole building's just an out-sized timepiece. You can hear BoskVeld ticking in its orbit. Listen . . . .

As for the huri, only one of last night's three remains. The original huri, I have to assume. It crouches on the uppermost node of the pupa, the point at which the braid breaks through, and rides The Bachelor's mummified head as it used to ride his shoulder. Each time the wrapped body turns this way I feel the huri's staring at me, taking my measure. If I had a pistol, I'd shoot the damn thing, I swear I would. Even if it meant that the concussion would split the seams of this temple and send it crashing down on my ears—every fragile cabinet shattering, every eyebook bursting open. So help me, I would.

Which is probably why I didn't bring a weapon out here with me in the first place. . . . But now the little beastie's clawing nervously at the silken membrane, unhinging its wings and shaking their outstretched tips. I think, gang, we're going to get some action. Give me a few minutes, just a few. . . .

*[Several minutes pass.]* Action, indeed. The huri's moving in its own catch-as-catch-can fashion down the swaying cocoon that houses The Bachelor. As it moves, it peels back pieces of the membrane, snips them off with its feet, transfers the pieces to its greedy hands, and eats them. That's right, *eats* them. . . . I'd been wondering what the little bugger subsisted on, and I have to continue to wonder. Viable food chains do *not* result from a creature's feeding on its own excreta. Too much is lost. . . . Nevertheless, the huri's feeding on the husk of The Bachelor's metamorphosis, on the rind of its master's involuntary change. Maybe that's phrasing it a little too philosophically, but I can't help thinking the huri's eating The Bachelor's former self. . . . It's crabwalking in a spiral down the cocoon, a spiral mirroring the great corkscrew of the pagoda's staircase, and it furiously shovels in and gobbles up the membrane that it's snipping away.

Now the huri is at the hollow of The Bachelor's chest, and I can see the outline of my old friend's head through the milk-blue film that remains even though the silken outer layer has been eaten away. This film clings to his features like a hood. It's moist and trembly, and through it I can see the death mask of his face.

Ben, Ben, you can't expect me to stay here and watch this. Tell the others not to expect that of me. The bitch-goddess of xenology's fucked me over too many times already, and I'm nauseated with fatigue. With disgust. It's worse than last night. There's an odor in the temple, a smell like excrement and rot and the foul discharges of the glands. I don't know what I'm . . .

*[A retching sound, painful and prolonged. Then, a rapid succession of footfalls, suggestive of running.]*

The doors. I've got to get to the doors. . . .

## THE SECOND NIGHT

I. CHANEY *[his voice thin but genial]*: We're in the Wild again. Out in the open. Out among the singing leaves, the dancing moons, the glittering winds. The humidity's horrible.

It makes my sinuses act up. After spending one sore-necked night in the refrigerated vault of that Asadi warehouse, though—and one stomach-turning day in it when it changed from a warehouse into a charnel house—well, the humidity's a welcome relief. Let my nose run as it may, where it may. Even though I don't know where the hell the face it's running on is running to. Actually, we're not running at all. We're moving quite leisurely through the trees, The Bachelor and the huri and I. In no hurry at all.

*[Clinically]:* I feel pretty well now. The horror of this afternoon has evaporated. I don't know why it made me ill. It wasn't that bad, really. I should have stayed and watched. That's what I came out here for. But when the smell got so bad, well, I had to get out of there. My system's been under a strain.

I bolted for the pagoda's entrance, pushed aside the heavy doors, and ran down the tier of steps. The sunlight increased my nausea and I threw up again. But I couldn't go back inside, Ben, and as a consequence I'm not entirely certain what the final circumstances of The Bachelor's removal from the cocoon were. Like a little boy waiting for the library to open, I sat on the bottom step of the pagoda and held my head in my hands. I was ill. Really ill. It wasn't just an emotional thing . . . . But now I feel better, and the night—the stars twinkling up there like chipped ice—seems like my friend.

*[Wistfully]:* I wish I could navigate by those stars. But I can't. Their patterns are still unfamiliar to me. They don't tell me where we are. Maybe we're going back to the clearing, maybe elsewhere.

*[Throughout this section of Chaney's monologue the sound of wind and leaves corroborates his testimony that they are out of doors, out of the temple.]*

The Bachelor's striding ahead of me, the huri on his shoulder. I know, I know, you're wondering what he looks like, what his disposition is, what his metamorphosis accomplished for him. Well, gang, I'm not sure. You see, he looks. . . . about the same. As I said, I didn't go back into the museum, I waited outside until the sun had set, thinking all the while that I'd go back up the steps when the darkness was complete. I knew that my two disarming friends couldn't get out any other way, that I wouldn't be stranded there alone. At least I didn't see any other doors while I was inside. The ancient Asadi—the Ur'sadi, damn 'em—apparently didn't see

any need to leave themselves a multitude of outs. The end
they've come to supports that hypothesis. But before I could
steel myself to reentering the pagoda—just as the twilight
began to lose its gloss—The Bachelor, looking not much different, appeared on the highest step.

And came down the steps. And walked right by me.

He didn't look at me, and the huri, clinging to his mane,
had the comatose look I remember it possessing when Eisen
Zwei came into the Asadi clearing for the second time. Now I
know why it looked so bloated and incapable of movement—
it had just ingested the old man's huri-spun pupa, if indeed a
trio of huri had for reasons of their own so encased Eisen
Zwei. God help me. I still haven't figured this out. I may
never figure it out. . . . Anyhow, I noticed only two small
changes as he stalked by me in the jungle, two small changes
in The Bachelor, that is. First, his mane's now a full-grown
collar of fur, not just a bib under his throat. It's still a little
damp from the filmy blue substance that lined the chrysalis.
And second, a thin cloak of this film stretches between The
Bachelor's naked shoulder blades and falls in folds to the
small of his back. Probably it just hasn't dropped away yet.

And that's it. His eyes are still as mute, as white, as uncommunicative, as they ever were.

We're in a kind of tunnel. We've been walking, slipping
beneath the vines and hanging bouquets of flowers, for about
thirty or forty minutes. A while ago we came upon what seems
to be a footpath, a beaten trail where we can walk upright.
The only such trail I've seen in the Synesthesia Wild, ever.
The Bachelor's moving down it easily, and once again I'm
having no trouble keeping up.

> *[Singing softly]:*
> *The Wild is lovely, dark, and deep,*
> *Its grottos free of war's alarms—*
> *But would I were in my bed, asleep,*
> *And all Earth in my arms.*

I'm lost. *[Pensively]:* All the time I've spent in the Asadi
clearing, all that time watching them amble around and wear
down their heels to no purpose—it seems like centuries ago.
No kidding, Ben, Eisen, that time in the clearing just doesn't
exist right now. Lost as I am, I feel I could follow The
Bachelor down this narrow trail forever.

But his metamorphosis—or lack of it—bothers me. I've been thinking about it. My considered, but not necessarily considerate, opinion is that the old grey mayor—mayor, chieftain, what's the difference?—is exactly what he used to be. Anatomically speaking, that is. Maybe the very brief time he spent hibernating in that homemade sleeping bag altered him psychologically rather than physically. Perhaps it put him more closely in tune with his huri and his huri with him.

Who's to say, gang? Who's to say?

*[Ten minutes of wind, water, and shush-shush-shushing feet.]*

II. CHANEY *[whispering]*: There's something in the trees ahead of us. A crouched grey shape. The Bachelor just turned on me, Ben—he wouldn't let me approach with him. If I don't stay fairly close, though, I'll be lost out here. Damn you, you hulking boonie, I won't let you sneak away. . . . We're off the trail, we've been off it a good while, and the trees, the lianas, the swollen epiphytes—hell, everything's the same, one spot's like another. . . . I'm disobeying the bastard. I'm staying close enough to keep him in my sight. He's out there in a ragged hallway of rainthorn leaves moving toward the thing in the tree. A tumor in the branches, a lump that the moonlight gives a suspicious fuzziness. . . . You should see the way The Bachelor's approaching the thing. He's spread his arms out wide, and he's taking one step at a time, one long easy step. Like an adagio S.S. man. The membrane between his shoulder blades has opened out, too, so that it makes a fan-shaped drapery across his back. Shadows shift across it, shadows and moonlight. . . . What a weird goddamn boonie. You should see him. He's a kind of moving, blown-up version of the drunken huri clinging to his mane. . . . We're closer now. That thing up there, whatever it is, it's either dead, or inanimate, or hypnotized. Hypnotized, I think. It seems to be one of the Asadi from the clearing. A grey shape. Ordinarily you don't get this close at night. You just don't. The Bachelor's hypnotized it with his slow-motion goose step, the filmy rippling of the membrane across his back and arms, maybe even with his empty eyes. . . . Now we're just waiting, waiting. I'm as close as I can get without jeopardizing the purity of this confrontation. . . . I can see eyes up there, Asadi eyes, stalled on a sickly but reflective amber. *[Aloud, over a sudden thrashing]*: The damn thing's just jumped out of the branches! It's one of the Asadi all right, a lithe grey female. The Bachelor's wrenching her backward to the ground, the huri's fallen sidelong away from him! It's fluttering, fluttering in the thicket beneath the rainthorn tree! *[A heavy bump. Continued thrashing. Chaney's voice skyrockets to an uncontrolled falsetto]*: I knew it! I knew what you were! Dear lord, I won't permit this! I won't permit your hideous evil to flourish! DAMN YOU! *[Scuffling. Then, indignantly]*: Stay where you are. Don't approach me. Stay where you . . . *[Violent noises. Then a hum of static and prolonged low breathing.]*

III. CHANEY *[panting]*: My head aches. I've been sick again. I didn't think I could throw up again, my stomach's so tight and empty, but somehow I managed. . . . It's sweet here, though. I'm kneeling in fragrant grass under the lattice-sail trees by the edge of the pagoda's clearing. . . . I've been sick again, yes, but I've done heroic things. *Semi*heroic things, perhaps. In any case, I'm vaguely proud of myself. . . . Even though I'm sick, down on my hands and knees with the cramps. . . . You can hear me, can't you? I'm talking out loud—OUT LOUD, DAMN IT!— and he's not about to stop me. He's just going to sit there opposite me with his long legs folded and take my reproaches and evil stares. Aren't you, boonie? Aren't you? That's right, that's a good boonie. . . . He's appalled by what I've just done, Ben. As a matter of fact, so am I. I've freed him from that scabby little battlecock of his. . . . There's blood on the grass. Dark, sweet blood. Too sweet, Ben. I've got to get up.

*[Chaney moans. A rustling of clothes, then his strained voice]*: Okay. Fine. A little bark to lean against here, a tree with spiny shingles. *[A stumping sound.]* Good, good. . . . I refused to let myself get disoriented, Ben. We came slogging right through that opening there, that portal of ferns and violet blossoms. . . . Oh, hell, you can't see where I'm pointing, can you? Never mind, then. Just know that we slogged to this place from that direction I'm pointing, and I kept my head about me all the way here. My head, by the way, continues to ring from the bashing The Bachelor gave me back in that—that other place. He bloodied me, damn him, when I tried to stop him from slaughtering this poor woman here, the one lying here butchered in the grass. . . . He knocked me down and I couldn't stop him. Then he whirled her up over his

shoulder, grabbed the huri out of the undergrowth by its feet, and took off through the jungle. Because of my bruised head, my aching eye, the Wild rang like a thousand wind chimes. To keep from getting lost, I had to follow him. Dear God, Ben, I had to hobble along after that crazy Asadi crew. . . . Then we reached this little patch of grass among the swaying lattice-sail trees—the pagoda's right over there—and The Bachelor threw the dead woman on the ground and disemboweled her. He opened her belly with his teeth. I saw him hovering over her as I stumbled up through the root gnarls and hanging tropical moss after him. I got to this place just as he was making an incision down her abdomen with his canines. . . . I collapsed and watched. The enormity of what he was doing scarcely fazed me. Holding my bad eye and squinting through the other, Ben, I watched. In ten or twelve minutes I'd forgotten what it all meant, and the woman didn't look like an Asadi any longer—but a deep-red, a blood-black slab of meat. Now the grass is littered with her, and I didn't even attempt to interfere. But, Ben, I couldn't help that, it was all owing to my fatigue and my bruised head, I wasn't thinking straight, I didn't realize he was butchering a human being. As soon as I could, I remedied the situation. And that's why I'm still a little sick. . . . But my head's clear now; it aches, but it's clear. And the boonie isn't about to strike me again. Are you, boonie? All he can do is sit and stare at me. I've intimidated the hell out of him. He thought I was some kind of maneless Asadi vermin, apparently, and now he's unable to reconcile that image of me with his memory of what I've recently accomplished, poor mute bastard. My semiheroic deed kicked him right in his psychological solar plexus.

[Bemusedly]: As the night is my witness, Ben, I killed the huri. No, the boonie can't believe it either. Nevertheless, it's true.

Look at him. He's making slow figure eights with his chin. He thought me just another low Asadi dog, but I've boggled him past recovery. When he was finishing carving up that pitifully helpless woman, that sweet, long-legged lady, he set the huri atop her carcass and busied himself devouring her viscera, the sweet discarded bones of her limbs and skull. . . . I had to do something then, of course. I pulled myself up—but the huri was sitting there on her butchered body staring at me blindly and daring me to move. I wasn't supposed to move, you see; I was supposed to be a good cannibal and wait until dinner was properly served. . . . But I'm not an Asadi, and I paid no heed to the boonie's stupid sentinel, Ben. I killed it. That's the heed I paid it. I ran up and kicked the huri with my boot, it fluttered backward, and I was upon it with my reinforced heel, grinding its filthy little no-face into the grass. Its body split open. Pus spilled out of the lesion like putty from a plastic tube, stinking to the skies. Strands of the stuff coagulated in the gelatinous mass, grew silken and feathery in the air. The smell was intolerable. . . . That's what made me sick, I'm afraid, the sight and the stink of the huri's silk-making innards. I stumbled away, fell to my knees, and heaved until I thought my guts would wrench loose inside me. You can't imagine what it felt like. . . .

The Bachelor never moved. Killing the huri had given me a hold over him, a power. He just sat, like he's sitting now, half hunkering, half flat-assed on the ground, and watched me be sick. The smell of the grass revived me, convinced me of my own feeble heroism, and that's when I had to tell you about it, when I started talking through my sickness and the heavy, too-sweet smell of the grass.

*[A period of silence, during which only the wind in the tropical vegetation and an ambiguous, intermittent rustling are audible.]*

Hello. Are you still there, still with me? The Bachelor just stood up, uncoiled from his crouch, and faced me like an enemy. I thought I was dead, I really did. I know that's a turnabout—you don't have to require consistency of me under these circumstances, do you? . . . But he didn't attack. He merely stared at me for a minute, then turned and walked across the open clearing toward the temple. He's climbing the steps right now, very slowly, a grey shape remarkably like the grey shape he killed.

Every moon is up. The three of them ripple his shadow down the tier of steps behind him. Balthasar, Caspar, and Melchior arrayed in virtual conjunction. The pagoda itself, in this light, scarcely has substance. It looks to have been built of water, water frozen not into cloudy masonry blocks of ice but into a transparent crystalline structure contiguous with the very atmosphere. How to say this? It seems to be merging with the jungle, Ben, Eisen, everyone. The pagoda is slipping out of my vision like a scarf slipping from my hand, just that easily and casually.

*[Shouting]*: Damn you! You can't leave me here in this gut-strewn glade! I'm coming after you! Do you hear me! I'm coming!

IV. CHANEY: Where is it, Eisen? You said we could see it from this hemisphere, you said it was visible. But I'm standing here, standing out here in front of the Asadi's fading temple where there aren't any branches to block my view, and, damn you, Eisen, I don't see it! Just those blinding moons dancing up and down and a sky full of flaming cobwebs. Where's Sol? Where's our own sun? Nowhere. Nowhere that I can see.

*[Suddenly resolute]*: I'm going back into the temple. Yes, by God, I am. The Bachelor's abandoned me out here. Twenty minutes I've been out here alone. I don't intend to die in this place. I killed his huri, and my suspicion is that he wants me to die for my deed. But is a man who kills a huri the sort to accept a passive death? I hope not, Ben. I've taken too much shit, heaved up too much of myself, to sit cross-legged under the trees and wait for either my own death or the onset of the corrupt hunger that would keep me alive. . . . I won't eat his offering, and I won't stay out here in that poor butchered lady's company. I can't.

There's a beautiful golden cord in the pagoda, a beautiful golden cord. That should do it. If the boonie's still too shaken up with his loss, his stinking bereavement, to lead me back to the clearing—the Asadi clearing—well, that plumb line ought to serve. I've worked with my hands, I can fashion a noose as well any dumpling-hearted boonie. And then carry it through where he couldn't. . . .

*[The movement of feet in the dirt, Chaney's short-windedness as he climbs the temple's steps, the groaning ut-terance of a heavy door. From this point on, Chaney's each word has the brief after-echo, the telltale hollowness imparted by the empty volume of a large building's interior.]*

It's cold. You wouldn't believe how cold it is in here, Ben. Cold and dark. There's no light filtering through the high, jewellike windows, and the chandelier—the chandelier's out! My eyes aren't accustomed to . . . *[A bump.]* Here's a cabinet. I've scraped my elbow. The shelves are down, and I scraped my elbow on one of the shelves. The cabinets give off their own faint light, a very warm faint light, and I'll be able to see a good deal better if I just stand and let my pupils adjust. *[A* *scraping sound, somewhat glassy. \*]* Wait a minute. The bottom petals of this cabinet have been broken off, torn away. I'm standing in the shards. And I'm not the vandal, Ben. That little bump I gave the cabinet couldn't have done this. Someone had to work energetically at these shelves to break them away. The Bachelor, maybe? The Bachelor's the only one in here besides me. Did he want an axe to stalk me with? Did he need one of his ancestors' ornamental knives before he felt brave enough to take on the pink-fleshed Asadi outcast who killed his huri? *[Shouting]*: Is that it, boonie? You afraid of me now? *[Echoes, crashing echoes. When they cease, Chaney's voice becomes huskily confidential]*: I think that's it, Ben. I think that's why the globe lamps are out, why this place is so dark. The boonie wants to kill me. He's stalking me in the dark. . . . Well, that's fine, too. That's more heroic than the cord, an excellent death. I'll even grapple with him a little, if it comes to that. Beowulf and Grendel. It shouldn't take very long. The lady he killed felt amost nothing, I'm sure of that. *[Shouting]*: Over here, boonie! You know where I am! Come on, then! I won't move!

*[A forceful crack, followed by a tremendously amplified shattering sound, like a box full of china breaking.]*

My God! The pagoda's flooded with light now, flooded with light from the three globes in the great iron fixture that yesterday hung just beneath the dome. It's different now. The iron ring's floating almost two meters from the floor, it's humming oddly, you can hear the hum if you listen, and The Bachelor's inside the ring stabbing at one of the globes with a long-handled pick. . . . He's already chipped away a big mottled piece of its covering, and that piece has shattered on the floor. . . . All three globes are pulsing with energy, angry energy, they're filling the temple with electricity. A deadly chill. Anger . . . I'm sure they've generated the field that's keeping the iron ring afloat, the ring hovering like a circular prison around The Bachelor's shoulders. . . . The plumb line whips back and forth as he jabs, it's damn near entangled him, and he's caught inside the ring and keeps jabbing at the foremost globe with his pick. . . .

*[The jabbing sounds punctuate Chaney's headlong nar-*

*Just one of the many apparently unsimulatable sound effects that convince me of the authenticity of the tapes. How much of what Chaney reports is hallucination rather than reality, however, I'm not prepared to conjecture. T.B.

*rative. Apparently, another piece of the globe's covering falls to the floor and shatters.]*

What's he doing? Why the hell doesn't he duck out of there? Is he trapped in that field? I can see he's too damn busy to be worried about me, gang. Too damn busy to want to kill me. Instead, he seems to want to kill the pagoda, to destroy its energy source and free himself from the odd hold it has over him.

I think his actions are having precisely the opposite effect, though. All the cabinets are open, all the shelves are down. I can see them. The temple seems to be alive again. Angry. Indignant. All it took was the dark and a little violence. . . . The foremost globe's split wide open; The Bachelor has knocked the crown off it, and spilling from that artificial caldera in the globe, erupting from it and flowing into the pagoda's central chamber with us, is a terrible, violet radiance! It's almost more than I can look at. . . . He persists, though. The ring is canting to one side, and his shaggy body is a flaming silhouette behind that hellish radiance! What does he think he's doing? . . . There's a smell in here, an odor that seems almost to be a concomitant of the light. It's like . . . like the smell when I ground out the guts of The Bachelor's huri. Terrible!

*[A fluttering which is distinctly audible over both Chaney's voice and the persistent tapping of The Bachelor's pick.]*

Lord, they're driving him out of the lofty darkness of the dome—two or three enraged, murder-intent huri. Clumsy beasts a little larger than the one I killed. They're stooping on The Bachelor as a raptor stoops on a field mouse, diving upon him with their claws wide and their wings canted so as to slice him up maliciously each time they pass. He's trying to fight them off, waving the pick overhead, swinging it madly—but they perceive its presence and somehow compute the length and direction of its arc and thereby manage to elude its blows and inflict their anger physically upon The Bachelor. Despite their seeming clumsiness, he's no match for them, no match for them at all. . . .

I'm getting out of here, Ben. I'm going to go tumbling down the steps and out of this place while it's still within my power to do so. What a madhouse, what a sacred, colossal madhouse. Ole Oliver Oliphant should bless the solitary comfort of his grave for sparing him from this. BoskVeld crawls with a strangeness we don't want to be a part of. . . . Or perhaps it's a world beckoning to us across thresholds of insanity and terror for which our sweet lost Earth already has sufficient analogues. . . . Why commit ourselves to a madness the likes of which we've been trying for millennia to flee? . . . Don't listen to me. Who knows what I'm saying? I've got to get out of here. . . . I'm coming home, I'm coming home to you. To you, all of you, my kinsmen. . . .

*[Footfalls, a heavy wooden groaning, and then the unechoing silence of the night as Chaney emerges into the Wild.]*

V.  CHANEY *[exhilarated]*: God, look at them go off! I'm unloading my backpack. I'm lobbing them toward old Sol, wherever the debbil he at. Another Independence Day! My second one. *[Four or five successive whooshing sounds.]* I'm coming home, I'm coming home. To you, Ben. To you, Eisen. To Morrell, Yoshiba, and Jonathan. You won't be able to say I didn't perform my duties with a flair. *[Laughter.]* God, look at them stain the sky, look at 'em smoke, look at 'em burn away the reek of Asadi self-delusion and the stench of huri arrogance!

No, by God, we don't destroy every race we come across. Maybe the pygmies, maybe we did it to the pygmies—but the Asadi, bless 'em, they're doing it to themselves, they've been doing it to themselves for aeons. With help, perhaps. With assistance from their weird, imported familiars from beyond this solar system. It's not ourselves at fault, though. No one can say it's us.

But, God, look at that clean phosphorescent sky! I only wish I knew which direction Sol was in; I'd like to see it. Eisen, you said we could see it. Where? Tell me where. I'd like to see it like a shard of ice glittering in the center of those brilliant, beautiful, flaming cobwebs. . . .

## LAST THINGS

*Thomas Benedict speaking:* We saw the flares and picked Chaney up. Moses Eisen was with me in the copter. We had come out extremely early on the morning of Day 140 in order to complete Chaney's customary supply drop and then to circle the Asadi clearing with the thought of making a naked-eye sighting of our colleague. Captain Eisen had ordered this course of action when it became apparent that Chaney wasn't going to communicate with us of his own accord. Eisen wished to apprise himself of Chaney's condition, perhaps by landing and talking to the man. He wanted Chaney to return to base camp. If it had not been for these unusual circumstances, then, Chaney's flares might have gone off for no audience but an empty sky. As it was, we saw only the last two or three flares he set off and had to reverse the direction of our copter to make the rendezvous.

By the time we reached him, Chaney was no longer the exhilarated adventurer that the last section of his monologue paints him. He was a tired and sick man who did not seem to recognize us when we set down and who came aboard the copter bleary-eyed and unshaven, his arms draped across our shoulders.

By removing his backpack we came into possession of the recorder that he had used for the last two days and the eyebooks he had supposedly picked up in the Asadi temple. And that night I went back to the Asadi clearing alone to retrieve the remainder of his personal effects.

Back at base camp, however, we committed Chaney at once to the care of Doctors Williams and Tsyuki and saw to it that he had a private room in the infirmary. During this time, as I've already mentioned, he wrote "The Ritual of Death and Designation." He claimed, in more than one of our conversations, that we had picked him up not more than four or five hundred meters from the pagoda which he describes in this brief paper. He made this claim even though we were unable on several trips over a large area of the Wild to discover a clearing large enough to accommodate such a structure. Not once in all of our talks, however, did he ever claim that he had been *inside* the pagoda. Only in the confiscated tape does one encounter this bizarre notion; you have just read the edited transcript of the tape and can decide for yourself how much credence to give its various reports. One thing is certain: The eyebooks that Chaney brought out of the Calyptran Wild with him *do* exist. And they had to come from somewhere.

The eyebooks are a complete puzzle. They look exactly as Chaney describes them in the tape, and they all work. The cassettes are seamless plastic, and the only really efficient way we've been able to get inside one is to break the bulb—the glass eyelet—and probe through the opening with an old-fashioned watch tool. We've found nothing inside the cassettes on which their dizzying spectral patterns could have been programmed and no readily apparent energy source to power such a rapid presentation of spectral patterns. Morrell has suggested that the programs exist in the molecular structure of the hard plastic casing themselves, but even this intriguing hypothesis resists confirmation. To date, computer analysis of the eyebooks' color displays have established no basis for "translation" out of the visual realm and into the auditory. We lack a Rosetta stone, and because we do, the eyebooks remain an enigma.

As for Chaney, he apparently recovered. He would not discuss the tape that I once—only once—confronted him with, but he did talk about putting together a book-length account of his findings.

"The Asadi have to be described," Chaney once told me. "They have to be described in detail. It's essential we get down on paper every culture we find out here. On paper, on tape, on holographic storage cubes. The pen's mightier than the sword, and paper's more durable than flesh."

But Chaney didn't do his book. Three months he stayed with us, copying his notes, working in the base-camp library, joining us only every sixth or seventh meal in the general mess. He kept to himself, as isolated among us as he had been in the Asadi clearing. And, I suppose, he must have done a lot of thinking, a lot of somber, melancholy, fatalistic thinking.

He did something else that few of us paid much attention to. He grew a beard and refused to have his hair cut.

Later we understood why.

One morning we couldn't find Egan Chaney anywhere in base camp. By evening he still had not returned. Eisen sent me to the dormitory quarters we shared and told me to go through Chaney's belongings to see if I could determine his whereabouts from an explicit note or a random scrawl— anything he might have left behind in farewell. Already, you see, we were beginning to believe Chaney had defected to the Wild.

"I really don't think he'll be back," Eisen told me. He was right about that, but he was wrong in supposing that Chaney would have left his farewell amid the clutter of our dormitory room.

It wasn't until the next day, when I checked my mailbox in the radio room, that I found what Eisen had told me to look for. Knowing that there had been no probeship deliveries or private light-probe transmissions, I checked my box merely out of habit. And I found the note from Chaney. The only comfort it gave me was the comfort of knowing my friend had not decided to commit suicide—that he had successfully fought off a subtle but steadily encroaching madness.

Eisen disagreed with me in this assessment, believing that Chaney had committed suicide as surely as if he had taken poison or put a bullet through his brain.

Read the note he left behind, however. It expresses a peculiar sort of optimism, I think, and if you don't see the slender affirmative thread running through it, well, I would suggest that you go back and read the damn thing again. Because even if Chaney *has* committed suicide, he has died for something he believed in.

### CHANEY'S FAREWELL

I'm going back to the Asadi clearing, Ben. But don't come after me, I won't let you bring me back. I've reached a perfect accommodation with myself: Probably I'll die. Without your supply drops, that seems certain, doesn't it?

But I belong among the Asadi, not as an outcast and not as a chieftain—but as one of the milling throng. I belong there even though that throng is stupid, even though it persists in its self-developed immunity to instruction. I'm one of them. I feel for them.

Like The Bachelor, Ben, I'm a great slow moth. A tiger moth. And the flame I choose to pursue and die in is the same flame that slowly consumes every one of the Asadi. Don't forget me, Ben, but don't come after me, either.

Good health to you,
Egan

# CHAPTER ONE

# Moses Eisen

After rereading *Death and Designation Among the Asadi* for the umpteenth time, I slept only a little. Denebola's rising spread a radiance through Frasierville that automatically dimmed the streetlamps and set their vanadium-steel poles glinting like silverware in the hands of hungry pioneers. Maybe it was the noise of their flashing that sliced through my dreams and woke me up.

In my austere little debussy I relieved myself and drew enough water through the vacuum tap to slap away the numbness in my cheeks and crow's-feet. The mirror showed me a man whose every encounter with his mattress leaves him imprinted as if by a waffle iron. I dressed hurriedly and banged down the steps to hunt up Moses Eisen.

Eisen now lives with his wife and two children, both Bosk-Veld-born, in a house whose grounds jut into the Calyptran Wild like a barren peninsula. Three-quarters of the house lie below the surface. An unpainted wood verandah fronts the ground-level roof, and a ventilation tower rises above the jungle canopy behind the verandah. By default, this residence constitutes our planet's "Governor's Mansion"—for three years ago Kommthor elevated Eisen from the captaincy of the Third Denebolan Expedition to the post of interim administrative head of the BoskVeld Colony. When we were engaged in matters of official import, then, I was supposed to call him *Governor* Eisen and refrain from indecorous displays of intimacy.

That had never been hard. Eisen had no aptitude for either

small talk or jokes, and although old hands were able to barge in upon him without risking a stiff rebuke or an imperious stare, they could never accuse Eisen of trying to make them feel themselves a part of the family. Usually, weather permitting, he came outside to receive callers; and in the four and a half years since Civi Korps engineers had excavated his home from the rain forest's crumbling humus, I had set foot inside it exactly twice—for small but formal parties commemorating the births of his and Rebecca's children. I envied Eisen his family, but not his status or his disposition.

I walked down the little forest-locked peninsula to his house and mounted the steps to its deck. Dressed in dappled coveralls and smelling of an astringent homemade cologne (or "pore opener"), Eisen was somewhat testily awaiting me.

"You're late," he said by way of greeting. "I thought I was going to have to send someone after you."

We were going out to Chaney Field together. One of Eisen's duties was to greet all incoming colonists and support personnel, a duty he performed with grudging conscientiousness.

Late or not, I had to stand beside Eisen on his gallery as Denebola poured its copper light into our eyes from far beyond Frasierville's eastern perimeter. He seemed in no hurry to make up for the tardiness of which I was supposedly guilty. Instead, he nodded over his shoulder at the forest sighing and photosynthesizing at our backs.

"How long has it been since anyone did extensive field work among the Asadi?" he asked me, knowing the answer as well as I. The question—I was certain—had specific reference to the arrival of Chaney's daughter.

"No one does it full time anymore, Moses. You haven't permitted any of us to submerge ourselves in their culture since Egan disappeared." I'm sure I gave *culture* a disparaging inflection. Emotional identification with an alien species isn't always possible, even for people trained to repress their ethnocentric prejudices in the interests of a clinical objectivity. Egan Chaney knew that as well as anyone.

The Governor revolved his noncommittal face toward me. "But you and others continue to go in there occasionally, don't you?"

"Sure," I acknowledged. "I do, sometimes, and so does Yoshiba when she gets the chance." But after Chaney's defection, my interest in the Asadi rain forest was perhaps less in the Asadi themselves than in the ecological integrity of the rain forest as a biome. The fact that the only living organisms we had ever found in there were botanicals, insects, and the Asadi had made me, against my training, something of a xenologist. As had my work on Chaney's tapes and notes.

"To what end?"

"Sir?" I asked, intimidated by Eisen's tone.

"What real progress in our understanding of the Asadi has been made since Chaney left us? What specific achievements?"

"Their behavior hasn't altered fundamentally in the past six or seven years. We reaffirm Chaney's basic findings. We note small changes in the size and makeup of the population in the Asadi clearing. . . . We're only in there by day, Moses, when we're in there, and it's tedious work. All our attempts at telemetered observation have been thwarted by the Asadi themselves. They won't tolerate mechanical systems in the Wild. They disassemble such equipment when they discover it or hurl it about like male chimpanzees engaging in charging displays. This discovery, by itself, is probably the most significant one we've made in seven years—it suggests a hostile but systematic response to our attempts at long-distance surveillance."

"Couldn't it just as easily suggest an instinctive dislike of things that don't naturally belong in their jungle? It doesn't require cognitive ability to recognize an intrusive wrongness, Ben. Back home, a sparrow seeing a piece of rope in its nest perceives the rope as a snake and refuses to land. You see, the *wrongness* registers."

Tactfully, I admitted that the Asadi's destruction of our telemetering equipment might well stem from its "wrongness" rather than our subjects' intelligent awareness that we were trying to record their life styles.

"Is that it, then?" Eisen asked. "One ambiguous discovery in six years?"

"There's Geoffrey Sankosh's film," I responded wearily. "From that we've learned that the Asadi bear live young, whom they leave during the day in nests high above the forest floor. We also know that their young don't come to the Asadi assembly ground until they've grown relatively imposing adult manes. As best we can tell, this takes more than seven years, maybe as many as twelve. Since the Third Expedition hasn't been here twelve years, Moses, it's hard to be much more accurate than that in estimating the age of initiation."

"The holographic film was shot by an outsider," Eisen murmured deprecatingly, squinting into the sun.

I hurried to counter the implications of this remark: "That's because you didn't have the authority to summon Sankosh back to Frasierville every night. The terms of his grant freed him to work independently of colonial authority, and he took full advantage of that freedom. Besides, he was lucky, Moses. If he had discovered the female already well advanced in her labor, he would never have been able to get his equipment into place in time to film the births. Had he arrived earlier, the female would have fled beyond him without a trace."

Eisen was smiling reminiscently. "I've seen it six or seven times, that film. A marvelous accomplishment. Once I set my projection cylinder down there on the patio roof"—pointing his chin at the expanse of leaf carpeting below the verandah—"and let little Reba watch it, too. The angle of apprehension was perfect. I've never seen her eyes so big."

To that I didn't respond.

Frasierville was beginning to stir. Doors flapped open, and 'bola-powered lorries hummed back and forth among the warehouses, import-processing plants, and the central solar station, a pagoda of tarnished mirrors. A caravan of newly indoctrinated colonists was departing for Amérsavane, the bitter-grass veldt country to the far southeast. Eisen and I watched its long train of veldt-rovers and settlement cars hitch jerkily along Dry Run Boulevard and out of sight beyond the power sails of the hospital.

"At least Sankosh came back alive," Eisen finally said. "We didn't have to send someone into the Wild to retrieve him."

"No, we didn't," I agreed.

Eisen moved silently along the deck and went down the steps at its opposite end. Obediently, and of necessity, I followed. He was halfway up the tree-lined peninsula of his yard before I could fall in comfortably beside him and pick up the gist of the monologue spilling from his lips.

". . . care for it, Ben. Not a bit. She may have a grant, too—autonomous institutional funding freeing her from my control. Even her father didn't have that. But what if she isn't as fortunate as Geoffrey Sankosh? What if she melts out there in the Wild and then can't reconstitute herself as a functional human being? I don't like this a bit, Ben, and I'm not particularly disposed to like her, either."

Still walking, he said, "Thank God, she's not the only one I'm going out to the shuttle field to meet—her daddy's *memorial* shuttle field, I suppose I should add. And thank God, you're her escort and surrogate daddy for the day, maybe even for the duration of her stay, and it's your bounden duty, Ben, to keep her out of my hair. Keep her out of trouble, too."

We walked to the lorry pool three streets beyond my own living quarters. A Komm-service guard, recognizing Eisen, drove a veldt-rover out of the fenced-in compound and picked us up. Another attendant, a young woman in a violet enlisted-grade jumpsuit, swung the gate shut behind us and locked it with a metallic pop. Purring, our veldt-rover leaped away.

"I'd almost made up my mind not to go this morning," Eisen said.

"Why?"

"I don't think Egan Chaney had very much in common with the author of *The Iliad*. And I don't think his interloping daughter is likely to have much in common with the excavator of Troy, old what's-his-name."

"Neither do I, frankly. Is that all that's bothering you?"

Eisen, the margins of his salt-and-pepper tonsure fluttering in the wind, regarded me with something like childish pique. "If I had my way, Ben, we'd move Frasierville to a coastal or a veldt location and leave the Asadi altogether to their own devices."

"But they warrant study. An intelligent ancestral species of the Asadi or an artifact-making collateral relative—the Ur'sadi—went extinct some time ago. But despite what Chaney babbled in his final tape about their being on the verge of autogenocide, the Asadi themselves seem evolutionarily stable at present."

"Then maybe we just ought to leave them alone."

"Thanks to you," I countered, "that's pretty much what we're doing. In any case, they're a"—I quoted to Eisen from the xenologists' handbook that Chaney had helped to write before his arrival on BoskVeld—"' 'Komm-protected indigenous species possessing either fully developed self-awareness or its demonstrable potential.' That being so—even if they aren't truly indigenous—we can't kill one of their number to examine its brain, and in all the time we've been here we've never had the opportunity to recover one of their dead."

"Pity," said Eisen, smiling faintly. "I hope you don't hold me accountable for that."

Our driver negotiated the washed-out surface of Calyptran Perimeter Road—which old hands irreverently refer to as Aphasia Alley, so difficult is it to speak while jolting along its three-kilometer length—and then headed northeast on the white, polymer-bonded macadam of Egan Chaney Highway. The veldt swallowed us, and off to our right we saw the convoy destined for Amérsavane crawling through the morning's dizzying veils of heat shimmer. You began to realize why the imperial British were so fond of pith helmets.

The veldt was vacant. A visitor could look in vain for impala, zebras, wildebeest, or gazelles. The African analogy worked only topographically, and the foliage clinging to the earth and tufting a thumb's length above the surface in prickly beige or cream-colored flowers had no known counterpart in the Serengeti or the Ngorongoro Crater. Only a few tussocks of the many nondescript clusters flamed out in gaudy reds and oranges, and those, of course, caught and captivated the eye.

Traveling them, you wondered why the savannahs had spawned no animals to graze there. You wondered how the Asadi could have evolved on a world whose biota seemed so limited and niggardly. *Prodigal* is not a word you would have used to describe the Creative Animus that undertook the husbandry of BoskVeld's plains and forests. Hence, the utter anomalousness of the Asadi. (As for the batlike huri that Chaney mentions in his journals and tapes, no one but him had ever seen a specimen of those elusive, nasty-sounding critters.) I sometimes found myself believing that forty million years in the future, when humanity had passed away from the universe at large, the bacteria we left behind on BoskVeld would have evolved into ethically self-aware hominids and that the Asadi would still be there on the planet to confute their logic and boggle their understanding. . . .

"We're going to arrive well before the probeship's shuttlecraft," said our driver. He was a dark-complexioned young man whose name was embroidered in purple thread on the shoulder of his violet sleeve: Bahadori.

"Fine," said Eisen listlessly.

The shuttle field's colossal, and useless, probeship gantry had been visible to us for ten or twelve minutes already. Like a titanium cat's cradle, it reared up fifteen stories in the desert shimmer, defining the surrounding countryside by both its size and its geometric complexity: The veldt around it seemed to exist for the sole purpose of providing the gantry with a place to rest. Its interior struts glistened like the threads of a giant spiderweb, and the cylindrical passenger and cargo cars poised on the gantry-to-ground diagonals resembled dewdrops trembling in the webbing. A field of whilais, irrigated by vacuum pumps, grew behind the gantry and gentled the terrible but stunning monotony of the veldt. To the north, beyond the field's main landing strips, sat a colossal, and useless, probeship hangar. This building, which had been vandalized and inscribed with weird graffiti repeatedly over the past four years, looked like a vast but isolated slum. I was fascinated by it. Several times in recent months I had toured the hangar just to be by myself in its echoing emptiness.

Much nearer, a cluster of flat-roofed buildings with translucent green walls provided housing for the shuttle field's support personnel and temporary shelter for the new arrivals. Chaney Field, in fact, had become an important suburb of Frasierville. Many had had hopes that it would soon take its place in the hierarchy of Glaktik Komm as a bonafide lightprobe port. Hence the folly of the unusued gantry. Hence, too, the folly of the immense probeship hangar which was now in use principally as a warehouse for imported colony supplies.

"Whom else must you meet?" I asked Eisen as we neared the complex.

"A new group of colonists," he responded without looking at me. "And, as I understand it, a friend of Elegy Cather's whom I may wish to put in quarantine for a while."

"Quarantine!" I exclaimed.

"So the *Wasserläufer IX*'s captain informed me by radio last night."

"What the devil are you talking about?"

"Patience," said Eisen. "Have patience, Ben."

# CHAPTER TWO

# Jaafar, Elegy, and Kretzoi

Outside the terminal in the blistering midmorning heat we stood—Jaafar Bahadori and I—while Eisen awaited the shuttlecraft's coming in the comfort of his air-conditioned Chaney Field office. He had invited us to join him without much enthusiasm, and we had politely declined in order to watch the shuttle put down on the landing strip.

Cracking his knuckles in anticipation, Bahadori shifted from foot to foot and peered into the pale recesses of sky above the Calyptran Wild. The wind blew in gusts past the field's green-glowing support buildings, setting up an eerie lament in the titanium lyre of the gantry.

At last the shuttle appeared: a huge white fuselage descending on the treetops to the northwest and banking into the wind to align itself with Chaney Field's main landing strip. It got down quickly. Then, distorted by heat haze, foreshortened by distance, the shuttle bumped toward Bahadori and me at high, whining speed.

Despite having watched a hundred such shuttles land, I was always surprised by how ungainly they appeared on the ground. In the newer probeships the shuttles slot into the cargo nacelles underslung aft and so become merely another modular component of the whole—but, independent of their parent ships, they have all the grace and aesthetic appeal of wounded pelicans.

Baggage lorries and passenger vans departed the shade screens of the terminal and scooted competitively across the polymac. The shuttle, meanwhile, began putting out its tubelike extensible ramps—a trio of them. Bahadori and I caught a ride on one of the passing baggage trucks. Then we jumped from its running board only ten or twelve meters from the shuttle's central ramp.

Many of those disembarking were women—more women than men, in fact—and I knew that it was going to be no easy task finding Elegy Cather among all the attractive candidates. I understood, though, why the young Iranian had been so keen to greet the shuttle—he was nineteen or twenty and a long way from home. He blustered into the crowd surging out of the extensible tube opposite us and fought his way upstream like a randy salmon. I didn't see him again for another forty or fifty minutes.

As soon as Bahadori was gone, I started asking each young woman who approached if she were Elegy Cather. No luck. My candidates shook their heads, or smiled and raised their eyebrows in apology, or gave me haughty looks as if I had indecently propositioned them. The men among whom they walked either grinned or pretended not to notice me.

One fellow, however, stopped and took my arm. "Go up the rear ramp," he told me, nodding. "Cather's back there now, trying to get something straightened out with a Komm-service steward."

This ramp was on the other side of the shuttle. I walked beneath the craft's bloated, silver-white belly, then entered the antiseptic-smelling tube leading upward to the passenger compartment.

"Who's going to guarantee his safety?" I heard a female voice demanding evenly. "You? Governor Eisen? Who?"

The steward responded, "If it *isn't* quarantined, young woman, who's going to guarantee the lives of the inhabitants of BoskVeld?" This man, who was facing me from the rear of the passenger compartment, stood a good head and a half taller than his diminutive adversary. He looked, in his less-than-heartfelt belligerence, amost as old as I. My heart went out to him.

"Not *it*," the young woman corrected him. "Kretzoi's an utterly unique intelligent being who deserves your respect. Have the decency to use the masculine pronoun." She paused to glance over her shoulder at me before resuming her argument with the steward. "And who do you mean by 'the inhabitants of BoskVeld,' anyway? The Asadi? If so, no one thought to quarantine the members of the First, Second, and Third Denebolan Expeditions before turning them loose like a . . . a *swarm* of renegade bacteria." That wasn't the word she wanted, but she emphasized it nevertheless.

"I didn't mean the Asadi," the steward wearily parried. "I meant the *human* inhabitants of BoskVeld. The civkis, the colonists, the scientific and military support personnel. Would you care to be responsible for turning this planet into a ghost world?"

"Kretzoi had a clean bill of health before we left Dar es Salaam. Do you think he contracted a plague virus aboard the *Wasserläufer?* Do you think he's going to expose everyone here to some mysterious and lethal contagion?"

"Civ Cather, *I* don't think anything," the man tried to begin.

"Apparently not," the young woman declared, ignoring the real import of his inflection. "I wonder who does."

"I mean," the haggard steward began again, "that the decision isn't mine. It's Governor Eisen's. He wants to confine Krikorian—or whatever its name is—until your, ah, companion is thoroughly acclimated and at home. He also has the safety of others in mind."

"Acclimatize Kretzoi!" the young woman exclaimed. "Why, this is almost exactly the sort of climate he grew up in!"

I edged my way along the aisle until I was standing at the young woman's shoulder. "Elegy Cather," I said, "I'm Thomas Benedict."

The steward's face betrayed relief and gratitude; he took the occasion to excuse himself and trudge past us toward the pilot's cabin.

The glance that Chaney's daughter had thrown me a moment earlier had imprinted only her eyes in my memory. They were as large and brown, and as potentially dangerous, as chestnuts in an unbanked fire. They radiated intelligence and indomitability. Her other features, by comparison, seemed soft and unprepossessing. Elegy Cather looked like a feminine, mulatto version of her father, compact and unadorned. The packaging promised nothing extroardinary, but her eyes transformed her deceptive plainness. Her eyes and her warm, no-nonsense voice.

She unhesitatingly extended her hand, addressing me as Dr.

Benedict. I refrained from avuncularly suggesting that she call me either Thomas or Ben. After all, I was several years younger than her father.

"Who's supposed to be quarantined?" I asked her instead.

"Come along," she said, "and I'll show you."

She took me deeper into the shuttle's tail section and then down a cramped helical stairway into the cargo bay. The bay's exterior doors were open by this time, and the lift operators in their lorries on the plymac were keying instructions into the mechanical stevedores rearranging the goods and equipment in the bay. The heat of the veldt poured in through the open doors.

"This is where he had to ride," Elegy Cather told me, picking her way among the crates, transport cylinders, and naked machines packed against one another in the cargo section. We halted in front of a small pressurized closet against the port bulkhead. "Right here," she emphasized, "Caged. As if he'd murdered somebody or plotted with known subversives to disrupt the authority of Glaktik Komm's legally appointed agents. Aren't you appalled? Aboard the *Wasserläufer*, Dr. Benedict, he shared my stateroom. My stateroom!"

Chaney's daughter fiddled with the latch on the closet, sprang it expertly, and eased the rounded door aside.

My first thought was that someone had kidnapped Elegy Cather's traveling companion and by some insidious legerdemain replaced him with—well, one of the stupid and brutal Asadi from our native Wild.

I took a step or two backward.

The creature in the pressurized cargo closet was revealed to me in hunched profile, squatting on the floor and clutching its knees like an autistic child. The tawny mane and the powerful, sinewy limbs of the beast, however, suggested a Calyptran origin.

"Kretzoi," the young woman murmured. "Are you all right?"

When the creature turned its head to look at us, I felt certain it was an Asadi. Its head seemed overlarge, but its eyes consisted of two circular lenses as thick and rippled-seeming as old-fashioned bottle glass. I expected to see the irises behind these lenses change colors in rapid, unpredictable sequence. Instead, behind the fitted lenses, I saw eyes like mine or Elegy Cather's—brown irises in a matrix of coagulated albumin. This, too, unsettled me.

Kretzoi—to lend the creature Cather's distinguished name for him—blinked behind his artificial eye bubbles and made a rapid sign with his right hand. Then he let his hand fall limply aside.

Chaney's daughter signed to the creature in turn, even though he had apparently understood her spoken question. Then she leaned inward as if to help Kretzoi out of his place of confinement.

"He's hot and thirsty and cramped," Elegy Cather said. "Which isn't particularly surprising under the circumstances, is it?"

"Civ Cather!" shouted a voice from aft.

We turned and saw the weary steward staring down on us from the helical stairway in the shuttle's tail. He was ducking his head and contorting his neck in order to bring us into his line of sight, and I briefly feared he might fall. The fact that Chaney's daughter had gone so far as to free a passenger bound for quarantine was such a shock to him that he paid no attention to where he was putting his feet and saved himself a concussion only by reaching out and grabbing the narrow handrail. Once down, though, he managed to get to us over the crowded cargo floor in a matter of seconds.

"What are you doing?" he demanded of Elegy. "What do you think you're doing?"

Kretzoi, out of his closet, ignored the steward but raised himself to a tentative standing position and looked about as if peering over a field of waist-high grass. Elegy was touching his arm reassuringly, trying to persuade him merely by tactile suggestion to go with her back the way the steward had just come. Kretzoi continued to peer about warily, taking in everything at once, his doglike muzzle revolving toward the open bay doors to scent the humid rankness of the laborers on the polymac and then swinging back across the jumble of supplies to brush against Elegy's shoulder. He was half crouching, half standing, with his arms or forelimbs cocked at the elbows in front of him and his hands hanging limp.

Completely upright, he would have been as tall as the young woman who tried to direct him out of the cargo bay—as tall, I estimated, as many adult Asadi. His mane, I felt sure, was the result of some kind of sophisticated hormonal treatment, while the hard transparent carapaces shielding his eyes were undoubtedly nothing but surgical implants. His body fur was thin and, in contrast to his mane, silver-grey. I decided on the spot that Kretzoi was a hybrid terrestrial primate genetically altered or eugenically manipulated to yield an individual with the characteristics of both a Gombe Stream chimp and an Ishasha River baboon. Recently he had undergone the relatively minor physical "adjustments" that had grafted to these unusual hybrid characteristics the distinctive external features that would identify him to the Asadi social until as one of its own.

These, at least, were my on-the-spot deductions about Kretzoi's singular anatomy, and even as the Komm-service steward interposed himself between the three of us and the stairway at the rear of the shuttle, I began to formulate a dim idea of how Elegy Cather proposed to succeed where all other potential rescuers of her father had failed. She had brought her own spy and infiltrator. . . .

All our dismayed and harried steward was thinking about, though, was the likelihood of Kretzoi's infecting the world with a deadly simian virus. He fisted both hands and held them like fragile porcelain eggs in the pit below his breastbone.

"Very lax security," I told him. "Do you propose to put all three of us in quarantine? Make that all *four* of us—I'm afraid you've exposed yourself to the possibility of infection, too." As soon as these words were out, I regretted the smugness of my tone and the small irrational joy I was taking in baiting the man.

His hands still fisted in his stomach, he responded with painful tact: "Would you at least do me the favor of waiting here until I can find out what the Governor wishes us to do now?"

"In this heat?" Elegy demanded. "It's fortunate Kretzoi didn't die in this sweatbox your captain had him placed in."

"Let us go upstairs to the passenger section," I urged the steward. "I promise we'll wait there until you can discover what to do with us."

"Why are you worried about the heat?" the steward asked Elegy, ignoring my suggestion. "I thought this was 'almost exactly' the sort of climate your Kirkorian grew up in." He unfisted one hand and began clenching and unclenching his fingers as if seeking purchase on an invisible neck.

"It's Kretzoi, not Kirkorian! He's named for the Hungarian paleontologist, not some Armenian figment of your curdled imagination!"

"I'm Armenian myself," the steward said. "I don't see that—"

Envisioning an absurdly heated exchange of genealogical insults, I told the man that we were going back up to the shuttle's passenger compartment—with Kretzoi—in order to free the steward to do his duty, whatever that might be. If he wished, he could find us there after consulting with his pilot and radioing the news of our intransigence to Moses Eisen in his air-conditioned office. In the meantime, we were going to take advantage of a little air conditioning ourselves and wait for some authoritative final word on our disposition. That said, I led Elegy Cather and her persecuted traveling companion through the cargo hold and up the stairway to a pair of comfortable aisle seats and a sweet pervasive coolness. Kretzoi squatted on the floor.

*

Within five minutes Moses Eisen himself had boarded the shuttle. He approached us up the long aisle from the front of the craft, his eyes trying to adjust and his dappled coveralls giving him less the appearance of a Colonial Administrator than of a balding adventurer who had wandered by accident out of some reptile-infested backwater. He looked seedy.

When he spotted Kretzoi sitting in an alert, baboonlike posture against Elegy's starboard aisle seat, as if silently imploring the young woman to groom and soothe him, Moses halted and stared. He obviously had no idea what to say, and my own inclination was to laugh. At last the Governor of all BoskVeld, former captain of the Third Denebolan Expedition, eased himself into a row of portside seats just in front of mine and propped his chin on arms folded atop the cushion of a chair back. Now he resembled a small child attempting to survey surreptitiously all the other passengers around his own assigned in-flight island of shuttle space.

"Elegy Cather," I said, making introductions, "this is Governor Moses Eisen. Governor Eisen, this is Kretzoi."

"Pleased to meet you both," said Moses. It would be a heinous distortion of the truth to say he sounded sincere. He was just barely on the acceptable side of civil.

"You're not really going to try to put Kretzoi in quarantine, are you?" asked Elegy. "That sweatbox downstairs was surely indignity enough for him to have to suffer." She groomed the back of Kretzoi's head, parting the tangles of his mane and drawing her fingers from crown to nape in graceful combing sweeps. Inside the lenses shielding them, I noticed, Kretzoi had shut his disconcertingly human eyes.

"No," said Moses. "Not now."

"Because you've been exposed to him yourself," I said. "Along with me, the steward, Civ Cather, and possibly the workers in their cargo lifts. It's either confinement for everyone or no one. Nothing else makes sense."

"I'm aware of that, Dr. Benedict." His inflection and choice of words were so cold that I felt my face crimsoning with both anger and humiliation; embarrassment, too, maybe. Then, addressing Elegy, Moses said, "This is a stupid way to begin our acquaintance and one for which I apologize. The captain of the *Wasserläufer* led me to believe your 'friend' was an experimental animal that had not been immunized against the various catarrhs and minor infections that newcomers to our world often contract, and my decision to quarantine was for the animal's benefit as much as for the citizens of BoskVeld's. It takes a couple of weeks for the full battery of immunizations to take effect, you see, and during that time your"—he struggled to find the appropriate expression—"your *ward* would have been vulnerable."

"My 'ward'—I wish you'd call him Kretzoi—was immunized at the light-probe medical facilities outside Dar es Salaam, just as I was, sir, and I can't imagine how *you* could imagine his getting so many light-years through id-space without having first cleared the Komm-galens Earthside."

"The captain of the *Wasserläufer IX* told me that . . . that Kretzoi had not been immunized, that there'd been a complicated mix-up before the departure of your shuttlecraft from Nyerere Field."

"Blather-tripe!" Chaney's daughter exclaimed eloquently, ceasing to groom her companion and imparting a veneer of stricken bafflement to our poor Governor's otherwise imperious features. "When did Captain de Lambant tell you this?"

"Yesterday afternoon," Moses responded cautiously, "soon after maneuvering the *Wasserläufer* into orbit."

"How incredibly disappointing and petty," Elegy said, her

voice scarcely more than a quiet hum. "My recompense for failing to give over my person. A little practical joke, in reward for my recalcitrance. I would have thought de Lambant above *that* sort of smallness." She shook her head.

"Isn't Captain de Lambant a woman?" Moses asked, trying to orient himself and crimsoning only faintly in the attempt.

"Yes, sir. Very much so. In the prime."

"Well, then—" The Governor ran down, stymied and flustered. His jowls gleamed fiercely, and the top of his head might have been the globe of one of Frasierville's streetlamps. He had forgotten that although pairbonding by members of opposite sexes is commonplace everywhere, it truly dominates human relationships only on frontier worlds like BoskVeld. A great many vestigial assumptions about sex and procreation haunt the old man, and at last I did laugh at him, rather loudly.

"Shut up, Ben!"

"At least we're back on a first-name basis," I said, still laughing in spite of his warning.

Moses cut his eyes away from me and looked at Elegy Cather. "In any case, you're here. Even though you're on a research grant permitting you a good deal of personal autonomy, Civ Cather, I hope you'll have sufficient wisdom to take the advice of old-timers like myself and Ben. The Calyptran Wild isn't going to go anywhere for a few thousand years yet, and there's a lot in Frasierville to see and learn."

"My father isn't in Frasierville, however," said Elegy pointedly, "and I've studied so many street maps and holographic constructs and eyewitness histories of your capital that I feel—maybe a little cockily—that I already know it firsthand."

This declaration did nothing to pacify Moses's fear that we would soon have another lost soul spooking us from undiscoverable recesses in the Wild. He turned his peevish gaze on Kretzoi, but addressed the young woman.

"I take it—from your familiarity with Frasierville and the appearance of your quasi-simian friend here—that you intend to seek out the Asadi even before you unpack your bags."

"Almost that soon. Yes, sir."

"Look. You've waited quite a long time for this opportunity. You can wait two or three more days. Give Dr. Benedict a little time to outfit your expedition, find out something about your plans, and work up an official prospectus for my perusal and peace of mind. I don't like to say hello and good-bye to visitors to BoskVeld all on the same day."

Elegy Cather inclined her head a degree or two to express her grudging consent. Then she resumed grooming Kretzoi's great tawny mane, and Moses and I silently watched her.

\*

After I had enticed him away from the three young civki sirens who had enchanted him in the Chaney Field terminal, Bahadori drove us back to Frasierville. Elegy and I rode in the veldt-rover's wide backseat, on split and sagging imitation-leather upholstery of a faded carrot color, while Kretzoi kept poor Jaafar company up front.

I had no iron-clad notions about the young Iranian's mood, for he said nothing at all on either our trip across the sizzling polymac or our swing along the liver-jouncing length of Aphasia Alley. Nevertheless, the rigid set of his head and the impenetrability of his silence gave me to believe he considered himself the victim of a terrible insult. He had taken Kretzoi for a genuine Asadi, and he completed our trip back into town only by submerging his outrage in the corrosive acid of "duty." I resolved to explain nothing to him, however, until later—for I was no more inclined to talk than he was. Even Elegy, whose vivacity and spirit had seemed so unquenchable in the probeship shuttle, was silent.

But as we rode, my silent wish for Jaafar was that in one of the enlisted-grade bars on Night Drag Boulevard that night he would find a wide-eyed female civki on his arm and a healthily requitable passion in his heart. My wish—sincere as it was—failed to get through to him telepathically, and his mood remained sour and uncommunicative. Only Kretzoi, of all of us, seemed unaffected by it.

Eventually Jaafar dropped the three of us off at the hospital, where I went in to arrange guest accommodations for Elegy and Kretzoi in one of the first-floor wings. The two of them nearly bollixed this operation by following me inside to the admissions desk. As soon as the three of us appeared, an astonished Komm-galen tried, altogether peremptorily, to order us off the premises. I forestalled him with an official communication from Governor Eisen and a poker-faced testimonial to Kretzoi's complete mastery of human toilet facilities. Reluctantly, the man installed them in adjacent rooms down the appropriate corridor and retreated back to the admissions desk wearing a look of haggard, hunch-shouldered resignation.

The Komm-galens didn't like it. Janitorial personnel were scandalized. And one of the residents of the guest wing slammed his door in our faces as we first strolled down the corridor in search of the Cather-Kretzoi suite. So be it, I told myself, thoroughly enjoying the experience. So be it. And after bidding them both good day, I left the hospital and walked leisurely back to my quonset and took a quiet lunch.

# CHAPTER THREE

# Once, Upon the Japurá River

I called for Elegy at the hospital the following morning, but waited for her at the first-floor admissions desk rather than going directly to her room. Interns and orderlies regarded me sourly, I thought, as if they'd been informed of the outrage I had helped effect against their institution. I didn't relish swaggering past them with Kretzoi in tow. The new day had sapped me of both my bravado and my humor. Nothing but business lay ahead, the dismaying and tedious logistics of adventure, and I feared what Elegy was going to make me do.

In a moment she was coming toward me from her room, and Kretzoi was conspicuous by his absence. She wore cream-colored jodhpurs, lightweight calf-high boots, and a poncho of paisley silk that lifted and eddied with each step she took. Lovely.

"Kretzoi?" I asked her when we were face to face.

"He's studying."

"Studying?"

"Governor Eisen sent us a projection cube yesterday afternoon and a copy of Sankosh's holofilm of the births of the Asadi twins. Kretzoi's going to spend the day reviewing it. Research, I suppose you could say. Neither of us had seen the film before."

"The film lasts twelve, maybe fifteen minutes," I told Elegy. "He'll wear it out."

"Intensive research." She laughed nervously and glanced around at the hospital personnel. "And I'm not ready to subject him to these people's stares, frankly. Yesterday took its toll. Let's let him recuperate.''

''He's likely to have it worse in the Wild. Human hostility is a pretty low hurdle in comparison to Asadi indifference.''

''Let's go,'' she said, apparently to deprive the interns and orderlies of the stimulant of our conversation. ''I'll show you how well I know Frasierville by taking you to Enos's for breakfast.''

All at once, then, we were out in the sun-bright streets, where Elegy, recalling her Earthside preparations for life in BoskVeld's capital, oriented herself like a native and led me away from the lofty aluminum sails of the hospital. We stalked together down a dusty little alley debouching eventually on a boarded-up cafe. The sign over the shop had been pulled down, and a stray dog—some pioneer's gone-awry eugenic attempt at creating a hairless, mole-snouted canine burrower for dog days on the veldt—was licking a mauve stain on the sidewalk tiles.

''This is supposed to be Enos's,'' Elegy said, her voice almost indignant. ''I'm sure it is.''

''Sure you're not lost?'' I taunted her gently.

A shimmer of doubt flashed in her eyes, like sheet lightning on an otherwise clear horizon. How could she expect to navigate expertly the byways and back alleys of an alien city she had never before set foot in? Maps and guidebooks, studied at a distance of so many abstract light-years, were poor substitutes for firsthand experience. Perhaps no substitute at all. Poor Elegy. She wavered, mistrusted her instincts.

Then she said, ''This place *used to be* Enos's, didn't it? Tell me the truth. I haven't gone wrong, have I?''

''This used to be Enos's,'' I acknowledged. ''You haven't gone wrong.'' The mole-snouted dog eyed us suspiciously from undoggish eyes, then limped off down the street fronting the boarded-up restaurant.

''What's happened to it, then?''

''Enos and his family pulled up stakes eight or ten weeks ago and left for Amérsavane with a newly arrived contingent of colonists. Colonial Administration helped equip them for the veldt by buying them out.'' I folded my arms and squinted back down the alley we'd come by. ''It's all right. I wasn't hungry, anyway. It's a little late for breakfast.''

"But I got here, didn't I? I found the place."

"You're not suggesting an analogy with our imminent search for your father, are you?"

Elegy Cather turned toward me so that her silk poncho inscribed a graceful manta-wing undulation in the air. "I wasn't," she said. "Not consciously."

"I hope not. Because in finding Enos's you've found nothing but the shell of your expectations and something you didn't expect to find at all."

Elegy favored this Nestorian counsel with laughter. "It's a little early for such pessimism, isn't it, Ben?" All of a sudden I was Ben. Good, grey Ben. I didn't really mind.

"It's six or so years too late for optimism," I rejoined.

"Or twelve. Or twenty. Depending on your degree of fatality and your personal perspective, of course. A guidebook to Frasierville's back-alley eateries isn't exactly a monograph on sacred Asadi places and rituals. Guidebooks are forever going out of date."

I said nothing. Brilliant morning sunlight flaked off the turrets of a nearby extrusion plant—as if Denebola itself were being whittled to a spear point. The Calyptran Wild, however, seemed either parsecs or centuries distant. A long way off.

"You've got an office, don't you?" Elegy asked, taking my arm. "We have a prospectus to draw up and plans to make."

*

My office was a miniature ecosystem of accidental design and haphazard self-perpetuation. On the days that I inhabited it—a ramshackle prefab from the days of Frasier's original Expedition—I was its most conspicuous life form. My secretary was a dictaphone device with communication relays and information-storage-and-retrieval components, and the placard on my desk read *Thomas Benedict, Head / BoskVeld Ecological Research and Administration.* A bureaucrat in an ersatz biome.

The force of habit was my ecosystem's principal energy source, and its other major life forms included several droopy botanicals (which I only intermittently took care of), assorted and sundry protozoa and bacteria (I cheerfully assumed), and a bevy of pugnacious cockroaches (imported, I was sure, by probeship shuttles as tiny egg pods in the boots and baggage of a thousand incoming colonists). These last were predators that had not yet run me to ground. They left specklike droppings on my windowsills and rattled the crumpled paper in my trash cans, and I never did discover exactly what they fed on.

When I introduced Elegy into this "environmental house," I half expected her to suggest that we return to the guest suite in the hospital to map out our plans. Instead, she thumped the old-fashioned air conditioner purring laboriously in one of the prefab's ports and pulled up a chair so that she could look through the picture window behind my desk. Just beyond the plasma-lamp barricade on Frasierville's eastern perimeter, I knew, she could see the flat, purple-veined palm leaves, evil-looking scarlet flowers, and irregularly corrugated boles of the trees in the Calyptran Wild. Once, like her father, I had done field work for extended periods amid that jungle's sense-distorting luxuriance.

Swiveling in my chair, I said, "That's what you'll have to fight, Civ Cather, that and six years' utter wastage of Egan Chaney's spoor."

"Why does it stop there?" she asked, staring intently into the foliage. "Why is it that half the planet's land mass is veldt and half's tropical rain forest and both regions abut each other without any real gradation?"

"There's an abrupt discontinuity in soil types between the two biomes," I said, "and the rain clouds scudding in from the ocean, Calyptra, west of the Wild, seem generally to dump their moisture well before reaching the veldt. Lush forest growth continues to the edge of the veldt, we assume, because of the permeability and moisture-conducting capacity of the forest soil, a kind of—well, as odd as it may sound, a kind of porous laterite beneath two or three centimeters of amazingly rich humus. The variations in soil types and the differences in rainfall account for the topographic features of BoskVeld."

"Couldn't the permeable laterite and the humus you speak of be symptoms rather than causes of the planet's topographic division? Couldn't the soil pattern in the Wild *result* from the fact that a tropical rain forest has overlain it for so long?"

"Theoretically, I suppose. I'm not sure it's very likely. Your reasoning suggests an ecological equivalent to artistic debates about the separation of style and content. More than likely, the two go hand in hand." I swiveled away from the window and looked at Elegy. "Why does the subject interest you at all? Does it really have anything to do with finding your father?"

But she asked, "How many native animal species does BoskVeld boast?"

"The Asadi are the principal one," I responded, as if saying a catechism. "Discounting a wide variety of marine forms we're only now beginning to study, some native insects, and a few vaguely reptilian land-going creatures. Why?"

"How likely is it, then, that the Asadi originated here?"

"The argument of an extra-Denebolan origin isn't a particularly new one, Civ Cather. In fact—"

"I'd prefer that you call me by my first name."

"All right," I said tentatively, without saying it. "In fact, Frasier himself was the first to propose it. He argued that the technologically advanced ancestors of the Asadi, from whom they supposedly *devolved* as solar and climatic conditions changed, must have come from another planetary system. Nobody has any idea which one, however, and the archaeological record here on BoskVeld isn't all that helpful. At times, to tell the truth, it's downright muddled and self-contradictory."

"Is it possible that the Asadi's ancestors could have terraformed—maybe 'engineered' is a better word in this case—BoskVeld to suit their physiological and cultural needs? Hence, vacant prairie out there"—she gestured with her poncho—"and sheltering rain forest over here."

"Anything's possible, Elegy. But probability is another matter, and I'd say you're roaming aimlessly around its edges."

Elegy got up and circled my desk so that she was standing at my picture window gazing into the Wild. "Edges," she murmured ruminatively. "Edgewise. On edge. Edge-yoo-cated." Her voice grew louder: "I'm ready to get off the uncertain edge of this enterprise, Ben, and go straight into the jungle after my father."

"Why?" I pushed myself and my chair away from the desk so that I could scrutinize Elegy's attractive but somewhat shelf-browed profile.

"Because it's what I came here for," she declared almost defiantly.

Sitting, I felt at a disadvantage—even more so when a cockroach scurried over my boot, then sculled beneath my desk and across the floor toward the other end of the prefab. After heaving myself out of my chair, I paced away from Elegy to assassinate this fellow inhabitant of my sleazy private ecosystem.

"I still don't understand," I said, grinding my toe on the cockroach. "You don't even share your father's name, Elegy."

"I do, however, possess a goodly number of his genes."

"And that's enough to commit you to a wholehearted but probably doomed attempt to uncover his bones?"

"Not merely his bones, Dr. Benedict—his person."

With the edge of my boot sole I scraped aside the crushed carapace of the cockroach. Then I looked at Chaney's daughter. She was nimbused by the light pouring in through my window, and, momentarily, it was as if I were holding a conversation with either a hologramic image or a ghost. The unreality of the young woman's presence disoriented and upset me.

"You're not likely to find him mummified or turned conveniently to stone in a climate like the Wild's," I said.

"That's not what I'd want, in any case. What would you say if I told you I have hopes of finding my father . . . alive?"

"Dengue fever, maybe. I'd urge you to return to the hospital for metaboscanning and treatment."

"I've had all my shots," she said, laughing. "Kretzoi, too." She sat down in my chair, and the light gentled and transfigured her features, making her again a creature of flesh and blood.

I approached the desk. "After six years? Not bloody likely, Elegy. How can you even justify such a hope to yourself?"

"Even though my father believed that by returning to the Asadi he was signing a warrant of self-execution, he had a friend out there. A friend."

"The Bachelor?" I asked incredulously.

"The Bachelor," she affirmed, "who became the Asadi chieftain or dominant male upon the death of Eisen Zwei."

I shook my head. "No one's seen The Bachelor since your father's disappearance. And we've had a few people in the Wild doing daytime field work—nothing so intensive as when Egan was in there, admittedly, but enough to confirm or deny The Bachelor's continued existence, I'd wager."

"Then maybe they're together, Ben."

"More than likely, they're both dead. That's a pretty

unappealable, and unappealing, form of togetherness. Wouldn't you say?''

"Alive or dead, well, that's what Kretzoi and I are here to find out.''

\*

After that, we worked to prepare the formal prospectus that Eisen had demanded of us at Chaney Field. Elegy knew exactly what she intended to do and how she wished to go about it, and, as a consequence, the document we contrived together was apparently little more than an abridged reprise of her application for the Nyerere Foundation grant that had brought her to BoskVeld. It came to about two and a half pages of double-spaced text, neatly paragraphed and speedily printed in triplicate by the computer console atop my desk.

My suppositions about Kretzoi, formed at hazard in the cargo bay of the probeship shuttle, were for the most part confirmed. He was a hybrid primate who had undergone a series of surgical adaptations to make him resemble the Asadi, and Elegy intended to have him coptered into the Wild, to the Asadi clearing itself, there to act as her personal agent-in-place.

"He's going to require supply drops," I said, "just as Chaney did."

"Perhaps not. We've adopted to Kretzoi's gut and intestinal tract a colony of protozoa capable of breaking down cellulose; they're dormant now, but a single meal of bark or hardwood will activate them and evoke the programmed symbiotic response. And if you look closely at Kretzoi's teeth, you'll see they're fashioned to make stripping and chewing the Wild's most common plants a relatively easy task. He'll eat what the Asadi eat. Or so we hope."

"For how long?"

"Not long at all, if things go right. Just long enough for him to learn the location of the Asadi pagoda and to lead us directly there. I'm not anxious to sit forever behind the lines waiting for that revelation, you know."

As we worked, I had to answer several long-distance inquiries from the veldt about optimum times and methods for sowing whilais in unbroken savannah soils of varying pH measurements. Other such inquiries I patched through to the agrogeneticists house of Chaney Field. Carryover projects from previous days I dealt with hastily and peevishly, either setting them aside or feeding them back into the computer for further notation and editing. My attention was fixed on Elegy Cather and her passionate commitment to her self-imposed quest.

"The last time I saw Egan Chaney," she said when we had finished drawing up our prospectus, "I was eleven years old, and we'd been living on the northern bank of the Japurá River in what used to be western Brazil. After the deforestation of the Congo, during the last days of the African Armageddon, a small group of blacks and whites had worked together to evacuate from the Ituri a dozen members of the BaMbuti people with whom my father was so obsessed. These were the last pygmies, Ben, old and sterile and utterly joyless in their forced relocation to a rain forest half a world away from the one in which they'd been born. There was no hope that they would take hold in the New World and replenish their numbers to their pre-Armageddon strength, but if they stayed in the cratered and poisoned ruins of the Ituri, my father and his colleagues knew, they would die just that much sooner. They'd be gone from the face of the earth as surely as trilobites, pterodactyls, and the Irish elk. Scarred and sickened, then, the BaMbuti survivors were rounded up against their will—for their own good, and the world's too, as Egan Chaney saw it—and airlifted out of the Congolese battle zones to another continent and a tropical reservation in an immaculate clearing along the Japurá."

Elegy paused in this recitation and removed a book from one of the metal shelves suspended precariously from the prefab's ceiling. She turned the book in her hands—the first Swahili edition of *Death and Designation Among the Asadi,* one of fifteen or twenty different editions of the monograph I kept on display in my office.

"Did my father ever speak to you of the Japurá Episode?" the young woman suddenly asked me.

"Never," I responded. "The only comments about the BaMbuti he made here on BoskVeld, Elegy, are in the monograph you're holding."

"And he never spoke of my mother or me?"

"We all assumed him a bachelor—with the possible exception of Moses, who must have known something of his private life before assigning him on as the Third Expedition's xenologist."

"Do you want to know what happened in Japurá Camp, then?"

"Please."

"The pygmies—six or seven old women and about that many aged men—began dying. Homesickness, nostalgia, disorientation. I don't know exactly what they were dying of, except that it wasn't anything you could cure with a hypodermic or oral antibiotics. And my mother, who was a doctor, tried to minister to the BaMbuti with medicines as my father, the anthropologist, tried to minister to them with mercy. My mother's name was Celestine Cather, and to join Egan Chaney at Japurá Camp in an enterprise he probably recognized as quixotic, she uprooted the two of us from our life in the Tri-Mesa Archipol in the Colorado River Sector of the old Rural American Union. She threw over her practice there. You see, even though their 'marriage' was based on intermittent intellectual companionship, Chaney had appealed to her for help. They had a no-strings understanding in regard to everything in their relationship but the nurture of their daughter." Elegy put both hands on her face and held them there as if to test the reality of her flesh. "My mother once told me that she and Chaney had never slept together. Not once."

I raised my eyebrows.

"I was an *in vitro* baby—conceived of the union of displaced and literally disembodied sexual cells, carried through gestation by mechanical proxy, and born of a merry virgin crystalline canal in an utterly sanitized laboratory." Elegy laughed at this parodic catalogue, but her laughter was ambiguous.

"You feel personally diminished by the circumstances of your birth?" I hazarded.

She dropped her hands. "No, not in the least. That isn't what I was trying to imply at all—only that Egan Chaney and Celestine Cather had a very strange relationship, even by the comprehensive standards of the latter-day West. Until the BaMbuti relocation, you see, they had never lived in close proximity to each other for more than a week or two at a time, usually at seasonal intervals of three of four months. They preferred it that way."

"You had an absentee father, then?"

"I had a succession of solicitous fathers in the Tri-Mesa, short-term uncles and surrogate daddies. And until the last pygmy died and he severed all contact with my mother and me, I had either Egan Chaney's genuine presence or his cassette-recorded image as a fatherly model. Twice a week— without fail while we were living in the Tri-Mesa—a cassette addressed exclusively to me would arrive at our E-cube. I'd hurry to click it into the player to see what fairy tale or exotic myth or stumblebum joke my father was enacting for me this time. There wasn't one I didn't enjoy, and most of them, without being preachy, had a kind of quiet moral to impart. In fact, when we left the Tri-Mesa for Japurá Camp, I asked my mother if the cassettes would stop coming now and she said Yes and I was both indignant and chagrined.

" 'You'll have your father in person,' my mother told me. 'Why do you think you'll still require the holotapes?'

"I didn't know—but when we got to the camp, via a final sweltering trip along the Japurá in a ramshackle motor launch, I discovered that I really didn't *have* my father in person at all. He was too preoccupied with saving the last BaMbuti to favor me with anything more intimate than an occasional weary smile, altogether in passing, and my mother was finding her time similarly monopolized.

"I dug in the mud, shot feather darts endlessly out of a blowgun into improvised targets, or tagged along after the mestizos from Lago Pariçá who kept our camp going. The pygmies I saw only rarely, and I knew they were dying—dying in spite of everything Egan Chaney and Celestine Cather could do. . . . It's a measure of my mood, Ben, that I'd begun to think it served the sad, poisoned buggers right."

Just then an inquiry from SteppeChilde—a veldt colony to the far northeast—was patched through my computer from the relay at Chaney Field. I tapped out the communication code indicating preemptive priority business. There was nothing I could tell BoskVeld's impatient SteppeChildren that demanded an immediate response, and Elegy seemed, at the moment, more perilously in need of my ear and my unspoken sympathy.

"When we'd been in the jungle nearly half a year and it was clear the BaMbuti were bound for extinction, Egan Chaney proposed that my mother preserve tissue samples from the last three shell-shocked pygmies. He thought it might be possible to clone replacements for them when we could get back to facilities permitting that exacting procedure.

"The other nine or ten diminutive Africans had been given

Viking funerals on the Japurá, cast adrift at night in oil-soaked canoes and cremated in cindery bonfires above the river. I remember those funerals very well, Ben—I can still see the reflections of the flames in the dark water and hear the provocative crackling of their bones. There was some fear, you see, that the pygmies had been contaminated by unknown biological agents during the African Armageddon. Even burial seemed an insufficient precaution against the spread of their undiagnosable and wholly conjectural disease. Hence, Viking funerals. I can remember that I enjoyed these festive boat burnings immensely. They were events, every one of them.

"Anyway, my mother—even though she had both the equipment and the know-how to take the tissue samples my father wanted—felt ethically compelled to refuse. There was a quarrel, one that I overheard because I happened to be in my mother's tent in a cot draped with mosquito netting. They woke me up quarreling. My father kept repeating the phrase 'the death of diversity,' muttering it over and over like an incantation, while my mother framed arguments that seemed to me, groggy as I was, young as I was, rational and humane.

"First, my mother told Chaney, it might be that the cloned pygmies would carry in their genes the inheritable malignancy to which their parental donors had fallen prey. Who knew what kinds of insidious microscopic warfare the kols and autoks were waging in Central Africa? Second, she said, supposing the clones grew to healthy adulthood, what kind of life would they have? The Ituri was a radioactive swamp, and the pygmies' entire cultural milieu had been obliterated irretrievably—as irretrievably as some crippled whore's dreams of paradise. And third, the BaMbuti deserved to die out with as much dignity as they had lived. Japurá Camp, my mother finally declared, had been from first to last a praiseworthy but foredoomed exercise in altruism. Why the hell couldn't Egan Chaney throw in the towel without first waving it over his head like a battle flag?"

"And this argument eventually led Chaney to sever all contacts with your mother and you?" I asked.

"In part," Elegy replied, staring sightlessly at the open monograph in her hands. "During the following week, the last three pygmies died, one at a time. My mother was in attendance on all but the very last, a grizzled old woman with dugs like goatskin wine sacks. She wasn't with this last one because I had taken sick the day before and she refused to leave my cotside to watch the old woman's inevitable demise. Instead, Chaney and a mestizo named Estanislau sat by the BaMbuti woman, and the next day, when I was suddenly quite well again, Estanislau reported that Chaney had wept all night, even biting a hunk of flesh from his forearm when it dawned on him they were keeping vigil over a corpse. Indeed, in the preparations for the old woman's funeral on the river Chaney showed up with a bright gauze bandage above his right wrist. My mother hadn't applied it, either, and he answered no one's questions about the wound it concealed.''

"And you?" I asked. "What had been wrong with you?"

"Nothing, Ben. Nothing at all.''

"Nothing?"

"'Well, something, I guess. I had feigned being ill to keep my mother beside me on the final night, dimly aware that Chaney would suffer more than anyone because of my ruse—out of both genuine worry for me and his heartfelt involvement with the old woman whose death he would make himself witness.''

"You hoodwinked your mother to spite Chaney?"

"It wasn't terribly hard. She was primed by Japurá Camp to see illness at the slightest symptom, and I complained of stomach cramps while holding bars of lye soap in my armpits to raise my temperature. The soap gave me a terrible rash that lasted for days, but I never told anyone about it. Just as Chaney never explained the wound on his forearm. Nevertheless, when we were safely back in Rio, the BaMbuti extinct and my father's hopes for somehow preserving their genetic heritage utterly dashed, he took me aside at the airport and said, 'I know what you did, Elegy, and one day you'll know, too.' I looked at him, Ben, and realized he *did* know. A fever that had nothing to do with lye soap concealed in my armpits spread through my chest and face, and, as things turned out, those were the last words he ever spoke to me. Mother and I returned to the Tri-Mesa, and Chaney disappeared without a trace from our lives. No visits, no cassettes, no word from him or anyone who knew him. Nothing.

"My doing," Elegy Cather concluded with quiet self-incrimination. "His disappearance from our lives was at least partially my doing."

"You probably ought to remember," I pointed out, half

amused by her assumption of responsibility and half irritated by it, "Chaney was a grown man and you were a little girl of eleven."

"I realize that. But I had a pretty mature ethical awareness at that age, and all it took to trigger my guilt was Chaney's revealing to me that he knew what I had done. In one sense, it was a small thing, pretending to be sick. But in another, taking into account the relocation of the last BaMbuti and my father's depth of commitment to them, it was equivalent to a kind of murder. If you and others can't understand that, it's probably because you aren't me. You don't *really* feel how terrible it is to know you could have acted in some more noble and compassionate way, child or no child."

"I have an abstract grasp of what you're saying, Elegy." I watched her replace the monograph on its shelf and silently resented her for consigning me to a kindergarten for the morally obtuse. "So all that business about taking your father's monograph literally is just so much argle-bargle to disguise the fact you have an *emotional* need to find him, and find him alive?"

We were both surprised by my tone. "No," she said carefully. "I believe in the literalness of the monograph because I don't think my father—whether sane or absolutely bonkers—was hallucinating out there. He recorded what he saw."

I tried to turn the conversation away from my sudden crankiness. "What happened to your mother, Elegy?"

"She was unable to resume her practice in the Tri-Mesa because people were afraid to put themselves in her care. Stories circulated about her being subtly infected by a kol or autok virus, some horrible artificial pathogen with an unpredictable incubation period, and even the favorable ruling of the archipol's highest medical board wasn't enough to remove the stigma attaching to Celestine Cather in the popular mind. She was the doctor of pygmies who had lost every one of her patients, and who was probably fatally ill herself. Nothing undoes reason like the specter of an exotic and incurable disease. The furor eventually died, and my mother now holds a government medical post at a mall-garden clinic—but for three or four years we lived only a little better than the gutter prols, siphoning off the income of past investments and scraping by. Egan Chaney contributed nothing to my 'nurture,' as their contract had it, and on this point in particular my mother grew more and more bitter. Even so, she never attempted to trace him. It was only when *Death and Designation* was published that she wrote The Press of the National University in Kenya to ask that a percentage of the residuals be set aside for my education."

"And here you are," I finished for her.

"Thanks to you," she acknowledged, smiling faintly. "It's been a long, strange trip. And it still isn't over."

At mid-afternoon I walked Elegy back to the hospital. As I was bidding her farewell at the admissions desk, it occurred to me that six years ago her father had spent several weeks convalescing in the primitive infirmary that had then occupied the hospital's site. I was struck again by how much Frasierville and BoskVeld had changed.

Later, I carried Elegy's prospectus to Moses Eisen. He met me on the deck of his better-than-half-buried house and read through the report with what seemed to me like deliberate inattention. It was already twilight, and he still hadn't had supper. Besides, he knew what the prospectus contained; by asking for it, he had merely been attempting to delay the inevitable. He had gained a day. That was all. Not much of a victory and therefore no cause for jubilation.

"You intend to take her and that animal into the Asadi clearing tomorrow?" Moses asked ruefully.

"With your permission."

"I'll have to put a stand-in in your office for you. It seems the folks in SteppeChilde and Amérsavane can't live without your advice."

"Lord, Moses, we both know I've just been marking time until something like this happened. I've been expendable for six years."

Moses glanced up from Elegy's prospectus and grimaced so that crow's-feet made overlapping tracks around his eyes. "Not to me, you haven't," he said in an admonitory whisper.

"Like hell," I responded, whether earnestly or banteringly I'm still not sure. "Bring Jonathan over from Colonial Administration. He'll miss the gab, but he and the computer won't have any trouble handling the colonists' basic geological and land-use inquiries. When he's stumped, the agrogs at Chaney Field'll take up the slack. They always do for me."

"I expect you and Cather back two evenings from now."

"We'll see," I said. "It's impossible to know what the situation may require of us."

After saluting informally, I listened to my toes make a tap-dancing sound down the wooden steps of Moses's verandah. As I strolled up the naked peninsula of his yard, the plasma lamps encircling Frasierville began coming on, glowing like pale-green melons atop their vanadium poles. I looked back and saw Moses staring lugubriously after me, a stick-figure silhouette in the steadily encroaching shadow of the forest and the night.

# CHAPTER FOUR

# A Visit to the Museum

Back in my own quarters I put through a telecom to Jaafar Bahadori's Komm-service barracks. During the course of our uneasy opening chitchat, I tried to assuage his wounded feelings with an explanation of Kretzoi's origins. Surprisingly, he came around rather quickly and asked me several insightful questions about Elegy's and my intentions with regard to Kretzoi and the Asadi. That gave me my opportunity to ask him to prepare a helicraft for us for the following day.

"The three of us are going into the Wild," I told the young enlisted man. "Outfit the BenDragon Prime and stock her with supplies."

"Yes, sir," he responded. Then: "Ah, an adventure."

"I suppose so," I said. "An adventure." Whereupon I said a crisp good night, broke our connection, and lay down atop the scrambled layerings of papers and dirty clothes on my bed. About two minutes later, it seemed, it was morning, and the telecom unit was buzzing again.

Elegy came on the line. I had no televid unit in my sleeping quarters, but I envisioned her as looking vibrant and alert. That was certainly the way she sounded.

"Would it be possible for you to bring an eyebook with you?" she wanted to know. "One of those my father supposedly found in the Asadi pagoda and brought out of the Wild with him."

"All but one of them were taken off-planet to computer research facilities at various Earth institutions," I answered.

"The idea was to crack the mystery of their operation and the significance of their spectral patterns. As I understand it, Elegy, molecular physicists, communication specialists, radioscopic technicians, spectrum analysts—just a whole bunch of folks—have alike all gone down for the ten count. If you'll remember, the bulb of one of the eyebooks was broken here on BoskVeld soon after Chaney brought it out. Three of the four eyebooks shipped home to Earth have ceased displaying—it's as if they got tired of being probed and picked at."

"I'd imagine they just ran down, wouldn't you?"

"I guess I would, primarily because that's the consensus of the men and women who were trying to unravel their secret. I'd also point out that Earth is an awfully long way from the source that initially charged and powered the eyebooks."

"Where's the remaining one, then? The sixth?"

"In the special-collections room of the Frasier Archaeological Museum of Indigenous Artifacts, just off Christ's Promenade, near the Administrative Kommplex. It's a single-story structure of only seven or eight rooms."

"I know right where it is."

"Of course you do."

"What are the chances of our taking the eyebook into the Wild with us? I want Kretzoi to have a chance to see it."

"Nonexistent," I said. "What are the chances of hanging King Tut's corpse in your closet as a conversation piece?"

"We'll have to go over there, then."

"With Kretzoi?"

"He's the one who'll be facing a battery of spectrum-displaying Asadi eyes when he enters the clearing. I think he should have some foretaste—or foresight, I guess—of what he'll encounter. In Dar es Salaam we had no access to any of the imported eyebooks."

"All right," I said. "I'll meet you on the Promenade in forty minutes."

*

Christ's Promenade derived its name from the immense thermoplastic pietà given to BoskVeld's Colonial Administration four years ago by the cultural-arts commission of Glaktik Komm. The statue sat on a tiered granite pedestal in the center of the Administrative Kommplex square. When

Denebola topped the modular onion domes of the archive buildings east of the square, the statue seemed to liquefy and evaporate, the grief of the Mother of God shimmering as elusively as a heat mirage above the veldt. At night, under a moon or three, the pietà focused and redirected the alien lunar light so that the luminous architraves of the various government buildings and the Promenade's streetlamps were were all but engulfed by the glow. Day or night, the effect was disturbing. You forgot that the statue's presence was considered decorative and historically instructive rather than sacred. You forgot that the civkis who walked past the pietà every day and gazed out their windows upon it during their meal or meditation breaks were wholly blasé in its beholding. Nearly everyone else, though, fell victim to the involuntary genuflection of his or her awe.

When I entered Christ's Promenade forty minutes after talking with Elegy, I saw her and Kretzoi in the mouth of Mica Strike Street staring at the massive, icelike monument. In turn, a number of curious or startled pedestrians were staring at them. Elegy and her shaggy, hybrid primate looked very small and out of place, and I felt a sudden swelling of shame at my reluctance to approach and greet them. To many of those on the square, encountering an Asadi on Christ's Promenade must have seemed as outrageous and unlikely as sitting down to a breakfast of bagels with the reincarnation of Adolf Hitler. The disbelief and repugnance on several faces almost made a coward of me—but at last I sucked in my breath and crossed the open court below the statue.

Kretzoi, without taking his weirdly capped eyes from the pietà, was talking with Elegy in rapid sign language, his stance the tentative upright stance of a vigilant baboon.

"It reminds him of something he saw in the Gombe Stream Reserve before being transferred for surgery and genetic alteration to Dar es Salaam," the young woman told me even before I had asked. "He once saw a male chimpanzee catch a baboon juvenile and dash out its life by swinging it against a tree. Usually the corpse is quickly dismembered and the skull cracked open so that the chimp can eat the limbs and brain. On this occasion, though, Kretzoi watched as several males of the baboon troop mounted a screaming counteroffensive on the murderer. It was more a pride-salvaging bluff than anything else, but the result was that the surprised chimp dropped the dead juvenile and lost it to the quick hands of the baboons. There was more screaming and bush shaking, but eventually the dead animal's mother reclaimed the corpse. She took it off into the bushes clutching its twisted body to her abdomen. Then she spent a brief half hour or so mourning it—as the Mother of God in that statue is mourning her broken Son.''

"Good morning," I said to Kretzoi's interpreter as Kretzoi himself, after only a brief pause, resumed signaling with his hands.

"She was a new mother and inexperienced," Elegy continued, unmindful of my greeting, "but after she had somehow made the intuitive leap to certain knowledge that her child would never move again, she tossed it aside and went off with the remainder of her troop to forage for food.''

Kretzoi stopped "talking," but his eyes remained fixed on the pale deliquescing bulk of the pietà.

"Is there a moral in that?" I asked. "And did Kretzoi really say 'intuitive leap'?"

"In free translation, yes, I think he did." Elegy was outfitted for the Wild: a beige jumpsuit with strips of perforated mesh along its legs, flanks, and midriff. Her dark hair was held back by a thong of hard red leather. "If there's a moral, it may be that you have to get on with things."

But it seemed to me that Kretzoi hovered between the amoral pragmatism of the baboon mother's "getting on with things" and the spiritual dignity of Mary's static carven grief. Our prospective emissary to the Asadi, then, was a creature floating in evolutionary limbo. I wondered if Elegy knew what she had done in having him tailored so specifically for this mission. Obviously, she could have had nothing to do with his hybridization—for Kretzoi was a full-grown "chimpoon" or "babanzee" (to use the whimsical terminology of the new primate ethologists and crossbreeders) of at least sixteen to twenty years of age, and Elegy was therefore almost his contemporary. But at the Goodall-Fossey Extension Center near the Gombe Stream Reserve she was apparently given leave to select Kretzoi out of a small pool of experimental animals; and the way he looked now—mane, optical carapaces, pronounced bipedalism, coloring—was a direct expression of Elegy's desire to find her father. How did she justify exploiting his anatomy in this fashion, especially when Kretzoi himself seemed to have at least as much intellectual awareness as some of the "human beings" I had worked with there on BoskVeld and elsewhere?

But I held my tongue.

Down Mica Strike Street I led my charges, over its dully glittering veldt-turf flagstones, to the Museum of Indigenous Artifacts.

This single-story building is notable for its smooth, hard facade of interswirling umbers and earthy yellows, like some kind of enormous rectangular clay vessel coated with a protective glaze and baked in a giant-sized kiln. A pair of tall rubber plants stands sentinel at its entrance, and the prefabricated building across the street—a small chemical-assay facility—is so nondescript and inconsequential in comparison that you can walk down Mica Strike Street several times before noticing it at all. In fact, but for its glazed and colorful exterior, the museum itself provokes very little notice. If you have been there once, the only reason to go again, I'm afraid, is to ascertain that it still exists. I did this regularly, primarily because the special-collections room housed an interesting array of Egan Chaney memorabilia, including representative copies of our monograph and the last of the mysterious eyebooks.

Robards de Feo and Chiyoko Yoshiba were the cocurators of the Frasier Archaeological Museum, de Feo up front and Yoshiba in the special-collections department.

When we entered, I immediately regretted not having forewarned them by telecom or televid of our coming. Kretzoi's appearance in the museum foyer caught de Feo completely by surprise, frightening him so badly that he fumbled something in his hands and narrowly missed dropping it to the floor. (It was a small stone effigy from the ruins of the only verifiable Ur'sadi structure in the Wild, a foundationless pagoda thoroughly excavated and described by Frasier and his First Expedition colleagues. A great many people supposed that Chaney had erected his illusory pagoda on the ruins of Frasier's real one.) De Feo relaxed a little when he saw me behind Kretzoi, but his face stayed the color of a rotten turnip's heart.

I introduced de Feo to both Elegy and Kretzoi and told him why we had come. He escorted us through the antechamber's spindly display cases—attempted duplicates of those described in Chaney's monologue—to the special-collections department, where Yoshiba, a heavy-set, middle-aged Japanese-Dutch woman with a remarkably serene and beautiful face, raised her thin eyebrows ironically and gestured us to several high-backed metal stools.

Kretzoi, discerning in a glance that he could not comfortably sit his stool, wandered into the center of the room and squatted. Hunkering, he regarded the three of us—de Feo had already returned to the front—with the same kind of bewildered attention he had given the pietà.

Elegy, meanwhile, gazed down into the glass cabinet in front of our stools. Several photographs of her father and a small fan of pages from one of Chaney's private journals were on display under her hands.

"This is his daughter?" Yoshiba asked.

I nodded.

"And she wants to see the last of the eyebooks?"

"Please," I said.

"Altogether my pleasure, she's come such a long way." With that, Yoshiba went through an archway behind the cabinet and returned a moment later carrying a white velvet pouch with equally velvety navy-blue drawstrings. She withdrew the eyebook from the pouch and laid it on the cabinet directly in front of Elegy, who looked up smiling and reached toward the alien cassette with a cautious—indeed, a reverent—forefinger.

"You're not permitted to activate its spectral display," Yoshiba warned gently. "We don't know how many more times it will work."

"She's come such a long way," I reminded Yoshiba.

"And I'd like Kretzoi to see it"—Elegy nodded meaningfully at her eerily attentive companion—"before he goes into the Wild today."

"Come on, Chiyoko," I pleaded.

The woman's serene, full-cheeked face betrayed neither suspicion nor sympathy. "For old time's sake, I suppose?" she asked me sardonically, then relented and said, "Very well—once." Not so much a concession as a restricted mandate. "You'll have to sign and date the register, Thomas. Nor do I think that the make-believe Asadi should perform the program activation."

Elegy, I believe, started to protest this judgment as bigoted and discriminatory, but Yoshiba retreated through the archway again and came back with the register. I held my thumb in the first open square on the page, just long enough to draw my print out of the paper. Then I signed my name with a blunt-tipped stylus. Yoshiba promptly closed the register and transported it back to its resting place in the farther room. Then, once again at the display cabinet, she indicated by a nod that I could take the eyebook to Kretzoi and show him how it worked and what it had to reveal of Asadi communication methods.

"If it fails to display again after this run-through," Yoshiba said matter-of-factly, "your signature will not save my position, Thomas."

"We're a good deal closer to its power source than were the university technicians and specialists who lost theirs," I replied, hunkering down beside Kretzoi and holding the eyebook under his muzzle. "Not to worry, Chiyoko."

Elegy dismounted her stool and came around behind the two of us. To Yoshiba, almost as a rebuke, she said, "In any case, we'll bring you several more. My father took only a few out of the Asadi pagoda with him. Others remain, maybe as many as 150,000."

Chiyoko laughed and lifted the velvet pouch by its drawstrings. "I'd better begin cutting material for more of these, hadn't I? Maybe I'd better file an import requisition, in fact."

I pressed my thumb over the right half of the rectangular tab beneath the bulb on the cassette.

The eye immediately began displaying. Colors swept in crazy sequence out of the Asadi crackerbox on my palm. I looked at Kretzoi and saw this rainbow rampage reflected in the lenses of his eye coverings. A staccato, ragtime piccolo parade of brilliant primaries, cunning blind pauses, and pyrotechnic shadings between the primaries. Kretzoi, tilting his head, peered at the flashing bulb and began to quake.

"Maybe you'd better shut it off," Chiyoko advised, but to preserve the eyebook's motivating energies rather than to spare Kretzoi his strange St. Vitus tremors—of which Chiyoko seemed totally unaware.

I put my thumb over the left half of the cassette's control tab, and as suddenly as it had begun, the spectral display ceased. The bulb in the wafer's center might just as well have been the glazed-over eye of a dead fish. Chiyoko took the eyebook from me and deposited it carefully in its velvet pouch. When I looked back at Elegy, she was kneeling in front of Kretzoi with a hand on his still-trembling shoulder.

"Could you read the pattern?" she asked. He seemed not to hear her, and she repeated the question.

Kretzoi made a sign that plainly meant No.

"What, then?" she demanded. "What happened to you?"

This time Kretzoi revolved a degree or two toward Elegy and began making hand signs with a deliberate, desperate verve.

Elegy translated for Chiyoko and me: "He says he read the eyebook's emotional content—not its specific message, not its philosophical or narrative import, but its . . . its emotional content." This disturbed her. "He says the spectral sequence evoked in him a deepening pattern of—well, of *fear*."

Kretzoi looked away from Elegy and "grinned," briefly exposing his altered teeth and mottled gums. The grin, in Old World monkeys, is a sign not of joy or potential aggression but of fear, and Kretzoi's grin was as involuntary as his hand signs had been deliberate. He seemed embarrassed and ashamed.

"Perhaps he's afraid to go to the Asadi clearing," Chiyoko said.

Elegy shot the woman an annoyed glance, but kept her hand on the animal's shoulder and asked quietly, "Are you, Kretzoi?"

He turned his wrist outward from his body so that his knuckle-dragging hand briefly exposed its palm. A shrug. His face remained averted, but his long upper lip finally dropped, eclipsing the fearful grin.

"We'd better go," I said, "if Kretzoi still wishes to go. Jaafar's holding a Dragonfly for us at the port near the lorry pool." It was extremely important to me that Kretzoi have a choice in the matter—as, apparently, it was also to Elegy, who was regarding the creature with genuine anxiety.

But Kretzoi's long, muscular body moved out from under her hand and flowed toward the door on all fours. Before going through into de Feo's territory, he paused, reared back, and made a beckoning sign at us with his right hand.

"He's ready," Elegy said in evident relief. She thanked Chiyoko for showing us the eyebook and allowing me to activate it.

"Altogether my pleasure," responded Chiyoko placidly.

"However, I'm not sure his seeing it has done him any good."

We headed back through the museum to Mica Strike Street. De Feo acknowledged our passage with a word and a nod of the head, but didn't budge from his post to see us to the door. Ordinarily he escorted every visitor out, talking animatedly all the while and encouraging an early return visit. It wasn't hard to deduce what had discouraged him from such commonplace but courteous behavior that morning.

\*

The helicraft—a modified Kommthor-Sikorsky Dragonfly with an iridescent red-orange fuselage for easy sighting from the air—stood ready on the central square of polymac at Rain Forest Port.

It took us only twenty minutes to walk there from Christ's Promenade, but Jaafar was fidgeting impatiently in the dispatch shack when we arrived. We were better than an hour and a half late.

"I'm supposed to drive a Kommthor official in from Chaney Field at noon," he told us. "What took you so long, I wonder." The "I wonder" was there to keep his impatience from sounding crudely insubordinate.

I nodded toward the BenDragon Prime. "Did you outfit it as I asked?"

"Last night," Jaafar replied. "On my off-duty time."

I informed him that no one on a colony world is ever truly off duty and watched him roll that overripe chestnut on the palate of his mind. "How many days' supplies?" I demanded.

"A week's—for three." He glanced sidelong at Kretzoi, who was peering out the dispatch-shack door toward the glinting and simmering helicraft.

"A week's?" Elegy said, startled.

"A hedge against accident," I said, knowing that she expected to drop Kretzoi off, observe him from afar for no more than a day or so, and then return in eight to ten days to see what he had managed to accomplish. After that she planned her own intensive campaign in the wild, maybe even attempting herself to go among the Asadi.

But I had grown impatient waiting for something—anything—to develop. What harm if we immersed ourselves in the jungle from the beginning? I had almost begun to feel that Elegy's Nyerere Foundation grant belonged in part to me, that I deserved some small say in its implementation.

"It's standard operating procedure when you overfly the wild," I repeated of the week's supplies aboard the helicraft. "A hedge against accident—just like the Dragonfly's coloring."

Elegy looked at Jaafar for confirmation. He wiped sweat from his forehead with his sleeve and maintained a noncommittal silence.

"We'd better go," I said.

Across the heat-deflecting surface of the polymac Elegy, Kretzoi, and I approached the sleek, evil-looking body of the BenDragon Prime. A moment or two later we were in the air, the forest revolving beneath us like a weird floral arrangement on a prodigious lazy Susan.

# CHAPTER FIVE

# The Wild

It goes on and on, the Calyptrań Wild. You gaze down upon a canopy of interlocking flowers, leaves, and lianas, myriad greens and blues transmuted from instant to instant by Denebola's steadily streaming but variably constituted copper-colored light. The mantle of the forest canopy drops off to the west, drops and drops without ever giving way to some other recognizable feature. The veldt behind you is an illusion, and the ocean Calyptra, near whose eastern shore Frasier and the First Expedition discovered the ruins of an Ur'sadi pagoda, is apprehensible only as a surf noise that may in reality be the droning of your Dragonfly.

Once up in the air I was ready to rebequeath to Elegy my secretly purloined portion of her grant. No wonder none of us had found Chaney. No wonder even the renowned Geoffrey Sankosh had failed. A human being attempts to embrace eternity when he puts his arms around the alien bigness of the Wild.

In less than an hour, not long after midday, I banked the Dragonfly over the Asadi clearing and gave both Elegy and Kretzoi their first glimpse of the unfathomable creatures who trudged there. Elegy sucked in her breath at the sight of the Asadi, and Kretzoi, in almost imperceptible reprise of his behavior at the Archaeological museum, lifted his hairy upper lip. The tips of his teeth gleamed dully.

"It's real," I said. "But since your father disappeared, Moses Eisen hasn't allowed anyone to stay out here doing field work—not for protracted periods, anyway."

"Kretzoi will take up where Egan Chaney left off," Elegy said.

The BenDragon Prime carried us beyond the clearing and out into the shimmering airspace over the Wild itself. I banked us again and circled back for another look-see. It struck me during this second flyover that one thing about the Asadi *had* changed in six years—they were no longer completely insusceptible to evidence of the human presence on BoskVeld. Whereas once they had acknowledged our existence only by fleeing when one of us approached on foot (the exception, of course, being their reaction to Chaney's methodical insinuation of himself into their little clearing), today they recognized the intrusion of our technology and were often open in their appraisal of and their hostility toward it.

As we came back over the assembly ground, I noticed that several of the Asadi had left off their intramural staring matches or brutal sexual gymnastics to watch the Dragonfly go by.

"Where'd you make my father's supply drops?" Elegy asked.

I pointed through the cabin's bubble to the immediate east. "Over that way. Chaney didn't want the helicraft to disturb his subjects. I used to believe that I could land among the Asadi without disrupting their lives or threatening their sanity—if you assume them sane."

"But no more?"

"But no more. Didn't you see them watching us as we flew over?"

Elegy confessed that she had.

"So that's new," I told her. "And I'm half convinced it has something to do with your father's having once been among them."

Out of the corner of my eye I saw Kretzoi make a series of hand signs for Elegy's benefit.

"He wants to know, Ben, if that's going to make it harder for him to gain acceptance among them this afternoon."

"Tomorrow morning," I corrected the two of them. "Tomorrow dawn. We'd be idiots to try to introduce Kretzoi into their midst after buzzing them as we've just done. We'll camp out tonight."

"Where?" Elegy asked.

The Wild's buckling, blue-green canopy knit itself together beneath us like a chlorophyl afghan.

"Right here," I responded, lowering us vertically out of the sky through an opening in the foliage seemingly not much larger than a doughnut hole. "At your daddy's old supply drop." The Dragonfly stuttered, stopping in midair several times as I maneuvered it down. Meanwhile, lianas and exotic flowers twined together around us as the sky closed up overhead. "This is the spot from which Chaney first walked into their clearing," I said when we had all ceased vibrating. "This is the spot where I weekly replenished his supplies of Placenol and moral courage."

"He had plenty of the last, didn't he?" his daughter said challengingly. "Who else has ever stayed out here longer?"

"The longer you stay the more surely it's consumed."

Elegy said nothing. We got out. It was interesting to poke around the old supply drop. In our first ten minutes of rummaging we found an unused flare packet, good for signaling up to eighty kilometers away, so high did the flare rockets carry their charges, and a number of self-heating food canisters that Chaney had probably scattered about contemptuously just after my last delivery.

Kretzoi swung himself up into a tree and began brachiating away from the helicraft into the jungle, more like a gibbon or an orangutan than a chimp or a baboon. For the first time since his and Elegy's arrival on BoskVeld he seemed at home, in his element, and I knew without being told that he was merely exercising the luxury of his freedom, that in a moment or two he would come swinging back toward us and deposit himself triumphantly on his haunches not far from either Elegy or me. Which is exactly what he did.

I dragged a nylon lean-to assembly out of the Dragonfly and began making camp, using the helicraft's fuselage as our tent's rear wall. Elegy set aside her awe and excitement long enough to help me.

Later, as night fell, we heard the Asadi dispersing into the Wild on every side, streaming past invisibly in the arabesque, three-dimensional maze of the rain forest. Where did they go? How did they avoid stumbling in upon us when we had taken such pains to conceal ourselves, even to the point of nearly thwarting the Dragonfly's gaudy, iridescent paint job? Why couldn't the Asadi remain together at night? What did they do, separately, in the dark? Those were questions that suddenly seemed new again.

\*

None of us was really able to sleep that night. I used the time to record the accumulating episodes of our adventure, hoping, eventually, to knit together a fabric at least as cohesive as the overarching vegetable roof. Kretzoi huddled nervously on a patch of ground outside the lean-to. It amazed me anew to realize that he anticipated the morning in the same way that students anticipate the advent of a major examination in their academic specialty. To calm him, Elegy sat down behind him and began tenderly, caressingly, grooming his mane. . . .

\*

But Kretzoi needn't have worried. The following morning he infiltrated the Asadi clearing with stunning ease, just as Egan Chaney once had; and Elegy and I, when we stooped beside the clearing, had trouble determining which Asadi was in reality Kretzoi and which were bonafide bubble-eyed aliens. But that was later.

That morning, at sunrise, the Wild began to fill with a noise like radio static—in truth, this was nothing more than the Asadi abandoning their solitary nests and heading homeward at great speed, brushing foliage aside and padding over the crumbling humus among the palms and lacy jungle hardwoods. Either running or brachiating, they flashed past our encampment.

"Go!" I told Kretzoi. "Now!"

"Maybe he needs a weapon," Elegy suggested belatedly. "A stunner or a knife. Something."

"Nothing!" I shouted in an angry whisper. "Kretzoi, get going!"

Off he went, without an instant's hesitation, and by the time either Elegy or I knew that he was gone, we were alone in the rising dawn.

Elegy had tears in her eyes—whether out of fear that Kretzoi was lost to her forever or joy in the imminent fruition of her plan I couldn't have said. Except for the tears, her face was blank and unreadable. We stood side by side and peered like voyeurs through the impenetrable curtains of the forest.

"What now?" she asked matter-of-factly.

"We wait a time."

"What for? Shouldn't we go after him, check to see that he's not been torn limb from limb or had his mane cut off or maybe just gotten lost?" But she framed her questions clinically rather than emotionally.

I told her we were waiting for the last stragglers to reach the clearing, that we didn't want to encounter an Asadi on its way in, that once we ourselves arrived we would have to take care to prevent our discovery.

Elegy listened to this counsel calmly, acceptingly, and when we at last set off, she wove her way with such skill through the tangled foliage that I finally yielded the lead to her and whispered only a few minor course corrections to keep her on track. It took us approximately twenty minutes to come within hailing distance of the clearing. Glimpsed through strange geometries in the tropical lacework, the Asadi trudged or flitted unceasingly across this clearing.

"Where is he?" Elegy whispered.

We were crouched side by side beneath an umbrella of silvery roots cascading down from the limb of a rainthorn tree. I shook my head helplessly, and the umbrella swayed above us like a living thing.

"I've got to get closer," Elegy told me after we'd been watching for a long time. "This is no good at all."

Before I could protest, she moved away from me, duck-walking forward, one hand occasionally reaching out to maintain her balance, her head as still and upright as a periscope casing. I followed her. The red leather thong in her hair gleamed at me through the undergrowth like a migrating orchid. At last I was beside her again. Asadi went by so near to us I could hear their measured breathing and see the spinning colors in their eyes.

"Listen, Elegy," I began—but she put her fingers to her lips and silenced me. Detection seemed almost inevitable. We were crouched in a shallow crumbling pit from which the huge bamboo-ridged bole of a tree grew up, and what cover we had was really little more than a swatch of falling shade.

Close up, the Asadi seemed to be performing some kind of nightmarish Sisyphean labor. The rock they pushed up the hill every day, only to have it roll crushingly back down upon them, was their commitment to an endless daytime sociability in their jungle clearing. At the same time, they were—by human standards—devastatingly alone in their commitment to this life. Interactions beyond brutal, random coitus and ferocious bouts of staring were rare. Indifferent Togetherness Chaney had rightly tagged the unifying principle of the Asadi social order, but I had never felt that principle so keenly as I did that afternoon. I pitied Kretzoi his initiation into such an irrational system, and I wondered briefly if he might not be better off failing to gain the Asadi's acceptance and actually suffering some grievous physical punishment at their hands.

"There he is," Elegy whispered excitedly. "There." She pointed at an Asadi slouching along the clearing's perimeter, heading south amid a number of lackadaisical Asadi, and at first all I could tell about him was that he looked like all the others.

"No. I don't think so."

"Yes," Elegy insisted, gripping my arm and turning her head so that she could read my expression. "He's perfect. He's one of them." When she looked back at the Asadi, she corroborated her own testimony by failing at first to pick out the one she had labeled Kretzoi. "Damn. I've lost him. . . . No. There he is. Look, Ben, that one right there."

A tawny mane amid the silver, silver-blue, and thick orange-gold ones. A body somewhat less gnarled and scarred than the others.

"You're right, Elegy. We've seen him. Now let's get out of here."

She wouldn't budge. Then, suddenly, she stood up and took an incautious step forward.

"Elegy!" I cried, half aloud.

Her movement and my voice betrayed us to the Asadi. Their procession halted abreast of us, six or seven Asadi bunching up in file and then disengaging from one another in order to fall to all fours and appraise us with madly pin-wheeling eyes. I grabbed Elegy's arm and pulled her back. One of the large silver-blue Asadi males lunged tentatively at us, staying well within the clearing and erecting the hairs on his back and upper arms. Elegy shook off my hand.

"*Get out of there*," I advised her fiercely. "The least you're likely to lose is your hair."

I had a vivid memory of the way the Asadi, upon accidentally discovering our equipment, had savagely wrecked a holocamera and a recording device installed one night in a tree near their clearing. . . .

But instead of retreating or standing stock-still and hoping to be spared, Elegy grasped the limb of a tree and, hooting threateningly, rattled the fronds with such animation that not an Asadi on BoskVeld could have remained unaware of her presence. The silver-maned male hurriedly backed off, and several nearby Asadi did likewise. The tribe's mute remainder gazed toward us in immobile surprise and perplexity.

"If I had a pair of garbage-can lids," Elegy said aloud, glancing back at me, "I could give 'em all heart attacks."

"You've given *me* one," I said angrily. "Maybe Kretzoi, too."

"We really should go, shouldn't we?" Elegy acknowledged.

I didn't say anything. I crept forward, touched her elbow, and eased her away from the tree whose fronds she'd just deployed in our defense. I noticed that the eyes of the nearest Asadi were radiating colors as quickly and as dizzyingly as had the eyebook in the Archaeological Museum—with the result that the Asadi's physical selves were dimmed by the racing spectral patterns and made to appear as transparent and colorless as water. The creatures in the foreground, in fact, seemed all eyes. Their bodies were ghostly outlines, nothing more.

Illusion, I told myself, backpedaling the two of us discreetly into the forest. A trick of the light; a brief, irrational perception born of crisis and fear.

Indeed, as we got deeper into the Wild and farther from the clearing, the nearest creatures' bodies took on substance again, fur and pigmentation emerging from wherever they had disappeared to.

"Did you see them fade?" I asked Elegy as we turned and fled toward the drop point and our encampment.

"I saw it—I'm sure I believe it."

The Asadi didn't attempt to pursue. Either Elegy had frightened them too badly or their commitment to the clearing was too strong. Maybe both.

Scraped, and bruised, and drenched in our own sweat, we reached the drop point, having run or trotted nearly the entire distance. Elegy began grinning like a maniac and pounding on the Dragonfly's fuselage in a primitive outburst of joy and triumph. I slid beneath the awning of our tent and lay flat on my back trying to breathe. My exhaustion and Elegy's pounding were so well synchronized they almost comprised a single, unmerciful pulse.

"He's in!" *Boom, boom!* "He's in!" *Boom, boom!* "He's in!" *Boom, boom!* And so on unto, it seemed, the very collapse of Time.

"Have pity," I managed feebly after this had been going on for ages. "Elegy, have pity."

"Sorry, Ben." The pounding stopped and Elegy knelt above me with a warm and beatific expression. Leaning forward and reiterating what I already knew, she whispered, "Kretzoi—he's in."

"Boom, boom," I replied.

\*

Later, recovered from our run, I turned on a fan in the Dragonfly and used my hand typer to transcribe several pages of notes. While I was working, Elegy climbed into the helicraft and interrupted me. She sat down in the cone of wind blowing from the fan and waited patiently for an opening. I looked up.

"He's in—but he could be in there for months, maybe even years, without a significant break in their behavior."

"That's right," I said. The bloom was off the rose.

"Do you think their seeming to fade means anything?"

"Only that it gives me an idea why your daddy liked to call this place the *Synesthesia* Wild. For him, trapped in this jungle, colors made noises, sounds had a tactile quality, smooth was sweet and rough was spicy. Or maybe we were just hallucinating."

"But has this ever happened to you before? My father doesn't mention anything quite like it—their fading, I mean—in his monograph."

"Nothing *exactly* like it has happened to me before," I admitted. "Or, so far as I know, to any of Chaney's part-time successors. But they didn't stand on the edge of the clearing and rattle branches at the Asadi, either."

"You think we were hallucinating?"

"It's possible. A function of the Wild, Asadi hysteria, and our own fear. Who knows?"

"Do you think Kretzoi will hallucinate, then?"

"If he does, Elegy, I'd guess that having been accepted as one of them, he'll participate in the *group* psychoses of the Asadi. He won't draw undue attention to himself by suffering conspicuously solitary mind trips."

Elegy stared at me thoughtfully.

"That's supposed to be comforting," I assured her. "It may be that their discovering us on the edge of their clearing triggered in the Asadi a process that triggered in us a tendency to see *the thing which is not*."

"I don't like that, Ben."

"Why not?"

"It has certain nasty implications about the accuracy of what my father saw in the Wild and reported in his ethnography."

"Not if you assume that as one of the Asadi—which, in his role as an outcast, Chaney paradoxically happened to be—he could hallucinate only what the Asadi hallucinated. In which case he reported, as accurately as it's given a human being to do, the subjective reality of the Asadi themselves. Or a portion of it, anyway."

"That's clever enough to be off-putting, Ben."

I shrugged, looked at my hands. "You don't like it because it undermines the objective reality of your father's reports."

"All right, then. Do *you* really believe my father shared the group psychoses of the Asadi?"

"I don't know. It's almost impossible to verify, isn't it?"

"Except, maybe, through Kretzoi."

We sat facing each other in the cargo section of the Ben-Dragon Prime, sharing the sultry windiness of the fan and thinking divergent thoughts.

"If," Elegy finally allowed, "the Asadi only do or hallucinate something *significant* while Kretzoi's among them. Otherwise, nothing. We'll be wasting our time and the Nyerere Foundation's money."

"That's supremely possible."

"Damn," Elegy said.

"In which case I'd suggest taking action outside the traditional tactics of mere observation and reportage."

"Like what?"

"Let's wait and see how things develop," I urged her quietly.

Her face took on an expression of mild pique. Without

another word she got up, brushed past me and the rattling fan, and exited the helicraft into the tight little bowl of our clearing.

\*

Denebola, somewhere, was sinking into the tepid waters of Calyptra, extinguishing itself in a vast caldron of brine. The Wild came alive in the settling darkness. The Asadi rushed from their assembly ground like children let out of school, and the forest's twilight trees, arrayed in ragged choirs against the coming night, began seething inwardly with the eerie music of glycolysis.

Kretzoi—almost as we had given up looking for him—came creeping back into camp and asked Elegy for something besides hardwood and bark to relieve his hunger. His eyes were distant and unutterably weary.

# CHAPTER SIX

# Lovers

Elegy gave Kretzoi a flask of water and an orangish purée of protein and potassium. He ate and drank languidly, then swung off a short distance into the Wild and prepared to make his first outdoor nest since arriving on the planet. Elegy and I finished our own small meal, and I went back into the helicraft to fetch a couple of stems of lorqual for an after-dinner drink. As I was opening the stems, the radio in the Dragonfly began making high-pitched summoning noises.

"You answer it," I told Elegy.

"Why?" She was closer to the helicraft's cabin than I was, but she had encumbered herself with the reptilian folds of an air mattress while I was fetching the drinks.

"Because it's Moses Eisen, and you'll do better with the old man than I would. Turn up the outside speaker, though—I don't want you have to repeat the epithets he hurls at me."

"Won't the Asadi hear, too?" she protested.

"That's all right. I'm not particularly worried about what the Asadi think of me, Elegy." A witticism strictly from lorqual.

"Answer it yourself," Elegy said, parent to child.

Because she was clearly determined to refuse me, I stumbled into the Dragonfly and took Moses's radioed rebuke. He was self-possessed and rational in his anger, but he wanted to know why we had not come back to Frasierville that evening and how we proposed to explain our continued presence in the Wild. Kretzoi, Moses said, was supposed to be our in-the-field agent, and if he wasn't, what was the purpose of our having

143

introduced him into the Asadi clearing, assuming of course that we had? Finally, still angry, he backed up and inquired sheepishly about the status of our mission. I told him where we stood. Justified in his initial gut appraisal of our duplicity, he again demanded to know why we were where we were. I began to feel a raw, inadvisable rebelliousness rising in my throat.

At which point Elegy slid into the Dragonfly's cabin and took the radio away from me. "We couldn't go off and leave Kretzoi without determining that the Asadi had accepted him," she said irrefutably.

*"Your prospectus seems to indicate you believed his acceptance among them a foregone conclusion,"* accused Moses's distance-thinned voice.

"That was intentional, sir. But the certainties of theories and expectations have to be confirmed in practice. It would be ridiculous to permit Kretzoi to die because of the abstract optimism of a project paper."

*"He didn't die, though, did he?"*

"No, but we had to be here to monitor his initiation into the clearing and his return this evening to my father's old drop point."

*"Tomorrow you and Dr. Benedict will come home to Frasierville."*

Elegy looked at me by the glow of the Dragonfly's instrument panel. When I shook my head, she smiled conspiratorially. "No, sir. We have supplies for nearly a week, and we'll spend our days here recording and studying the reports Kretzoi gives us each evening when he returns to our camp. We're his moral support, you understand. The Asadi ritual of Indifferent Togetherness is truly fatiguing, and he's not used to it. It may take him awhile to adjust. Tonight, Governor Eisen, he could tell us only that the experience both terrified and exhausted him. At dawn he has to go back in. To desert him for even a day under such circumstances would be ethically reprehensible and scientifically counterproductive."

Then, to turn the tables on Moses, she asked a single precisely pertinent question: "Why are you so set on getting Dr. Benedict and me back to town when we can best do our work in the Wild?"

A silence—as if we were subtemporally radioing another planet and had to endure a brief transmission lag. Into this silence I read the archaic Victorian and modern neocolonial social biases of Moses Eisen, as well as his very human chagrin at being so logically defied.

At last he said, *"I just don't want to lose anybody else to the boonies, Civ Cather. Your father was plenty, I think."*

"Nor do we want to lose Kretzoi to the Asadi, Governor Eisen," said Chaney's daughter.

*"I'll expect you and Dr. Benedict back in Frasierville in five days. Six at the very most. Good night, Civ Cather. Good night, Ben."*

The radio clicked off, and we were alone again in the claustrophobic coziness of the Wild.

\*

Asadi males, when they indulge their brief but vicious sexual appetites, mount from the rear. Almost all terrestrial primates also approach their partners from behind. It seems possible to conclude—a posteriori, if you will—that on whatever world it has evolved, the basic primate morphology demands this approach. Moreover, in many primate social units the responsibilities of paternity are principally a matter of begetting rather than of nurture. Wham, bam, thank you, ma'am, and daddy's duty's done. Did Asadi males play any part in the upbringing of their species' infants? Chimpanzee fathers do not, although upon occasion an older male sibling will take an inquisitive interest in his mother's most recent issue and later attempt to involve it in friendly, fraternal roughhouse. Closely spaced brothers often become fast friends as adults. Other males, however, are either only briefly curious or almost totally indifferent to new arrivals.

Among the Asadi—beyond Sankosh's film proving that birth did indeed occur on BoskVeld—we didn't even know to what extent the *females* were involved in the nurture of their offspring. Females as well as males had been seen to mount their partners from the rear, however, and large females climbed parodically aboard diminutive males at least as often as they themselves suffered such assaults. In the Calyptran Wild the sexual act always seemed as degrading and faceless as rape. It took place in public, on the assembly ground, and its social context resembled that of an altercation between masked strangers. On BoskVeld, as on Earth, genuine love between consenting adult primates of opposite sexes was even rarer than the private, face-to-face sexual embrace that is almost exclusively specific to humankind. . . .

Why do I inject this comparison/contrast of terrestrial and alien primate sexuality precisely here? Primarily because it was on my mind that night. I was trying, perhaps within a grandiosely encompassing frame, to interpret the meaning of what happened to Elegy and me after Moses's voice had faded off into the garble of interstellar static.

Face to face in the Dragonfly's cabin, we smiled at each other—as content in the triumph of the moment as we were comfortable in the knowledge that Moses had been embarrassed by the thought of our manifold chances for intimacy. Elegy's smile encouraged me, and I leaned toward her and brushed her lips with mine. I, the male, initiated this contact, keeping my eyes open to see what effect it would have on her. Her eyes remained open, too. She watched as from an Olympian height, her gaze steady and penetrating even when we were nose to nose in the follow-through of my calculating kiss. My temples pounded, my hands began to sweat, and I felt fifteen again. Meanwhile, her face—illumined by the glow of the instrument panel—grew to oceanic dimensions and wavered in my vision like a mist. Then, still without closing her eyes, she returned the pressure of my lips.

Tentatively pleased, I drew back and looked at her.

"Lust?" Elegy inquired with straightforward curiosity.

"Probably," I admitted. "With at least an equal measure of purely romantic feeling deriving from—well, the situation itself." I nodded upward through the windscreen at the jungle and the frond-veiled moon.

"All right, then. Come on." She jumped to the clearing's floor and ducked out of sight beneath the nylon awning supported by the helicraft. I got out of my chair and followed her.

Sitting cross-legged on the uninflated mattress she'd been struggling with earlier, Elegy nodded me to a place at her side while pushing determinedly at the heel of her right boot. "De Lambant's problem was lust unmixed with any feeling but the desire to subjugate and possess," she said, at last getting the boot off and beginning to work on the other.

"De Lambant?" I eased myself down.

"The Wasserläufer's captain," Elegy reminded me. "I refused her, though, because she enjoyed implying that Kretzoi and I—'' She stopped. ''Maybe you can deduce the rest for yourself.''

''I believe I can,'' I said.

''Once she asked me point-blank what it was like, and I told her thrilling beyond belief if you were surgically adapted for the experience—a response I thought might discourage any more overtures but which really just increased de Lambant's curiosity about both of us. As you know, my refusals eventually led to her nearly getting Kretzoi quarantined by your credulous Governor.''

''You don't have to entertain me on that account. I'm not the sort to hold grudges or seek a petty revenge, Elegy.''

''Who said you were?'' Both boots off, she smiled. ''Are you going to take part or just watch?''

I drew up my feet and began keying open one of my boots.

''My mother, in an enlightened age, believed she could affirm the 'spiritual' portion of her makeup by ignoring what she considered the 'animal' portion,'' Elegy told me, peeling her jumpsuit down from her shoulders and revealing the brown half circles of her upper breasts. ''Technically, she's still a virgin. Chaney honored her hands-off policy to the very end—I don't know, he may have believed exactly as she did. For that matter, the policy may have originated with him. In any case, I'm convinced that by striving so hard for the angelic and turning their backs on the animal, they never quite edged over into the fully human.''

''I never knew that Chaney,'' I said. ''He always seemed to me a man trying to define himself as best he could under circumstances that distorted his every definition. But he came closer than any of the rest of us, Elegy, and I admired him for the attempt.''

Elegy was gracefully out of her clothes, and our tryst beneath the bright nylon awning seemed both to illustrate and to mock her story of her mother's division of human nature into spiritual and animal halves. Highfalutin words floating in gyres above the primitive lusts. The trick seemed to be to get them spiraling through each other in precision concert. But for the moment Elegy's hemispherical breasts had me hypnotized and unmanned. I stared at them with mute, little-boy pleasure and they stared unabashedly back.

''Go ahead and look,'' Elegy said indulgently. ''They're a sexual signal at least as much as they're a maternal adaptation.''

I knew what she was referring to—the supposition that the human female's breasts have evolved as they have in order to mimic the fleshy buttocks used aeons ago by female hominids to signal adult males of their readiness to mate. The gradual development of an upright posture and efficient bipedalism selected for similar anatomical signals in front. Hence, hairless, rounded breasts in the female descendants of those still unplaceable ancestral hominids of ours. Not to mention the frontal self-mimicry of the red genital labia inherent in the protruding lips of our mouths and the ever-recurrent tendency of human females to paint them pink or scarlet. Originally, such disquieting evolutionary suppositions imply, we were designed to copulate belly to butt and to take our pleasure with the impersonal animal efficiency of baboons or chimpanzees. Maybe that's why women, at one time more thoroughly socialized in tenderness and nurture than males, often seem to find regressive variations on frontal intercourse degrading or animalistic. I don't know. All I know is that by inviting me to look without embarrassment on her naked breasts Elegy set off in me a free-associational nightmare of Asadi belly-to-butt gymnastics that embarrassed me mightily.

"What's the matter, Ben?" She was concerned rather than simply amused—although I think she could have easily burst out laughing, had she not held herself back—and that helped blanch the redness out of my face.

"It's been awhile," I told her lamely. And the last time, I recollected gloomily, in a ball booth on Night Drag Boulevard with a middle-aged woman whose secret peccadillo was biting savagely into a crème-de-menthe nougat at the moment of orgasm. She only got to do that once. Once was enough.

"Don't worry," Elegy counseled me. "It's like riding a bicycle. You never forget how."

"People get too old to ride bicycles, Elegy."

"You haven't, have you?"

So I finished shedding my clothes, and with no one watching but my cool, astrally disembodied self and the Pock-Marked Man in Melchior, I discovered that I truly hadn't. . . .

\*

I was still asleep at dawn. Elegy had to awaken me to say that Kretzoi had departed for the Asadi clearing and that we had a full day ahead before he came back to report his progress.

Elegy behaved toward me as she always had, neither more doting nor more aloof than usual, the only difference being her freeness in touching me as we strolled about the camp or talked with each other in the helicraft. These touches gave me a sort of grinning pleasure (except that I suppressed the grins) and a ridiculously improved opinion of myself. At the same time, I began to worry about what failure would do to Elegy. Her single-minded desire to discover both the Asadi pagoda and the fate of Egan Chaney had sustained her for the last several years, and now that desire—that commitment—was irrevocably on the line.

We spent the morning writing and transcribing notes. During the afternoon I again raised the possibility that Kretzoi's monotonous labors among the Asadi might fail to turn up anything new or useful about them. This discussion led me to plot strategies for the future. I suggested a trek northward, in the supposed direction of the pagoda. I proposed that Kretzoi might eventually act as something of an agent provocateur. Perhaps if he suddenly began behaving in anomalous ways, he would prod the Asadi into rare but revealing behaviors of their own. The prime argument against this unorthodox tack, Elegy pointed out, was of course the risk to Kretzoi himself.

"We're going to have to do something," I told her in turn. "I don't expect the Asadi to spill their innermost psychological secrets to us in the next few days. They haven't in six years, Elegy, and your father learned as much as he did, I feel sure, only because he happened to go among them during a cycle in which they were preparing to designate a new absentee chieftain. And the time of his arrival was pure chance."

"He also had patience and persistence on his side."

"But I don't, Elegy. And although you and Kretzoi may, I really don't think those things are the open sesame you're looking for. Six years of patience and persistence have brought the rest of us up against a brick wall."

"You're forgetting this is only Kretzoi's second day in there. Yesterday we saw something no one else has apparently ever seen before, too."

"Touché," I said.

"Patience," Elegy counseled, as people, in those days, seemed to delight in counseling me. "Patience and persistence, Ben."

\*

An hour before sunset, emptied of words and aerodynamically naked in the sticky heat of late afternoon, Elegy and I returned to our pallets beneath the Dragonfly's orange-and-white awning and made patient, persistent love. Then, like newlyweds expecting the arrival of a sensitive and lonely guest, we pulled on our clothes and chastely waited for Kretzoi.

# CHAPTER SEVEN

## A Captive

Little of consequence happened in the following days—if you discount the fact that Elegy and I continued to be lovers.

Each evening Kretzoi, progressively more disoriented and fatigued, came back to us for a meal and a rigorous debriefing session. After greedily devouring the packaged fruit and protein substitutes we had waiting for him, he would sit on his haunches in the hard, cold light of the Dragonfly's kliegs and make shadow pictures on the forest wall with his hands. Without Elegy's help I was unable to follow these exchanges. The signal system they employed—a special "dialect" of American Sign Language, or Ameslan, developed by the Goodall-Fossey primatologists—was still unintelligible to me, and I'd made only a halfhearted attempt to learn it. As a result, Elegy would translate Kretzoi's ramblings aloud and I would operate the recorders.

What we principally learned was that the Asadi, with a certain inarticulate skepticism, had accepted Kretzoi as one of their own. They allowed him to troop about the clearing, they engaged him in a couple of intial staring matches, and they invited him by angry gestures and whirling optical displays to take part in coitus. So far, because of his size and his maleness, he had escaped sexual assault. The inability of his eyes to pinwheel through a series of chemically motivated color changes had identified him unequivocally as a "mute," however, and despite the fact that human surgeons had given him the thick, tawny mane of an Asadi Brahman, Kretzoi's status among the Asadi was not high. His eyes, Kretzoi felt, disconcerted and even annoyed them—but he had not yet violated any of their ritual taboos and they tolerated his presence as they had once tolerated that of the clayey-eyed Bachelor who eventually befriended Egan Chaney. Although the Asadi had shaved The Bachelor's mane for leading Chaney to their temple, Kretzoi had neither any idea where this temple was (if it existed) nor anyone but us to lead there (should he somehow discover the way). The result was that Kretzoi saw stretching before him an eternity of Indifferent Togetherness in the Asadi clearing. Nothing could have dismayed Kretzoi more. Nor did either Elegy or I look upon this prospect with unmitigated delight.

What else did Kretzoi tell us in these debriefings?

Something curious and perhaps significant. Although he hadn't again experienced the rising queasiness of fear prompted in him by the eyebook we'd activated in the Archaeological Museum, his unwilling staring matches with Asadi antagonists had done odd things to his perception of time. More than once, caught unawares by a mesmerizing spectral display, Kretzoi had disengaged several *minutes* later to find that the sun had clocked off an *hour* or more's worth of arc overhead.

"Have you ever witnessed any of the Asadi going transparent?" Elegy asked Kretzoi after this revelation. "Have you ever noticed their bodies fading, losing outline and substance?"

Kretzoi crisply signaled No.

I suggested, "Given what he's just told us, Elegy, maybe Kretzoi's the one who's been losing outline and substance. Maybe, as a result of these vampiric staring contests, he's the one who does a fade-out."

Although Kretzoi appeared to have no conception of what I was implying, Elegy touched his shaggy wrist and asked, "What does it feel like—when you're hypnotized by the spectral displays, I mean?"

He stared off vacantly into the Wild for a moment, then made a desultory series of signs with one limp hand.

"That he's holding his own," Elegy translated for me. "That's it—that he's competing very well, indeed."

"But he can't hold his own," I said. "He doesn't have the anatomical equipment. All any of us can do is intercept the sensory output of those displays and try to interpret the data on an emotional level."

Kretzoi made another small flurry of half-formed signs.

"On an emotional level, Kretzoi says, he's too tired to 'talk' any longer. And he doesn't have anything else to tell us."

With that, after moving off wearily, he installed himself in an upright sitting position on Elegy's pallet, closed his eyes, and soon began making asthmatic sleep noises. This was our second-to-last night in the Wild before returning to Frasierville, and I had begun to feel like a blacking-factory owner slowly squeezing the *joie de vivre* out of one of my poverty-ridden juvenile laborers. It was time to try something else.

\*

Elegy yielded her pallet to Kretzoi that night and slept in the Dragonfly. I stayed awake, mulling our options and agonizing over both the legal and ethical ramifications of what I had in mind. There was one strategy I had purposely not broached to Elegy for fear she would veto it out of hand, counseling me again—maybe even angrily, preemptively—to the patience and persistence of that model field-worker, her father. I didn't want to risk her unqualified refusal. Her possession of a Nyerere Foundation grant, with its built-in exemptions from various Kommthor directives and regulations, gave her a degree of official elbow room that I, as an employee of Bosk-Veld's Colonial Administration, didn't have. Watching Kretzoi sleep, then, and tasting the sour bile of my own frustration, I decided to act on Elegy's behalf, invoking the explicit powers of her grant.

One small klieg continued to shine outward from the helicraft's door. Dust motes swam on the peripheries of the brilliant white cone, and the tangled jungle receded into nonexistence behind it.

Crouching in front of Kretzoi, I prodded him awake. It took three gentle pokes to get a response, so exhausted and sleep-drugged was he.

"Elegy and I have just had a talk," I told him as soon as he had nervously oriented himself to my presence. "Tomorrow's our last day before going back to Frasierville for a while."

Kretzoi made a one-handed inscription in the air, like a child jabbering objections to some arbitrary adult decree.

"I don't understand you," I whispered, shaking my head. "I won't be able to understand you, Kretzoi. All I want you to do is listen. Elegy's as worn down as you are almost. We've got to let her sleep."

Another rapidly executed sign.

"No," I quietly scolded him. "No more of that. I don't understand it, you see. Will you keep your peace and listen?"

One hand rose and twitched before Kretzoi could suppress the inclination to answer.

"I know you want to stay out here," I said with genuine sympathy. "You don't like what you're doing, but you're committed to it—and it's admirable you're willing to make such sacrifices for Elegy's sake."

Kretzoi's eyes shifted almost imperceptibly back into darkness. This time he had no response to make, no words to inscribe on the air.

"I suppose we could leave you out here, to keep from interrupting the continuity of your presence among the Asadi—but I've told Elegy you need to come out for a while. You need a break, maybe even a comprehensive metaboscanning at the hospital. You're a valuable resource, Kretzoi, and we can't let your sense of commitment be your undoing. Do you understand?"

Although Kretzoi could make a number of subtle discriminations among moods and concepts, in some things he was almost painfully literal-minded. He rested his hands on his upjutting upper thighs and regarded me with a cryptic immobility.

"Do you understand?" I whispered again, at last realizing he was merely practicing perfect obedience. "Nod, Kretzoi. Or signal Yes."

He signaled Yes. At the time, though, I wondered how much of what I was telling him was getting through. More than once on Christ's Promenade I had seen civkis blotto on theobromine or lorqual discoursing cozily with stray dogs. That image mocked me as I spoke to Kretzoi.

"All right, then. Tomorrow's your last full day in the Asadi clearing—at least for a while. If nothing world-shaking occurs, there's something we want you to do just before sunset, something very important and maybe a little difficult. Don't worry, though. We'll be there, Elegy and I, to help you. You're not going to be alone in this, not by any means.

"Before the dispersal of the Asadi into the Wild, Kretzoi, we want you to pick out a likely candidate for capture. We think it ought to be a male—the females may be nurturing infants in hidden nests and we don't want to endanger the lives of their young. So make it a male. And make it one of the smaller ones. You're going to have to overpower him at sunset, just before he rushes off with the others. A young, small male, then. That's good because the specimen's youth may give him the flexibility to bounce back from the shock of being forcibly detained. Ideally, we'd take an infant out with us for its adaptive potential—but that's impossible. There aren't any in the clearing, none.

"Are you following what I'm saying?" I finally asked, an audible hoarseness in my whisper. "This is very important, Kretzoi, you've got to keep it all straight. Signal Yes or No. Do you understand what we're asking of you?"

Kretzoi signaled that he understood.

"Do you think you can do it, then? It involves a certain clear risk to yourself. Suppose the other Asadi turn back to aid the one you've overpowered. Suppose the creature himself has enough strength to resist you. We've never tried anything like this before. I can't predict exactly what's going to happen. We want a healthy specimen, Kretzoi, but not a mighty mite. This depends very much on you. Do you think you can do it?"

Kretzoi indicated that he could do it. His optical carapaces reflected the brightness of our helicraft's tiny klieg, and the eyes inside them were pricked into alertness by what I had proposed.

I began to feel strangely ashamed of my ruse, as if I had betrayed rather than upheld a loved one. Kretzoi, I learned at that moment, was utterly without guile, or suspicion, or irony, or any of the other cerebrally duplicitous tendencies of human beings. Believing that I had talked with Elegy about capturing an Asadi, he intended to fulfill our requests of him as well as he was able.

"Try to get back to sleep," I urged him in my ugly-sounding, strangled whisper. "We only just made up our minds to do this, you see. Elegy would have outlined it all for you in the morning, but I told her she ought to try to sleep in." Obsessively even in the face of Kretzoi's silent but ready acceptance of everything I had said, I went on fabricating rationales for his convincing. . . .

*

It wasn't until late the following afternoon that I told Elegy what I had done. We were sitting at the pullout table where we typed and transcribed our notes. The fan's hard plastic blades made a rhythmic and continuous popping noise.

"It's illegal," Elegy said, avoiding for the moment the fact that I had gone behind her back. "The Asadi are a Komm-protected indigenous species. They may be within an evolutionary eyelash of full moral and intellectual self-awareness. That's why you've kept your hands off them this long, Ben."

"Your grant gives us extraordinary privileges," I countered. "We have the right to step outside standing Komm regs if orthodox procedures fail to produce results."

"It's *my* grant."

"I've read it very thoroughly."

*"It's my grant, Dr. Benedict!"* She studied me with outraged bafflement. Beads of perspiration formed a bridge of tiny diamonds above her upper lip. "Not yours," she emphasized more calmly. "Mine."

"I know that."

"The responsibility for fuckups and legal violations and squandrered funds lies heavy on the head of the Nyerere Fellow, Dr. Benedict—not in the lap of overzealous surrogate daddies or washed-up colonial officials who've kicked away their own best chances."

"Now you're playing rough."

But her steady, reasonable tone contradicted the harshness of her words, the unbaked fire in her eyes. "A kiss to build a scheme on," she said. "You had this in mind our second night in here, didn't you? Even before, perhaps."

"No," I answered, altogether truthfully. The pulse in my temples had begun to keep pace with the rhythmic popping of the fan.

"Then *why* are you doing it?"

'We need a breakthrough, Elegy.'

"This is only our sixth full day out here," she said. "My father spent the equivalent of more than four Earth-standard months out here before he witnessed the Ritual of Death and Designation."

"If I remember correctly, you were in such a helluva hurry to achieve a breakthrough when you first arrived that Eisen had to order you to spend that night in Frasierville. True?"

"There's a difference between enthusiasm and insanity. I

was in a hurry to get *started*. You seem in a hurry to turn my grant inside out, to do exploratory surgery on the Asadi's souls.''

"If they have any. —But, yes, I'm in a hurry for that breakthrough. My hurry's come upon me gradually over the last six years.''

Elegy went to the door of the BenDragon Prime. She raised one arm along its casing and stared into the Calyptran Wilderness. ''I don't know what my attitude toward you's going to be, Ben, if anything happens to Kretzoi.''

"Then I suppose we'll both find out at the same time, won't we?''

Without turning her head Elegy responded tightly, ''You've been on BoskVeld too long, Dr. Benedict. Too damn long.''

\*

In camouflage suits and light-absorbent facial makeup, Elegy and I made our way through the snaky lianas, hanging umbrella roots, and serrated fronds of the Wild. We each carried a tranq launcher and a backpack of netting with which to help Kretzoi subdue his chosen victim. There was no red leather thong in Elegy's hair, and our progress through the rain forest was so cautious and inchmeal that I wondered briefly if we could reach the clearing before sunset.

Neither Elegy nor I spoke. We were afraid to give the Asadi even the smallest hint of our approach.

The Asadi clearing was over a hundred meters long and about sixty wide. It was situated in the forest so that one ''end zone,'' as Chaney liked to term them, lay to the north-northwest of the other. From the air the clearing looked like a red-brown label on an amorphous billowy garment of green, blue-green, and even shiny purple. In order to help Kretzoi capture an Asadi, Elegy and I were going to take up places on either side of the clearing. There was no telling where Kretzoi would be when the aliens' twilight exodus began, and if Elegy and I were squatting beside each other nearly a hundred meters from the struggle, our nets and our tranq launchers would be useless. Even if we separated and tried to cover different territories, Kretzoi still might tackle his victim at a point equidistant between the two of us, putting us both too far away to intervene effectively.

At last, breaking our mutually imposed silence, I touched

Elegy's arm and told her that I was going to stake out a position on the clearing's western perimeter. She nodded, and we separated.

Denebola's last light was quivering in the foliage. I worked my way along the northern "end zone" and down the clearing's western boundary, careful not to alert the doggedly trudging Asadi to my presence but afraid that my nervousness would do just that. The smell drifting to me from the aliens' bodies was both suety and sweet, like rancid fat boiled in syrup. But I kept going and crept to a hiding place about thirty meters from the south end of the clearing.

It was strange—literally unearthly—how the Asadi, almost as a single conscious entity, registered the setting of their planet's sun, the precise moment at which Denebola had fallen altogether beneath a "horizon" that their rain-forest environment didn't even permit them to see. You would have thought a switch in their heads had been depressed and locked into place, a switch that only sunrise the following morning had the power to release. One or two observers have suggested that a single Asadi registers this moment and that his resultant dash for the Wild triggers the fleeing response in his conspecifics. This explanation merely narrows the mystery to one undiscoverable individual; it doesn't account for the mathematical accuracy of the Asadi perception that not a ray of Denebola's light is any longer coming to them direct. Nor does it explain the observation that even in thunderstorms the Asadi dispersal takes place on its same sunset-dictated schedule. The response seems built in, innate. Triangulations made from the air on both the Asadi clearing and the line along which BoskVeld's curvature sets a mathematically verifiable horizon in relation to the clearing—these meticulous surveys had demonstrated that full sunset and the Asadi's twilight dispersal are almost invariably coincident events.

You began to believe that on BoskVeld there thrived an unforthcoming species of sun worshipers whose very genes coded them to a reverence for the Light. Each individual was clocked to the sun, attuned to its passage.

The moment came. The unending Asadi shuffle ended, and individual animals began sniffing the air and staring skyward. Then they broke. The sound of their feet padding for safety or concealment or God-knows-what in the thickets of the Wild erupted like a sudden tattoo of drums. Anonymous Asadi bodies crashed past me on all sides. I crouched lower and lower. At the same time, I tried to find Kretzoi in the clearing. All I could see was bobbing heads and hairy backs—but the clearing was emptying rapidly and soon I'd be able to see nothing in there except the dust.

I got up, moved forward, and revealed myself to ten or twelve swift, heedless stragglers who were instantly gone.

Kretzoi was to my left, closer to me than to Elegy, and he was wrestling with a terrified Asadi male whose back he was riding with one foot dangling down as a brake against the other's efforts to free himself. It was comic, this wrestling match—except that blood streaked one of Kretzoi's forearms and suddenly he was hoot-screaming so loudly that the echo reverberated in the trees.

At last Kretzoi bulled the small Asadi to the ground, and there the two of them thrashed and bucked like bloodthirsty lovers. About the comic opera of their coupling, Kretzoi's aria of panic soared anguished and soprano.

"Ben!" Elegy cried, almost in counterpoint. I saw her running forward from the eastern woods, the parallel silver rods of her tranq launcher glinting in her hand. A few strands of her weighted net had been pulled out of her backpack and down across her right breast so that she could grasp the ends and shake out the entire net almost instantly.

At that moment, though, neither our tranq launchers nor our still tightly furled nets were of any use to us. Seeing the blood clotted in Kretzoi's wrist hair, Elegy cried his name and halted dead.

I was upon the two animals. *You don't need a tranq launcher*, I told myself, holstering it. *What you need is a water hose.*

The smell of both Kretzoi and the small Asadi male was overpowering, glandular. Suet and syrup steaming in the same pot. I reached into that musky confusion of pelage, though, and yanked back the only handle I could find—Kretzoi's unhurt arm. He howled, and I pulled him aside. The Asadi male scrabbled away several meters toward the Wild as I tried to free my tranq gun again and take aim.

*You've lost him, Benedict,* I told myself. My stomach slid sickeningly into the first coil of my upper intestines. *You've lost him. . . .*

Then, almost dreamily, Elegy's weighted net was spiraling down out of the air and enveloping the Asadi like a collapsing parachute. Tufts of hair protruded obscenely from the net's reticulations as the Asadi dragged it westward while clawing, biting, and frenziedly pirouetting. I tranq'd him with a single shot, and by the time he'd reached the Wild he was half asleep in his own sputum and piss. A downed Yahoo.

Before either Elegy or I could move to examine him, Kretzoi dashed forward and began pummeling the Asadi with his open hands. *Bam, bam; bam, bam.* Right through the twisted netting, as if he hoped to crack several ribs and reduce the alien's internal organs to holiday pudding.

Elegy hurried to Kretzoi's side, squatted beside him, and draped an arm over his shoulder. He quieted immediately and looked at her. Standing apart from them, I felt, suddenly, the fearful nakedness of our presence there in the Asadi clearing. The twilight sweeping like impalpable snow into the empty clearing only heightened my uneasiness.

"You'd better go back for the Dragonfly," Elegy told me. "It'll be dark soon, and you may have trouble finding the way."

I plunged reluctantly back into the rain forest, conscious now that at every step I was perhaps walking beneath the nest or past the camouflaged burrow of an Asadi. They were out here with me, and I had no idea where they were. We never did.

We had forgotten to take down the awning attached to the Dragonfly. I did that hurriedly, sloppily, wadding the nylon against my chest in a huge pie-dough lump and then heaving it into the helicraft's aft section. The twilight had taken on the color and the floating wispiness of bourbon dregs. I staggered about inside the Dragonfly either securing gear or kicking aside what I couldn't secure. Then I sat down inside the forward cabin and punched the long-dormant overhead rotors into life.

The surrounding forest thrashed and whipped as if a storm had blown up. Despite my inclination to let the BenDragon Prime rip its way out of the drop point, I eased it upward like a man picking a coin out of a box with a pair of remote-control pincers. My hands stayed steady.

Once fully airborne, I activated the spots on the Dragonfly's undercarriage and let them play giddily on the darkening canopy below. Almost immediately, it seemed, the Asadi clearing came tilting up at me out of the jungle, beckoning me to put down beside the three tiny figures huddled near its western boundary. In a flurry of revolving lights and upchurned dust, I landed as close to them as I could. Elegy was at the open door even before I could wedge myself through to meet her. The helicraft's rotors were still spinning whicker-ingly above us.

"How long will the tranquilizer keep the Asadi un-conscious?" she shouted at me, turning back toward Kretzoi and our poor downed Yahoo. God, did she look young! Her face had an unearthly bronze sheen.

"I don't know," I told her, running beside her, feeling the lead flowing moltenly in my gut and upper thighs. "I wasn't sure it would have any effect at all. Asadi biochemistry"—I paused to catch my breath, huffing and puffing gigan-tically—"it's probably a good deal different from that of terrestrial forms."

Elegy caught my arm. "You didn't even know the tranqs would work?"

"Not for sure, no. How could I? We've never done anything like this before. It's always been illegal, taboo."

She looked at me searchingly, casting about for an ap-propriate response. "It's *my* grant," she finally declared. "Mine."

\*

We got the Asadi male into the helicraft and netted off the aft section so that if he awoke on our way home he would be imprisoned there. (While moving his limp, bony body, I noticed that the "irises" inside his transparent eye coverings were composed of a number of small concentric rings, each ring itself oddly subdivided and faceted. In the Asadi's un-consciousness they were all a varnished oyster color, and it was hard to imagine them putting on a prismatic light show under any circumstances.) Elegy saw to Kretzoi's wound, cleaning it with an astringent bactericide and wrapping it in gauze. She also gave him, prosaically enough, a tetanus booster—despite his having had, at the light-probe port near Dar es Salaam, "all his shots."

If Kretzoi had almost been quarantined upon his arrival on BoskVeld, I suddenly thought, what's likely to be Eisen's reaction to the arrival of an unvaccinated and far from aseptic specimen of Asadi? Indigenous to BoskVeld or not, this new guest would create a commotion even more unpleasant than had the advent of Elegy Cather and Kretzoi. I hadn't even considered this disagreeable likelihood, not once during the time I was hatching our plan to bring an Asadi back alive, and now we were flying eastward toward the veldts and the melon-green lights of Frasierville—with an alien out cold in the rear of our Dragonfly. I was up front alone, and the sense of haunted isolation I had experienced that evening in the Asadi clearing settled upon me again, icily.

I radioed Rain Forest Port, the helicraft facility within the city limits of Frasierville. "BenDragon Prime to RFP Deliverance," I said wearily into the speaker unit. "Come in, please."

*"RFP Deliverance"* a voice hissed at me almost immediately—it wasn't Jaafar's. *"Go ahead, BenDragon Prime."*

"I won't be returning this copter to Rain Forest Port," I told the disembodied voice. "I'm going to land at Chaney Field. Notify Governor Eisen that we're on our way and inform him of my intentions."

# CHAPTER EIGHT

# In the Chaney Field Hangar

Approaching Chaney Field at night from the air, you find most of your attention drawn to the winking webwork of colored lights superimposed on the skeletal probeship gantry. This structure sits on the veldt like a great leafless Christmas tree, an anachronism and a reproach. The shuttle terminal and the flat-roofed support buildings southwest of the gantry, on the other hand, are delineated by strings of luminous pearls laid out in precise but elegant geometric patterns. The main thing about the entire complex, though, is that it looks lonely.

Even before we had passed over Frasierville, radio operators at both Rain Forest Port and Chaney Field were trying desperately to solicit responses from me. Although their voices crackled with competitive purpose, I ignored them. By the time I was preparing to set down on Chaney Field's most far-flung and little-used landing strip, almost a kilometer from the terminal complex, they were hinting apologetically at my dismissal from Colonial Administration and threatening a preemptive laser bombardment—this last on the grounds that having no clearance to land, and adamantly refusing to explain our peculiar behavior, the pilot and passengers of BenDragon Prime were a potential menace to the safety of the personnel at Chaney Field.

Moses, I knew, might well dismiss me from my post, but he would never authorize an attack on our Dragonfly—it contained the sacrosanct person of Elegy Cather, who was under his protection. The laser batteries surrounding the field would therefore remain poised but cold in their bunkers, and I could put us down on the polymac with almost certain impunity.

That's what I did. Elegy joined me up front, bemusedly, and in less than three minutes we were witnessing the arrival of a contingent of armored lorries and security vans. Headlights roped us in with their crisscrossing beams, and a loudspeaker atop one of the vehicles conveyed the unnegotiable demand that we surrender ourselves.

"This is Chaney Field," Elegy said, still bewildered. "Did you come out here because of the Asadi?"

"You don't want me to try to get him a room at the hospital, do you?"

"If you'll remember, *I* didn't even want you to try to capture him. The one who may require hospitalization is Kretzoi. Isn't that a major reason we all came back?"

The loudspeaker demanded again that we surrender ourselves.

I activated our own outside speaker unit and informed the dutiful people holding us hostage that I was waiting for Moses Eisen. Although fully dark, it was still relatively early. Good. Moses wouldn't have to drag himself from his bed in order to confront us. . . . And within a matter of mere seconds, it seemed, a veldt-rover was speeding toward us from the terminal facility over the deserted runways.

Moses leaped from the veldt-rover and strode into the overlapping circles of light just below the Dragonfly's cabin. Squinting, he gazed up at us.

"I've brought an Asadi back with us," I told him over the outside speaker unit. "At the moment, he's unconscious. Tranq'd."

"Everyone all right?" Moses shouted.

Prepared for either a formal rebuke or an informal display of temper, I stared down speechlessly at my superior.

"Is everyone all right?" he repeated.

"Kretzoi's hurt," I told him. "He sustained cuts and lacerations to one arm while subduing our Asadi captive. He's fatigued, too—badly fatigued. Otherwise, we're fine, Elegy and I. Everyone's fine."

"What made you land out here?" Moses shouted.

"The Asadi," I offered tentatively. "I didn't think you'd appreciate my bringing it into Frasierville."

"I don't much appreciate your bringing it out here, either. What are we supposed to do with it? You're in flagrant violation of Article Twelve of the GKR's, you know, and I'm less worried about the need to quarantine a native animal away from human population centers than I am about the breach of regulations." He cupped both hands around his eyes to cut the glare. "Do you mind if I come aboard?" he called. "I feel like I'm on criminal display out here."

"There's an Asadi aft," I reminded him over the outside speaker. "I thought that's why you hadn't already boarded."

Still cupping his eyes, he shouted, "If I were afraid of Boonie Fever, I'd've put in for reassignment seven years ago." He turned, passed out of view, and came clambering aboard the BenDragon Prime so enthusiastically that his entry rocked the entire craft.

Elegy and I met him in the rear, where Kretzoi was hunkering dazedly amid the ration kits and inflatable pillows littering the floor. Our Asadi, screened away in the tail section, had not moved in the last two hours—he resembled a small pile of animal pelts shoved against a bulkhead and left there to breed moths.

"Sure it's not dead?" Moses asked.

"No," I admitted.

"What do you propose to do with it if it isn't? I don't recall anything in Civ Cather's prospectus about capturing an Asadi."

"The terms of my grant gave us that option," Elegy said, almost as if I had worked a psychic ventriloquism upon her. "You asked us our second night out, as a courtesy, to return to Frasierville today. Since we weren't getting terribly far with our preliminary methods, we invoked the direct-intercession clause of the grant. I don't think you'll have to worry about a Komm inquiry into the legitimacy of what we did, Governor Eisen. The Nyerere Foundation's on extremely good terms with the bigwigs of Glaktik Komm."

"That still leaves the question of what to do with the critter," Moses said. "Frasierville doesn't have a zoo."

"I want Kretzoi to work with him," Elegy declared. "As soon as he's had his wounds tended to and taken a rest."

"Where?" Moses wanted to know. "I'm not happy about Ben's bringing the Asadi out of the Wild, but I'm willing to concede he showed a modicum of savvy landing out here instead of bang-smack in the middle of town."

"What about the probeship hangar?" I suggested. It was east of us in the dark, lit only by its own artificial battlements of red-orange paint. Phosphorescent paint. So far as I knew it had never been used as anything but an auxiliary warehouse for goods eventually transshipped by helicraft or settlement cars to Amérsavane, SteppeChilde, Prairie View, or one of the other veldt colonies. Otherwise, the hangar was of no use to anyone.

"The probeship hangar?" Moses said musingly.

"Yes, sir," I responded. "We'd be isolated from Frasierville, but we'd have plenty of room and almost immediate access to the civkis and Komm employees out here at Chaney Field."

Surprisingly, he agreed.

The Chaney Field security force permitted me to taxi the BenDragon Prime in toward the translucent green support buildings, and I spent that night in the terminal complex, lying awake on a cot in the antechamber to Moses's plush private office.

Elegy and Kretzoi rode back into Frasierville with the Governor in order to admit Kretzoi to the hospital—not as a resident in the first-floor guest wing, but as a patient.

As Moses's party drove off, I heard two young civkis outside the terminal joking that the Komm-galens at the hospital would be surprised to find that their Governor regarded them as little better than "cit vets." It had been a long time since I had heard that local epithet given such a vicious intonation. Even the civkis' youthful, ebullient laughter failed to gentle the nastiness of their repartee. If they found Kretzoi such a distasteful creature, what must they think of the Asadi we had just brought out of the Wild?

For that night—still unsummonably zonked—the Asadi was confined in the debussy of Governor Eisen's upstairs suite. I had carried him there myself, marveling again at the softness of his matted fur and the almost reedlike flimsiness of his body. Moses had insisted that I lay the Asadi out on the floor of his majolica-tile shower stall and then lock the creature in with the sliding, shatterproof door. That way, the Governor told me, if our guest got caught short during the night, it would be quite easy to clean up his mess by a remote activation of the shower spray.

My cot in the antechamber to Moses's office was only a few meters from the debussy, and one of the reasons I lay helplessly insomniac that night was that I kept waiting for the

Asadi to wake up and begin violently protesting his internment. I don't know whether it was a relief or a torment to me that he never did.

*

When I went into the debussy the following morning, I found that the Asadi had recovered consciousness. He was sitting motionlessly in the shower cage, a distorted two-dimensional blur behind the milky glass. Not even my purposely noisy entry had been enough to animate him.

Suddenly I was frightened.

How was I going to get him out? I didn't want to tranq him again, even had that option appeared an easy one to execute—which it didn't. Nor did I simply want to slide back the door and offer to shake hands.

Because it was still early, I returned to the antechamber where my cot was and sat down on its rumpled bedding to wait for help. Outside, the morning bustle of Chaney Field lifted its already monotonous drone, lulling me into a state of apathy almost totally untainted by fear.

Then I heard a small—a downright modest—thump in Moses's luxurious debussy. My fear came back. This was the only sound that had emanated from the debussy all that morning, and when I finally worked up enough courage to go back in, I found that my problem had solved itself. The Asadi, after having briefly revived, had collapsed again. I slid back the ripple-glass door and stared at his slender, crumpled body. When Moses came, we had no trouble getting the creature out—although by this time I had begun to fear that he would die.

*

That afternoon, with Elegy and Kretzoi still in Frasierville, Moses permitted me to relocate some of my personal effects in the probeship hangar north of the terminal building. He even accompanied me out there. We carried the Asadi in the air-conditioned cargo section of one of the airfield's armored vans. A Komm-service paramedic, riding with our captive in the back, fed him glucose intravenously on the dicey say-so of a portalab analysis of a tissue sample taken from the sole of his right foot. She also insisted on administering along with the glucose what she termed "an extremely mild sedative" in order to insure that her patient didn't awaken en route. It was impossible to scold her for a misbegotten apprehension—I remembered how fearful of the creature I had been that morning.

The probeship hangar was a monolithic slum. That description, even in retrospect, seems very nearly perfect. The building was longer and wider than the Asadi clearing, but, crisscrossed with swaths of luminous paint, it had a tarry-looking exterior that took it altogether out of the natural order of things. Doors as large as rain-forest thunderheads rumbled aside on metal tracks on the north and south flanks of the building, while smaller doors—for people—punctuated the hangar's length like the spaces between a comb's teeth, so numerous were they. Across the lower right-hand corner of the hangar's southern wall swept the beginnings of an embarrassingly erotic mural, laser etched at midnight by a bored Komm-service guard who was summarily court-martialed and reassigned to another colony planet. Satyr. Maiden. Stag. Two years before, a perfunctory attempt to fill and smooth the laser scars had been abandoned before the guard's artwork succumbed utterly, and now—even though nobody remembered his name—the man was a legend in Frasierville's Komm-service barracks as well as in most of the major pleasure houses on Night Drag Boulevard.

Inside, volumes of space. Automatically self-polarizing skylights permitted the passage of light while aiding in the maintenance of a consistent internal temperature (approximately 30°C, fairly warm). We weren't going to have air conditioning, Moses had said, but at least we probably wouldn't fall victim to heat stroke, either. Three catwalks made of metal dock plates and extensible steel platforms went around the hangar's interior at different but adjustable heights. In addition, one end of the facility boasted a recreation area for the higher-ranking probeship engineers (the ones who had never made it to BoskVeld, and never would), with carpeted pathways running among tubs of artificial botanicals and simulated teakwood flower boxes. A kidney-shaped swimming pool nestled at an off-center confluence of the meandering carpets—but a structural defect kept the pool from holding water and Moses had never given anyone authorization to repair it.

The probeship hangar embarrassed Moses. Everything about it recalled for him the folly of BoskVeld's rising expectations after Glaktik Komm's decision to colonize. Only the fact that the hangar's floor and mezzanines provided Chaney Field with a good deal of needed storage space had prevented Moses from having the building razed. The gantry, I sometimes thought, he allowed to stand as a symbol of popular gullibility—but the hangar, well, it simply gave him a headache.

Using a stretcher, the paramedic and I carried the Asadi into the recreation area, where we lowered our burden to the green all-purpose carpeting near the swimming pool.

The young woman, looking about critically, said, "This place is sort of a cross between a tropical paradise and a veldt-rover factory, isn't it?"

Moses thanked her for her help and told her she could return to the van, which, after canting the Asadi to the floor and collapsing the stretcher under her arm, she did with almost overobedient cheerfulness.

"I'd suggest you put him in the swimming pool and unroll one of those prefab soft-wall fences with the plug-in gates," Moses said. "That way, you'll have him confined and under control. If you want to, you can extend a ramp from the lowest catwalk and sit guard over him. A hose will take care of most of your sanitation problems."

Moses, I thought, seemed almost obsessed with sanitation problems. He must have seen the amusement in my face.

"Your Asadi stinks," he said defensively. "I'm just trying to get you settled in, under reasonably favorable circumstances. This isn't anything like quarantine, you know. It's more an adaptation to available resources."

"It ought to do," I said placatingly.

"How long do you intend to be here, anyway? You seem to have thrown over your initial prospectus."

"I suppose that depends on the kind of 'work' Elegy wants Kretzoi to do with our friend here." I nudged the Asadi gently with my boot. "And on the results of that work."

"Do you think you can keep him alive?"

"We'll need an assortment of plants from the Wild to provide him the basics of the Asadi diet. After that . . . well, it's up to him."

"I'll see to it you have what you need," Moses told me. "I'll also send in some people to help you get up that fence."

Moses gave me an odd half wave, and left me alone with my Asadi in the immense, solitary hangar. I carried the creature down the steps of the empty swimming pool and deposited him gently on the bottom of the deep end.

Ten or fifteen minutes later a crew of civki laborers came into the hangar, found a roll of soft-wall fencing, and installed it around the pool with a double gate near the shallow end and several swan-necked supports to keep it from falling. The fence was bright yellow—Sol-colored—so cheerful in its juxtaposition with the pastel-green interior of the pool that, looking down upon the scene from an extensible catwalk ramp, I simply had to smile.

\*

Elegy and Kretzoi joined me late that afternoon, long after the Asadi had recovered from his second drugging. They entered the hangar's recreation area from the south, saw me beckoning from my vantage overhead, and found a metal stairway by which to ascend to the first lofty mezzanine. I was taking notes at a desk assembled from a square of plastic dock plating, and when they had squeezed along the catwalk to places on either side of me, I nodded down at the pool.

"How is he?" Elegy whispered.

"Weak and bewildered—not too surprisingly. After he came to, he spent most of his day crouched in the deep end, up against that wall there, staring at the skylights. He knows I'm up here, but he avoids looking this way. You've arrived in time to witness his reaction to his first sunset away from the Asadi clearing."

"Do you want to know how Kretzoi is?"

I looked at the hybrid primate, saw the clean bandage on his arm and the various places about his body where the hair had been shaved to permit the attachment of sensors. Poor Kretzoi. The victim of a whimsical precision plucking.

"Hypoglycemia," Elegy said.

The word didn't register. I blinked. Nothing more.

"Low blood sugar," she explained. "When we arrived at the hospital last night, he fainted—actually fainted. A combination of the loss of blood and his hypoglycemic condition."

"And today he was well enough to be released?"

"They treated his lacerations and gave him a unit of

glucose. They also chemically inhibited his own insulin-producing capability in order to permit the natural glucose level to build back up. I don't know what else they could have done, really. Besides, they were ready to have us both out of there. We made 'em even more nervous as patients than we did as guests."

"Glucose?" I belatedly echoed her.

"To restore the normal sugar-content levels of his blood." Elegy gave a sharp, sardonic laugh. "Very elementary. Even a 'crit vet' knows the reason for that procedure, Ben."

"That's what the paramedic gave Bojangles this morning," I said, randomly coining a name for our Asadi. "From a quick determination she made from a skin scraping. Glucose."

"That doesn't seem terribly odd. Glucose is a pretty basic reservoir of potential energy in most carbon-based life forms, isn't it? If your tranquilizer worked, why shouldn't glucose prove effective, too?"

"How similar to the Asadi are we?" I asked aloud, not so much of Elegy as of the early-evening sky still brilliantly agleam in the panes of the hanger's skylights. The immensity of the hangar and the cloudless grey-blue vault overarching it reduced all of us, in my mind's eye, to proud but presumptuous specks. And then Denebola set.

"Look," Elegy whispered, touching my arm.

Bojangles stood full up on the bottom of the empty pool. He lifted his snout to the skylights and sniffed bronchially. Then he performed a kind of spinning run that carried him out of the kidney-shaped pool and headlong into the soft-wall fence. Bojangles was unable to claw or bite his way through. Belted internally with microscopic polymer reticulations, the soft-wall skin didn't even tear—just pinched, unfolded, and returned to its former mocking yellow smoothness. At last, spent, Bojangles lay down on the narrow margin of the pool and assumed a fetal position reminiscent of Kretzoï's two nights before.

"And what did you say he did all day?" Elegy asked me.

"Tried to track Denebola's progress through the skylights. He kept staring up. You can see he didn't eat any of the liana bark or foliage we tossed in to him earlier this afternoon."

"We're fortunate he's still alive, Ben."

"So is he, assuming he values life away from the Asadi clearing."

"We've doomed him, you know. He's small, but he's an adult, and adults of most parahuman species don't take kindly to having their psyches rearranged at so late a date. He'll quite likely die in our keeping." The unspoken implication was that my own impatience had subjected Bojangles to a gauntlet of unnecessary cruelties.

"We had to get Kretzoi out," I defended myself. "They've diagnosed his condition as hypoglycemia, right? Suppose we'd stayed, Elegy. Suppose his condition had deteriorated to the point of his actually collapsing in the clearing."

"All right," Elegy said tonelessly.

And those two words, spoken in just that way, shut me up. The hangar was growing dark. I got up, squeezed past Elegy on the narrow extension ramp, and tottered between its rails to the northern mezzanine. Here, throwing four different light switches, I flooded the hangar with cold illumination. Far off to the east, beyond the recreation area, barrel upon barrel and crate upon crate of surplus matériel were arrayed in honeycomb patterns across the hangar's floor. Shadows cobwebbed the distant recesses and catwalks as well, drooping like silver-edged parachutes or shrouds.

Kretzoi was signing something urgent to Elegy.

She turned to me and translated: "He wants to go down there now, Ben. He wants to introduce himself into the Asadi's compound tonight."

"Why? They're diurnal creatures, obviously. He won't be able to do anything until tomorrow. If then."

Kretzoi made several more succinct gestures.

"He'd simply like to be ready," Elegy translated. "He believes that if—what are you calling him, Bojangles?—that if Bojangles awakens to find him there, it'll be better than if we make a show of introducing him later on. I think he's right. Bojangles has already suffered shocks aplenty."

Grudgingly, wondering if Elegy hadn't been putting words in Kretzoi's hands, I consented. I had to. Elegy was, in truth, the director of our project. And grudgingly I escorted Kretzoi down to the hangar floor in order to admit him through the fence's twin gates into the presence of our sleeping captive. . . .

# CHAPTER NINE

## Bojangles

Bojangles didn't eat. Although Komm-service personnel brought him fodder from the Wild—succulent fronds, skeins of prodigal epiphytic roots, the pale egglike pods of the lorqual tree—nothing that we put before him tempted him. Each evening when Bojangles fell asleep, Kretzoi would bring out of the compound the wilted remains of that day's menu. I burned the noxious leftovers in a pit behind the hangar, offended by the smell but thankful for an opportunity to stand outside in the evening air. Sometimes, burning them, I would request another delivery of the Komm-service guards who patrolled the perimeters of the hangar and who dropped by at set times to see if there was anything we needed. So well did these guards suppress their curiosity about our "experiment" that I often wondered if they were human.

Be thankful for small favors, Elegy told me. She referred in particular to the fact that Bojangles listlessly drank all the water we set out for him, apparently absorbing most of it into the mitochondria of his body cells. He pissed infrequently, usually in the dribbling fashion of a human male with prostate or urethral difficulties. (A hose, as Moses prophesied with a degree of inadvertent irony, was more than adequate to the task of poolside sanitation. Elegy and I alternated custodial duties down there, usually after releasing Kretzoi each evening for food and rest.) But Bojangles's readiness to quench his thirst seemed to be indicative of an *involuntary* will to live. Sometimes it was hard to tell whether he wished to live or to die.

When Bojangles wasn't focusing on Denebola's passage from skylight to skylight, Kretzoi managed—astonishingly enough—to establish something like a personal relationship with him. Elegy and I, in light of this, began to feel that the presence of a great many Asadi might have acted to inhibit meaningful intercourse—in all that term's appropriate connotations—among small numbers of individuals. We supposed this because Bojangles behaved almost congenially toward Kretzoi.

On his first day in the compound Kretzoi sat down so that Bojangles would see him immediately upon awakening. The result was a display neither of fear nor of aggression, but instead Bojangles's gradual uncurling to an awareness that in his strange captivity he was not alone. On that very first morning, we believed, he took Kretzoi for an Asadi. If he remembered that it was Kretzoi who had helped capture him, he bore no grudge—he permitted Kretzoi to touch him without displaying the characteristic fear grin of terrestrial primates, and, upon occasion, he sought to touch Kretzoi gently in turn, maybe as an abreaction of some long-dormant Asadi urge to deny the mechanisms of Indifferent Togetherness. On that first morning in the pool, for instance, he presented his back to Kretzoi in the manner of a baboon or chimpanzee seeking to be groomed. No one had ever witnessed grooming among the Asadi.

"Is that a breakthrough?" Elegy wanted to know.

"Maybe not to the location of the Asadi temple," I told her. "Then again, maybe that's exactly what it is. Especially when you consider that it could be the beginning of genuine communication between the Asadi and another intelligent species not of their world."

Elegy's slow smile was beatific. *"Another?"* she said.

As we watched from our ramp, filming the episode with holographic equipment mounted the night before on four different extensible catwalks, Kretzoi began searching Bojangles's scraggly mane for vermin. In fact, the Asadi's vestigial assumption of the grooming posture implied that either recently or once in his species' enigmatic past his "people" had played host to one or several varieties of parasitic insect. In any case, Kretzoi groomed Bojangles, and Bojangles, appreciatively soothed, watched Denebola roll across the sky.

Eventually Kretzoi tried to initiate a less one-sided form of communication. He tugged at Bojangles's arm, slapped and pinched him importunately. Bojangles resembled a bounce-back toy—punishment-prone but unflappable. After a good deal of bootless entreaty Kretzoi ran all the way around the pool, turned with outspread arms, and made the circuit in reverse. Then he squatted with his back to the compound's gates and looked up at us as if to say, I'm stymied.

"So much for interspecies communication," I whispered.

Elegy leaned over the catwalk rail and in their specialized dialect of Ameslan urged Kretzoi to return to action. Kretzoi shook his head, his mouth hanging loose and sacklike before him. A boonie. An ignorant, contemptible boonie.

Even Elegy's sympathy for Kretzoi evaporated. She stopped making hand signs and, heedless of the possible effect on Bojangles, raised her voice so that its echo reverberated eerily.

"You're doing fine, Kretzoi! You've done something no one else has ever been able to do!"

The echoes lapped at us like waves from a cold and distant sea.

"Now go back to him, I'm telling you—go back to Bojangles and let him do for you what you've already done for him! Go on, damn it, you're doing fine! There's no one else on BoskVeld who can do any better!"

Finally Kretzoi moved. He returned to Bojangles. But instead of plucking at his arm or gouging him in the chest, Kretzoi sat down with his back within reach of Bojangles's hands. Then he waited. Before too long the Asadi began absentmindedly stroking Kretzoi's mane. He never dropped his eyes from the skylights, but the contact, once made, was sustained for well over an hour, to both animals' mutual pleasure. Kretzoi eventually fell asleep.

"Maybe we're back in business," Elegy said.

"Or maybe we've simply got a bushed and temporarily zonked Kretzoi on our hands," I countered.

"Reciprocity, Ben. A beginning."

*

Subsequent events proved Elegy right. Although Bojangles did cease grooming Kretzoi, taking his eyes off Denebola just long enough to visit a corner of the pool he had designated his privy, that afternoon he permitted several interruptions of his sun worship. Having groomed and been groomed in turn, Kretzoi was able to distract Bojangles from his Denebola watching for minutes on end—sometimes by turning his head virtually upside down to look at Bojangles, sometimes by an inquisitive poke at the other's eye carapaces, sometimes by nibbling playfully at the Asadi's ears. To most of these exotic stimuli Bojangles responded favorably: He turned to Kretzoi and sought to touch him.

At one point in the afternoon Elegy said, "This suggests that if you just get them out of that infernal clearing, the Asadi may not be the brutal, single-minded demons we've come to view them. Their clearing is their hell, Ben—as if they've fallen from a state of grace, or believe they have, and so deliver themselves up to their punishment day after day without protest."

"Would *you* go voluntarily to such a Gehenna?"

"I didn't say they go voluntarily. I said they deliver themselves up without protest. They're genetically and behaviorally programmed to do so, and their willingness to suffer 'hell on BoskVeld' must have survival value. A specific kind of photoperiodism has been the evolutionary result. They're safe by day on the Asadi assembly ground. They're safe by night in the Wild. Don't you think?" she concluded enthusiastically.

"Elegy, day or night, there *aren't* any predators on BoskVeld. There's some evidence for occasional cannibalism among the Asadi, though."

"What about the psychological predation of their own past? Don't you think the past's out there with them, even in their present-day slogging and trudging about? The past is their most remorseless predator. It's the avenging angel that's condemned them to their rain-forest hell."

"You've gone awfully damn metaphorical on me, Elegy."

"All right. You mentioned cannibalism. That's a kind of predation too, isn't it? Maybe their gathering together in a common place during the day and then dispersing to the wind's twelve quarters at night are defense mechanisms against an innate tendency—born of past genetic developments whose triggers we haven't yet guessed at—to prey on one another. The Asadi seem to be in a precarious evolutionary equilibrium between autogenocide and meaningless self-perpetuation. Indifferent Togetherness and Frenetic Dispersal are the modes by which they sustain life, Ben. The fact that they still live at all is the only real meaning their past has bequeathed them.''

"You think Bojangles's a candidate for salvation?''

Elegy glanced at me to see if I were baiting her, and decided her suspicion was groundless. "I don't know. But today, suddenly, he seems less alien, more comprehensible. That's comforting, isn't it? Nobody's comfortable with the truly alien, are they, even if they find it exciting and go out of their way to pursue it. Secretly, you know, primatologists are looking for similarities between themselves and their subjects. Differences are scrupulously noted and analyzed, yes, but it's the points of contact you live for." A moment later she added, "I'm speaking for myself, of course. That's all I can do.''

And Bojangles's amiable susceptibility to the japes of Kretzoi *was* comforting. We began to feel that the mystery of the Asadi was about to open to us like a flower.

*

On his second full day in the swimming-pool compound Bojangles stopped staring wistfully, compulsively, after Denebola and got down to the business of exploring his immediate environment, which just happened to include Kretzoi. (Our cameras did, however, record his recurring panic at sunset—but this reaction diminished on each successive evening, until, finally, his only observable response was a rapid alternation of the common fear grin with the "threat face" often employed by Earthly rhesus monkeys: front and side teeth glinting nastily and the mouth full open to screech or howl. Bojangles, however, never made any sound at all.) At first, his forays around the pool's perimeter and interior made us think he was merely adapting the Asadi assembly-ground behavior to his new surroundings. We weren't dismayed by this development, though, because it was so striking a departure from the first day's intense sun worship that we believed even bigger surprises had to be in store.

We expected Bojangles to eat. In this he disappointed us. But he didn't disappoint us in his newfound readiness to jettison old Asadi behavioral patterns for exploratory ventures of his own.

Ninety-four minutes of marching around and through the empty pool—while Kretzoi sat bemusedly by the chrome ladder at its deep end—were all Bojangles required to survey his artificial clearing. Then he stopped, located Kretzoi, and hurried to him for what we supposed would be another session of mutual grooming. Even Kretzoi was of our opinion in this, for he reached to begin combing the other's fur—only to have Bojangles deflect his hands, catch them firmly at their wrists, and hold them before him. Kretzoi's strength was sufficient to permit him to break the hold, but he didn't move. Then Bojangles voluntarily released his hands.

"This gets better and better," Elegy whispered.

Again, she was right. Kretzoi inscribed a simple gestural communication in the air. Bojangles, whose back was partially to us, leaned forward and stared not at Kretzoi's hands but deep into the protruding lenses over his eyes.

"Kretzoi's getting a spectral display," Elegy said. "We're picking it up on the third monitor, Ben."

This monitor, attached to the catwalk rail to the right of our desk, gave us a telephoto closeup of Bojangles's grimacing face. So sharp was the picture's resolution that I could even make out the individual colors in his pinwheeling eyes. But the message in those colors, however eloquent or Homeric, was all of a piece to me: pitiless Greek.

"Where does he get the energy for that kind of display?" I wondered aloud. "He hasn't eaten anything for a good sixty to seventy hours."

"What about the sun?" Elegy responded.

This was old speculation, an early theory of Moses Eisen's as a matter of fact, and the only thing wrong with it was that Komm decrees of, first, the Martial Arm and later, Colonial Administration had never permitted us to put it to a test. Because Bojangles had gone so long without taking food, evidence for some sort of photo-driven organic battery in the optical equipment of the Asadi mounted inexorably. If this hypothesis had any validity, I knew, it might offer the beginnings of an explanation for the present absence of prey and predators on BoskVeld. The Asadi ate low on the food chain; also, they might share with green plants the ability to synthesize chemical energy from direct sunlight, thereby abstracting themselves from any crass dependence on carnivory. Why, then, did they sometimes choose to be cannibals?

Kretzoi suddenly shoved the Asadi in the chest, thrusting him away. He then made a series of angry gestural signatures.

"What's that all about?" I asked.

"He's telling Bojangles, *You have Kretzoi hands, but I*

*don't have Bojangles eyes*. It's a rebuke. If they're going to communicate, he seems to be saying, it'll have to be by means of an anatomical common denominator.''

"The hands?''

"So he's arguing. The trouble is he's outlining the necessity of employing Ameslan in Ameslan itself, which can only be—''

"Greek?''

"Yes, which can only be Greek to Bojangles.'' Elegy leaned forward to watch both the live action below and the screens of the four closed-circuit monitors on the catwalk's rail.

Kretzoi grabbed Bojangles's wrists, as if remembering that the Asadi had been the first to compare their hands and to imply a willingness to bridge the evolutionary chasm separating them. With only that to go on, then, Kretzoi pulled Bojangles off his butt and began forcibly twisting the Asadi's hands into some of the basic alphabetical and symbolic gestures of Ameslan.

Bojangles hunkered before Kretzoi in a rapture of studious incomprehension, allowing his hands to be manipulated like modeling clay, his eyes (according to Monitor No. 3) glowing a mute pale silver.

After ten or fifteen minutes of this he yanked one hand free and made the sign for "frightened.''

"He's smarter than you are,'' Elegy whispered. "He's an absolute linguistic genius in comparison to you.''

*Frightened*. The sign hung in the air, whether by a random concatenation of muscle responses or a deliberate attempt to frame that very message—well, my skepticism inclined me to the former view.

"The sign for 'afraid,' '' Elegy excitedly mused. "Ordinarily you start with objects—'cup,' 'book,' 'chair,' 'eyes,' and so on—because you can define them by pointing. Bojangles has begun with an intangible, Ben, with an abstract emotion. That's incredible—it's spine-tingling.''

"Maybe he selected randomly among the signs Kretzoi showed him,'' I proposed. "He's mimicking, after all, and he had to start somewhere.''

"No, no,'' she countered. "Look at the monitor. Bojangles knows exactly what the sign means, just see if he doesn't.''

In closeup, Bojangles's baboonish face: lips skinned back in the primate's characteristic fear rictus. Tenor and vehicle of the gestural metaphor conveyed together in a sick, scary grin.

"It's nothing supernatural," Elegy said huskily. "Kretzoi probably drew his own lips back when he made the appropriate sign. Did you notice?"

"No, I was watching Bojangles."

We used our playback monitor and confirmed that Kretzoi had indeed displayed the fear grin while making the sign for "afraid" or "frightened." My stomach's squadron of butterflies found roosting places and fluttered less energetically. But my hands were clammy.

"Nothing supernatural or occult," Elegy repeated. "Bojangles simply picked up on the facial expression and the hand sign together. God, though, wasn't it quick of him?"

The conversation at poolside continued, Kretzoi repressing his surprise at Bojangles's nimble-wittedness and reeling off so many vocabulary signs that it was clear he was going overboard. For definition's sake he pointed, pouted, shrugged, and played mime, Ameslan and digital dumb show getting bollixed up together like yarn in a box of fishing tackle. Bojangles paid strict, even slavish heed.

Then he made the fear sign again.

"But he doesn't *look* frightened," Elegy observed. "Outside of sleep periods and grooming sessions he's as calm as we've seen him."

"It's a frightening thing, having the combined past and present literatures of Earth dumped on you in sign language in three minutes' time," I said, both fascinated and amused by Bojangles's supposed fear.

"Do you remember, Ben, at the museum, Kretzoi told us the Asadi eyebook had invoked in him a disturbing fear pattern?"

"I remember."

"Maybe, in both cases, the fear derives from the head-to-head clash of two different cultural units at the level where compromises have to be reached. Their own discrete systems of conveying information and knowledge, I mean. Kretzoi's emotional reaction to the eyebook program may have been a measure of his hopelessness in confronting so alien a system as the Asadi's. That system, being mechanical, refused to compromise."

"Then, why is Bojangles afraid? Kretzoi's beginning to show a little consideration, he's slowing down. That's compromise for you, isn't it?"

In fact, Kretzoi was now forming signs like an elocution

teacher pooching out the lips and curling the tongue to demonstrate *precisely* how a sound ought to be made; and Bojangles was watching with rapt studiousness, hardly a heart-tugging picture of fear.

Elegy said, "I don't know why he's afraid, if he really is. Maybe because the compromise—if that's what it is—is taking place entirely within the terms of Kretzoi's system. Bojangles is having to set aside the polychromatic optical language that's the Asadi heritage. That's a loss, it's really a kind of self-negation. Why shouldn't he be afraid? What if you found yourself among a tribe of extraterrestrials who insisted you communicate with them by, say, conscious control of the passing of intestinal gas."

I laughed out loud. "Unless they offered to assist me, I don't think I'd be afraid." But suddenly the butterflies in my gut rose en masse and performed a clumsy wing roll. "In Bojangles's case, Elegy, I think you're taking too restricted a view. He's not frightened by the Berlitz course Kretzoi's giving him."

"He doesn't *seem* to be," she confessed. "Maybe it's homesickness, and the sense of disorientation, and the newness of—" She gestured sweepingly at the gloomy interior of the hangar.

"Probably," I agreed.

And for nearly ten hours, with time-outs only for water and comfort breaks, Kretzoi and Bojangles played pedagogue and pupil. By midafternoon the two were exchanging information, groping toward interspecies understanding, and, in the process, amusing the hell out of each other. Elegy and I watched them with mounting wonder and a certain envious admiration.

*

"What did you learn, Kretzoi?"

Elegy interpreted the signs he made: "That the pagoda exists. That Bojangles himself has seen it and knows it exists."

"Where?"

"Bojangles wouldn't tell him that. The penalty for revealing its location is—well, pariahhood. The mane is shaved, the betrayer ignored."

"What else, Kretzoi? What else?"

Our debriefing was taking place on the movable mezzanine where the three of us had established our sleeping quarters. A pyramid of white planvas sat atop the factory flooring of the mezzanine, providing a translucent interface between ourselves and the honeycombed storage areas of the hangar.

Inside this pyramid Kretzoi regarded me numbly from a bench that looked to have been made from an outsized erector set. Physically drained, he was taking a transfusion of gluocose; he could sign with only one hand, his left, and that hand had suddenly stopped gesturing.

"Did you ask them how they feed, or why he isn't taking solid foods, or what role cannibalism plays in their—?"

"Whoa," Elegy said. "They've just started kindergarten and you're already giving Kretzoi a graduate-level exam."

"He's already found out about the Asadi temple," I protested, waving my arm and accidentally gouging the planvas wall. "Why not a few of these others?"

"Even Ameslan prodigies can't discuss everything the cosmos holds in a single day. And Kretzoi's exhausted, weak. He's on medication to suppress insulin production, and he's got a needle in his arm. Have mercy, Ben."

Kretzoi regarded me appraisingly, but not, I felt, without sympathy. How strange. Sitting in judgment of me, a chimpoon with a urine-colored bag of glucose suspended over his head from an aluminum monopod.

"Why don't we give him a day off?" I suggested.

Kretzoi shook his head, his mouth hanging open like a pouch.

"*You* could go down there with Bojangles," I told Elegy. "Kretzoi's taught him the finger talk; you could continue the lessons—make the sort of inquiries that might lead us directly to the temple."

Elegy squinted at me, then shook her head and looked away. "The only trouble with that is . . . Bojangles probably won't believe I'm an Asadi. I'm convinced he thinks Kretzoi's a kissin' cousin if not a prodigal sibling. Do you really want me to risk going in there tomorrow to see if I'm accepted as readily as Kretzoi's been?" Elegy's eyes, opening wider and flaring like hot acetylene, again intercepted mine. "Maybe you'd like me to cut off my hair and pretend to be an Asadi outcast. That would gain me acceptance, more than likely, but it wouldn't make me a very popular confidante."

"I'm sorry," I said, meaning it.

"What we're doing now is extremely important, Ben. We're learning things no one else has learned, ever. In two days we've justified both my grant and our rashness in abducting an Asadi from the Wild."

"Patience," I counseled myself sagely. "Persistence."

Elegy's eyes torched me with flames of exasperated admiration. "God, you're just like a little boy."

"Not in everything, young lady. Not in everything." I ducked my head and went through the pyramid's doorway to the mezzanine platform outside.

"Where you goin'?" Elegy called.

"For some air," I said. "To burn the weeds Bojangles turned up his nose at today. We all need a vacation from me, I think."

I went down the perforated metal steps and across the gloomy hangar floor to the recreation area. My own weariness was like a drug in my veins.

# CHAPTER TEN

# The Experiment Ends

The umbrellalike roots of the epiphytes smelled the worst. They burned along their nodulous ganglia like a tangle of gravid snakes hoisted over charcoal and prodded into writhing incandescence. The odor was a blend of curdled mayonnaise and mint-scented feces. All that made their burning bearable was the open veldt country sweeping away to the northeast of the knoll behind the hangar, that and the freshness of BoskVeld's winds blowing across the pit. The stars looked like microscopic screw heads rotated into the hidden template of the universe. I stood on the knoll poking at the mass of coal-bright roots and staring toward the empurpled, northeastern horizon.

"Dr. Benedict!" a voice hailed me.

A figure with a high-powered hand lamp was approaching me from around the northwestern corner of the hangar. A solitary figure. He had nearly a hundred meters to go before we would be close enough to converse in anything other than shouts. All I could do was watch the white-blue beam of his lamp stutter around the landscape until he arrived. Usually, it crossed my mind, Komm-service guards patrolled in pairs.

It was the young Iranian, Jaafar Bahadori. Over one shoulder he carried a lightning-emblazoned laser half rifle, exactly the sort of weapon with which our hangar's legendary muralist had etched his erotic masterpiece. Jaafar's boots, I noticed, were of the stalking variety favored during field maneuvers and commando assaults.

"That stinks," he said by way of greeting.

184

"I didn't know you had to pull guard duty, Jaafar. I thought you were safely ensconced in the lorry pool or over at Rain Forest Port."

"I am doing a friend a favor, sir."

"Someone talked you into taking his duty?"

"I talked her into letting me take it for her."

"Such altruism."

Jaafar nudged the burning epiphytes with his boot toe. "That really stinks. How is it you are standing it?" But he squatted near the pit as if to inhale the full unadulterated aroma and told me, "There's been some talk in her Komm-service barracks, says my good friend, about putting on night face and staging a commando raid on the hangar. Much of it is lorqual loquaciousness, as they say, mere silly drunk talk, but some of it is truly serious."

"A commando raid?" I exclaimed. "What for?"

"To capture the Asadi and put it to death. A war game, you see. Boredom is rife these days, she says. Her barracks-mates' last maneuvers were three months ago, and carrying vegetables out of the Wild every morning for your alien has given some of them nasty ideas. They don't like to play at catering service for your . . . well, your—"

"Boonie?" I suggested.

"Yes, sir. For a boonie." Jaafar stood and gazed up at the sky—a moon was rising. "I have a partner on the other side of the building, sir. I told him he could patrol that side and go googly over the lovely laser scrawls if he'd just give me time to make my circuit. I had been pretending a limp until I got clear of him, you see, and so he thinks I'm slow."

"Is your partner one of the conspirators?"

"I don't know. He doesn't talk to me very much. He did not wish to talk to you, either. He was very happy, this one, to let me come around here and fill my nostrils with this . . . this . . . this terrible effluvium," he concluded, pleased with himself.

"Why hasn't your friend reported the mutinous talk?"

"Oh, no. Impossible. She's a daughter of the Martial Arm, Planetary Command. Her loyalty to her comrades-in-arms prevents her."

"What about her loyalty to Colonial Administration, Jaafar? Maybe her priorites are badly scrambled."

"Aren't I here? Didn't she let me come in her place tonight, knowing I would do the necessary?" Jaafar seemed to think these rhetorical questions settled the matter. "It's time for me to go, sir."

"They'd be crazy to try anything so foolish," I said to Jaafar's back. The barrel of his half rifle topped his shoulder like an evil smokestack.

He turned. "Some of them, she says, are truly crazy." With that he went off halt-footed down the knoll, getting in practice for the partner who believed him temporarily lame. "Good night, Dr. Benedict." The words were partially muffled by a long, warm gust off the veldt. The crinkling epiphytes smoldered in their pit. After watching them a time, I went back into the hangar.

*

"Do you believe him?"

"Do I believe there's been talk in the barracks of a lynching party, or do I believe they really mean to throw it?"

Elegy made a moue of distaste at my semantic fussiness. "The later, of course. Do you really think they'll do it?"

"The talk I'm certain of, Elegy—it's typical barracks talk. But the other's dicey. Jaafar's friend is right, though. Some of the Martial Arm's planetbound E-graders are hotbrows, even with off-duty tranqs, thetrodes, and lorqual to keep 'em cool. They don't like it here, but they're indentured for life. If they rev themselves into it, they might risk courts-martial or even a big half-C of Punitive Sleep."

"Just to get Bojangles?"

"Apparently."

"Then there's danger to Kretzoi, too. I wouldn't trust them to distinguish between an Asadi and an imported replica, especially if it's dark and they're all spring-wound like cuckoo clocks."

"Do you want to get out of here?"

"Where would we go? This is the perfect place for the sort of work we're trying to do, Ben. Why don't you call Governor Eisen? Tell him what you've learned. Surely he'll send out a special unit to protect both us and the hangar—for at least the next few nights, anyway."

"That special unit would probably be partially comprised of some of the very guards who've been volleying about the notion of a raid."

"Fine. Let 'em know someone in authority knows what

they've been plotting. That by itself might be enough to keep
'em honest. We'd be stuipid to take the chance their in-
barracks bravado *isn't* going to spill over into a real working
out of their fantasies. There's too much at stake to hope
they're all just swaggering in their socks, Ben.''

"If I tell Moses, there'll be restrictions and punishments
among the Komm-service guards and even more resentment
of our presence out here."

Elegy's So-what? expression was as direct, eloquent, and
humbling as a kick in the coccyx. "Let 'em resent us. They
already do, anyway. What's a bit more? The restrictions, the
punishments—dear God, Ben, it's only what they deserve for
their loose talk and their contemptible disregard of their true
duty!''

She crossed the bright interior of the pyramid and sat down
by Kretzoi, who was asleep on his cold metal bench. She
stroked the big primate's mane and stared at me angrily.

Everything she had said was straightforward and ir-
refutable. I descended from the mezzanine, crossed the
hangar floor to a glassed-in closet housing a televid unit,
and put through a call to Moses's home.

The Governor heard me out emotionlessly, his face pasty
and impassive on the tiny screen. But he promised that within
twenty minutes we'd have a six-guard contingent stationed
around the hangar. This matter disposed of as if it weren't in
the least extraordinary, Moses asked if we'd made any
progress with our "trouble-making" Asadi. To show that his
choice of words was intended humorously, he gave a wan
smile. I told him that Kretzoi and Bojangles had become fast
friends, but didn't mention the latter's startling adeptness at
picking up Ameslan. Moses nodded amiably, assured me the
talk in the barracks would be squelched, along with any conceivable possibility of a raid, and, saying he had a few
pointed televid calls to make, almost apologetically broke our
connection.

Easy. So easy.

I didn't begin to feel better about things, though, until, less
than twenty minutes later, standing in one of the hangar's
small southside doorways, I saw the headlights of two
armored vans boring through the night across the salt-white
brightness of the polymac. Civki security police, independent
of the military guards who usually stand sentry duty at
Chaney Field. Behind them, the pearly lights of the terminal

building and the green-glowing panels of its support shacks. Because I didn't want to talk to the newly assigned police—who would take up their positions whether I greeted them or ducked inhospitably out of view—I closed the door and moved through the hangar securing dead bolts and checking the many other possible points of entry. Then I returned to Elegy and Kretzoi.

"You were gone quite a time," Elegy said.

"Everything's taken care of, though. Moses knows what's happening and we've got six laser-toting bodyguards strolling our estate."

"Good." The annoyance of a possible commando assault behind us, Elegy's relief was little greater than if we had just replaced a broken skylight through which the rain had been inconveniently falling. "I think Kretzoi's all right," she told me. "A urine test I administered a few minutes ago shows his blood-sugar levels are back to normal. The work with Bojangles hasn't exhausted him anything like his time in the Wild."

"Tomorrow—" I began.

"Tomorrow we'll let them resume, Ben. During all his time studying the Asadi, Egan Chaney never had a true informant—not even The Bachelor, who probably disclosed as much as he did only out of accident and a happy dim-wittedness. Now, though, we're developing an informant of our own. At the rate he appears able to learn Ameslan, in a week's time we may be transcribing answers to some of our questions directly from Bojangles's own hand signs. And it's Kretzoi's accomplishment, Ben."

"Three cheers for Kretzoi."

Elegy darted me an up-from-under look. "What's the matter? Feel slighted?"

"No, not really. At least I don't think so. It's just that I think we'd better move as fast as we can. Kretzoi's already managed to ask Bojangles about the Asadi temple, Elegy. If he can do that, he can do more tomorrow. Much more, believe me."

"That may have been sheer serendipity, the pagoda business. Kretzoi made a series of gestures imaginatively translating this hangar into the heart of the Wild and then demanding to know if Bojangles had ever seen anything like it out there. Bojangles made an intuitive leap and replied that he had."

"That's not serendipity, that's intelligence. I want to give Kretzoi a list of questions to ask Bojangles tomorrow, just to see how far he gets with them. . . . What objections can you have to that?"

"None," Elegy said almost sullenly, believing, like most twenty-two-years olds, that Time is an unestrangeable ally. "Make your list."

*

Time isn't an unestrangeable ally. It runs out on you. And this time, to my sorrow, it wasn't the youthful expectations of Elegy Cather that prevailed, but the actuarial pessimism of Thomas Benedict. Sometimes the cost of being right is heart-breakingly high.

My list was long. Damn long. It began with relatively simple questions about observable Asadi behavior, proceeded to matters about which we had been fruitlessly speculating for six or seven years, and concluded with a series of inquires about the Asadi past and its influence on their present-day lives. I touched on feeding habits, social relationships, the Asadi "chieftaincy," the batlike huri, and so on for a total of nearly sixty questions, many with overlapping areas of concern. I might have gone on manuscribing all night, but Elegy touched my hand and made me stop.

"Select the ten most important ones," she said, "so that I can relay those to Kretzoi in the morning."

"They're all important."

"I won't have time to brief him on sixty, though, and even if I somehow managed, interrupting his sleep to do it, it's not very likely he'd have time to ask them all tomorrow. How do you expect him even to *remember* so many?"

So I winnowed, snipped, and collapsed my questions until there were ten, and the next morning, well before sunrise, Elegy sat down in front of Kretzoi and shaped them for him as he took his breakfast.

In the swimming-pool compound the day began exactly as had the previous one, with Bojangles marching ritually about the interior perimeter of the fence and back and forth through the empty pool itself. Kretzoi sat with his back to the compound's gates, his wrists on his knees and his hands hanging limply between.

But Bojangles soon began swaying playfully from side to

side, finally spinning himself out of his march and bringing himself up short in front of Kretzoi—where he leaned forward and stared unflinchingly at our shaggy field agent.

Kretzoi looked away. A stare is a threat signal among Earth primates. During his time in the Asadi clearing, one of Kretzoi's most difficult adjustments had been learning to meet the eyes of the aliens who wished to engage him in their habitual staring contests. The stress of locking eyes with the Asadi, in fact, may have accounted, in part, for his lapses of strength and his hypoglycemic vertigo. When the Asadi decided he wasn't worth taking on as a staring partner, his stress levels fell—even if his body never wholly regained its former homeostatic condition. But the Evil Eye, as exemplified by the stare, still retained its ability to discomfit Kretzoi; and even during the previous day's gestural tête-à-tête with Bojangles, he had made a point of frequently averting his gaze. You don't face down the Evil Eye.

In this respect, as well as many others, the Asadi had evolved differently. Their staring matches were not merely threat displays and acts of aggression; they were also televid chats, poetry readings, bull sessions, songfests, lectures. An Asadi could communicate on a complex informational level with another member of his species only if he looked him directly in the eyes. A few theorists suggested that the Asadi inhabited their clearing only during the day because only during daylight could they meaningfully exchange information. Vocal communication works at a distance; it carries in the dark as well as it does in the daylight. Gestures and other visual signals, however, depend on proximity and visibility for their effectiveness, and night neutralizes them as surely as does a blindfold. Hence, argued these theorists, the sunset dispersal of the Asadi and their evolutionary triumph over the typical primate phobia of the face-on stare.

Maybe.

At any rate, Kretzoi looked away from Bojangles, and kept his face averted until the Asadi lightly slapped his chest and made the Ameslan signs for "ugly-silent-lazy-friend." Kretzoi responded. Bojangles broke in. And soon the two were gabbing gesturally at great speed. It was too swift and complicated for me, hand-jive gossip at a high level of informational exchange. The conversation also had ongoing pedagogical significance, for Kretzoi continued to augment the Asadi's rapidly growing repertoire of signs.

"They're going like torrential sixty," I told Elegy. "I think they could have handled *all* my questions, don't you?"

Elegy scrutinized the monitors noncommittally. "We're lucky we've got a hologramic record, Ben. I'm not keeping up very well on my own."

And I exulted, confident we had come through where so many others, including Egan Chaney and earlier temporal projections of myself, had all had to settle for partial answers or no answers at all.

A pounding interrupted these self-congratulatory musings. My heart leaped numbly. Kretzoi and Bojangles stopped conversing and lifted their snouts toward the source of these repetitive, echoing thuds.

"What the hell is that?" I whispered.

"The door's locked," Elegy told me. "It's our morning delivery." Of plants from the Wild, she meant.

She cleared one of our four small monitors and activated the controls of an exterior camera so that we could see the visitors at our door. Foreshortened by the camera's overhead lens into macrocephalic dwarves, two Komm-service guards stood seeking entrance to the hangar, each carrying an armful of plants. They each bore weapons, too.

A heavy-jowled, olive-complexioned man and a pale woman with bright, hawklike eyes. The woman, against regulations, was using the butt of her half rifle to knock on the door. She wore a violet scarf around her neck, an optional piece of uniform for the idiosyncratically debonair. The set of her brow revealed her distaste for the duty she was performing, and the slammings of her rifle butt against the door occasionally buffeted a skein of roots or a few flower cuttings out of the crook of her other arm.

"Bojangles isn't going to eat," I told Elegy irritably. "I don't know why we're still bothering trying to supply him."

Elegy gestured at the monitor. "*They're* the ones who're supplying him, Ben. And whether Bojangles eats or not, you're going to have to go down there to open the door. There's no automatic release, unfortunately."

"Do we even want to let them in?"

"I don't, not really—but they're obeying orders and we'd better not alienate the ones who still have the good sense to do that."

So I went. The poundings came at about five-second intervals, the echoes reminding me of depth charges. Negotiating the catwalk, I saw that Kretzoi and Bojangles still hadn't resumed their dialogue. Their heads were tilted quizzically.

Once down, I reached the recreation area's door and cast aside its sequence of heavy metal bolts—only to find myself looking square at the drawn-back butt of the woman's half rifle.

"Today's food supply," she announced, expertly recradling her weapon. In the place on her sleeve where her name should have been there were only a few frayed tufts of purple thread. The man's embroidered name was right where it was supposed to be—but in Arabic characters I was unable to decipher. Although these anomalies registered, they didn't set off in me a chain reaction of increasingly more insightful suspicions.

As soon as they had entered the hangar, the young woman dropped her bouquet of vegetables into my arms, just as if I had asked for them, and closed and secured the door. Its bolts fired shut like a battery of pneumatic nutcrackers. My first thought was that this woman knew to take every conceivable security precaution to protect us. Hence, her conscientious bolting of the door.

"I'm Jaafar's friend," the raptor-eyed woman told me suddenly, confirming me in my opinion of her motives. "E-3 Filly Deuel."

"Technically," I told her, glancing at her sleeve, "you're out of uniform, E-3 Deuel. Your name's no longer legible there."

"She only recently made her new rank," the man said in a well-modulated, faintly accented baritone. "Yesterday the blouse belonged to an E-3 who has also just gone up a grade. That's why Deuel hasn't stitched her own name in yet. You wouldn't report such a minor infraction of the GKR's, sir."

"What's your name?" I asked the man abruptly.

"E-5 Spenser Pettijohn."

"Pettijohn? Why have you rendered your name in Arabic characters, then? That's a right reserved for ethnic personnel, isn't it?"

"My mother was a Hindustani, sir, and before coming to BoskVeld I pulled a five-year tour on GK-world Quattara II in the Veil. I exercise the option by right of both ethnic derivation and past service, you see."

We stood appraising one another with an uneasiness I couldn't identify. Something seemed wrong. Deuel's face in particular betrayed a hint of repressed hysteria. Her lips were slightly open and her cheeks glowed. At that moment, I tentatively began to wonder if Pettijohn and Deuel were really Pettijohn and Deuel.

"Have you had any trouble, sir?" Pettijohn asked.

"Not yet."

"That's good." He gestured with his bouquet. "Why don't you let us take these to the Asadi? I know your previous deliveries were all made earlier in the morning, but last night's arrangements for a permanent detail here at the hangar played havoc with our schedule. If you'll show us the way, then, we'll drop these goodies off and get out of your hair."

My own arms laden, I led Deuel and Pettijohn into the recreation area, through a labyrinth of tubbed plants and carpeted pathways to the clearing where our bright-yellow fence made its kidney-shaped circuit around the swimming pool. Elegy watched us from the catwalk, but I kept my head down and instinctively avoided pointing out her position to the Komm-service guards.

Once beside the fence I unceremoniously heaved the roots, flowers, and fronds in my hands up and over. They landed on the other side with an audible thump, although a few cascaded back down the wall onto my feet. Deuel, more duty-conscious than she'd been outside the hangar, helped me pick them up.

Pettijohn, however, simply stood beside us. His jowls had begun to glisten with sweat, and his eyes now resembled those of a thetrode addict.

"I'd like to take mine inside," he said sweetly, distantly.

"Why?"

"They bruise when you drop them like that, sir. They're fragile. The cell walls collapse. The nutrients spill out. It's simple common sense, if you think about it."

"Pettijohn, you're overestimating the frailty of these plants. I've studied several dozen varieties from the Wild, and there just don't happen to be that many goddamn shrinking violets among them."

"I'd like to take mine inside," Pettijohn insisted sweetly.

"That won't be necessary. You'll disrupt the progress of our experiment. You're disrupting it right now."

"I'd like to take mine inside."

"Give 'em to me," I said, with as much artificial patience as I could muster. "I'll do the dirty work you're too fastidious to do yourself."

Upon a warning flash of Pettijohn's cold, stoned eyes, E-3 Filly Deuel used the butt of her half rifle on my head. A whip cracked through the convolutions of my grey matter, and my eyes bulged like a hooked trout's. I fell sidelong, plunged in throbbing confusion but still vaguely conscious of the events unfolding around me.

Pettijohn cast aside his bundle of plants, stooped over me to find in my eyes a welcome (for him) but blessedly false (for me) deadness, and then threw himself against the compound's double gate. Even lying flat on my back, I could see that he was almost immediately successful in gaining entry. A section of the pool's pastel interior loomed as large in my mind and vision as the morning sky overhead.

"There's the woman!" I heard E-3 Filly Deuel shout. "She's running along that catwalk! Hurry, Spenser, damn you!"

"Shoot her!" Pettijohn commanded from the pool.

"With what?" Deuel countered shrilly. "With what, you great turd? All this thing will do is knock on doors and old men's heads! You wouldn't trust me with a fully operable rifle and you're lucky me didn't!"

"Then shut up!" Pettijohn called. "I'm going to do what I came to do, I'm doing it now, and you can just shut up!" He screamed piercingly, a warrior's cry, and a brutal droning noise—followed by a brief alteration in the quality of the light—filled the hangar. Afterward, a pervasive smell of ozone.

Pettijohn, I knew, had just discharged his own half rifle, the one he'd brought into the hangar slung infantry fashion over his shoulder. My nausea grew deeper, even more intolerably complicated.

Then, like great multifaceted eyes with metal lids, the hangar's skylights closed, and the building was suddenly dark. I surrendered to the darkness. . . .

\*

In our pyramid atop the movable mezzanine platform, I awoke on Kretzoi's bench. Someone had applied a thin gauze bandage to my right temple. The hangar had apparently opened its eyes, too, because light suffused the building's interior and illumined the triangular panes of our pyramid as if they were church windows. The face above mine belonged to Jaafar Bahadori.

"I told them you didn't need a hospital," he said.

I shifted my gaze to the left and tilted my head back: There was Kretzoi, staring out the pyramid's doorway in the direction of the swimming pool.

"Your Asadi is dying," Jaafar informed me tenderly. "It's on its way to the hospital in Frasierville, but no one, I think, holds out much hope. That Pettijohn performed some very vicious surgery with his half rifle."

"Your friend," I managed bitterly, "the one whose sentry duty you took last night—she helped the bastard."

"She didn't want to. Pettijohn brought her along as punishment for speaking to me. The rifle he gave her was a company discard. He made her pluck her name off her uniform sleeve because this morning's duty roster, which the civki security police check before they let anyone in, showed that E-3 Ludmilla Meddis and E-5 Krishna Mai were supposed to make the food delivery. Pettijohn impersonated Mai and forced Filly to impersonate the woman called Meddis."

I sat up. The pyramid tilted around me as I did, and Jaafar, standing to give me room, towered away toward the pyramid's apex. That struck me as odd—Jaafar was not very tall.

"She didn't want to help him, my Filly didn't."

Anger began pressing up beneath my numbness. "Then why did she?"

"He had a hand weapon concealed amid the plants in his arms. He would have shot her, sir, had she tried to refuse him. In the barracks, before they came out here, he half throttled her to death as a foretaste of what he would do if she didn't obey. The madman."

"She was wearing the optional scarf—" I began.

"To conceal the bruises," Jaafar finished. "They're terrible." His wince conveyed the gaudy painfulness of poor Filly Deuel's contusions.

"She slammed a rifle butt into my head, Jaafar."

"Only hard enough to knock you down. Happily you had the strength of mind to pretend unconsciousness when Pettijohn bent to examine you."

"Unconsciousness wasn't a difficult thing to pretend just then, Jaafar."

"No, sir. The real thing caught up with you, I think, when

the lights went out. Maybe, too, the power of suggestion was involved in that."

Suddenly I felt the absence of Elegy, realized the overwhelming truth about Bojangles. The alien—our Asadi—was dying of wounds inflicted upon him by a Komm-service enlisted man whose intense personal hatred of the Other had overcome both his early indoctrination in the Komm regs and his fear of a long, nightmare-riven Punitive Sleep. Hatred and boredom. The two had worked together to rob Bojangles of his life.

I struck the edge of the metal bench with such violence that I sliced the heel of my hand. Crimson flooded the pale upholstery of my flesh and smeared the knee of my trousers.

I looked to Kretzoi for help. "What happened in there?" I demanded of him. "What happened?"

With melancholy deliberateness Kretzoi started to shape a pantomime of the morning's events.

"No," I said. "I won't understand you."

"Young Civ Cather," Jaafar jumped in, "reached the controls operating the mechanical skylight covers and shut them all as fast as she could. She had no weapon with her on the catwalk, and that was all she could think to do. Very, very happily, it worked. Kretzoi and Filly reached Pettijohn before he could perform any more nastiness with his half rifle. Utter darkness, you see. That one"—he indicated Kretzoi—"took a giant chunk from the madman's upper chest and unsocketed his right arm. Didn't you hear the bastard screaming, sir?"

"I didn't hear him," I confessed, surprised that Jaafar had pronounced "bastard" with no more emphasis than he would have given "uncle," or "xenologist," or "wife."

Kretzoi was looking toward the recreation area again, remembering the things that had happened there and shrugging off my hastily withdrawn invitation to narrate the story for me. He didn't appear to be physically hurt. But I regretted having cut him off so imperiously. Bojangles was dying, and Kretzoi had more than an abstract understanding of this fact.

I reached beneath the bench and found the same first-aid kit from which Jaafar had scrounged a bandage for my head. I wrapped a piece of gauze around the heel of my hand and held it there until the bleeding stopped.

Jaafar began to pace. "Filly shouted that everything was under control, you see, and although Civ Cather wasn't inclined to believe her, seeing what she had done to you, eventually she was persuaded to take a chance and throw back the skylight covers. After that, the civki police were admitted and the various damages assessed. Worst, you already know, was your Asadi. Yes, worst of all was your Asadi, and I arrived with Governor Eisen to—''

Wobbly in the knees and sick at heart, I stood up and approached Kretzoi. Jaafar finally hushed. Although he tried not to show it, he was more than mildly surprised when I reached out with my uninjured hand and began combing Kretzoi's mane. . . .

# CHAPTER ELEVEN

# Autopsy

Bojangles died in Frasierville. Elegy and I repressed our bewildered grief and urged Moses Eisen to ask Kommthor's permission to subject the body to both an autopsy and a full anatomical/biochemical computer analysis. It took three days, time during which Bojangles's corpse lay in a refrigerated chamber in Frasierville's hospital, but at last this permission came through—whereupon the body was enthusiastically attacked and dismantled. Three mechanic-surgeons and a glass-and-chromium array of transistorized medical equipment attended Bojangles's dismantling.

Elegy and I weren't permitted to watch any of these exacting procedures or to record for our own curiosity or use any of the initial laboratory results. Truth to tell, we didn't much care. We were like squeamish fathers, the sort who don't want to be on hand for the birth. Bojangles was dead, and the issue of his autopsists' labors would be a long catalogue of anatomical and biochemical comparison/contrasts demonstrating the precise statistical degree of his *alienness*.

Your baby, the doctors would tell us, is *different*, folks. Pull down the blinds and prepare yourselves for an unsettling shock.

When Moses finally came to us with the preliminary results, Elegy and I were seated over an old hardwood table near the hangar's swimming pool. The soft-wall fence had come down the day after Pettijohn's attack on Bojangles, and we had spent the week since the Asadi's death talking desultorily about a new expedition into the Wild and playing card games.

Moses tossed three or four laminated folders onto the table and pulled up a chair.

Behind him in the artificial shrubbery sat Kretzoi. It would be tempting to say that Kretzoi was mourning Bojangles's death, but, more probably, he had simply surrendered to the ennui of our long confinement. His tendency to lurk in shadows and wander aimlessly through the tubbed botanicals was symptomatic of his boredom.

I tapped one of Moses's folders. "Anything startling?"

Moses held his hands in his lap, below the surface of the table, and spoke to the skylights. "Several confirmations of past speculation. The Asadi have a carbon-based biochemistry, and, in almost all respects, they appear to be BoskVeld's equivalent of terrestrial primates. That confirms past speculation, as I say, but it also happens to be startling."

"A far-flung example of independent evolution?" Elegy offered.

"Far-flung? Far-fetched? I don't know which better describes the case," said Eisen, still gazing skyward. "Bojangles's cells each contained twenty-four pairs of chromosomes. That's one more pair than you'll find in the cellular makeup of human beings. But it's still remarkably close."

"White rats have twenty-two pairs," I told Moses with ill-concealed annoyance. "And there's a friggin' one-celled rhizopod with better than 850 pairs. The number of chromosomes doesn't mean as much as the type and quality of the genetic information stored within each strand of DNA."

"What about this, then?" Moses retorted, still without looking at me. "The DNA molecule comprising the Asadi chromosome has a structure almost identical to that of the human chromosome. In fact, the differences are often minuscule—simple displacements of one or two amino acids in the linear sequence of various kinds of protein molecules. Human beings and chimpanzees share an identical arrangement of the 141 amino acids comprising the alpha chain of the hemoglobin molecule—good evidence for a common ancestor somewhere back in the Miocene."

"So?" I said. "The Asadi aren't chimpanzees."

Moses finally looked at me, his eyes alert and penetrating.

"The alpha hemoglobin molecule in Bojangles's blood tested out with the same 141 amino acids in precisely the same sequence."

That rocked me, but I didn't like to show it. "You're proposing that chimps, human beings, and the Asadi all have a Ramapithecan daddy from good ol' Sunshine III?"

"I'm not proposing anything!" Moses flared, leaning toward me and unexpectedly catching my wrists on the tabletop. "I'm trying to detail for you and Civ Cather the results of nearly seventy-two continuous hours of analysis and speculation. I'm telling you what's been discovered. Your flippancy merely demonstrates the degree of your own confusion, Dr. Benedict. If you expect the Governor of BoskVeld to come to you with a personal briefing on this unpleasant topic, you've got to have the decency to hear him out with both civility and respect!"

Moses's face collapsed. He slammed my wrists against the surface of the table, stumbled from his chair, and stalked resolutely toward the door by which Pettijohn and Deuel had entered our hangar nearly a week ago. In the sparse, self-parodying foliage of the recreation area, Kretzoi moved discreetly out of his path.

Stunned, I thought of an instructor in my undergraduate days whose favorite disciplinary strategy was to leave the room and wait for an apologetic student to come to his office with a general appeal that he return. When I saw Elegy hurrying across the carpet after Moses, the prophecy inherent in my recollection seemed to be fulfilling itself: Elegy and Moses talked briefly, then locked arms and came strolling back toward me. I stood to greet them, cowed more by Moses's vulnerability than by his unusual display of strong emotion.

"Moses," I began; "Moses—"

He waved his hand, freed himself from Elegy's daughterly grasp, and sat down again. "I feel as old as God's little brother," he said to the tabletop. "Kommthor's been giving me hell about the death of an Asadi at the hands of an E-5 with a history of xenophobic tendencies—even though Pettijohn's psychological profiles were apparently lost or misconveyed during his most recent transfer." Moses sighed.

"They've also been on my back about your invocation of the privileged-intervention clause of Elegy's grant," he added wearily. "In fact, they seem to fear that the whole damn cosmos is going to unravel because you went beyond the bounds of xenological convention in capturing a highly evolved and maybe even self-aware variety of alien. I'm exaggerating Kommthor's position some, but not much. Worse, their response to our first light-probe communication about the Asadi's physiological gestalt indicates they may move very soon to *invalidate* the privileged-intervention clause of grants like Elegy's. They'd do so on the basis of the Golden Rule provision—suppose intelligent aliens decided to investigate *you* by means of capture and confinement.

"As a consequence of recent events," Moses concluded, "I seem to be in some small danger of early retirement. Relocation of my family and me to, say, Amérsavane or Steppe-Childe isn't altogether unlikely—not as hard-scrabble pioneers, mind you, but as 'esteemed wards and wardens of the community.' That's still not a prospect I cherish, Ben."

We sat for a time without saying anything. Occasionally I caught glimpses of Kretzoi in the foliage, eyeing us cryptically from behind a planter or a stone sculpture.

Then, almost himself again, Moses flipped open one of the laminated folders and began running his finger down a double column of figures. "Brain volume is 923 cubic centimeters," he said matter-of-factly. "Since Bojangles was a small adult male, the supposition is that Asadi endocranial volume may run as high as 1300 cc's. That's well within human parameters. In fact, the two figures pretty closely approximate the range of brain sizes among known specimens of *Homo erectus*, contemporary humanity's great-grandparents, so to speak." He looked up, glancing first at Elegy and then at me. "I'm not sure what significance that has, only that the statistics reveal the similarities."

"It may mean the Asadi are self-aware after the fashion of human beings," Elegy said. "*Homo erectus* tamed fire and had something approaching a knowledge of the mystical finality of death. They ate the brains of their dead as a means of maintaining spiritual contact with their departed relatives."

"Or as a means of incorporating and subjugating the essence of their enemies," I added. "It's hard to reconstruct intentions from five-hundred-thousand-year-old skulls with holes near their brain stems."

Moses looked back down at his folder. "The organization of the Asadi brain also appears to have a good deal in common with ours. A triune evolution and structure—but four principal lobes in the neocortex, with a bridge between hemispheres similar to our corpus callosum. Bojangles's brain, however, has no recognizable counterpart to Broca's area in its left hemisphere, the specific region in which resides our ability to formulate the symbolic structures of language.''

"That's not surprising," I said. "The Asadi don't speak—at least not with their tongues.''

"What they do have," Moses went on, "is a structure in the right hemisphere of the parietal cortex—or superassociation area—that may have a *functional* correspondence with Broca's area even though it controls the muscles of their eyes rather than those of their lips and tongues. Call it 'Bojangles's area,' if you like—that's how it's recorded in this white paper.'' Moses tapped the printout. "Anyway, Bojangles's area may act in the Asadi as Broca's area acts in us. It's a source and a repository of the structural grammar of the Asadi's polychromatic optical 'language.' It also appears to perform the function of Wernicke's area in human beings—that is, it stores sensory images, particularly visual ones, and permits the Asadi to communicate with one another in a complex visual code we haven't yet broken.''

"This area—Bojangles's area—exists in the right rather than the left hemisphere of the Asadi neocortex?'' I asked.

"According to this," Moses acknowledged, looking with undisguised awe at the white paper in his hands and riffling its pages. "This entire folder has to do with the anatomy and function of the Asadi brain. The whole damn thing.''

"In human brain lateralization," Elegy said, picking up my cue, "the left side is the digital computer that formulates the objective personality, the rational self. The right side is the analogue computer that links up the various counterstreaming visions and nightmares of our subconscious self; it's the residence of our intuitive and more recognizably mystical personality. The ego lives in the left brain, the 'not-I' in the right. If the same bicameral correspondences hold in the Asadi brain, then their polychromatic optical language derives much more immediately from 'ancestral voices' than does human speech. The implication—isn't this what you're driving at, Ben?—is that they communicate with one another on a much more intuitive or even artistic level than do human beings?''

Moses wrapped his feet around the front legs of his chair

and leaned back in it like a little boy tempting gravity. He gave a derisive bark and shook his head.

"What?" Elegy asked him.

"What's 'intuitive' or 'artistic' about staring contests in a humid jungle clearing?"

"How can we possibly answer that," I asked, "until we know what kinds of information they're exchanging? Even if the Asadi brain superficially resembles ours, the location of Bojangles's area suggests that their intelligence—their entire neuro-symbolic attunement to the world—may be of a different order of reality from ours. The physical similarities, the anatomical matchups, even the amazing correspondence of the amino-acid sequences may mean nothing at all in the face of the Asadi's totally alien perception of their place in the Infinite Scheme of Things."

Moses clumped forward and put his elbows on the table again. "That's Thomas Benedict talking out of *his* right brain," he told Elegy. "What the hell is your friend driving at?"

Elegy—for the sake of argument, I think—took Moses's part: "Kretzoi and Bojangles did manage to get on the same wavelength for a while, Ben. For the short while, I'm pretty certain, they . . . well, *touched*."

"If they did," I said, "it proves only that Bojangles was able to cross an interspecies Rubicon unfordable by you or me. Bojangles made the crossing, Kretzoi didn't. And *we* may never be able to make it—for the same reason iguanas can't fly or hippopotami sing."

That shut us all up for a while, even me.

Then Moses pulled another folder toward him and opened it. "This one has to do with the eye," he announced. "Not the areas in the brain that store visual memory or the Asadi's indecipherable optical grammar, mind you—but the structure and function of the eye itself. Photoreception, the willed conversion of photosynthetic pigments into spectral displays, and the breakdown of sunlight into chemical energy usable as metabolic fuel. The eyes of the Asadi, you see, have at least three distinct functions—they see, they communicate, and they feed. They may do other things as well, but we're not certain yet what they are."

"Then the Asadi eye *is* capable of photosynthesis?" Elegy asked.

"So it appears," Moses responded, "although we still don't completely understand the mechanism. Their eyes capture sunlight in specialized cellular structures containing energy factories similar to the chloroplasts because they contain light-absorbing pigments in addition to chlorophyl, some of which we've never seen before—convert light energy into electrical energy and electrical energy into chemical energy. Some of the chemical energy is radiated in the Asadi's special displays, which may be either willed or random—although the consensus at the hospital seems to be that the Asadi *control* them. Just as your father surmised, Civ Cather, and just as we've all along assumed on the basis of simple observation and the empirical evidence of the eyebooks.

"The remainder of the chemical energy produced in the Asadi's optical chromoplasts goes into the manufacture of ATP and, ultimately, of course, glucose. The efficiency with which their chromoplasts use absorbed light energy appears to be nearly one hundred percent, and the oxygen that in plant photosynthesis is given off as a waste product the Asadi manage to channel back into their systems as an agent in the purely animal-specific energy-producing process of the Krebs cycle. In a sense, then, the Asadi even *breathe* through their eyes. That's why, when we first began examining the optical photosynthesis theory, our tests for especially high concentrations of oxygen over the Asadi clearing always proved negative.

"Now, apparently, the theory's been confirmed, and that confirmation suggests a reason for their staying in the jungle clearing only during the hours between sunrise and sunset—that's when their eyes photosynthesize most efficiently, and that's when they're best capable of communicating with one another through their spectral displays. The two processes complement each other, setting up a positive feedback loop in the same way that the tendency to bipedalism in early terrestrial hominids and the need to carry objects reinforced and further developed each other. But a positive feedback loop can dictate and drastically limit behavior, too, and that seems to be one of the reasons the Asadi have fallen into such a stagnant and repetitive life-style during their recent history. Perhaps the structure and function of their eyes have been the undoing as well as the making of the Asadi as a viable species."

"They're completely viable," Elegy put in. "Their numbers are small, but they don't appear in danger of extinction. What you're really saying is that by the standards of Sol III's arrogant human primates, they're not readily *comprehensible*. Isn't that it? Besides, the Asadi aren't absolute slaves to this physiological and biochemical process; at some point, they must have *chosen* to assemble at dawn and to disperse at sunset."

"Why?" Moses asked.

"Because visible light exists prior to dawn and after sunset. Their eyes, if they really operate at almost one hundred percent efficiency, could easily photosynthesize at these times, too."

I got up, clasped my hands at the small of my back, and stared at Kretzoi's half-concealed form in the poolside foliage. "That still doesn't suggest conscious choice, Elegy. The pattern—you suggested this yourself when you implied we could redeem the Asadi by taking them out of their clearing—the pattern may be part of a genetically dictated behavioral program. An instinct. You said yourself their willingness to suffer the monotony of the clearing must have survival value. Don't you remember your speculations about cannibalism?"

"All I know is that we've lost Bojangles, Ben, and that I'm tired of theory and speculation."

"That's why I've come to you with facts," Moses said, again riffling the pages of a report. "Look. Look here. Do you remember your father's account of the Asadi 'chieftain'—Chaney called him Eisen Zwei; a typical Chaney impertinence—who did battle with Denebola, staring directly at it and wrestling the sun with his hands?"

Yes, said Elegy, she remembered.

"The result was that the old Asadi's eyes burned out, became like two blackened holes in his head." Moses shook the report. "The evidence here is that blindness is *equivalent to death* for the Asadi. And those among them who are handicapped by an absence of photosynthetic pigments in their eyes—like The Bachelor, like the chieftain Eisen Zwei—are regarded with either passive repugnance or worshipful terror, as we might regard a zombie, one of the living dead. These handicapped Asadi have to depend on sources in addition to sunlight to feed themselves, you see, and they're unable to communicate with their fellows in the usual Asadi way. Hence, they're not simply 'mutes' to the community at large, they're walking dead men. That's why, after Eisen Zwei's ritual suicide, The Bachelor—a former pariah—was chosen to succeed the old man as 'chieftain.' ''

"You're theorizing again," I reminded Moses.

"All right," he said. "Listen. The evidence indicates that direct observation of Denebola definitely burns out the Asadi's eyes. They realize this themselves, and for the most part they prudently avoid staring matches with their sun. Unless, of course, they *wish* to blind themselves, as Eisen Zwei apparently did."

"But why did he want to blind himself?" I asked.

"Figuratively, he was committing suicide. He was old and sick and weary of the rigors of his absentee chieftaincy. If blindness is an absolute metaphor for death, the Asadi who purposely puts out his eyes is symbolically killing himself. In Eisen Zwei's case, according to Chaney's monograph, actual biological death followed this metaphorical death by less than thirty hours. The metaphor hastened the reality, in fact—just as Eisen Zwei wished it to."

Elegy's face took on a sudden jaundiced glow. "Bojangles stared at the sun, or tried to, almost the entire first day we had him in here!"

"Exactly." Moses cocked his finger at Elegy as if she had just solved an especially difficult equation. "His behavior wasn't an involuntary manifestation of Asadi photoperiodism, but Bojangles's own conscious attempt to kill himself. He wanted Denebola to burn his eyes out."

"It didn't," I said.

"That's because the hangar's skylights—to keep the temperature in here bearable—filter out most of the radiation in the yellow and green parts of the spectrum. An inadvertent result of this process was that Bojangles was unable to blind himself. Ironically, even though he didn't eat the plants that were hauled in for him, his staring upward helped keep him alive. He was 'feeding' in the red and violet parts of the spectrum, you see, and photosynthesizing all the nutrients he required from air, water, and sunlight. Even when he and Kretzoi started conversing and he gave up trying to blind himself, Bojangles was still deriving all the sustenance he required from Denebola's filtered light."

"He wanted to kill himself," Elegy murmured.

"That's not hard to believe, is it?" Moses asked her. "Look at this place we're in. You can't expect a creature who's never seen anything like this hangar to adjust to an abrupt and unexpected confinement within it. Bojangles had spent his entire life in the Calyptran Wild. You tore him up by the roots and relocated him in an environment terrifyingly alien."

"But Bojangles *had* seen something like this hangar before, Moses." I walked along the edge of the pool toward the place where I had last seen Kretzoi lurking.

"He had?" Moses pushed himself away from the table and maneuvered his chair about so that he could see me. "What?"

"The Asadi pagoda," Elegy whispered in a throaty way that carried. "Or the Ur'sadi temple, if you prefer." Then, in her normal voice: "Of course Bojangles may never have been *inside* the temple. So it's entirely possible you're correct, Governor Eisen—the hangar's strangeness may have been enough to prompt him to try to blind himself. Suicide, if you like."

"Kretzoi!" I called. "Kretzoi, come out here!"

He emerged reluctantly, walking on all fours like a baboon on open savannah. The fact that he could go upright as well as most human beings was lost in the disdainful animality of his approach.

Half to show my concern, half to bedevil him, I put my hand on Kretzoi's mane and walked him back to the table.

"Bojangles told you he'd seen the pagoda described in Chaney's monograph. He told you that on his second day in here, didn't he?"

Kretzoi nibbled at a tuft of hair on his shoulder, then smoothed it with his tongue.

"Kretzoi, I'm talking to you. Bojangles told you he'd seen the pagoda. He told you a good deal more, too. Information you haven't shared with us in the wake of his . . ." I let my voice trail off.

"Murder," Elegy finally said. "In the wake of his murder."

At that, Kretzoi reared back and promptly made the Ameslan sign for "murder." Then he looked accusingly at each of his human interlocutors in turn.

"This from a hybrid creature," I told Moses, "whose progenitors sometimes bashed open the skulls of infants to get at their brains."

"His genetic makeup is partially chimp, partially baboon," Elegy countered angrily, "but human beings also happen to be one of his 'progenitors'! His intelligence was augmented and, apparently, so was his capacity for sensitizing himself to that voice in the neocortex we call conscience. The same thing should happen to you."

Moses laughed. I exhaled audibly and held up my hands in mock—no, in genuine—surrender.

"We're going back into the Wild," Elegy enthusiastically told Moses, ignoring me. "No more field studies among the Asadi. No more windy speculation about origins and endings. We're going to look for the temple, where all our answers assuredly lie."

"Wonderful," said Moses. "How are you going to find it? Geoffrey Sankosh, if you'll recall, spent the better part of a year in there looking for that building and the remains of your father. And he didn't find either."

"He didn't have Kretzoi."

"Do you 'have' Kretzoi, Civ Cather? And even if you do, what can he accomplish for you if you don't remove another Asadi from the Wild for him to tutor in the basics of Ameslan?"

"Look through the carapaces over his eyes, Governor."

Moses hesitated.

"Go on. Look at Kretzoi's eyes and tell me what you see."

Moses drew back from the creature and said, "I know what his eyes look like, Elegy. To some extent, like mine. Or like yours. They're not the eyes of an Asadi."

"Unless you suppose they're malformed in some basic way, Governor—as if congenitally lacking in a full complement of photosynthetic pigments. In the Wild, the Asadi accepted Kretzoi's presence, but after they'd discovered his . . . his handicap, they treated him pretty much as my father said they treated The Bachelor. That is, they tolerated him among them, but they found his presence disturbing. The cause of their uneasiness was his eyes."

"All right," Moses said, waiting to be convinced of Kretzoi's future usefulness but altogether skeptical of the accomplishment.

I wandered away from the table and squatted at poolside, transfixed both by their conversation and the snaky fissure running across the bottom of the pool's deep end.

"The Asadi regard Kretzoi," I heard Elegy tell Moses, "at

least on a subconscious basis, but maybe even on a sociological level, as one of their walking dead. That's why, at first, Bojangles kept telling Kretzoi he was afraid.''

"All right," Moses said again.

"That means we may be able to induce in them, all of the Asadi, not only a 'passive repugnance' of Kretzoi but a 'worshipful terror.' Weren't those the terms you used? Why must we send him among the Asadi as a lowly Sudra, is what I'm asking, when we could just as easily send him into their midst as a supernatural Brahman?"

I looked at the figures in dim tableau at poolside. Moses Eisen was leaning back contemplatively in his hardwood chair. Elegy had insinuated the fingers of one hand into the golden pelage of Kretzoi's mane. The primate, meanwhile, sat beneath her touch with the regal composure of a lion.

"So that's what we're going to do," I heard Elegy say with youthful assurance. "Kretzoi's going to impersonate an Asadi king."

# CHAPTER TWELVE

# A Time Between Times

That evening, by sheer chance, I happened through the central lobby of the Chaney Field terminal at the same time a pair of Komm-service guards was escorting former E-5 Spenser Pettijohn to a detention area in one of the field's outbuildings.

Moses Eisen had sat in summary judgment of the man on the second day after Bojangles's death, convicting him of the malign abduction of E-3 Filly Deuel, the forcible implication of E-3 Deuel in the commission of a high felony, the misappropriation and criminal use of Kommfleet weapons, and, most tellingly, the "malicious homicide" of a representative of a Komm-protected indigenous alien species.

When I saw Pettijohn in the airfield lobby, I knew he was going off-planet to a GK-world with rehabilitative/punitive Long Sleep facilities. Provisionally sedated and mind-tamp'd, he already looked like a zombie. As Kretzoi, in Elegy's view, was one of the Asadi's "walking dead," Pettijohn was one of ours. When he approached between his guards, I stepped out of the way. The next time he awoke to life he would find himself on an unfamiliar world among strangers, an E-1 again, newly indentured and as stingingly raw as an April onion.

Reborn.

Fifty years of time-released, salutary nightmares lay ahead of him. Dreams that beneficially terrorize the immobile sleeper. Hypnopedagogic visions that insinuate a dawning ethical awareness through a series of varied reenactments of the crime itself. Painful neurological appeals to the heart and the head . . .

Only within the past three decades had the process become economically feasible, and Pettijohn, by his murder of Bojangles, had made himself an heir to Kommthor's distressing mercy.

I stood in awe of the killer as he passed—not for what he had done, but for the sweet, dread justice of what was about to befall him. Then I hurried through the terminal lobby into the twilight and found a driver to take me to my sleeping quarters in Frasierville.

\*

Although we had continued to share with Kretzoi our mezzanine accommodations in the probeship hangar, Elegy and I had not slept together since the Asadi's death. Our relationship was strained, only superficially cordial. Kretzoi's disaffection with human beings had something to do with this, as did, certainly, the lingering trauma of Pettijohn's killing of Bojangles. . . . Maybe Elegy and I had just been too close to each other for too long. Our faces were as familiar as a mismatched pair of shoes you can't bring yourself to throw away; our smells were as inextricably woven together as the strands of a wet hemp rope.

The morning after Bojangles's death I had asked Moses to let me move back into town, but he had insisted that all three of us remain where we were until he assessed the reaction of Frasierville's population to the murder. Rumors would bruit the news about, he said, even if we tried to keep a lid on it; we were safer where Komm-service guards could keep a regular watch on us. I argued that they hadn't prevented Pettijohn and Deuel from finagling their way in and doing their worst—but Moses merely murmured, "Once wounded, twice wary," and that was the end of my request.

Now, though, I was on my way home.

The lights of Frasierville welcomed me, and even my ratty sleeping quarters, so in contrast to Moses's bedecked and arcaded "mansion," seemed luxuriously appointed. The fusty closed-in smell that greeted me was a perfume, and even the clamminess of my unmade bed exuded a delicious welcome. I was glad to be alone. I kicked around in the dark, tossing my clothes and listening to the inarticulate gurgle of the toilet in my debussy. I could even hear the Wild sighing, a mysterious whisper of growth and decay.

I wasn't sure I wanted to go back out there. Bojangles's death had dampened my fervor. Kretzoi's regal contempt had soured me on his company. Elegy's formal politeness, in combination with her renewed faith in her own foresightedness in bringing Kretzoi to BoskVeld, had taken the edge off my desire to accompany her into the Wild again. Besides, it was good to be alone with my imperfections. So good, I confess, that I spent four whole days lounging about intractably with them.

\*

"Wake up, Ben! You're holding us up, you wretched slugabed!"

Elegy was on my tiny porch banging at the door and calling my name. She sounded her old impertinent self. Squinting, I opened the door and stared down at Jaafar Bahadori and Kretzoi coexisting in the front seat of a lorry-pool veldt-rover. Buddies. They had just arrived together from Chaney Field, all three of them. Elegy squeezed past me into the room, urging me to get dressed (I was wearing a sleeping jacket whose hem fell to midcalf) and surveying my quarters like a traveler who has unexpectedly stumbled upon the scene of a massacre.

"We're going on over to Rain Forest Port to prepare the BenDragon Prime!" Jaafar shouted from the veldt-rover. "Governor Eisen has given me permission to go, too, sir!"

The vehicle spun out, wheeled left around the southern corner of my quonset, and disappeared. Morning sunlight glittered in the jungle, and, when I shut the door, I faced back into an overmastering dimness.

"It stinks in here," said Elegy's voice from somewhere in front of me.

My eyes readjusted and I found her. "I've been burning epiphytes in my bathtub," I said.

"What?"

"Nothing. You just reminded me of Jaafar. Good thing *he* didn't come in. What's this about his going with us, anyway?"

"We may be able to use a little help this time," Elegy

said seriously. "He knows how to handle a weapon, he can fly a Dragonfly, and he'll stay on the radio for us. Besides, Ben, he's being subtly harassed by persons unknown. They've ripped open his bunk closet and shredded his uniforms. They've posted threatening messages to his Komm-service box. Governor Eisen thinks he'll be better off in the rain forest."

"Jaafar? In the rain forest?"

"Jaafar made the suggestion, but Governor Eisen approved it and I wholly concur. What about you?"

"Fine. I guess. But where's E-3 Deuel these days? She being harassed, too?"

"The day of Pettijohn's trial Eisen sent her to SteppeChilde with a helicraft shipment. She'll pull a duty tour out there. I think it's the Governor's way of punishing her for handling the situation less expertly than she should have."

"Elegy," I said abruptly. She looked at me with raised eyebrows, and I asked, "Do you really intend to send Kretzoi into the Asadi clearing in the guise of one of their chieftains?"

"Not right at first. We have some things to do before that."

"But eventually?"

"Yes. That's why we're going back."

"How do you intend to send him in there? Just as Eisen Zwei entered the clearing on the final three occasions before his death?"

"As much like that as possible, yes."

"Carrying, each time, a dressed-out carcass with which to feed either the Asadi multitudes or himself?"

"That's right."

"What do you plan to use for meat, Elegy?"

"Meat. What else? Governor Eisen has given us a couple of sections of imported beef from a recent shipment, and Jaafar's outfitting BenDragon Prime with a refrigeration locker. If these substitutes don't give Kretzoi the credibility he needs, we may simply have to use the genuine article."

"The genuine article?"

"Before he was killed, Bojangles told Kretzoi what the Asadi eat when they return to the Wild at night and how it may be possible for us to find their nests. Sankosh lucked into his solitary moment of glory, Ben, but Kretzoi's going to lead us to our discoveries on the basis of a certain knowledge."

"The Asadi are truly cannibals, then?"

Elegy took a tunic off the seat of the cane chair next to my bed, wrapped the tunic around the chair back, and sat down in the midst of all my dwelling's sweet-and-sour debris. "Part time," she said. "Nocturnal cannibals. Moonlighters, if you like. Where else in the Calyptran Wild could they possibly find meat? My father came to understand their secret, you know."

Elegy seemed smug again. I wanted to puncture her smugness. "We've never really considered the possibility that he may have been eaten," I said with swift irreverence.

She gave me a puzzled look, then fell into quiet contemplation. After a while she said, "Ben, I don't think that happened."

I was a prisoner in my own house, trapped by the pathos Elegy generated and the comic dishonor of my early-morning dishabille. It suddenly struck me that this was *not* where I wished to be.

"Elegy, you've forgotten one very important thing about your father's description of Eisen Zwei's various appearances in the Asadi clearing."

"The huri," Elegy said.

"The huri," I echoed her.

"I haven't forgotten at all," she said. "I really haven't. Eisen Zwei's batlike little familiar has been much on my mind, Ben. But do *you* happen to know a huri personally?"

My expression as neutral as I could make it, I stared at her.

"Scratch that," she said, standing up so quickly she had to grab my chair to keep it from falling. "I'm sorry, Ben. I realize no one's ever seen a huri except my father. Kretzoi tried to ask Bojangles about the creatures, but either the Asadi didn't understand the sign Kretzoi had to invent or else he didn't wish to discuss the subject. In any case, the existence of the huri remains conjectural."

"You believe in them, though?"

"As surely as children believe in magic animals and toy-toting old men with long white beards. And for the same reasons, too. My father once told me in earnest they exist, and my father didn't lie. What about you?"

"Likewise. But I'm not sure it was my father who told me. I'm getting too old to have ever had a father, don't you think?"

She approached me, put her arms around me. We embraced, my chin resting on the top of her head. I stared about the cluttered room in dismay, cursing myself for presiding with such brassy equanimity over the refuse heaps of my past and present selves. In comparable surroundings, I reflected glumly, only jackals or vultures would manifest anything even remotely like passion. But here I was yearning toward Elegy again; and, miracle of miracles, blind to the ruins about her, she was responding in kind.

After we had twisted together to my bed, though, she raised her head from the half-sloughed linen and gazed about briefly before subsiding back into my pillow. When I tried to kiss her, she began to giggle. Hiccups. Tiny convulsions. Muffled Gatling-gun laughter.

"Elegy, what's the matter?"

Still convulsed, she finally managed, "I never thought . . . never thought I'd sink so low."

# CHAPTER THIRTEEN

# Bojangles's Brother

Twelve hours later I let the BenDragon Prime sink to a resting place in the Wild. Chaney's old drop point. Only this time there were four of us rather than three, and we had planned our arrival to coincide almost exactly with Denebola's setting. We were barely able to get our nylon awning into place before the Wild erupted in a percussive caroling of snapped twigs and rattling fronds. The Asadi were fleeing into the jungle and the gathering night as they had every sunset since, we sometimes supposed, time immemorial.

"Abstracting Bojangles from their number doesn't appear to have had any effect on their behavior," I told Elegy.

Elegy stood mute in the down-sifting dark, waiting. Kretzoi, too, seemed apprehensive and nervous. Once night had securely settled, we were going to leave Jaafar at the Dragonfly's radio and strike out through the jungle in search of one of the nests Bojangles had told Kretzoi we might be able to find.

In the past—specifically, in the years since Chaney's disappearance—we had never had any success on these quests. We had failed for the same reason that primatologists have still not compiled detailed studies of the drills and mandrills of post-Armageddon West Africa. The Asadi's nocturnal habitat is virtually impenetrable to ground-going observers, and the Asadi themselves, out of their clearing, are so retiring as to seem mere phantoms.

But now Elegy believed we could accomplish something,

and her optimism derived from the fact that Kretzoi had learned a few things from Bojangles about Asadi behavior in the Wild.

When the stars at last came out, we said our farewells to Jaafar and set off. I carried a high-powered hand lamp with three beam intensities and a small tranq launcher. Elegy also had a hand lamp but, in addition, twenty meters of rope and a backpack full of assorted wilderness gear. We were each equipped with a "hearing-aid" radio receiver in our ears and a small, button-touch transmitter at our throats. Kretzoi carried nothing; he used the vines and tree limbs spotlighted by our lamps as a pathway through the forest, moving almost casually among the lower branches in order to keep from out-distancing us. Even so, Elegy and I often had a difficult time keeping pace.

Always, just as we were about to lose sight of him, Kretzoi slowed, or dropped to the jungle floor, or hung by one arm from a glistening branch, revolving there like a carcass on a furry hook. As soon as Elegy and I had nearly closed the distance, though, Kretzoi invariably went ghosting away again into the rank, humid copses of the Wild. And our lamps' beams went careering desperately after him, frail luminous extensions of ourselves.

After this had been going on for two hours or more, and I had checked in at least eight times with Jaafar (in scrupulous observance of the fifteen-minute interval we had agreed upon), Kretzoi suddenly dropped out of a thick-boled, mangrovesque hardwood and squatted among its curved, stiltlike roots without moving. Elegy and I went in to him by clambering over and ducking under the root arches barricading the tree's gnarled foot. Shortly, all three of us were crouched shoulder to shoulder in the eerie, dryadic chapel of the mangrove, listening to the wind and computing the dimensions of our solitude.

"Is this the place?" Elegy whispered.

Why couldn't she talk aloud? The Asadi, if any were about, knew exactly where we were by the telltale brilliance of our hand lamps, which shone aslant through the mangrove bladelets above us.

Kretzoi turned and dug at the clumpy soil at the base of the tree. A handful of this dirt he held beneath his nostrils, like an inspector sniffing coffee beans. Then he patted the soil sample back into place and felt about the trunk of the alien mangrove in several different places. This done, he swung back and spoke with his hands.

"He says this is where Bojangles sometimes slept," Elegy interpreted.

"How does he know?" Like Elegy, I was whispering.

"Bojangles marked the place with his urine; he also gave Kretzoi explicit directions to this tree and a description of its surroundings." Elegy gripped the hybrid animal's shoulder. Then, as she made pidgin gestural commands with her free hand, she whispered, "Go up, Kretzoi. Find his nest—Bojangles's nest—and see what you can see."

Standing up, Kretzoi gripped one of the weird root arches bracketing the tree. He did a languorous flip, pulled himself onto the arch, and sprang nimbly into the tree itself. He melded with the leaf cover so seamlessly that neither the moon shining down nor our lamps shining up could distinguish him from the foliage.

I got up and made to join Kretzoi aloft, gripping the same root arch he had gripped. The bark was as smooth as sharkskin.

"What're you doing?" Elegy demanded.

"I'd like a firsthand look. This cuts out the need for an interpreter, too. Eliminates the middleman. No offense, Elegy."

"You'll break your idiot neck," she whispered savagely.

Two meters off the ground I was already dizzy. Elegy lifted her hand lamp and held it for me as I climbed. The mangrove had thick but resilient limbs at fairly regular intervals, and when the canopy of bladelets above me had become a treacherous carpet under my groping feet, I could still see the eye of Elegy's lamp burning whitely in the leaves, giving them a leprous incandescence. Once, when I slipped, a hand caught my wrist and pulled me to the safety of a right-angle limb. I clung to the tree's central trunk, breathing rapidly, as Kretzoi held me in place with one hand.

"Thanks," I whispered, feeling like an idiot whose idiot neck has just been mercifully spared.

My cheek pressed against smooth, silver bark, I peered out at the reeds, tufts of woven grass, assemblages of fitted twigs, and quilts of tropical flower petals comprising the Asadi nest cantilevered between several branches to my right. By its smell I knew the nest for what it was. It smelled as Bojangles had on the day of his capture; it smelled like the Asadi in their clearing.

Kretzoi made a sign at me, which, still trying to compose myself, I waved off. Whereupon he released me, climbed higher, and draped himself over a bough so near Balthazar that the moon appeared but a single step beyond him. From this limb Kretzoi stared down into the nest. At last I leaned out cautiously to peek at what Kretzoi was confronting with neither flinch nor cry.

The nest contained something with eyes.

They coruscated in the moonlight, and they scared the residual bejesus out of me. They seemed disembodied, and vaguely saurian, and chillingly close to death. Closing my own eyes, I told Kretzoi in a whisper that I was ready to go down.

*

"You already knew what we'd find?"

"I had an idea," Elegy responded when Kretzoi and I again sat with her in the twisted root arches under the mangrove. "Bojangles told Kretzoi, and Kretzoi told me. But I wanted it confirmed."

"That's an Asadi up there," I said. "It's still alive, but it's been reduced to little more than a head and a truncated torso."

"That's Bojangles's twin, his sibling, his 'meat-brother.' "

"Whom Bojangles has cannibalized to this horrifying stage of dismemberment and incipient rot?" I looked with unseeing eyes back up into the mangrove. "Sibling rivalry's played for keeps among the Asadi, isn't it?"

"The meat-sibling is simply a twin until the two juvenile Asadi are old enough to warrant their mother's making a determination about which is the more robust, which has better sustained itself through optical photosynthesis. Mother's milk and photosynthetic nutrients are all the infants feed on for the first two or three years of their lives, you see."

"And the more robust animal is automatically designated the cannibal, the weaker its perpetual victim?"

Elegy and Kretzoi exchanged a brief flurry of hand signs. "It may be the other way around," she said, looking back at me. "Kretzoi isn't sure. Bojangles gave some indication that the *stronger* becomes the meat-sibling—because it's better able to sustain the continuous depredations of the next several years.''

"How can it survive them a week, much less a number of years?" I asked aloud, my voice rising out of a whisper into almost Chaneyesque indignation at the infuriating *alienness* of the Asadi.

"The Asadi mother uses ready-to-hand herbal coagulants to stanch the bleeding of the meat-sibling and other herbal drugs to anesthetize her sacrificial child to the day-by-day feasting of its weaker sibling and herself. In fact, long periods go by when the sacrificial child is permitted to recuperate, even given a chance to regenerate limbs and organs already partially consumed. This is a reptilian characteristic that the Asadi have apparently retained. . . . Then the love feast begins again, quite tenderly and touchingly, an act of reverence and solicitude you'll never see enacted in the Asadi clearing— because, on the assembly ground, tribal allegiance takes precedence over private family ties and Indifferent Togetherness is the order of the day.''

"You're saying the ritual cannibalism of the meat-sibling by its twin and its mother derives from a love impulse?''

"Why not?" Elegy shifted positions, supporting herself on one outstretched arm and gesturing modestly with her free hand. "For the most part, cannibalism among the Asadi takes place at night, when they can't photosynthesize. The dispersal that occurs every sunset, then, frees a few individual Asadi to rendezvous with other creatures with whom they share family ties. In some cases, at least.

"The old and the prematurely bereaved, I'd imagine, simply retire into the woods to sleep or to look for dying or dead tribesmen. These last, once discovered, are probably greedily cannibalized. Then their bones are buried. They aren't given the care the Asadi female and her cannibal offspring lavish on the sacrificial child because, ordinarily, an immediate family tie doesn't exist between the eater and the eaten. And because, even when drugged, the old and sick can't withstand a nightly cannibalism over a protracted period.

"But the Asadi child who is being eaten and sustained, in order to be eaten and sustained again, engenders nothing but devotion in its mother and its cannibal sibling; they prize and cherish it, they rush to it at sunset—not only to feed from its body but to tend its wounds and raise its threshold of apprehensible pain by giving it herbal anodynes. They also feed it nuts and other protein-rich sources of plant matter—but in paste form, pre-chewed so that it will be easily ingestible by the semiconscious victim of their love.

"Look, Ben, what you saw up there frightened and revolted you. It would have me, too, if I'd gone up there. At first, in fact, I'm probably not going to be of much use when we take it out of the tree in order to carry it back to the Dragonfly. But—"

"Back to the Dragonfly!" I exclaimed.

Startled by my voice, Kretzoi moved away and took up lodging in an adjacent root-arch chapel partially concealed from our view. Elegy watched him go with a finger laid across her lips, to shush and calm me.

"Ben, you're reacting to this out of its proper context; you're passing ethnocentric judgments. If you'd—"

"I want to know what you mean by saying we're going to carry that thing up there back to the BenDragon Prime."

"Do you remember my father's fondness for the twentieth-century anthropologist Colin Turnbull, the author of *The Forest People*? In that book Turnbull rejoiced in the lives of the Ituri pygmies, who at the time he went among them were still a viable but pristine society."

"What's this got to do with the Asadi and their nocturnal cannibalism?"

"Turnbull in later years went among an East African people called the Ik," Elegy said, ignoring my question. "He wrote a scathing book about them called *The Mountain People*. The state regime of that period had forbidden the Ik to hunt, even though they'd never before been agriculturists and lived in an arid and infertile region of the country. The result was that in their individual struggles to stave off hunger and survive, the Ik came to treat one another with cruelty and derision. All fellow feeling was lost; they behaved toward their compatriots only as a private selfishness and the main chance dictated. Turnbull was appalled.

"He concluded that the Ik were a mirror of the corruption at humanity's heart—once you had stripped away the veneers of 'civilization.' He recoiled in disgust from the implications he drew. He forgot that to some extent the degradation of the Ik had been externally imposed. He forgot that his own cultural biases were undoubtedly shaping the philosophical thrust of the conclusions suggested by his field work. The

Turnbull who laughed joyously with the Ituri pygmies was in this subsequent book a disillusioned and oddly embittered man—all because he had reached some dismaying conclusions about his entire species on the basis of his disgust with the Ik.''

"Because that thing upstairs appalls me, I'm like this older and more cynical Turnbull? Is that what you're suggesting, Elegy?"

"You're like him because you're ignoring contexts, that's all I'm saying. My father did the same thing, and like Turnbull he was trained in the exacting empirical methods of the cultural anthropologist. The Ik fell from grace because of changing ecological conditions and the meddlesomeness of a state trying in good faith to preserve its native wildlife. The Asadi have fallen from grace for reasons still opaque to us.

"But their nocturnal cannibalism isn't necessarily a sign of their present-day corruption; it could be evidence of an evolutionary recovery. The stronger is sacrificed to the weaker, out of both altruism and a grisly pragmatism. Since both infants receive the devotion and care of their mother, a bond of real affection is at work here, Ben. It's the only one that now seems to exist among the Asadi.

"Ritual cannibalism—probably because of population pressures and severe protein shortages at some point in their past—became the medium for this unique expression of tenderness. It undoubtedly began as a desperation measure. The intensification of production methods and subsequent increases in population led to ecological disruption, which led to food shortages and a loss of essential protein intake, and these in turn led to the adoption of infant cannibalism as a means for a select few to survive the ecological catastrophe. The old were probably always eaten, out of love as well as necessity.

"The planet has never had any herd animals, it seems, or any other kind of land-going creatures, for that matter, except those the Ur'sadi brought to BoskVeld with them when they arrived here from another solar system. So they took their requirements of amino acids from either native plant forms or protein-rich plants whose seeds they'd carried here with them, and they intensified agricultural production to heighten yield. One result was that much of BoskVeld was deforested. Some of the planet's veldts—today such conspicuous features of the topography—were once thick with trees. The sociological result, just as I've said, turned out to be the cannibalism of one or maybe even both of the infant twins born to the immigrant Ur'sadi females. Twin births were, and continue to be, the rule among the various evolutionary lines of our present-day Asadi.''

A wind scouring the Wild from the western ocean jostled the treetops, making the foliage sigh. Elegy shivered, clutched her knees self-protectingly. In a matter of mere minutes a front of towering storm clouds had blotted out the nighttime sky. The hand lamps provided our only illumination.

"It's going to rain," Elegy said. "We'd better get moving."

"Wait a minute. What's your time scale, Elegy? How long ago are you proposing all this happened?"

"Three to seven million years," she answered at once.

"Dear God, woman, you're certainly putting it back a ways. Why three to seven million years?"

"Because between seven and twelve million years ago," she said, going off on another tack altogether, "the Ur'sadi may have dropped off on Earth a small contingent of colonists-explorers. They did so with the idea that their representatives would successfully cooperate or compete with a number of our presentient terrestrial primates. In fact, the Ur'sadi may have genetically and biochemically altered these pioneer specimens so that selective interbreeding could take place. Their motive was as much altruism as self-preservation; they believed they could spare their primate counterparts on Earth some of the more wasteful and tragic consequences of a purely *random* evolution toward intelligence.

"But evolutionary factors and innate differences in the nature of the beasts they were dealing with did them in. There was an explosion of speciation among the terrestrial primates, followed by a number of outright extinctions of some of the 'higher' forms. Whatever of themselves the Ur'sadi had hoped to preserve on Earth was submerged and lost within a period, oh, of four to five million years. One thing that remains, though, is an exact correspondence of the amino-acid sequence for hemoglobin in both their human relatives on Earth and their Asadi descendants here on BoskVeld." Elegy rose, wiped her hands on her thighs, and gazed up at the alarmingly booming canopy of leaves.

I stood, too. "Elegy, have you ever heard of Occam's razor?"

"You don't have to believe me, Ben," she said conciliatorily, even though her eyes were fierce in their shadowy sockets. "You'd be crazy to believe me, in fact. How the hell do *I* know what happened twelve million years ago? How the hell does *anybody* know, for that matter?"

"Ideally, people make intelligent suppositions on the basis of concrete evidence and proven research techniques. Sometimes a strong imagination doesn't hurt. You just have to make sure it's not operating independently of the facts or in a complete absence of any empirical data."

But now Elegy was ignoring me, probably for good reason. She summoned Kretzoi back from his hiding place and put into his hands the rope she'd been carrying on her belt. With rapid hand signs she told Kretzoi she wanted him to go aloft and then lower to us the nest containing Bojangles's semiconscious meat-sibling. Alive with wind, the alien mangrove and all its graceful kin swayed and whickered.

Jaafar's voice sounded in my ear: "*You'd better return to the drop point, Dr. Benedict. A rain, I think, is blowing up. Our Dragonfly is waltzing a little, sir.*"

"We're coming," I told him, activating the transmitter at my throat. Then, gesturing at the obediently climbing Kretzoi, I told Elegy, "He's liable to get shaken out of that damn thing. And he's probably going to need some help."

"Hold your hand lamp up for him, then."

I shone my lamp up through the virtually impenetrable foliage, not knowing where exactly Kretzoi happened to be or whether he truly had the skill to fashion a basket-sling from the nylon rope Elegy had given him. To allay my irritation, I said, "You've put the Asadi's ancestors on Earth between seven and twelve million years ago, and here on BoskVeld between three and seven million. Is that right?"

"I don't know if it's right," Elegy responded indifferently, playing her lamp's beam from side to side among the chattering leaves, "but it's what I speculate. The Ur'sadi sent representatives to BoskVeld precisely because it was a virgin planet with no advanced evolutionary sequence of land-going fauna to alter or disrupt by their presence. Burgeoning speciation had undone their representatives on Earth, after all, so they opted for a world with a compatible botanical ecosphere and only a few primitive animal forms as potential competitors. Many of these they exterminated, for this time they were relocating portions of their population not from any altruistic research motive, but because deteriorating solar conditions in their own planetary system—''

"Made it imperative that they find a brave new world upon which to lay their burden down," I concluded for Elegy. Drops of rain began pattering down, staccato annotations of my impatience.

"Yes," Elegy said, shielding her face with her forearm. "They came to BoskVeld with their polychromatic optical language intact. They'd even invented an extrasomatic means of conveying the language—their eyebooks, I mean—maybe a million or more years before their ill-fated experiment on Earth. That experiment may have failed, in fact, because the processes of evolutionary speciation on Earth selected *against* the complicated optical equipment that had allowed the Ur'sadi to achieve mastery of both their own distant world and the corridors of interstellar space.

"Of the twin children born of Ur'sadi mothers who copulated with terrestrial primate males, only the child with eyes more nearly like its sire's managed to survive. And not all of these. Radiation was a factor. So was primate prejudice. Because copulation took place from the rear, the male protohominids servicing the Ur'sadi females didn't have to deal with the disconcerting appearance of their partners' alien eyes. But socialization requres many face-to-face contacts, and juvenile primates with threatening Ur'sadi optical structures were killed long before they could reach maturity. The prospect of a visual 'language' for you and me died with them, Ben."

Kretzoi began hooting above us. So seldom had I heard him vocalize that at first I simply mistook the sound for some weird intensification of the storm.

"What does he want?" I cried.

"Keep your hand lamp focused on that spot right there, Ben!" Elegy grabbed my wrist and pointed the beam for me. "I'll try to light him a pathway on the other side of the trunk!" She ducked beneath a root arch and took up a position almost immediately opposite mine.

I was in no hurry to greet Bojangles's half-eaten brother. The longer Kretzoi took to lower the nest the happier I'd be. I was even prepared to spend a night licking rainwater off my lips if that's what so long a reprieve required. For now—all too soon—the rain was coming down torrentially.

But my mind wasn't on the storm or Kretzoi's efforts to ease down to us the Asadi nest. I was helplessly mulling everything Elegy had said and trying to fit the jagged pieces together.

"What do you think happened to the Ur'sadi who arrived on BoskVeld, then?" I shouted at Chaney's daughter. "What, besides a depletion of resources, brought them down?"

Her hair plastered to her forehead and water running from her jumpsuit, Elegy showed me her ill-lit, rain-blurred face. "What?" she called. "What did you say?"

Like a fool I repeated my questions.

"Not now, Ben! It's impossible!" Her shoulders went up in an uncomprehending hunch. "Look—there's the nest! There's Kretzoi!" Her beam stabbed upward into the dripping, chattering mangrove bladelets; and I saw Kretzoi emerge from the higher limbs stiff-backed and straining, for in front of him, balanced across his matted thighs, was the huge, twiggy disc of the Asadi nest.

Kretzoi had shaped a complicated cradle of rope to hold the nest, and the ends of the rope were wrapped in a harness around his neck and upper torso. As he came down through the mangrove, lowering himself branch by branch, the strain in his triceps and neck muscles seemed almost to be unbearable.

"Help him!" Elegy shouted as I watched Kretzoi's display of willful physical strength. "Ben, reach up and help him!"

After holstering my hand lamp so that the beam still shone upward, I stretched to receive the prickly-slimy bottom of the Asadi nest. Surprise—it was as light as a big inflated doughnut of rubber or plastic. But only at first. Its lightness had to do with the fact that Kretzoi, even after I'd slipped my arms beneath it, was supporting the nest entirely by himself. Only when he had dropped all the way to the ground did I begin to experience the nest's full weight. I staggered back with it as Elegy helped Kretzoi free himself of the harness he had made.

There in my arms, a nightmare. The Asadi's lower viscera outlined themselves in the downpour as if in rippling neon. The creature had no limbs to speak of, although stubs where its arms should have been may have signaled the beginnings of an arcane regenerative process. The eyes were empty bubbles, glinting with oily highlights. I could feel myself on the edge of a breathtaking faint.

Then, suddenly, Elegy's thumb was pressing against my teeth, and before I could resist the violation, she had wedged something round and smooth—an anti-nausea tablet—into my mouth. I swallowed, and my queasiness began to subside.

"Let's go!" Elegy shouted. "Back to Jaafar and the Ben-Dragon Prime!"

From out of her backpack she materialized a tarp with a crimped, self-sealing edge. This she applied to the top of the Asadi nest—almost as if she were covering a gigantic pie with a piece of tinfoil. Rain began pooling in the tarp's depression and rills, then gathering and spilling to the ground. Four plastic handles spaced about the circumference of an additional tarp—this one slung beneath the nest—gave us a means of sharing the burden.

Gripping these handles, Kretzoi, Elegy, and I set off through the gnarled root arches of the mangroves and into the dense, streaming foliage all about them.

We trudged for thirty minutes, rested briefly, took up our burden again, trudged another demoralizing half hour or so in the thickening mud, stopped a second time. We continued in this way until the rain had dwindled to a mist indistinguishable from our own prolific sweat. When we were less than an hour from Jaafar, whose off-trail words of cheer kept breaking into our struggle, we finally allowed ourselves a decent interval of rest before the final push. As we rested, the rain stopped completely. This development gave us enough heart to start moving again.

Seven hours after we had left the drop point, we came back into the tiny clearing so exhausted and muddy-brained that Jaafar had to undress Elegy and me and put us to bed. Kretzoi, I was later told, slept on his side on a narrow dry spot under the helicraft's tail section.

# CHAPTER FOURTEEN

# The Love of Cannibals

"You probably have Asadi blood flowing in your veins," I told Jaafar at our high-noon breakfast the following day.

Although aware that I was joking, Jaafar had no good idea how he was supposed to react. "Why do you say that?" he asked me gravely, a spoonful of reconstituted honey halfway to his lips.

"Because Elegy believes we all do. Our hemoglobin is Asadi hemoglobin. And vice versa. Blood's thicker than the hydraulic pressures of evolution, it seems."

Jaafar looked at Elegy for denial or confirmation. She was noncommittally sipping her juice.

"Later," I went on, "the Asadi's ancestors came to Bosk-Veld and cut down all the trees but these. Hence, the veldts."

Elegy gave me a swift, appraising look over her cup. Kretzoi was in the Wild somewhere. Bojangles's half-eaten brother lay in his nest in the helicraft's cargo section. Only a few minutes before joining us at table, Elegy had removed the tarp covering the nest.

"The Ur'sadi lived for several million years on their own planet," I persisted, still watching Elegy, "without suffering any major evolutionary or cultural upheavals. With the fruits of a self-perpetuating and incredibly advanced technology, they lived in near-perfect social and moral equilibrium. Very intelligent, very temperate folk. Then they botched an evolutionary experiment in our solar system, leaving behind their hemoglobin's molecular structure as a calling card. A million or so years later they decided to come to BoskVeld to escape

228

the expansion of their sun into a menacing red giant.''

"Pure speculation," Elegy said. "Space opera."

"But you're its scenarist, aren't you? You're the author?"

Elegy said nothing. She sipped her juice and studied me as if I were a pet that has just demonstrated its untrustworthiness indoors.

"I'm synopsizing, Elegy; plagiarizing. You know that."

"I wasn't talking for the record!" she suddenly flared. "I certainly didn't expect to have you quoting me verbatim once we got out of that goddamn mangrove thicket and back into the light of day!"

Embarrassed, I looked at Jaafar, who immediately renewed his acquaintance with the honey bowl before him.

"Haven't you heard of ghost stories?" Elegy demanded. "Or tall tales? Or epic adventures? My father had. He used to package them up in visicom 'settes and send them to me when I was a little girl in the Tri-Mesa. Once a week they came. They made life in an E-cube bearable. I didn't confuse them with reality, either. They were full of marvelous notions, those stories—but you didn't have to believe in the marvelous notions, just entertain them for a while. So that you, in turn, could be entertained by your private pretense of belief."

"You were trying to *entertain* me last night?"

"Not just you," Elegy said. "Myself, mostly."

"I'd like you to finish your story, then. You didn't explain what you thought happened to the Ur'sadi to bring them to ruin—beyond an intensification of production that depleted resources and a population explosion that made the burden even worse. How could such a stable, intelligent folk get themselves in such a bind?"

"We'd better check Bojangles's meat-sibling," Elegy said, nodding aft and putting down her cup.

"He'll be all right. He's survived this long without Bojangles's aid, or ours, or anyone else's. Come on, Elegy— the rest of your story."

"Please," Jaafar suddenly put in. "I would like to be . . . to be *entertained*, too, Civ Cather."

"All right," Elegy said, leaning back and blowing a puff of air toward her forehead. "What I think happened is this:

"BoskVeld, despite being habitable to the Ur'sadi, wasn't by any means a 'carbon copy' of their home world. Denebola, too, posed problems for them. After they'd been here a millennium or more, it began radiating in unpredictable sunspot cycles disruptive of the sensitive workings of their eyes and their blood chemistry. The sunspot activity caused lymphocyte deficiencies, and these deficiencies, in turn, caused a variety of diseases the Ur'sadi had never experienced before. In addition, disturbances in BoskVeld's magnetic field—another result of the violent sunspot activity—played havoc with their eyesight. Their ability to communicate optically was subtly impaired. The same thing had happened to their representatives on Earth, of course, but not to such a pernicious degree."

"It wasn't the sun that did them in on Earth," I told Jaafar. "It was our devilish primate daddies."

Elegy favored me with a wan, semitolerant smile. "The Ur'sadi turned to genetic manipulation to save themselves. They equipped their circulatory systems with inheritable organic 'lymphostats.' The autopsy report, by the way, mentions this unusual adaptive feature in Bojangles's blood—or the vestiges of this feature, since Denebola is now in a protracted 'quiet' phase. And these freely circulating lymphostats regulated the production of lymph cells in the Ur'sadi's blood, no matter what Denebola happened to be doing. Storming or smiling.

"The Ur'sadi also moved to make extensive genetic alterations in their eyes. The most significant was to give their organs of sight and communication the ability to photosynthesize. Each individual optical cell was equipped with a chromoplast containing one or more photosynthetic pigments. Previously, as my father had incorrectly assumed was true of present-day Asadi, the optical cells had produced their spectral displays solely by means of minute, controlled chemical reactions. Now, though, the spectral displays employed the ancient chemical reactions along with the light-reflecting properties of the photosynthetic pigments added by the Ur'sadi geneticists. This tandem arrangement prevented a major rewiring of the brain—specifically of Bojangles's area—and it gave the Ur'sadi not only an immunity to Denebola's unpredictable radiation showers but a means of freeing themselves from their dependence on BoskVeld's dwindling resources.

"The familiar pigments our Komm-galens found in Bojangles's optical chromoplasts, by the way, include chlorophyll, carotenoids, and phycobilins. Substances that reflect light in either green or red wavelengths. But our surgeons also found BoskVeld-specific pigments capable of converting sunlight and water into energy—substances that radiate light in the blue, violet, and even brown frequencies. We don't even have ready-made names for them, Ben; they're new to us, just as Governor Eisen told us last week in the hangar. And it's these pigments—perhaps—that made the new Ur'sadi such efficient processors of Denebolan sunlight. So efficient they no longer had to depend on social cooperation for their survival. Each neo-Ur'sadi was a living factory capable of supporting itself anywhere on the planet—so long as it had access to sunlight and water.''

Kretzoi suddenly appeared in the helicraft's doorway. Stalking on all fours, he proceeded past our table and into the cargo section. Once there, he sat back on his haunches and scrutinized Bojangles's meat-sibling.

''You think the ability to photosynthesize was a major cause of the Ur'sadi's collapse?'' I tried to ignore Kretzoi, to disregard him in his bedside watch over our macabre guest.

''We ought to check him'' Elegy said. ''He probably ought to be outside. In direct sunlight. Where he can sustain himself.''

''Elegy,'' I asked her quietly, ''why the hell don't we simply let him die? Bojangles is gone, and that poor bastard back there's apparently got no affectionate family left to devour him. He's got no one to apply the medications he needs.''

''He's got us,'' Elegy said. She rose and walked into the cargo section. I shook my head in acquiescent dismay. Then, along with Jaafar, I joined Elegy and Kretzoi aft. Shoulder to shoulder, the four of us stared down at our charge.

Today the most amazing thing about Bojangles's meat-sibling was not his gnawed and mutilated body, but the fact that his eyes were lethargically pinwheeling through a spectral display. Baby talk, maybe. Or maybe the incoherent babbling of one in delirium. Although the pattern made no sense to any of us, it gave us all the feeling that we were eavesdropping on someone's dying words.

I nicknamed the creature Cy; short for Osiris.

''Look at him,'' I said, even though we were all looking fixedly at him. ''This is your proof the Asadi are on the road to an evolutionary recovery from barbarism?''

''He's in pain,'' Elegy murmured to herself. ''He's been seven or eight days without tending.'' Aloud she said, ''Jaafar, hand me that kit, please.''

Jaafar handed her a medical kit. From this Elegy extracted a syringe and a vial of the sedative we used in our tranq launchers. After diluting the substance with a measured quantity of water, she knelt over Cy and injected the sedative into a vein in his neck. The creature shuddered visibly; the rate of his optical baby talk accelerated nearly to the point of blurring.

Still squatting above Cy, Elegy said, "This is a recovery, Ben. No matter what it looks like to you, it's a recovery. You see, the Ur'sadi had purposely avoided speciation within their own genetic pool by maintaining deliberate proximity to one another. They also kept individuals moving back and forth from one adjacent colony to another to stress the psychological cohesiveness of the whole and to keep small pockets of divergent populations from springing up. Their ill-fated experiment on Earth had been one factor persuading them of the necessity of maintaining their genetic integrity no matter where they went. On BoskVeld, where things were proving especially hard for them, this policy seemed even more crucial. They had to emphasize solidarity—social, psychological, genetic—just to survive the hardships of their new world and its ornery sun." Elegy stopped stroking Cy's mane. "Let's get him outside. He's calming now. See his eyes?"

The creature's eyes had stopped displaying; a strange film occluded each concentric ring comprising his organs of sight. Jaafar and I then picked up the nest by the handles affixed to the tarp beneath it and struggled through the Dragonfly and out into the clearing.

Elegy suggested that we place the nest in a squat, broadleafed tree on the edge of the drop point, and that's what we did. As we carried Cy into the Wild and lodged his nest at waist height in the tree, Elegy tried to complete for us her private reconstruction of the Ur'sadi/Asadi past.

Her main argument was that the first Ur'sadi to receive the ability to photosynthesize broke the ages-old prohibition against separating themselves from the indivisible whole. They formed self-sufficient sects and splinter groups. These retreated into the remaining forests of BoskVeld and purposely maintained themselves distinct from their forebears. Their rationale was that their forebears had gone a long way toward destroying their adopted world before creating the savior race they embodied. Then the schismatics, unified at first by the habit of cohesiveness within another context, as well as by their common purpose and physiology, built elaborate temples and monuments in the Wild—not as centers of redistributive feasts (after the pattern of many of the mounds and megaliths of human prehistory), for these neo-Ur'sadi had no compelling need to accumulate and redistribute foodstuffs, but instead as museums of what they considered admirable in their past and as memorials to the ancient people who had created them. They stocked these temples with eyebooks stolen from their Ur'sadi settlements and with representative artifacts either manufactured in the Wild or carried out with them on their stealthy diaspora.

Constructed in approved Ur'sadi ways to withstand the erosive capacities of time and weather, these pagodas proved short-lived rallying points for the neo-Ur'sadi. They forsook not only the temples but the small forest communities around them in order to pursue a thousand separate individual quests for meaning. Their umbilical to the land severed by their new power to photosynthesize, their ties to one another frayed and weakened by this same miraculous force, they scattered, willfully distancing themselves from kith and kind. In this way the seeds of speciation were sown among the Ur'sadi for the first time in millions of years: The selective pressures of environment came to bear once more on their evolution. By coming back into harmony with nature through their creators' desperate manipulation of their genes, these neo-Ur'sadi had irrevocably surrendered their destinies to nature. Ahead of them, unknown to them, lay approximately three million years of painful retreat from civilization.

"Meanwhile," Elegy said, once we'd moved beneath the orange-and-white awning in front of the BenDragon Prime, "Denebola's disruptive solar activity continued, and the original Ur'sadi, seeing what was happening to their unmannerly offspring, decided to leave. They razed their settlements and cleared away the debris. Then they doctored the surrounding landscape so that no one could find a scrap of evidence they'd ever even *visited* BoskVeld."

"Why did they do that?" Jaafar asked. Sorting the various drugs in our medical kit, he held up vial after cut-glass vial for inspection.

"Because that's the only possible explanation for our not having found a trace of their existence on the veldts," I told Jaafar. "Unless you're silly enough to suppose they were never here at all."

Elegy laughed. "Because they wanted to *disguise* the fact they'd been here," she corrected me. "They wanted no part of their mutinous offspring. At the same time, though, they wanted to give them a chance to evolve as nature directed. They were bequeathing the planet to their ungrateful children, handing it over without strings or hindrance. . . . There's some evidence—in the partial ruins of the pagoda Frasier investigated, for example—they may have tried to carry off every last clue to their presence here by destroying the jungle temples of the neo-Ur'sadi. Something prevented them, though, and they had to leave BoskVeld without making the break as cleanly as they would have liked. Today's Asadi betray their ancestors' presence here, and so do the eyebooks my father brought out of the Wild six years ago."

\*

Under Elegy's guidance Jaafar prepared an anesthetic milder than the one she had earlier given Cy. We held this in reserve against the time the creature revived and again needed a painkiller. Periodically we traipsed to the edge of the clearing to check him. Each time we peered into his nest, his raw and mutilated appearance startled me anew.

Cy was a lesson in Asadi anatomy. His muscles gleamed in fiery knots, organs protruded lopsidedly, and scar tissue crazed his purplish-grey lower intestines like a network of varicose cabling. Because she feared the sedative she had given him was repressing his ability to photosynthesize, Elegy was anxious for him to come to.

Back in the Dragonfly, the three of us unfolded a metal table with a thick sealed-cork surface to use as a butcher's block. In the outdraft of the refrigeration locker we struggled to remove the beef haunches Moses had given us. Then, as we played at butcher, Elegy told us what she believed had happened to the Ur'sadi who scattered through the Wild after building temples to their past.

First, they discovered they still had strong appetites for solid food and occasional socialization. Their bodies, after all, were made to assimilate protein in the form of animal flesh as well as in nuts and other exotic forest products; and, photosynthesis or no photosynthesis, they still had to rendezvous occasionally to mate. So seldom did these sexual encounters occur at first, however, that twin births proved an especially adaptive feature of their reproductive strategy. More and more of the solitary proto-Asadi creatures were born, and they slaked their meat hunger by preying upon the old, the sick, the feeble. The proto-Asadi became their own scavengers. Because of steadily mounting population pressures, bands coalesced in the Wild, and these bands, in turn, took to warring with one another in order to establish territorial elbow-room. They also took prisoners, whom they ultimately sacrificed not to any cruel omnipotent god but to the less-than-godly yearning in their bellies. Moreover, to satisfy their reborn cravings for fat and animal protein, they embarked upon periodic binges of infanticide. These practices combined to reduce population levels again—until, finally, a proto-Asadi contingent with enough dim intelligence to perceive what was happening to it stepped in to mark off an area of jungle in which cannibalism was taboo during the hours of their highest photosynthetic efficiency. This clearing was the forerunner of the Asadi assembly ground. By outright designation it gave the Asadi a center for their absurd communal activities and a refuge from their tendency to feast on one another.

Collateral species of Ur'sadi—bands that failed to submit to the hallowedness of this primeval clearing—were hunted down at night, killed, and eaten. When only a single species remained, the proto-Asadi themselves, its individuals settled into a social ritual parodying the goal-oriented cohesiveness of their departed forebears. They became survival machines, automatons. Their optical language degenerated into a medium for conveying either invective or raw, unstructured emotion. Their few identifiable "customs" were nothing more than neurological engrams for enforcing conformity and penalizing innovation.

Elegy, laying out one of the beef haunches and trimming away a long snake of fat with a pair of soundless butcher's shears, compared the early Asadi to victims of prolonged sensory deprivation.

"They were the only animal species on the planet," she said, "of any intellectual development—even if they'd perverted it by isolating themselves from one another and then killing off those who conspicuously differed from them in behavior or appearance. In their original clearing the Asadi were like a man in a small black box or tiger cage underground. Their every physical response to the world was a reenactment of old and time-worn behaviors. They were at a remove from reality, just like the prisoner who can certify his existence only by biting his lip or clawing the inside of his thigh. That prisoner, you leave him alone long enough, finally goes insane. Well, that's what happened to the ecologically isolated Asadi—they grew into an overwhelming and seemingly irreversible community insanity. By default, Ben, their species was the measure of all things.''

And when Asadi numbers again began to climb, the clearing teemed anew with impatient and angry animals.

"At which time," said Elegy, "the females began to select their more robust infants as objects of family cannibalism, and for the first time since the departure of their ancient Ur'sadi forebears, the possibility of love reentered the complex of Asadi emotions."

"Love," Jaafar scoffed, the old prejudice resurfacing. "They love what they eat, is that it? Just as I 'love' honey, and hot fresh bread, and fried cephalopod tentacles. Spare me such love from a mother, though. Much better she should hate me inordinately but keep her teeth out of my liver and lights.''

"I don't say the practice *arose* from an impulse of love," responded Elegy, putting down the butcher's shears and using the bone saw I handed her to cut a blood-red hunk of meat. "It probably arose as means of easing population pressures in the clearing. It also gave the Asadi the promise of protein in a familiar and appetizing guise. The nutritional value of the sacrificial child wasn't really important. What was important was that the female subtracted one twin from each double birth by giving herself and the weaker child the *psychological* blessing of meat ready to hand. The cannibalism really didn't significantly improve the protein and fat content in the Asadi diet—it still doesn't—but it created an effective stabilizing factor in their population growth. It also reinforced the pattern of Twilight Dispersal by giving each adult Asadi a gruesome incentive to return at sunset to the Wild.''

Her hands slick with grease, Elegy gave me a long strip of fat and a section of bone with meat still clinging to it. "Take these to Kretzoi, Ben.''

I carried the offerings to the helicraft's door, spotted Kretzoi grooming himself beneath the tent awning, and tossed him both the ragged bone and the snaky, glistening rind. Kretzoi looked at me indifferently, then picked up the strip of fat as if it were a lei to be worn about his neck. I returned to the helicraft without waiting to see how he disposed of his meal.

Elegy was still working, still talking to Jaafar.

"... mothers learned it was more rewarding—both psychologically and nutritionally—to keep the sacrificial child alive as long as possible. To do this they had to expend energy and care; they had to search out, usually in full darkness, herbs and plants with which to heal and anesthetize the meat-sibling. The return in protein and fat wasn't large enough to justify so much labor. . . . Not unless you suppose, as I do, that Asadi mothers derive great satisfaction from caring for the Eaten One. For that matter, Asadi children, male as well as female, do, too. Those who are permitted to live are raised to cherish the meat-sibling, to eat of it only in the dark—and temperately, even then—and to nurture it at all other times. In four or five years, in fact, the meat-sibling becomes the possession and love object solely of the designated survivor—for the mother, by this time, passes out of her infertile lactation interval and becomes pregnant again. When this happens, she builds a new nest quite distant from the old one and begins a new family.

"The designated survivor carries on as it has been taught. Until its mane is full, it remains both day and night with the Eaten One. Then it ventures by itself into the Asadi clearing and undergoes its initiation into the social life of its conspecifics. Indifferent Togetherness. And Indifferent Togetherness strengthens the new arrival's desire to flee back to its meat-sibling at sunset. In just this way, then, it surrenders its identity to a well-established pattern and becomes another lost marcher in the Procession of the Asadi Damned."

With a long-handled, thick-bladed knife Elegy perforated one of the beef haunches and worked diligently to make the slits go all the way through the meat.

"But the seeds of affection, of tenderness, of love," she said through gritted teeth, "have been sown among the Asadi, Jaafar, and if they can break out of their rut and survive another hundred thousand years or so—maybe much, much less—they may be able to redeem themselves from the fatiguing hell into which they've fallen.

"Bojangles is evidence that—were we given the go-ahead to intervene—a delicate programming operation might be all that's necessary to put them right again. We could do it within a single Asadi generation. The only drawbacks to such a scheme I can see are that it violates GK regs and raises the possibility that the citizens of Frasierville and our colonists out on the veldts would have to *share* their planet with a species with a prior claim. And sometimes, Jaafar, human beings don't share very well.''

Elegy turned to me, her wrists bloody and her forearms a speckled burnt-umber color. "Could you get the straps out of that box, Ben? I want to fix this little package up right.''

From a box in the cargo section—a small teakwood trunk, really—I removed two wine-colored leather belts, one with a buckle, one with a cat-tongue overlap fastener of Velcro. At the butcher's table I threaded the belts through the slits Elegy had cut in the beef haunch. Jaafar was struggling to force the blade of his knife through another marbled slab, and his face, contorted by the effort, resembled that of a hired Levantine cutthroat. We had cut four packages of meat from the two beef haunches.

Wiping her brow with her forearm, Elegy said, "Call Kretzoi in here, Ben.''

So, from the cargo section, I shouted, "Kretzoi, come in here! Hey, Kretzoi!'' and Elegy and Jaafar looked at me as if I had just belched during an especially lovely section of Bach's *Christmas Oratorio*.

But Kretzoi leaped into the Dragonfly and swaggered with a pronouncedly baboonish gait to our makeshift slaughter-house.

"Kretzoi,'' Elegy said, approaching him, "try this hunk of meat on. We may have to adjust the straps.''

Quite composedly, the primate rocked back on his hind-quarters and made a series of hand signs.

"I'll comb the 'mess' out, Kretzoi. You can't be your old fastidious self if you go through with this tomorrow, though. The mess goes with the job. That's just the way it is.''

Elegy hefted the slab of meat by a copper belt buckle and swung the whole package around so that it thudded softly against Kretzoi's back. She got his forelimbs through the straps and did a careful cinching job in front.

"Stand up, Kretzoi. Stand up and walk. I want to see if that's going to be all right.''

Kretzoi stood. With his forelimbs—his arms, rather—bent provisionally before him like someone whose wrists have just been broken, he performed a gimpy minuet. Animal, I thought; only an animal. But Elegy, satisfied, asked him if he were reasonably comfortable. He signaled that he was.

Jaafar and I took the slab off Kretzoi's back. I unfastened both belts and replaced the meat in the refrigeration locker. The cold air whirling out took my breath away. We cached the other three dressed-out pieces with the first and saved back several small strips of meat for our evening meal. Protein and animal fat.

Thomas Benedict, carnivore.

*

Jaafar and I went out to the edge of the drop point to check Cy again. Elegy remained with Kretzoi under the awning, soaping the "mess" out of his lovely red-gold fur and scraping away the tangled lather with a comb and a wire brush.

Cy seemed to be stirring. The creature's truncated body hiccupped alarmingly; the eyes were no longer occluded by a film. Colors spun lazily inside his bottle-glass lenses—a spectral display reminiscent of a carousel whose operator can't decide whether to run it at three-quarters throttle or shut it completely down. Jaafar lifted his syringe and placed the needle on a vein standing visible in the sparse hair of Cy's throat.

"Victim of love," he murmured, ready to drive the needle home.

I caught his hand. A twitch of Cy's head had revealed something odd about the area around his brain stem. A small excavation, in fact. None of us had noticed it before. I gripped the creature's mane and pushed his head all the way to the right, exposing the neat, almost homey hole.

Through this, it was clear, Bojangles or his mother had withdrawn the medulla oblongata, the cerebellum, and other tasty portions of the neocortical grey matter. They had trephined Cy in order to get at the tempting sweet-breads of his brain.

"They probably left him his reptilian brain," I said; "his primitive R-complex and a good deal of the neocortical frontal lobes. That's all he's operating on, Jaafar. I doubt he's in pain. The twitches are nervous responses to the return of a low level of consciousness."

"His eyes—" Jaafar began.

"They left him Bojangles's area because they couldn't get at it. Or maybe because they knew he'd need it to protract this fetid death-in-life state of his. His spectral displays are ritualized patterns. I'd bet they emanate from some kind of roundabout hookup between his R-complex and Bojangles's area."

Fiercely, Jaafar said, "Let him return, then, to the good, sweet dark," and he plunged the needle into the vein in Cy's neck.

"We'd do better just killing him. His spectral display's a distress signal, more than likely—repeated, and repeated, and repeated again."

"*Pfyu!*" Jaafar spat into the leaf cover at our feet; then he tossed the syringe into the Wild with a savage, underhand flip that slammed his hand into the bottom of Cy's nest and jammed one of his fingers. He put the finger into his mouth and, turning back toward the Dragonfly in a crouch, sucked at the sudden hurt.

"I didn't expect," he said, speaking only half intelligibly around his finger, "to discover such sick-making things about these creatures." Then, as if it were an old-fashioned thermometer, he shook his finger in the air. "When we get back, I swear to you I am going to pull a Pettijohn and see if they can't find me beautiful nightmares on the punishment worlds. It couldn't be worse than these . . . these eat-your-own-issue *boonies!* Oh, no; indeed not."

I walked him back to the tent awning.

Two hours later, at sunset, he ate his slices of solar-broiled beef with as fine an appetite as if he had never seen what he had seen. For that matter, so did I.

# CHAPTER FIFTEEN

# Following the Script

I woke during the night to realize that Elegy had left our awning tent and gone into the Dragonfly to share a bed with Jaafar. Although I could hear nothing but the wind in the forest, I knew they were in each other's arms. Would Jaafar call her "Civ Cather, my sweet Civ Cather" at the moment of climax? It seemed quite likely. I grinned in bitter amusement at the prospect.

An hour before sunrise, I dressed, shook down the kinks in my bones, and strolled to the edge of the Wild. Cy lay comatose, or very nearly so, in his relocated nest. In solemn moonlight I cut his throat and lifted him out, as a person removes a new garment from its wrappings in a shallow box. A few of the creature's exposed intestines slipped free and dangled in the darkness like soft pendulums ticking off the minutes until dawn. I cut them loose and laid the carcass on the ground.

It took me only fifteen or twenty minutes to clean the Asadi meat-sibling, to cut away the hide, the lights, the head. When I was finished, I cradled the denatured meat of his corpse in my arms and carried it back to the helicraft.

Inside the Dragonfly I passed the sleeping couple's bunk and opened the refrigeration locker in the cargo section. As I was hanging the dressed-out carcass beside the other well-trimmed packages of meat, Elegy's head and shoulders rose from the anonymous contours of Jaafar's bedding.

"Ben?" she whispered. "What're you doing?"

"Showing mercy," I said in a normal speaking voice.

"Showing mercy and demonstrating my practical side as well. This is the genuine article I'm stowing here, Elegy, the genuine article."

Something about her silence suggested that she understood.

"What about you?" I asked her. "What're you doing?"

"Spiting you," she said aloud. "There's really no other way to describe it, I'm afraid."

"But why?"

"For failing to believe in what we're doing. For failing to believe in my reconstructions of the Asadi past."

That boggled me. Jaafar awoke and sat up in the bedclothes like a man revived from bitter death. He looked surprised but not particularly grateful.

"Do *you* believe in them?" I asked Elegy.

"In part."

"It's not that I don't believe them," I said quickly, maybe cutting her off. "It's just that I've almost ceased to care. One day, Elegy, I'd like to know why humanity has such a hunger to disillusion itself."

"My father's out here," Elegy responded, as if that explained everything.

"Good morning, Jaafar," I said.

"Good morning, Dr. Benedict," he managed coolly enough.

I closed and bolted the refrigeration locker. Suddenly aware of the foul stickiness of my hands and forearms, I quickly washed up at the vacuum sink, toweled myself dry, and left the helicraft without another word.

Outside, the first thing I saw was Kretzoi standing upright at the nest where Cy had lain and peering down into it with his arms extended before him like man with two broken wrists. When he turned to look at me, his eyes reflected the waning moonlight and his posture suggested a helpless hostility. I dropped my gaze and ducked into the tent. Dawn was painfully slow to arrive.

*

"Damn it, Kretzoi!" Elegy said sharply. "Hold still. We want to get there an hour after they do, exactly one hour, and you're not making this easy."

Jaafar and I were attempting to position a chunk of meat on the primate's back, using the belt straps to secure it, and

Kretzoi was twisting from side to side to see what we were doing. The meat was cold, its fat the consistency of candle wax. Kretzoi's nervous shruggings made the package slide in our hands and coat the fur on his back with sticky globules of grease.

"What's the matter with you?" Elegy asked. "We did this yesterday in the helicraft, remember?"

Kretzoi swung away from Jaafar and me so quickly that the meat slipped free of its straps and tumbled to the hard-packed dirt near our tent. Jaafar bent in groaning disgust to retrieve it, and in silent disgust rethreaded the greasy belts so that we could try yet again.

"*Kretzoi!*" Elegy exclaimed.

The primate made a series of sullen, sloppy signals with his hands.

"What?" I asked. "What's his problem?"

"He says you've got to get the package on his back so that he can undo it by himself. Otherwise, he says, we might as well stay home."

"His problem," said Jaafar astutely, "is that he doesn't appreciate Dr. Benedict's having shown Bojangles's meat-sibling the ultimate mercy. Nor does he appreciate having Dr. Benedict's hands on him."

Kretzoi confirmed this assessment with another abrupt but sloppy sign. Then he squatted so that Jaafar, who had finally got the meat strapped and reasonably well dusted off, could position it on his back. I stepped aside and stared intently through the Wild in the direction of the Asadi clearing. "Try to take it off," I heard Elegy tell Kretzoi, and out of the corner of my eye I saw the primate unbuckle the package and lower it gracefully to the ground with the exposed loop of the other belt. Then Jaafar, having again restrung the meat, lodged the package high on Kretzoi's shoulders while I reflected, altogether sardonically, that I was out of favor with an ape. . . .

"Two other problems," I said.

Elegy squinted at me in the coppery morning sunlight. At her throat and beneath her arms, sweat had already darkened the olive-green dapplings of her jumpsuit's camouflage. "What?" she asked me.

"We need a huri," I said, finally looking at her.

"That's one problem," she said. "What's the other?"

"The other's this: Eisen Zwei appeared to an Asadi congregation that had been behaving strangely for almost a week prior to his arrival. They'd split into two 'teams'—that's what your father called them—hugging opposite ends of the clearing and carrying on like so many possessed medieval orphans. Kretzoi's arrival among the Asadi may not have the same impact as Eisen Zwei's for the simple reason that conditions aren't the same now."

Elegy was unperturbed by my reasoning. "Maybe Kretzoi's arrival will *induce* the appropriate behavior."

"The strange behavior existed *prior* to Eisen Zwei's coming," I insisted. "You're ignoring the principal terms of the equation."

Elegy shrugged.

"Then what about the huri?" I asked her.

"Jaafar," she said, glancing at the young man as he wiped his hands down his thighs to clean them of grease, "Jaafar, Ben wants to know about our huri. Would you get it, please?"

Jaafar turned and leaped into the Dragonfly. A moment later he was back, carrying a laminated bag in which there appeared to be sleeping the embryo of a crumpled demon.

"Substitutes for everything," said Elegy with broad self-mockery. "For Eisen Zwei, for prime cut of Asadi, and now for my daddy's infamous and maybe even apocryphal huri. Apocryphal, that is, if you listen to skeptics. I don't, I guess. I wouldn't be here if I did." She unsnapped the bag and withdrew the repellent black folds of the mysterious "embryo" inside it. Then she shook out the folds, pulled a small metal pin at the base of the rubbery pleats, and watched in evident satisfaction as air rushed in to inflate the thing. In a moment she was holding a huri on the palm of her hand, supporting it against her breasts as if it were a hungry demon child. "I had this made in Frasierville," she told me. "Didn't take 'em too long. They did it from the plans I gave 'em the day after you left the hangar to hole up in your private, dry-docked garbage scow."

"Thanks," I said. "Just who did it for you?"

"A pair of workers at the civki synthetics plant. Governor Eisen intervened for us again, you see." The artificial huri had serrated wings, henlike feet, and a face that was featureless except for the lip- or beak-resembling prominences surrounding its predatory mouth. "Puncture-proof, Ben, and the claws are made to grasp." She approached Kretzoi and affixed the mock-huri to his right shoulder, bending the vulcanized claws so that they clung tenaciously. "It won't fly, I'm afraid—but we'll have to live with that. My father's monograph indicates that in the clearing the huri seldom did anything but ride Eisen Zwei's shoulder or squat insentiently wherever it was placed."

Kretzoi pulled his head as far to the left as he could, eyeing the little hitchhiker with distaste. I didn't much blame him, either. Eventually, he assumed a baboonish sitting posture, shut his eyes, and tried to pretend that the thing enthroned on his shoulder didn't exist.

"The Asadi 'teams' will take care of themselves once Kretzoi gets in there," Elegy assured me. "Wait and see. They probably simply consist of a number of Asadi mothers and several of their designated-survivor children. A daylight manifestation of the nest bond. Really, what so excites and flusters them is their anticipation of a chance to eat meat in the clearing in broad daylight."

"That still doesn't explain why some mothers go to one side, Elegy, and some to the other."

She ignored this. "Jaafar, we've got to get moving. Expect us back in about thirty minutes for a second piece of meat—or Kretzoi, anyway."

Jaafar nodded obediently and climbed into the cockpit of the BenDragon Prime. Elegy and I helped each other secure our equipment, including our transceivers and one bulky but lightweight holocamera. Then Elegy chucked Kretzoi tenderly under the chin, reviving him to the business of the day, and the three of us set off together toward the Asadi clearing.

\*

Kretzoi entered from the east, only a little over an hour after the Asadi had gathered there that morning. We were very careful about both the time and the direction of his entry. Once he had gone in, Elegy and I stayed well back from the clearing's eastern boundary. However, we chose a spot permitting us only a partially obstructed view into the very center of the assembly ground, where we believed Kretzoi would have to play out the greatest portion of his role as a second Eisen Zwei. I got my camera pointed through a narrow tunnel in the vegetation and rocked back on my heels waiting for the show to begin. Both Elegy and I hoped that Kretzoi's appearance among the Asadi would divert their attention from our ill-concealed presence nearby. Which, thank God, it unquestionably did.

At first the milling Asadi seemed unaware that something unusual had happened. All I could see through the sight of my sleek tubular camera was their marching bodies, dusty manes, and bobbing snouts, for Kretzoi disappeared into their midst like a diver into dark water, and I feared that he would fail to resurface.

"Where is he?" Elegy whispered, straining forward at my side, but in a moment she had her answer.

Kretzoi was apparently plodding out a circuit contrary to those of the Asadi themselves. This circuit, along with the huri on his shoulder and the packet of thawing meat on his back, soon made the Asadi aware that someone unusual had just crashed their party. Almost as a single being, then, they withdrew from the middle of the field, leaving Kretzoi plainly visible there. Soon, in fact, they lined the perimeters of the clearing.

I aimed my camera into the heart of the assembly ground. Its whirring attracted no attention. The Asadi were too busy gaping at Kretzoi to mount charging displays on the alien technological artifact recording their behavior.

Swaggering, employing a gait halfway between bipedalism and primate knuckle walking, Kretzoi entered the Center Ring and undid the buckle securing the meat to his left shoulder. Then he swung the packet free and set it on the ground.

The sight of the meat emboldened the Asadi. They began edging inward toward it—but as soon as they did, Kretzoi hunkered down, removed the mock-huri from his shoulder, and set the rubber beastie atop the meat. For a moment he had to struggle to keep it from toppling over—but at last he got the huri to stand on its own, its claws buried like fork prongs in the deep-red flesh. Again the Asadi ebbed away.

"You can smell their fear," Elegy whispered. "I swear, Ben, you can actually smell it."

Kretzoi came knuckle walking uncertainly across the clearing toward us, looking less graceful and more chimpish than I had ever seen him. A moment later he was beside us in the Wild, having flushed a bevy of Asadi back into the clearing to avoid contact with him. The grease in his fur was already growing rancid; in fact, the "fear" Elegy smelled was emanating at least as much from Kretzoi as from the stunned Asadi.

"We're going back for another piece of meat, Ben. Think you'll be all right while we're gone?"

"Fine. Just remember to have Kretzoi enter from the south next time." I cradled the unwieldy camera in my arms and prepared to find another position from which to shoot. "Hurry back."

Off they went. The Wild closed around them like a great green mouth, and beneath braided yellow runners and the gravid pods of a tree called boawort I crept southward along the eastern perimeter of the clearing. Most of the Asadi remained crowded together about the edges of the assembly ground, very near me, quarreling with their eyes and sometimes cuffing one another. I moved so deliberately, to prevent my being discovered, that it took better than twenty minutes to navigate a distance I could have skipped in a tenth the time.

I found a tree on the clearing's edge: a lattice-sail tree with well-spaced boughs for climbing and billowy, reticulate leaves for concealment. Securing my camera, I climbed to a vantage a good five meters above the ground. With luck I wouldn't have to move again, not even when Kretzoi and Elegy returned to the Dragonfly for a third packet of meat.

And, yes, Kretzoi was even now reentering the clearing, shouldering aside the puzzled, frightened aliens near the southern end zone. I began filming, with no idea at all where Elegy might be. The Asadi ceased quarreling among themselves—to watch in nervous bafflement as Kretzoi staggered regally into the middle of their field, removed the package from his back, lowered it beside the first, and squatted to arrange the mock-huri astride both slabs together. That done, Kretzoi left the clearing again.

A voice beside me whispered, "It's going well, isn't it?"

"Lord, woman, what you doin'?" Elegy had climbed into the lattice-sail tree as I was filming, and the mild whirr of the camera, along with my own concentration on Kretzoi, had kept me from hearing her. I wrapped an arm around the bole separating us and stared keenly at her dark, grinning face. She gestured at the Asadi pushing and squirming beneath us.

"We induced the appropriate behavior," she said. "Two 'teams'—north and south, even if they've run together a little—and utter milling confusion in both populations."

"You let Kretzoi go back to the Dragonfly alone?"

"He knows the way. Jaafar'll take care of him, Ben."

"And you're going to keep me company up here?"

"I think so," she whispered. "When Kretzoi gets back this time, he's going to stay. That's why we're liable to be up here for a while. If events unfold as they do in my father's monograph, we may have to sit patient and pretty a good five or six days."

"*Five or six days?*"

"Don't you remember?"

"I remember, Elegy—I helped put that snakebit monograph together. But I'm not about to become a permanent tenant of a lattice-sail tree just so Egan Chaney's dubious version of history can repeat itself!"

"Shhh," Elegy cautioned. "Maybe Kretzoi's acting will speed things up. I've told him to try to get everything done today—everything within reason, that is. Patience, Ben."

Gazing down, I had the distinct impression that several Asadi had become aware of us. One or two lifted their muzzles and sniffed the wind; three of four others cocked their heads, listening intently—but none looked directly at us or threatened assault.

Elegy and I fell silent. Eventually Kretzoi returned, entering the clearing from the west, a packet of meat on his back and two pieces of nylon rope looped about his neck. What he did then was exactly what Eisen Zwei, according to the witness of Elegy's father, had done more than six years ago: He lifted the mock-huri to his shoulder, laced lengths of rope through the slabs of meat on the ground, and pulled one slab into the southern end zone, leaving the huri to guard it, and the other slab into the northern end of the field, stepping aside here to act himself as guardian. The aliens clacked their teeth, tugged furiously at their manes, writhed their arms in wordless entreaty. Never had I seen them so agitated. Finally, mercifully, Kretzoi stepped back and made a strangling noise deep in his throat.

At this signal the Asadi all about the clearing, some so far away from Elegy and me it was difficult to distinguish among individuals, sat down and watched Kretzoi hobble back toward the center of the assembly ground. The meat he had brought them occupied most of their attention, but they refrained from falling upon and devouring it.

"He's got to fetch the huri before they'll do anything," Elegy whispered. "See, he's coming back this way."

Indeed, Kretzoi walked the length of the clearing, paused at the offering in the southern half of the field, and bent to retrieve the huri. Once it was astride his shoulder, Kretzoi returned to the center of the clearing and lifted his broken-seeming wrists toward the midday sun. Every Asadi eye was upon him, as was the telephoto lens of my holocamera; the just-perceptible whirring of the film was amplified in my head a thousand times. That no one could hear it but Elegy and me seemed so unlikely that for a brief moment I stopped filming.

"Don't stop," Elegy said fiercely. "This is one of the things we came for, Ben."

I sighted and began filming again. Kretzoi's face was turned directly toward Denebola—he probably had his eyes closed. He made a sobbing noise more protracted and higher-pitched than his previous call; and, in immediate response, the Asadi broke from their places around the clearing and swarmed like great hairy insects toward the pair of offerings. Sheer, brazen, scrabbling bedlam. Even seated high above the arena of the Asadi's gladitorial insanity, I was filled with fear, discomfited by the thought that at any moment they might espy us and drag us into the general melee. But I kept filming.

"Incredible," Elegy said aloud. "Absolutely incredible."

There was no reason for her to whisper. Each Asadi had but one thing in mind: the procuring of a bit of flesh and its swift, slashing ingestion. To this end, the Asadi tore at one another, kicked, butted heads, clawed, pulled fur, flashed their teeth—all without any accompanying sound but the thunderous grinding of tooth enamel, a vivid, ubiquitous panting, and the thudding of their feet.

The carcasses Kretzoi had dragged into opposite ends of the clearing were gone in a bloody twinkling. Like piranhas, Chaney had written. Well, in six years, that hadn't changed. None of the Asadi was injured irreparably, it seemed, but many did drag themselves away with broken bones and severely gaping wounds.

Kretzoi signaled a conclusion to the feast by sucking in his breath and calling his subjects to order. They obeyed readily. Even the injured turned their heads toward him. The victors, to whom had gone the spoils, sat back on their haunches and, wiping their muzzles with their hands, gave Kretzoi a keen and critical eye. Of all the milling Asadi, however, only a few had actually been fed.

"A far cry from loaves and fishes," I told Elegy *sotto voce*. "Makes you wonder why they simply don't make Kretzoi their dessert."

"No chance of that, Ben. Watch."

"He going to eat the packet on his back? 'S what Eisen Zwei did, I know, but I swear Kretzoi hasn't got the appetite of that old man."

"Shhh."

Kretzoi did as the script of Chaney's monograph obliged him to do. He removed the third well-whittled carcass from his shoulders, placed it at his feet, and then sat down behind it to tear off ropy morsels. He ate slowly—but not, I felt sure, merely because Egan Chaney's script required him to: The heat and his own nervousness made it impossible for him to gulp the overample meal. He ate as he had to. And as he ate, the mock-huri clinging to his mane, the Asadi regarded Kretzoi with decorous, respectful envy. The noise of my camera suddenly seemed intrusive.

"That's enough, Ben. A few of them seem to be tracking on the whirr. Save some film for later."

I lowered the camera's barrel, swung it across my back on its leather sling.

"Do you see what Kretzoi's eating, Ben?"

"Meat—what else?"

"It's Cy," Elegy whispered. "The carcass is small but it's almost entire. It's not a beef slab like the others."

I swung the barrel of my camera around and sighted through the scope of its automatic enlarger. The meat Kretzoi was so soberly devouring was indeed the meat I had rendered that morning from Cy's corpse—darker in color than the beef, less sinewy, stranger. I returned the camera to my back and looked at Elegy.

"I don't understand. This morning Kretzoi gave me the evil eye for ending that poor bugger's hopeless vegetable existence. Now he's cannibalizing the remains."

"In Bojangles's stead," Elegy told me. "Can't you understand that?"

"As if Cy were *Kretzoi's* meat-sibling? Is that what you mean?"

"Exactly."

My back and buttocks aching, I shifted nearer Elegy. "I still don't understand."

"Listen, Ben, what Kretzoi's doing he does because I've

asked him to. He knew he'd have to down the better part of a good-sized piece of meat as part of his impersonization of Eisen Zwei, but he wasn't entirely happy with the assignment."

"He's fastidious."

"He is, despite your tone. He's genuinely fastidious. In a way, Ben, you've inadvertently made his role in this charade easier for him—he's reaffirming his bond with Bojangles by eating the dressed-out carcass of Cy. He's not simply masquerading as an Asadi, he's not just playing a part—he's actively *identifying* with these creatures."

"Which is fine. If it doesn't go too far."

Elegy framed a contemptuous scowl, then looked back out into the clearing. Only her small, hard profile met my gaze. With the same noncommittal enduring patience as a coat rack holds coats, the lattice-sail tree held Elegy and me. For the next two hours—amazingly enough—we didn't exchange a single word. During this time Denebola moved into the western half of the sky and Kretzoi finished swallowing all but the gristle and bone of his adopted meat-sibling. Good-bye, Cy, good-bye. I was glad when the feast was over.

Then: "Get your camera ready."

I obeyed, and in the very next moment I was filming. Kretzoi lifted himself sluggishly from the ground and summoned the Asadi to attention by drawing a painful breath. Then he emptied the contents of his stomach in quick, sharp retches—like a slot machine paying out a series of jackpots. The artificial huri wobbled on his shoulder, but didn't fall. Afterward, dazed, Kretzoi stumbled away a few steps and collapsed into an exhausted crouch.

"That's in the script," I said, "but is it deliberate? Kretzoi's several days ahead of schedule, isn't he?"

"He's doing his best to accomplish the entire program for us in a single day." Elegy's knuckles were white against the striated, blue-grey bark of the tree.

"You think this is the beginning of the Ritual of Death and Designation?"

"Looks like, Ben. Certainly looks like."

I shifted again, leaning my back into a fan of boughs supporting an especially large reticulate sail, and arranged myself so that I could film without toppling headlong down.

The Asadi, as they had done at Eisen Zwei's nauseating prompting six years ago, came forward from the clearing's sidelines, approached Kretzoi in something like homage, and began taking away tiny morsels of regurgitated matter. They did this one after another, in so orderly a fashion they seemed lobotomized or drugged. Several of the first Asadi to pass through the center of the clearing carried their prizes into the jungle, there to eat in relative privacy or to stow their loot where it might not be easily discovered.

Meanwhile, the late-comers comported themselves admirably; they touched the moist place in the dust, then touched their fingers to their lips. Even though Kretzoi's huri could not fly, even though Kretzoi was different from them in subtle ways beyond the evident inability of his eyes to pinwheel polychromatically, the Asadi treated him with deference, even honor. Throughout the entire ceremony, in fact, he was continuously visible—no Asadi trespassed upon the little circle of ground he had staked out for himself, and none entreated him to contribute something more to the solemn festival of their homage.

"Now," Elegy whispered, "Kretzoi must die."

I ceased filming, glanced at her in surprise.

"Figuratively," she emended. "Theatrically, if you like."

Whereupon Kretzoi, savagely abridging the Ritual of Death and Designation, began wrestling with BoskVeld's sun. He rose out of his crouch to do battle with Denebola, and as his hands tore at the flaring corona of the sun, as if trying to pull the alien star into ragged filaments of taffy, the Asadi took note and retreated again to opposite ends of the field. From these vantages they watched the hand-to-hand combat between the sun that fed them and the chieftain who fed them, and I realized, for the first time, that the significance of the combat lay in the Asadi chieftain's presumptuous challenge to Denebola as his people's most important, most generous provider.

It was a combat no mortal Asadi could ever hope to win, of course, and any chieftain who entered upon it was in fact surrendering his eyesight and his life to the greater power of the sun. First, blindness; then, death—the first a metaphor for the second, and the second an inevitable consequence of the former. Meat was a mere mortal's gift, whereas the gift of Denebola to the photosynthesizing Asadi was the energy innate in sunlight: the virtually immortal fuel of solar systems, of galaxies, of the living, binding plasma of the cosmos itself.

This speculation by no means explained the Asadi to me, but it suffused their lives and their behavioral patterns with a towering significance I had never before recognized. I was suddenly elated. The contrast between the grubby physical spectacle below us and the redeeming philosophical import of that spectacle roared through me in combers of insight and perception. Had something similar happened to Egan Chaney before his ultimate return to the Wild? Maybe. "I belong among the Asadi," he had written, "not as an outcast and not as a chieftain—but as one of the milling throng."

Filming Kretzoi's reenactment of old E.Z.'s challenge to Denebola, I experienced the bewildering conviction that I, too, was a brother to the Asadi. Our fraternity was written not merely in the identical amino-acid sequence of our hemoglobin, but in the even more compelling miracle by which the cosmos had given us life and self-awareness. Chaney had defected to the Wild, I finally understood, for reasons essentially ontological and hence religious. Did Elegy understand that? Did she know that in seeking out her father we were knocking at a door that opened into other dimensions, other continua, other modes of knowledge?

"Let's hope he's keeping his eyes closed," she whispered.

"He's got 'em shut," I responded. "Kretzoi's not crazy."

At last, his act almost concluded, Kretzoi covered his head with his arms and slumped to the ground. He rolled so that his eyes stared sightlessly into the eastern portion of the Wild, his limbs tucked inside the rigid curve of his body. The mock-huri was thrown to the ground by his fall. It looked dead. Old E.Z.'s huri had flown, and I think both Elegy and I feared the remainder of the Ritual would fail to unravel as it ought because ours couldn't fly.

But the Asadi, bless 'em, gave the make-believe huri a wide berth; made no move either to examine it or to grab it up and hurl it into the forest. Instead, they suddenly began acting in concert to bring about a desired end.

A pair of aliens from each group came to the center of the field and lifted Kretzoi like pallbearers hoisting a casket. In the meantime, other Asadi gathered foliage from the Wild with which to make a pallet. Soon, so rapidly had the Asadi worked, Kretzoi was lying on a pile of rubber-tree fronds, his arms folded on his breast and his head tilted back as if to receive a final ambiguous blessing from the sun.

After a while, swinging my camera's barrel back and forth

between the two opposing groups of aliens, I saw that the eyes of every single specimen were radiating a mournful deep-blue color. Indigo, Chaney had called the color. It made the carapaces protecting the Asadi's eyes even murkier-seeming than usual. Moreover, the afternoon light sifting through the mosses and bearded lianas of the Wild daguerreotyped everything beneath us in subtle mercury vapors. Strange, passing strange, and lovely.

Heads began moving from side to side, snouts inscribing figure eights in the air. This went on—hypnotically, obsessively—for better than an hour. Denebola was sinking into the Calyptran baths beyond the western foilage of the Wild.

Indigo eyes. Everywhere, indigo eyes.

And then, so secretly that I scarcely had any consciousness of its arrival, twilight gathered in the rain forest and seeped out into the clearing like a flow of cyanide. Sunset. Evening star. And the inaudible bugle notes of twilight's poignant taps. A call to retire.

But no one retired.

# CHAPTER SIXTEEN

# Thus We Vindicate Schliemann

*"Dr. Benedict,"* a voice sounded in my ear. *"Dr. Benedict, are you there? You, too, Civ Cather—are you there?"*

It was Jaafar, speaking to us from the BenDragon Prime. He had held his peace all afternoon, but now that Denebola had set he wanted to know if we were still alive.

Elegy and I exchanged an ambivalent glance, having each forgotten about Jaafar. Now that events were progressing so rapidly, his reminding us of his presence elsewhere in the Wild seemed an unjustifiable distraction.

Before I could keep the words from coming out, I said, "Did he call you 'Civ Cather' last night?"

"Answer him," Elegy urged me angrily.

"Jaafar," I said, activating the transceiver at my throat, "we're fine, we're doing fine."

He wanted to know what was happening, why the Asadi had not come crashing back through the Wild now that the sun was down.

"We'll be in touch," I told him curtly. "Stay in touch with us, Jaafar, and we may soon take you to Chaney's pagoda."

*"Yes, sir,"* came the faint reply.

Below us in the clearing the Asadi had crept toward the crumpled form of Kretzoi, their ostensible chieftain. As daylight wearily disintegrated, I set my camera to record in the infrared frequencies.

What I saw and filmed was the younger and smaller Asadi moving inward to lift Kretzoi from his pallet and to bear him toward the north. They were bracketed on both sides by

255

larger, more handsome animals with fuller and more strikingly colored manes—as if at last a covert caste system were making itself manifest in this moment of crisis and rare joint endeavor. Chaney had likened the smaller specimens to workers, their protectors in the two exterior columns of the march to warriors, and maybe the dichotomy had a biological basis, maybe it grew out of some self-protective Ur'sadi sociological instinct dormant for thousands of millennia. In any case, Kretzoi floated northward above the heads of the Asadi workers while the silver- and tawny-maned warriors trudged along in their guardian columns keeping a conscientious lookout for who-knows-what likely or unlikely enemy.

"Let's go," Elegy said, scrambling down the boughs of the lattice-sail. A moment later she was beckoning me from the edge of the assembly ground.

I followed, repeatedly banging the barrel of my camera against both my head and the bole of the tree. When I was safely down, the last members of the Asadi parade were just about to disappear into the dusky foliage.

"Listen," I said, "I'm not going to be able to do any more filming. It'll be all either of us can do just to keep up."

"Forget the filming. Look—right out there—that's our artificial huri, Ben!" She ran to the center of the clearing and picked up the pleated, evil-looking thing. The Asadi had been careful not to step on it, and it was as good as new, if a little dusty. "I'll carry this," Elegy exclaimed. "Come on." And she jogged on ahead of me, her head thrown back and one raised hand beckoning me again and again to follow her lead. Camera barrel banging, I did.

The Asadi procession maintained a stately even pace, swaying as a unit through spaces I would have thought impassable to a single individual. The Asadi made a highway where no human being would have ever been able to perceive anything but creeper-clogged arches and tangled knots of squid-orchids and rainthorn. Elegy and I, though, found ourselves stepping through keyholes in the vegetation already unlocked by the Asadi's passage.

Chaney could not recall how long he had walked before the Asadi reached their ancient temple, but I made an effort to keep track. My best estimate is a little better than five hours, and my feeling is that we traversed a distance of some fifteen to twenty kilometers. In any case, by the time Elegy and I broke out of dense, clinging jungle and found the Asadi arrayed before a lofty shadow in the dark, we had outlasted the hour of midnight and worn down the leather sidesoles of our boots.

The three moons were up: Balthazar, Caspar, and Melchior. They receded into space one behind the other, staggered against the night like lanterns hung at different levels. The foliage of the Wild, I knew, was straining after this conjunction just as the waters of Calyptra strain toward the moons at the dangerous hour of flood called tri-tide. It happens once every five or six days in BoskVeld's equatorial zone, but I was surprised to see the conjunction now and disturbed by the eeriness imparted to the night by the polarized lunar light and the murmurous tidal sloughing of the trees.

An accident, this conjunction; mere coincidence.

But the Asadi swaying together in the clearing in front of absolutely nothing but open space and shadow (a shadow that should not have existed in such towering majesty) made me believe that perhaps it was Elegy, Kretzoi, and I who were being manipulated rather than the shrewd and unforthcoming Asadi.

"Do you see Kretzoi?" Elegy asked me.

"No, not yet." I pulled her around the outsized clearing to the east. A moment later we were looking inward from a spot where thick vegetation concealed us and we had an end-on view of each of the four Asadi ranks. The huge open space in front of the foremost rank stretched away to the north, to our right, for eighty to a hundred meters.

As we watched, a pair of Asadi, their manes silver-white in the moonglow, detached themselves from opposite ends of the front rank and approached the looming shadow ahead of them. The Asadi nearest us had sustained a wound in that afternoon's free-for-all over Kretzoi's meat offerings—its right arm was ripped open from elbow to wrist and coagulated blood glistened in the wound like a vein of caramel. I lifted my camera to film the scene.

"Don't," Elegy cautioned me. "There's too much risk—we don't want to undermine what we've already accomplished." So I eased the camera behind me on its sling.

At the instant, as if they had turned at right angles to the moonlight, or absorbed so much of it that its residual sheen actually cloaked them, the two advancing Asadi slipped out of my vision, *poof*. Elegy clearly saw what I saw, and yet we each seemed to believe that the Asadi had merely edged themselves simultaneously into our common blind spot; as a result, their disappearance had nothing weird or unsettling about it. We expected to see them reemerge into our vision as soon as we shifted our heads or a passing cloud subtly altered the moonglow. It was the vitreous humor of our eyes that was at fault, we believed, and not the basic paradigms of reality. To our relief, subsequent events confirmed that nothing *terribly* supernatural had occurred.

The two Asadi warriors reappeared at the precise moment the Asadi pagoda itself jumped into existence for us.

When two green flames on either side of the temple's hung wooden doors burst into view, we saw what had previously been invisible to us. The pagoda stood where before there had been only shadow. After slipping into that shadow, our two Asadi warriors had mounted the steps fronting the temple in order to light the iron flambeaux near its massive doors. Once lit, the green flames not only made the torchlighters visible again but drew the substance of the pagoda itself into a viable alignment with the strangely polarized light of the triple moons and the Wild's psychotronic polarization of our Asadi and human perceptual abilities. Some dormant energy inside the building had responded to the firing of the torches by negating the concealing polarizations of light and perception outside it. As a consequence, the temple had leaped into view like a television picture springing fullblown from a blank but highly sensitized screen. It happened almost like an explosion, but one with neither flash nor din.

The Asadi reacted by lifting their arms, shaking their heads, and falling back a step or two.

Elegy and I reacted by embracing and stooping to the ground together, as if a shower of sparks and debris might come cascading out of the air upon us. No chance of that, though. We were simply being given the chance to see what had existed in the clearing for the lifetime of the pagoda occupying it. We were seeing what Egan Chaney had seen before the light- and perception-polarizing powers of the structure, programmed into it a million or more years ago for enemies other than human investigators, had again plunged the temple into invisibility—as a direct consequence, apparently, of Chaney's trespass and The Bachelor's lunatic vandalism.

The pagoda was . . . well, magnificent. It combined the architectural qualities of several terrestrial styles from several historical epochs. Its central dome, of a weirdly translucent marble or travertine, recalled those on Islamic mosques, while a narrow spire rising from the dome might have been anything from a lightning rod to a radio antenna. The gem-shingled wings of the five successively smaller roofs, going from bottom to top, suggested the religious towers of Buddhist and Hindu Asia. From the outermost tips of all five wings hung reedlike tubes of several shapes and lengths, instruments through which the wind had once been free to concoct melodies that the temple had long since either muted or stopped. The flutes and bassoons, I told myself of Chaney's fevered "imagination." The stone tier rising to the Gothic doorway was Roman, while the panes of opaque violet glass set like monstrous but wafer-thin amethysts at intervals in the spaces between the top three roofs had no Earthly analogue at all. They did have the imperviousness of basilisk eyes, though, and they shimmered and changed in the moonlight as if a viscous colored liquid were oozing down their backsides in the pagoda's interior. The building, which had once been sleeping, was alive—alive and expectant.

"There it is, Ben."

Elegy's voice conveyed no smugness, only wonder and childlike belief. The verdigris coating the temple's facade—coating, too, the bas-relief carvings running like bredework in the stories between the lower two roofs and the high entablature—in no way degraded the temple in her sight.

She eased herself out of my embrace and stood. "They're carrying him up to the funeral scaffold," she whispered, pointing, and as I, too, stood, I saw six of the smaller Asadi bearing Kretzoi up the temple's steps to a carven stone catafalque. Here the corpsebearers laid Kretzoi out with a care approaching reverence, then took up positions behind the bier and faced their shaggy, shuffling people.

For the Asadi had begun to do ritual combat with Bosk-Veld's moons, now no longer in perfect conjunction, Balthazar having moved retrograde to the other two and Caspar having outpaced Melchior to the west. Not all of the Asadi took part in this pantomimic warfare, just a sufficient number to make shadows dance in the clearing.

"The huri designates the chieftain's successor," I told Elegy, shaking off my awe. "And our huri's incapable of that. Our entire elaborate ruse breaks down at this point, Elegy."

"Let's see, Ben. Let's see."

We must have waited—yes—another two or three hours as Kretzoi stoically bore the inconvenience of his "death" and lay unmoving on the catafalque. The moons were finally so far apart that two of them had fallen beneath the artificial horizon of the trees, Caspar west and Balthazar east. Melchior, more distant, dallied, but the Asadi dropped their snouts from its contemplation and began moving about the clearing just as they moved in their daylight clearing.

And it was now, Elegy and I both knew, that the dead chieftain's huri ought to come flapping above their heads in deadly earnest to decide a successor. It would dive into the throng and thrash an unsuspecting Asadi to its knees with merciless wing beats. The Asadi so chosen, usually a "mute," would have to separate itself from the others and keep body and soul together not only through limited photosynthesis, but also through the midnight cannibalization of its conspecifics and their hidden meat-siblings.

Elegy squatted and picked up the artificial huri she had carried with her from the other clearing. It was deflated now; a tiny, collapsed umbrella.

"You planning on throwing that among 'em, Elegy? As soon as it hits one, he'll know it's a—what would Eisen say?—a *wrongness*."

Still squatting, Elegy ignored me. She pulled the metal pin lost somewhere in the huri's multifoliate pleats, and the creature bloomed in her hands.

"The other possibility," I went on, crouching beside her, "is that they'll accept whichever Asadi it strikes as their new chieftain—after which our torchbearers up there"—nodding emphatically in their direction—"will put the green flame to Kretzoi. Is that what you want?"

"Just shut up and watch, Ben." Elegy handed the huri to me and I took it because I had no other choice.

We watched. The Asadi's movements grew sluggish, perfunctory. They'd been at it, this abortive ritual, for hours, and they were nearly as weary as we were. In fact, Elegy and I were still running on curiosity and adrenalin, whereas the aliens looked to have exhausted both. The flames in the heavy iron sconces on either side of the pagoda's doors had guttered almost to extinction. . . .

A faint buzz sounded in my ears. "*Elegy*," said a voice imploringly, "*Elegy, are you there?*"

"He *does* know your first name, doesn't he?"

"Give him coordinates, Ben," Elegy commanded me with steely self-possession. "He may need them. We may need for him to have them."

I gave Jaafar the coordinates.

"*Do you want me to come?*" Jaafar's thin voice inquired. "*Is there room for me to land the Dragonfly?*"

"There's room for you to land," I responded, "but we don't want you to come. Besides, even with coordinates, you might have a helluva time finding this place. The pagoda disguises itself, and from the air the clearing probably presents an illusion of continuous jungle. Stay where you are."

"Until we call," Elegy qualified my command, and it was the first time in the Wild, away from the drop point, she had allowed herself to speak to Jaafar directly. Three words; no more. They ended the conversation, and Jaafar receded into the radio white noise of the rising dawn.

"Do you know what's wrong with you, Thomas Benedict?"

I looked at Elegy as if she had struck me. *Good lord*, I thought, staring at her in numb fascination.

"You're trapped in your left brain," she informed me. "You're a prisoner of your 'rational' self. You're dying of a disease called formulaic digital logic—which doesn't prevent you from behaving like an animal in moments of intuitive sanity." Her anger was even more palpable than the blown-up huri in my hands.

"What are you talking about, Elegy?" I nodded toward the pagoda. "In no time at all they're going to be cremating Kretzoi alive and you're subjecting me to an off-the-wall character analysis."

"Your archaic jealousy's one of the few signs the disease may not be as far along as it sometimes appears."

"*Elegy—*"

"How many times have you and I . . . copulated?" she challenged me, settling on the final word with a deliberate but opaque irony.

I stared at her in disbelief, but my mind raced to compute, to tally, to come up with an answer. "Twelve or so. Less than fifteen."

"Which is it, Ben? Tell me exactly."

"Fourteen," I hazarded.

"Are you sure?" she pressed.

"Positive," I said in exasperation, believing Kretzoi mortally imperiled by our argument and our inattention.

"How many times must we copulate before you stop counting?"

"What?" I waved helplessly at the temple.

She grabbed my gesturing hand and pinioned it to the mock-huri clutched awkwardly against my chest. "Your left brain's keeping score," she whispered hatefully. "It counts off its ticks like a clock. There hasn't been a time we lay naked together, Thomas Benedict, you didn't start intellectualizing the experience from the perspective of an anthropologist, or a sociobiologist, or maybe even a fucking Komm-galen with a minor in psychosexual angst. Your mind's like a mirror on the ceiling. It records but doesn't participate. That's what's wrong with you."

"Much obliged," I raged. "Holy goddamn fucking obliged!"

"And that's why Jaafar and I had our way with each other last night, or the night before last, or whenever the hell it was!"

"Because he doesn't *intellectualize* the act?" I raged, glancing in harried disbelief back and forth between Elegy's face and the Asadi temple.

"Not in the least."

"Listen," I hissed, aching with both jealousy and chagrin, "I'll tell you what's wrong with me—if, incredibly enough, that's all that's on your mind."

"Go ahead."

"I've been living for six years in the shadow of a dead man. I've made his work my own, I've pursued his ghost as if it were a grail, I've even allowed his doubly obsessed daughter to dictate the terms of that pursuit. That's what's wrong with me. I've put my identity in an equation with Egan Chaney's and then factored myself totally out of the picture." I saw quite clearly that the two Asadi torchbearers were lifting the heavy iron flambeaux from their sconces and moving toward the bier on which Kretzoi lay. At last, half panicked, I stood up and stepped from our hiding place. "Maybe that's what's wrong with you, too, Elegy—you've lost yourself in your obsession to find a dead man! *A dead man!*"

I was naked in the clearing. My last angrily declaimed

accusation had drawn the eyes of the Asadi. But for the jungle at my back, I was beset and surrounded.

Elegy shouted, "Goddamn it, Ben, *do* something!"

I raised the mock-huri and shook it violently. Then, taking it by one tarry wing, I whirled it about over my head like a child flying some sort of strange toy aircraft. Dawn was almost upon us. Swinging the artificial huri, I advanced through the Asadi toward the pagoda. Elegy came with me. On every side, the beasts retreated from us in fear and bewilderment.

The corpsebearers and torchlighters on the pagoda's highest tier observed our approach with puzzlement and alarm. To save themselves they would either have to flee or fight. Those seemed the only options available to them; and when the creatures failed to show any readiness to flee—we had just set foot on the bottom step and begun our ascent—I feared they would defend with their very lives both the pagoda and the body of their chieftain. I stopped.

"What's the matter?" Elegy asked.

"Are you ready to take on all eight of those fellows?"

The amethyst eyes of the pagoda, streaming with a multifaceted ooze, stared down on us in macrocosmic parody of the indigo gazes of the Asadi attending Kretzoi's bier.

Then I heard Elegy say, "Look."

Half turning, I saw the Asadi behind us plunging back into the Wild in a thousand different places, one after the other. Denebola's rising had triggered their dispersal, an inversion of the usual course of things. But the corpsebearers and torchlighters awaiting us on the temple's broad, high porch had not yet fled. Maybe they didn't intend to.

Elegy and I resumed our climb. My arm aching, I continued to whirl the mock-huri above my head.

On the temple's highest step the Asadi formed a phalanx eight individuals abreast. Bending aggressively forward, they stared down with eyes spinning out of indigo dullness into spectral displays of such angry intensity that their faces seemed to be on fire. A moment later they all began to fade, their bodies emptying of color, texture, and substance—so that through the outlines of their torsos and limbs Elegy and I could clearly see the catafalque behind them, the mossy, rearing facade of the pagoda, and the rough-hewn massiveness of the temple's doors.

"Again," whispered Elegy, matter-of-fact and non-committal.

"Hallucination," I told her. "They're radiating a spectral pattern that polarizes or off-centers our ability to perceive them. They do it in concert for maximum effectiveness. It's a residual capability. The pagoda retains in its structure the essence of this power, and their resorting to it now, Elegy, means they're out of their boonie minds with fright!"

I hurled the mock-huri with all my strength up the sweep of the tier, fell helplessly forward, and watched as the huri's wings stabilized its stumpy fuselage and sent it cruising like a crazy kamikaze intelligence into the alien phalanx—sixteen pinwheeling eyes above eight ghostly bodies.

The eyes scattered, and the bodies beneath them were suddenly real again, every one of the shaggy Asadi stumbling down the steps in a direction that would spare it a confrontation with us. Casting aside their torches, they were gone into the Wild almost before we could blink.

"Kretzoi!" Elegy shouted. She threw herself up the remaining steps to the summit and knelt beside the granite catafalque. The artificial huri, I noted, had struck the pagoda's doors and plummeted sidelong to one of the upper steps, where it balanced precariously. Wearily I climbed to the nasty thing and kicked it down the steps. Then I joined Elegy at Kretzoi's bier.

The primate lay on his back with his knees bent and his sex exposed. He appeared either asleep or unconscious. Holding his receding chin between her thumb and forefinger, Elegy tenderly tilted his head first to this side and then to that, all the while crooning entreaties and prayers. I had to believe that the rhythmic, swaying progress of the Asadi columns through the Wild had hypnotized him, for Elegy was hard pressed to bring him back to our reality.

"Let me try," I said.

I eased Elegy aside and laid my ear to Kretzoi's chest. He was breathing as a hibernating animal breathes, all his bodily processes clocked down to the laggardly cadences of winter. I put my mouth over his wide hairy lips, covered his death's-head nostrils with my hand, and blew a violent puff of air deep into his lungs. He started as if he had been galvanized. I puffed again, tasting the unplaceable odors of his breath and immediately wiping my mouth dry. That done, I dragged Kretzoi off the catafalque and slammed his limp body against the temple's left-hand door. Holding him there with my hip and one trembling hand, I made a hammer of my other fist and struck him squarely on the sternum. Again, he twitched—like a frog administered an electric shock.

"Stop it!" Elegy cried. And, in truth, I don't know whether I was trying to revive Kretzoi or neutralize my long-pent anxiety and frustration. Maybe I was doing both. Kretzoi was the Asadi I had not been able to get my hands on a moment earlier, and I didn't want to let him go.

"Ben!" Elegy cried again, grabbing my arm. "Stop it!"

I shrugged her away, but relinquished my grip on Kretzoi. Amazingly, he didn't slide down the door. Inside their clear polymer carapaces his human eyes came open, focusing on me with slow-dawning recognition and cold disdain.

As Kretzoi's consciousness returned, he pressed himself defiantly against the door at his back—with the result that the door groaned inward on its hinges and revealed to both Elegy and me a tall, narrow slice of the pagoda's interior. Kretzoi fell quickly to all fours and bounded aside.

"Ben," Elegy said tentatively.

"What?"

"You did well just then, Thomas Benedict. You were working intuitively for a change. That was your 'not-I' performing, you know—your right brain."

"Then I hardly deserve any credit, do I?"

Elegy laughed, and there on the top step of the high Asadi altar her laughter sounded incongruously merry and sweetly apropos. "Of course you do. It's your 'not-I,' isn't it?" She stepped forward and took my arm. "The honor's yours if you want it," she said, gesturing at the lofty crack between the temple doors. "You've waited as long as I have, I guess, and I'll be damned if it matters to me who goes in there first. . . . . Kretzoi, *sit!*"

The animal was edging toward the opening, but at her command he stopped and looked at her inquiringly.

I felt a sudden piquant affection for Kretzoi, an affection born of shame and an ineffable backassward respect. My own unworthiness, in contrast, was almost strong enough to choke me.

"Let the hairy ape go first," I said. "There's always the nasty chance the first one in won't come out at all."

Somehow Elegy perceived that I was joking. "In which case none of us will," she said. "Go ahead, Ben."

I unstrapped my camera and laid it on the catafalque. Then I activated the radio at my throat. "Jaafar," I said, "we've found the pagoda and we're going in. Bring the Dragonfly to this clearing, if you can."

Jaafar's response was swift and static-free: "*Very good, Dr. Benedict. I certainly will.*"

That was the end of the conversation. I wiped my hands on my thighs and moved to push even wider ajar the door that Kretzoi had already set groaning inward.

Elegy's voice halted me: "Inside, we're going to find the 'dead man' in whose shadow we've both been living. And that discovery's going to liberate us both."

"All right," I said, mouthing the words.

"My prayer for you, Thomas Benedict, is that afterward you'll know what to do with your freedom." I started to speak, but she cut me off: "Move your butt, Benedict. Let's see what we've let ourselves in for."

I led Elegy and Kretzoi into the pagoda. . . .

# CHAPTER SEVENTEEN

# Inside

"Preternaturally cold." So Chaney had described the interior of the Asadi temple. The temperature was indeed several degrees below that of the Wild, but you could scarcely call the place "cold." More accurately, the pagoda was *cool*. This coolness undoubtedly traced to the height of the structure and the fact that a pervasive, silver-tinged gloom seemed to neutralize the jungle's heat. This gloom, meanwhile, derived its tarnished silver glow from the morning light seeping through the central dome and moving as if by osmosis through the amethyst windows.

"There's the stairway to the 'chandelier,' " Elegy said, not bothering to whisper. "Just like my father described it. And the globes of the metal ring, they've been replaced and hoisted back into position." A faint echo overlapped her each succeeding word.

I stared up at the globes. Although possessed of a dull, mother-of-pearl luster they emitted very little light. They were each, I estimated, about the size of a Bronze Age shield rotated through a third dimension; they were also quite heavy-looking. I didn't want to be standing under one of them if it suddenly took a notion to fall.

Huddled just inside the door, we saw many of the things Chaney describes in *Death and Designation Among the Asadi*—from the spindly display cabinets whose design the curators of the Museum of Indigenous Artifacts had attempted (unsuccessfully, we now saw) to reproduce from Chaney's descriptions, to the vast, glowing wall on which were hung the Ur'sadi eyebooks. We also experienced a number of things Chaney had neglected or not thought to mention.

First, a feeling that the pagoda had unexplored recesses beyond the central chamber in which we stood.

Second, an unsettling glandular smell as pervasive as the gloom inside the temple.

And third, a distant fluting sound—a kind of hollow cooing reminiscent of wind blowing across the mouths of empty bottles, or maybe even of the rattle of rice-paper partitions during minor seismic tremors in an Oriental city.

This last sensation seemed to suggest that the pagoda was occupied, that somewhere in its eastern or western extremities there dwelt creatures accustomed to the temple and secure in their knowledge of its layout and architecture. My curiosity had just about given way to fear. I could see the three of us captured and existing briefly as "meat-siblings" to the real Asadi chieftain, the one whom Kretzoi had merely impersonated. . . .

"We want some more of those eyebooks," Elegy said, squelching my hope that she, too, might have reservations about continuing our trespass. "We ought to take all those on a single rod. Maybe by taking a complete sequence of fifty—or however many each rod holds—we'll improve our chances of deciphering the damn things. The sequence may be as important as the individual spectral pattern of each book."

We crossed the pagoda's immense flagstone floor, circling to the left of the stairway spiraling upward to the energy globes in the iron "chandelier." Our footfalls echoed, and our breaths came as loud in our ears as if we were wearing oxygen masks.

The wall of eyebooks glowed uncannily. It prickled with the two or three thousand glinting rods protruding like brush bristles toward us, each rod supporting a sequence of eyebooks secured by a small, ornately flanged wingnut. Elegy removed one of these fasteners and scooped an entire sequence of eyebooks off its rod. Then she bound them together with a piece of elastic and deposited them in a pocket on the thigh of her jumpsuit. The weight scarcely made the pocket sag.

"Leave the others alone," she said. "There's no reason to take any more than we absolutely need. So far we haven't proved ourselves worthy of the first six my father brought out with him.''

"Fine," I said. "What now?"

"I don't know. . . . Maybe we'd better ask *him*." Elegy gestured at the stairway twisting down from the pagoda's dome.

Descending the steps was an Asadi who, more than likely, had just witnessed our theft of the eyebooks. His appearance, seemingly from out of nowhere, was as heartstopping as the sudden self-manifestation of a ghost. Kretzoi, his hackles fanning out behind his head like a peacock's tail, assumed a belligerent bipedal stance.

*The Bachelor*, I thought: *It's none other than Chaney's Bachelor*.

At the bottom of the immense, looping staircase—which rose, as if without support, toward the inverted bowl of the dome—the Asadi paused and stared at us across the open flagstone flooring. Perched atop his left shoulder, shifting from foot to foot, its claws rhythmically digging, was a huri—a *real* huri. The huri's gathered wings appeared wrinkled and squamous, its body as moist and smooth as raw liver, its eyeless head as fleshy as a mushroom cap. It could not possibly see us, and yet it knew we were in the pagoda as certainly as did the Asadi whom I had already identified for myself as The Bachelor.

Elegy had made the same private intuitive leap. Extending her hand toward the Asadi, she spoke to it:

"You can see what we are. You've met another like us. We believe he's here—that other one whom we resemble." She passed her hand back and forth between herself and me, excluding Kretzoi.

The Bachelor merely stared, his eyes inanimate and grey.

"Egan Chaney," Elegy said more loudly. Understanding that she might be trying to bridge an unbridgeable chasm, Elegy conversed rapidly with Kretzoi in Ameslan and urged the primate to intercede for us.

Kretzoi obeyed. But as he approached The Bachelor, the huri grew more and more agitated, lifting its wings and expanding its tiny, oyster-colored chest. All the while it scrabbled back and forth between The Bachelor's shoulders. Its activity confounded and alarmed Kretzoi, who finally halted and began making hand signs that the huri's own unceasing movements seemed to render pointless.

The Bachelor wasn't Bojangles. We weren't going to bridge the chasm separating us with Ameslan or anything like it.

But Kretzoi persisted. Ignoring the huri's frantic dance of annoyance, he crept forward, hunkered, spoke with his hands, crept forward again, hunkered, and so on—until he was virtually genuflecting at The Bachelor's feet.

Kretzoi's last approach so intimidated the huri that it threw itself into the air and disappeared with almost insulting swiftness into the vault of the temple, somewhere high above the ring of energy globes.

Abandoned to his own devices, The Bachelor panicked. He cuffed Kretzoi glancingly across the snout and attempted to run over him—past the wall of eyebooks and down the eastern corridor of the pagoda. He failed because Kretzoi, after recoiling from the unexpected blow, ran him to ground just abreast of Elegy and me. Almost indistinguishable, the two of them rolled about in the mouth of the eastern corridor.

"Kretzoi!" Elegy barked, and before I could stop her she was straddling the two animals, shifting her feet to keep from being toppled and pulling determinedly on Kretzoi's mane.

I joined her, and we got them apart. The Bachelor—my knee in the hollow above his left hip, my hands pressing his face against the flagstones—lay trembling but acquiescent beneath me. Kretzoi, meanwhile, shook free of Elegy's angry grasp, retreated several meters into the corridor, and, moodily, began grooming himself.

"Damn," Elegy mumbled to herself. The murmurous "voices" of the pagoda disguised their source by frequently ceasing and then abruptly resuming. The place was alive, and we were intruders in its sanctuary. . . .

From out of nowhere the huri dove upon me in a long, erratic sweep. A wing tip brushed my hair, after which the beast wobbled away down the eastern corridor, executed an amazing midair turn, and came gliding back toward us. I fell across The Bachelor, saw Elegy drop to her knees, and watched the huri go teeter-tottering above us, only to fall to rest on the floor of the central chamber. Here it tiptoed about with its wings spread, ultrasonically berating us, emitting high-pitched echolocation pulses in order to define us in space.

Visually blind, the huri "saw" us in three dimensions. It did so by means of a continuous biosonic scan and a brain so sensitive to the reflections and reradiations of its high-frequency pulses that its lack of vision was no handicap at all. The huri, I felt sure, possessed a sophisticated bioholographic neurological complex that made Elegy, Kretzoi, and me as palpable to it as three blocks of stone under a sculptor's hands. Strutting cryptically and bombarding us with orientation pulses that we could neither see nor feel, the creature held us at bay.

Kretzoi, on all fours, made a threatening move toward the huri—but Elegy put up her hand to restrain him. Whispering, I explained that the blind huri was not blind at all. "It 'sees' your hand," I told Elegy. "It 'sees' Kretzoi poised to spring. We're each one of us a three-dimensional auditory image with frequency, amplitude, and phase."

Elegy lowered her hand.

"And the pulses the huri emits to create temporal and spatial holograms of us," I went on, still holding The Bachelor down, "may also be either signals to its fellows or commands to the living machinery of the pagoda. Maybe both."

"All right," said Elegy. "And what does that mean?"

I took my knee from The Bachelor's hip and eased myself to a standing position, thus releasing my prisoner. "I don't really know—but look up there."

The Bachelor lay immobile at my feet, even though I had let go of him. Meanwhile, the wide iron ring supporting the temple's energy globes began to descend through the center of the helical stairway. The globes themselves grew brighter, and the entire vast apparatus produced a choral humming sound as the ring descended. The torus appeared to be completely free-floating, perhaps with a mechanism for the gyroscopic negation of gravity at spin in its interior—a mechanism that might also have been responsible, I reflected, for the ring's strange humming. Just as the huri was no doubt responsible for its descent.

At last The Bachelor moved. He rolled over and got to his feet as gingerly as I had. Then he walked past Elegy toward the pagoda's central chamber, limping almost imperceptibly. Before he could reach the huri, however, the ring halted a little over two meters from the floor and hovered there like a gigantic tiara set with three enormous glowing jewels. A painful brightness illumined the chamber, and the huri danced spastically in its sheen.

Then a section of the floor began to move. A grating sound filled the pagoda, a protracted groan punctuated by several deafening clicks. The moving section of floor was circular, about two and a half times the diameter of the torus floating above it. It clocked to the right and kept moving clockwise until it had screwed itself free of the surrounding flagstones. Then, on a carven stone stem resembling an Asadi with four huge, blind faces, this circular block of flooring rose toward the hovering ring and received the ring's weight on the tripodal arrangement of its energy globes. The huri, who had risen with the floor section, sat on it just outside the ring of the chandelier, flapping its wings at us. Meanwhile, a terrible organic stench boiled up from the catacombs beneath the pagoda, as did a geyser of spreading heat and a noise like angels at war.

The hole in the floor was almost eight meters across, cut as if to permit an army to descend together underground, and the tetravisaged statue supporting the block of flooring had the girth of a good-sized tree. The pillar had been hewn from a carnelian-colored rock with the texture of granite. The eyes of the statue—the two pairs that I could see, at any rate—were nothing but empty sockets, as if someone had long ago removed the stones or picked away the intricate lapidary work filling them. A tier of stone steps commencing at the lip of the hole's northern hemisphere led into the abyss. Peering into the hole from several meters away, I could see that beneath its rim was a pedestal—a thick stone sheath—from which the Asadi statue had risen and into which it would once again sink when it came time for the great circular floor section to fall counterclockwise back into place.

The huri atop the elevated block of floor suddenly swooped down and affixed itself possessively to The Bachelor's mane. Immediately, The Bachelor's nervousness and uncertainty seemed to evaporate. As the huri tiptoed to a perch on his right shoulder, the Asadi turned calmly toward us.

"Egan Chaney," Elegy said again, a four-syllable litany. "You know where he is—don't you?"

The Bachelor's first response was a dead, grey stare. Then, pivoting, he strode to the lip of the hole and dropped one foot onto the first semicircular tier. He looked back at us in invitation, then descended several more steps and halted again.

"Let's go," Elegy urged Kretzoi and me.

"One of us stays behind," I said. "In fact, we'd probably be smart just to get the hell out of here."

"You stay, then."

"Make it Kretzoi and we're off."

Elegy looked at Kretzoi and gestured wearily toward the pagoda's tall, half-open door. "Wait out there for Jaafar," she said. "We'll be back as soon as we can, just as soon as we—" She stopped.

The Bachelor was gone. The warring angels underground beckoned.

As Kretzoi sidled obediently toward the door, casting accusatory, baffled glances our way, I touched Elegy's shoulder and led her toward the pit. Then, beneath the massive elevated wheel of the floor, we went apprehensively down the tier of steps. A monster with four faces watched us with a cold eyeless gaze. . . .

\*

The steps formed a horseshoe—an inverted, steeply terraced U—against the northern half of the pit. This horseshoe arrangement persisted to a depth of about four meters, whereupon we could continue to descend only by walking along the bottommost tier until we had reached a narrow set of steps corkscrewing widdershins downward from the eastern base of the U.

Fortunately, we had The Bachelor going before us as a guide and enough pale, phosphorescent light to see him. Still, the going was hazardous, and I kept imagining that the wheel overhead was about to click stridently, rotate counterclockwise atop the countenances of the blind Asadi effigy, and grind into place like a colossal manhole cover, sealing us beneath the pagoda forever. That didn't happen, but each time I looked back up the well of the pit, the faces of the statue appeared to be turning and I was startled and discomfited anew—until I reminded myself that our own steady widdershins descent was responsible for the statue's apparent motion.

More agile than I, Elegy now had the lead. I kept my hand on her shoulder and squinted into the abyss, whose contours and dimensions were perpetually changing—at first because the pit opened out into a vast Plutonian cavern, and then because the stone steps gave way to smooth concrete platforms that had been reinforced with steel or titanium. The Bachelor, his huri settled comfortably on his right shoulder, was negotiating the fifth or six platform beneath ours. I gripped Elegy's shoulder hard and indicated that I wanted to sit down. The heat had caused me to sweat through my clinging undergarment, and a bout of nausea seemed imminent.

"We'll lose him," Elegy protested, peering downward—but she let me squat gracelessly at her side and put my head between my knees in an attempt to stave off my queasiness. Given five minutes, the treatment worked. I raised my head and tried to wipe the sweat from my face with the sleeve of my jumpsuit.

"It's not The Bachelor we've lost," I told Elegy. "It's the huri—the huri's navigating for him, sending out ultrasonic pulses and constructing temporal and spatial holograms from their feedback."

"We've lost the huri, then. The result's the same." Elegy sat down beside me on the smooth cantilevered platform and began idly to rub my back. "You're drenched through," she informed me, removing her hand to pick fastidiously at the cloth of her own jumpsuit. "So am I, for that matter."

"They won't leave us up here," I said. "Otherwise, they'd have never admitted us in the first place."

"They?"

"Not The Bachelor and the huri. The huri and all its catacombpent relatives, that's the 'they' I'm talking about."

Elegy didn't reply. As we sat in the high, hot dark, the sound of warring angels we had heard in the pagoda suddenly reasserted itself, and there wheeled before us in the divided cavern a vast, smoky cloud of huri—thousands upon thousands of them convoluting in the air in a shape reminiscent of a single prodigious member of the species, a superorganism duplicating on an Olympian scale the morphology and movements of its constituent organisms. Like herrings or mackerals, the huri were *schooling*, and the superorganism they made had all the crude, airborne agility of The Bachelor's own huri. It wheeled and plunged with such a thunderclapping of wings that Elegy and I were left dumbfounded when a banking movement at our left hands carried the school altogether out of sight. The huri were making a low circuit of the catacombs, but the stone column at our backs prevented our observing the entire orbit. The wind in the creatures' wake was the wind from a rotting forge bellows.

"Dear God," Elegy said.

"That's the 'they' I meant. Maybe we'd do better, though, to refer to the whole stinkin' crew as 'it'—one vast body, one vast mind."

"And The Bachelor's huri?"

"It's a monitor, a receptor/transmitter of the huri overmind. That's what each one of the creatures is, separated from the transcendent superorganism."

"Ben, how the hell can you suppose they're anything but some kind of hairless alien chiropteran? That was a flock of Denebolan bats that just flew by, not a great sentient cloud worthy of worship."

"What makes you so sure? Left-brain logic?"

Elegy put her hand on my sweat-drenched back and held it there. She looked at me appraisingly, not without compassion. "Do you want to get out of here, Ben? I'll go with you if you do—and I'm not just looking for an excuse to abandon this nasty business, either."

"Not now, Elegy. We're committed."

She kissed me on the cheek, then ran her tongue through the stubble spiculing my jaw. 'You're my salt lick," she whispered, and we both burst out laughing.

I stood, took Elegy's hand, and pulled her to her feet. Then she preceded me down the next three staggered platforms. As we got lower, the dimensions and the weird topographic furnishings of the chamber revealed themselves with striking clarity. Either our eyes had adjusted or the light beneath us had grown appreciably stronger during our descent. In either case, we saw that the chamber to the east was divided by honeycombed grids or walls of living amethyst like the windows in the pagoda. These grids or walls, laid out at varying angles to one another, were at least twice as tall as a full-grown Asadi, and they comprised an enormous labyrinth in the eastern half of the subterranean chamber. Although I had no way of knowing, I supposed that a similar labyrinth dominated the western half of the chamber as well.

As we stared down, the huri superorganism wheeled ventrally into view above our right shoulders—a huri thunderhead crackling with pale phosphorescence and stirring the slow, hot air. Its tremendous bulk scraped the chamber's ceiling, altering the very consistency of the light. Then it stooped and leveled out and rode like a bank of shredding black cirrocumulus toward the east, individual huri separating from the mass and gliding downward like grains of dark sleet. In fact, the superorganism—which kept reconstituting itself on a small scale as huri after huri broke free and plunged— sometimes seemed to be dropping not only living segments of itself but an erratic firefall of cinders.

"What in Christ's name is that?" Elegy cried.

At the moment, I wasn't absolutely sure. All I truly understood was that the superorganism was decaying before our eyes, hundreds of individual huri plummeting to hidden roosts in the labyrinth on the chamber floor. The cinders plummeting with them were . . . well, a special form of bioluminescence. The huri were defecating in concert. The grains of their excrement glowed because the huri sustained themselves on molds and fungi that glowed. Bioluminescence in, bioluminescence out. And if a degree of fire was lost in the digestive process, the huri absorbed it into themselves as a nutrient with brilliant side effects; namely, the hollow bones in their wings sometimes shone like gone-amok isotopes of plutonium.

Now, the wheeling superorganism, greatly diminished on our left, was sculling westward out of view.

I activated my radio: "Jaafar, can you hear me? Jaafar, can you hear me?" It seemed imperative to make contact with someone outside, even if he happened to be traversing great stretches of jungle in a Dragonfly. But Jaafar didn't respond.

"We're too far underground for that, Ben. Let's just hope he's able to *find* the pagoda—that it doesn't conceal itself as successfully again this morning as it's done these past six years."

"Maybe it won't. The huri control the pagoda, Elegy, and we've diverted their attention. They know we're here."

We gazed down. A good many of the honeycombed partitions constituting large sections of the labyrinth were draped with ruffled fungi or cottony spills of mold. These otherworldly thallophytes were antique gold, pale blue, death's-head white, and they shone with a radiant faintness that gave the whole scene a faery unreality. Moreover, broad compartments of the labyrinth were mounded with hills of lambent guano. Gardens of bioluminescent waste, landscaped and adorned with statuary.

We continued downward, dropping from platform to platform. The cavern's temperature dropped with us, and the noise of beating wings eventually ceased. Because the huri had disappeared into the labyrinth's myriad plastic dovecotes, a terrible silence and stillness descended upon their fetid underworld.

At last Elegy and I were down. The floor of the catacombs was aglow with the ghostly luminescence of the fungi and the amethyst walls. The column of stairs, scaffolds, and platforms by which we had reached the floor, however, disappeared into utter blackness above us. We were too far down to see its summit.

The Bachelor awaited us. He stood in the mouth of a nearby corridor, the huri riding his shoulder with its wings spread and its chest outthrown.

# CHAPTER EIGHTEEN

# Chrysalis

The corridor was wide enough to accommodate four columns of Asadi marching abreast. How long had it been since that many Asadi—or, more likely, proto-Asadi—had tramped these hidden corridors? Ages, certainly.

No thicker than a human hand span, the amethyst walls were just lucid enough to reveal inside them eccentric arrangements of tubes, lights, circuitry. A few walls were empty of anything but swirling glass, a few were packed with arcane equipment—but most alternated areas of empty crystal with areas of tightly organized and geometrically complex "plumbing." My only guess about the functions of the walls, aside from their utility as dividers, was that they comprised a sophisticated but far-from-compact computer network, with tie-ins to the pagoda overhead, the thallophytes growing in their plastic honeycombs, and the huri nesting in their own specialized wall cells.

The sections of wall not containing equipment were capable of subtly deforming and warping: Sometimes elongated or oblate "windows" opened in the glass, migrated a brief distance, and then closed up again. These short-lived windows permitted Elegy and me to see other parts of the labyrinth: nesting huri, pools of algae- and diatom-infested water, mossy fungi and molds, glowing heaps of guano.

Sometimes the walls themselves opened out to reveal these things. At one point, in fact, Elegy and I found ourselves in a doorway fronting the wide expanse of a guano garden. The chamber contained a number of vaguely humanoid figures—

statues, you had to call them—fashioned from the long-since-desiccated droppings of the huri.

Most of these statues were better than half buried in the accumulated muck of millennia, only a torso or a snout or a raised arm visible above the hellishly radiant mounds. One or two figures, however, stood atop the slag, their bodies perfect but for the warts and tubercles of fairly recent fecal bombardments. All of the statues in the garden were of Asadi. Among them were seven or eight huri hobbling about almost aimlessly.

Elegy tried to pull me down the corridor after The Bachelor, but I resisted.

"Damn it, Ben, come on. You can't stay here."

I shook her hand from my arm and stared into the garden, fascinated by the scene, curious about the statues. When the huri in the compound became collectively aware of our presence, Elegy renewed her efforts to rouse me.

"If you make me," she threatened, whispering, "I'll leave you here." I didn't respond. "All right—keep the wretched little demons for your own, Ben. I've got more pressing things to do."

A moment later Elegy abandoned me in disgust and followed The Bachelor.

The huri in the garden congregated on a mound directly opposite me. Treading one another's backs, knocking wings, and scratching at the hardened guano underfoot, they eventually settled into an arrangement that satisfied them all. Then they began fusillading me with echolocation pulses of such pitch and force I could actually *feel* them. Now I wanted to escape, to rejoin Elegy—but that option no longer remained. The huri's continuous, high-pitched piping had paralyzed me. Even though I tried, I was unable to move.

Breaking away the guano crust to get at the pliable matter beneath, the huri began to shape a simulacrum of Thomas Benedict. In less than five minutes they had lifted a life-sized, three-dimensional effigy of me out of their own fluorescing waste, positioning it so that my double and I stood face to face—a feat that required a one-hundred-eighty-degree transposition of the biohologramic data they were receiving from their cerebral sonar. The statue stood higher than I did—it lacked identifying detail—but even in my paralysis I knew that it was meant to be me, and I felt that the huri had stolen some of my private essence in erecting it. . . .

Then the fusillade of ultrasonic pulses ceased, my psycho-motor cortices were returned to me, and the huri scrambled off across the mounds in different directions. While I stood there numbly collecting my wits, they rose into the air and powered themselves over the deliquescing walls.

I turned to look in the direction Elegy had disappeared. The corridor ahead of me branched in an off-center V, and, frustrated, I murmured an expletive under my breath.

Aloud I cried, "*Elegy!*"

The entire subterranean complex rang. In answer, only a few moments later, a huri came swooping at me through the corridor from the right-hand branch of the fork. I threw up an arm to shield myself and pitched sidelong to the floor, which was as smooth and dark as obsidian. The huri, however, skimmed my head and landed atop the amethyst wall behind me. Then it skittered along the top of this wall toward the fork in the corridor, fluttered across the opening to the wall beyond, and resumed its tightrope walking. In this fashion it led me away from the compound in which several of its fellows had just memorialized me in bioluminescent shit.

This was The Bachelor's huri, I realized, and it had come to reunite me with Elegy. We soon passed an entire wall of dovecotes in which other huri nestled like rubbery, headless fetuses. Only a short while before, they had been wheeling overhead in a noisy cloud.

We also passed a section of honeycombed wall on which three or four wakeful huri were grazing. Like monstrous houseflies, they walked the vertical plane of the wall, scissoring with their beaks at a glowing tapestry of woolly gold fungus. Several empty cells in the wall revealed complicated networks of plastic tubing which I assumed to be conveyors of water and nutrients. The Bachelor's huri hopped single-mindedly along the wall, pausing occasionally to riddle me with ultrasonic birdshot. Finally, it lifted and flew again, disappearing over a wall into an open area containing a subterranean lagoon of considerable size.

I stumbled into this clearing and found Elegy and The Bachelor standing like old friends by the water's edge.

The surface of the lagoon was oily-seeming, but diatomaceous plants floated at various levels in the water, illuminating it to a depth of at least two or three meters. Far out on the lagoon, drifting facedown like alien water hyacinths, was a pair of huri. Apparently they were drinking.

Meanwhile, The Bachelor's huri settled out of the air onto his shoulder and Elegy came forward to embrace me.

"You get to look as long as you wanted?" she asked me.

"Longer," I said, and as The Bachelor led us along the margin of the lagoon I explained to her what had happened.

"But why did they do that?" Elegy wanted to know. "What possible purpose could a statue like that serve?"

"Maybe the huri are all sculptors manqué. —Hell, I don't know, Elegy. It's possible they were identifying me spatially and temporally for the benefit of their sleeping relatives. Only a few stay awake at a time, it seems, and when they're not functioning together as a single mind, individual 'brain cells'—individual huri, that is—may have to record intrusions for those who'll awake later."

"How does one of their statues identify an intruder temporally?"

"By its position in one of the guano gardens, I guess. Haven't you ever heard of archaeological strata? The deeper you go, the further back in time are the antiquities you unearth. A statue that's completely exposed is a recent statue."

"They didn't make a statue of *me*, Ben."

"You stayed with The Bachelor. You didn't give 'em a chance to triangulate on you. What else can I say? I can't even *pretend* to understand everything we've encountered down here."

We walked in silence beside the coruscating waters until, narrowing, they extended a snaky arm into a corridor bounded by neither a grid of dovecotes nor a wall of amethyst. The partitions here were ramparts of natural limestone, grey-green and wet-looking in the reflected sheen of the water. The Bachelor hugged the right-hand wall, and Elegy preceded me along this slender pathway.

After a time, the lagoon—or, better, its armlike tributary—died in a tiny delta where so many diatoms and their snowflake skeletons had washed up that the glow was stark and uncanny. Beyond this delta, straight ahead of us, was what appeared to be another guano compound. But immediately before it, partially blocking the opening, stood a biosonically engineered sculpture that grabbed our attention by stilling our hearts. The statue's subject was a human being.

"That's my father," Elegy whispered.

I recognized it as Egan Chaney, too, although in retrospect

I'm not sure how. Like the huri's recent sculpture of me, this one lacked individualizing detail. The body appeared clothed, but the drape of the clothing was merely suggested. The face had features, but the bioluminescence of the waste matter comprising the statue blurred and obscured them.

Maybe it was the set of the bearded jaw or the martial rigidity of the posture that identified the statue for us. Or maybe it was our knowledge that it couldn't be anyone *but* Egan Chaney.

A trail of diatoms and murky algal weeds to the base of the statue told us that lunar tides regularly moved the lagoon waters down here—without ever pulling them close enough to erode the statue itself.

Elegy ran to the thing and shoved it in the chest. As if it had been made at least partially of carbonized sugar, it crumbled and broke apart, its torso and arms cascading down in a cinder storm. This dismemberment accomplished, Elegy kicked at the upright stumps of the statue's legs. They, too, shattered and went whirling across the floor.

Unmoved by Elegy's violent display, The Bachelor stood to one side, his back still against the right-hand rampart of limestone. The huri, too, appeared indifferent, almost comatose atop The Bachelor's head.

Elegy threw back her head and breathed an audible sigh of relief. "I was afraid," she began, "that it might literally be my father—his corpse, you know, plastered over with huri crap." She raised her head and swung a foot across the debris. "It wasn't, though. You can see it wasn't. Not unless they crystallized his remains."

"He's in there, Elegy." I nodded toward the compound. "That's why they brought us this far—not to show us another biosonic sculpture."

Queasy and frightened, I entered the little compound ahead of Elegy and found that it was not another guano dump at all. Instead, it was both a crypt and an incubator. In its center . . . well, my first impression was of a mummy canted from the floor at a forty-five-degree angle in a macramé hammock of glistening silk.

I stared at the thing. "Your father, Elegy—not that other, but this." She was at my shoulder. We both stared.

A great fan of milky silk filled the chamber, gently cradling Egan Chaney's chrysalis. The threads at the top of the fan disappeared into, or fused molecularly with, the amethyst wall at the rear of the chamber; the threads converging below the chrysalis's feet ran tautly into a pit of dark but glittering water that may well have fed the lagoon behind us. Water or some more syrupy fluid oozed down the wall behind the chrysalis, disappearing noiselessly into the gravelike pit above which the hammock was suspended. Guy lines of silk—they resembled wings—supported the body on either side, running to left and right of the hammock and seeming almost to pass directly through the natural limestone of the compound. Meanwhile, beads of viscous water trembled in procession down the lines to the chrysalis's head and body.

"We've got to get him down, Ben!" Elegy broke free of me and ducked beneath the webbing to the left of the pit. She looked like a shuttle weaving among a fan of milky threads. When she had finally reached her father's head, she took a knife from her belt and leaned purposefully out over the hammock.

"You're liable to kill him!" I cried. "That's been his life-support system for God knows how long!"

Elegy's face was acrawl with reflections from the water. "He's as good as dead now, Ben. For whom or what is he living?" She began cutting at one of the support lines raying upward to the chamber's rear wall.

She wasn't thinking straight. If she did manage to cut her father loose, his chrysalis would plunge into the pit beneath him.

At this point The Bachelor's huri arrowed past me into the chamber and alighted on Elegy's father without stirring a single thread. Then it opened its wings and worked its beak in warning, frightening Elegy badly enough that she crouched back out of the creature's way. The Bachelor himself loitered nervously near the entrance to the compound.

"I want you to help me, Ben," said Elegy quietly, her eyes fixed on the huri as if it were a cobra preparing to strike.

"What do you want me to do?"

She beckoned with her knife hand.

Thinking it might be best to engage the huri on two fronts, I eased myself into the fan of silk on the right side of the pit and wove my way inward until I was crouching opposite Elegy. The huri turned to face me, turned back to keep Elegy in view, and set the entire hammock quivering in its lacework harness. The shrill piping noises the huri was now making were all too audible, brief but ear-splitting bursts of sound.

"Suppose the little bastard calls in reinforcements?" I asked Elegy in an even voice.

"That's something we're just going to have to chance. . . . I'm going to cut my father free of this, Ben—I'm going to midwife his resurrection."

Elegy thrust the knife viciously forward, nearly skewering the huri. It skittered up Egan Chaney's chest to his head, and Elegy lunged at it again, pulling back just in time to keep from falling. The huri flapped once and wove a miraculous zigzag to the top of the rear wall, where it sat facing inward, piping its fainter and fainter protests but recording our every move with pulses in the steep ultrasonic.

I stood, leaned forward, and steadied Egan Chaney's chrysalis. Elegy canted her knife blade and began digging at the cerements around her father's hips and bound hands. The silk—the extruded huri cable—comprising these wrappings was exceptionally tough; Elegy had to struggle to make a clean cut without plunging the knife into the body itself. At last, though, she made a neat incision and began peeling away the fiber around her father's right hand—not, oddly, in unending strings, but in scablike clumps that she lifted away easily and then dropped into the pit.

Beneath these silken scales was a thin bluish membrane, like a birth caul. Almost at once Elegy began scraping at the exposed membrane on the back of her father's hand. When a piece about two centimeters square bunched up in front of her knife blade, both she and I realized the membrane had either replaced her father's human skin or interpenetrated it to such a depth that the two were virtually indistinguishable. Black blood oozed from the scraped area, in which veins were now visible.

"It's impossible," Elegy said between her teeth, lifting her knife away. "They've fixed it so we can't unwrap him, they've fixed it so—"

Her voice broke, and with grimacing fury she flipped the knife into the pit. I worked my way around the foot of the tilted chrysalis to join her on the other side.

As I did, the huri dropped from the wall and balanced itself on Chaney's head. Soon it was peeling back scales of silk with its claws and transferring these to its ugly, scissoring mouth.

Elegy, seeing, started to shoo the creature away, but I restrained her, and in a few minutes the huri had uncovered her father's face. All that yet clung to his features was the bluish undercaul. We could see the man's nose, his stony beard, the sockets of his eyes. The huri tore a hole in the membrane where Chaney's mouth was supposed to be and put its beak to the hole. It flapped to keep from falling.

"Ben, goddamn you, let me go!" Elegy tried to wrench free, but I held her even more tightly. Our struggle swayed the cables around us. When she finally did escape me, the huri had returned to the top of the wall and her father was gargling a dark, syrupy liquid.

Obligated by the fear that Chaney would strangle, I brushed past her, got caught in the huri web, tore at it, then ducked beneath the clinging strands and pulled the hammock far enough over that the fluid in Chaney's mouth was able to spill into the pit. Digging with my forefinger at the viscous substance in his mouth, I held the hammock in this position until my shoulders ached and Chaney seemed to be completely drained.

This took several minutes, but Elegy joined me before I was finished and eased a little of the burden. Soon Chaney was breathing audibly, sucking the pale blue undercaul into his nostrils and then billowing it out again. With a fingernail I made a pair of gimlet holes in this membrane—Chaney's breathing grew regular, so systematic and sane that I half believed he had only been dozing in a peculiar sort of sleeping bag. I let go of the hammock and painfully straightened up.

Stunned by the sound of Chaney's breathing, we waited a long time. The Bachelor deserted us altogether, leaving his huri as sentinel atop the wall. We didn't miss him because we had other things on our mind.

"Go ahead," I urged Elegy. "Talk to him."

She crouched beside the chrysalis again and reached out to touch it with her right hand. "Father," she said, "it's Elegy. It's your daughter—I've come all this way to find you."

There was a brief hitch in Chaney's breathing, then the same, even, miraculous rhythm as before. After glancing bemusedly at me, Elegy tried again, repeating her name several times and assuring the transfigured man that she was actually beside him. Nothing. If Chaney was alive, he seemed alive beyond reach.

"Do you think he can hear?" Elegy asked me. "Maybe the caul's a hindrance, maybe that syrup's gumming up his inner ears."

"He's already heard you, Elegy."

"But he's not responding. He might as well be dead." She dropped her arm, pivoted toward me on the balls of her feet. Then her eyes flared and she exclaimed, "Like hell!

"*I'm* the problem, Ben. I'm too far removed from him in time and even in emotional attachment to establish my reality. He's in a subterranean vault beneath an Asadi temple on BoskVeld, and the daughter whom he last saw eleven years ago in a South American rain forest is trying desperately to kiss him awake." She slapped her forehead with the heel of her hand, not for emphasis but to rebuke herself for what she considered her stupidity. "At best, he's got to think me a dream, a disembodied voice without a single referent in the long dream of his adult life—before the Asadi did this to him."

"You think I'll fare better than you have?"

"Try, Ben. You were his only friend in Frasierville—in the Third Expedition's base camp, I mean. His last memories of human contact have to include you prominently. So, yes, you've got to give it a try."

Elegy and I exchanged places. As she had done before me, I extended a hand and touched Egan Chaney's shoulder. Then, not believing in my power to resurrect Chaney where Elegy had already failed, I said, "Egan, this is Thomas Benedict. I'm here with you beneath the Asadi temple."

Again, the telltale hitch in the transfigured man's breathing, a movement of the mouth. But no other response.

I repeated my name. I told Chaney what had happened to him in the Wild six years ago. I rehearsed for him the story of his disappearance from base camp. I narrated a little of Frasierville's recent history. I informed him that his daughter had indeed come all the way to BoskVeld from Dar es Salaam just to find him. I said that she was beside me at this moment. Then I repeated my stupid self-introduction and began the history lesson all over again—

Whereupon the man in the silken chrysalis murmured, "Ben." One word. Like his own body, it had an alien husk on it, this word, and it trembled in the air.

I leaned toward him. "Yes, it's Ben. You've been gone from us a long time. Do you remember where you are?"

Elegy's hands gripped my shoulders from behind, and I glanced up to see her scrutinizing the chrysalis's inhuman head for some evidence of the beloved face she recalled from her girlhood. But time, distance, and a terrible metamorphosis had interposed many veils between that face and the face before her now, and she seemed to be having trouble making the connection.

"Do you remember where you are?" I repeated.

We waited. Finally, the thing that had been Egan Chaney murmured another word, one cryptic word: "Halfway."

"Halfway?" I echoed him inanely. "Tell us what you mean, Egan."

"And I'll never," he confessed, almost before I had finished speaking. "Get. The remainder. Of the way."

At my ear Elegy whispered, "He's talking about his physiological condition. He's trying to say that his alien metamorphosis hasn't taken. He's halfway between his humanity and some other state."

I took Elegy's cue: "Egan, who did this to you? What were they trying to do? What went wrong?"

"You're going too fast," Elegy admonished me.

But Chaney's mind processed the questions in order, and his lips shaped the answers: "The huri did this. Through The Bachelor. They wanted to make"—Chaney's tongue, black in his mouth, licked at the tatters of caul surrounding it—"an Ur'sadi. Of me," he finally managed. "They wanted. To redeem the Asadi. Through a return to their past." Another long pause. "My metamorphosis. Into one of their ancestors. Was supposed. To do the trick. Everything. Went wrong."

"It was The Bachelor who strung you up like this?"

The black tip of Chaney's tongue protruded briefly, like a lizard's head emerging from a hole. "Paralysis. Came first. The huri did that. They—"

"They did something to the psychomotor areas of your brain," I said, attempting to aid him. "They jammed those areas with ultrasonic pulses."

"But they didn't. Steal my consciousness." His tongue made a leisurely circuit around his mouth, then disappeared again. "How long. Has it been." There was no note of interrogation in the words.

"Six years," I told him again.

"Forever," his voice corrected me. "Gestating forever. They won't. Let me abort."

Suddenly I was crying. The tears flowed copiously, and I let them come. "After the paralysis," I said, "you were bound and strung up?"

"It took. Forever. I was done. In stages. My face. Went

last. But always." The inevitable pause, lengthening painfully
until he managed in one burst: "But always I *knew*."

This final word was Chaney's first to convey the weight of
any real inflection or emphasis, and its effect on Elegy was
immediate. "We've got to get him out of this shithole!" she
exclaimed, digging her fingers into my collar bones. "We've
got to cut him down and carry him out!"

The man in the chrysalis murmured, "Who."

"Your daughter, Egan. I've told you about her already. She
came all this way to find you."

"Here."

I wiped my eyes, then tilted my head back to look at Elegy.
It took us both a moment to realize that that single word was a
question.

"Yes, I'm here," Elegy said quietly.

"Wrong sound," the voice from Chaney's mouth contradicted her. "It's a fever. That gives you. The lie." And, a
moment later: "My body's. Burning. From inside out."

"You're not delirious," Elegy insisted, close to either anger
or a crippling pathos. "I'm a grown woman. I've come a
long, long road, and I'm standing here beside you, Father."

The black tongue tip made its customary journey around
Chaney's mouth. "I'm stranded. Halfway. They detected in
me. Intelligence. Like that of their Ur'sadi symbionts. Who
brought them here." The man seemed to be warming up,
gaining fluency. "They also liked my blood. Found it compatible to their needs. But later it was somehow. Wrong. I'm
not sure how. Too much like that of the protohominids. From
whom we evolved."

Elegy seemed to be waiting for him to return to the subject
of her presence, but Chaney had either forgotten the matter or
else deliberately set it aside.

"Who told you these things?" I asked. "How do you know
them?"

"The huri. I hear. In the ultrasonic registers. That happened early. Afterward they schooled me. In the semantic
distinctions. Among the various pulses. I can hear and interpret. At all meaningful frequencies. Beyond a single
megacycle. It's a language. I couldn't hear before."

"Do the huri communicate ultrasonically with the Asadi?"

Chaney's voice was definitely shedding its huskiness, as if
the activity of speaking aloud were loosening his vocal cords.
"Not so well as they used to. With their Ur'sadi ancestors.

Each of the ultrasonic pulses. Corresponds to a color. If you can interpret huri. You can also interpret. The Ur'sadi spectral language.''

Vaguely chagrined that I kept grilling him even as the horror of his transfiguration drew my stinging tears, I asked, "The eyebooks, Egan? What about them?"

"Eyebooks," Chaney acknowledged. "If I could see one. I could read it. The colors are all. In my head. The huri put them there. But I'm halfway, Ben, and I'm stranded.''

"What went wrong?" Elegy suddenly asked. "What exactly?''

"It's the fever giving you the lie," her father responded enigmatically. "I'm neither fish nor fowl. No huri savior. The huri have intelligence. Only in the aggregate. It's taken them forever. To understand I'm not their savior. Nor are any of us." Chaney licked his lips. "Being what we are." Then, with a moan, he fell back into himself.

"Father!" Elegy cried, not in desperation but in an attempt to recall him to the present.

I spoke Chaney's Christian name a couple of times, but finally decided he was recycling emotionally and physically. In much the way that I had let the huri's viscous, metabolic antifreeze spill from his mouth, our brief colloquy with Chaney had also drained him. And so, for the moment, we let Elegy's father go. . . .

# CHAPTER NINETEEN

# Parturition

That was not a time of clear thinking for me. We had found Egan Chaney alive, but changed and apparently unrecoverable. The huri had attempted to transform him in the vain, perhaps even idiot, hope of recreating a specimen of the Asadi's ancient forebears, with whom, eons in the past, they had come to BoskVeld as symbiotic fellow travelers. In fact, the superorganism that the huri comprised may have been the motivating force behind that interstellar migration. They were manipulators and parasites, tiny slavemasters who fed on their chattels' bodies and minds. The Ur'sadi had been exemplars of intelligence, but the huri superorganism had used the individuals of that departed hominoid race as a Kommgalen uses the instruments of his surgery—as physical extensions of the will. Just such extensions of an external will had been the Ur'sadi in the motivational grip of the huri—except that the Ur'sadi were living creatures with living, if ultrasonically subverted, wills of their own.

Having small bodies and only rudimentary hands, the huri had evolved a joint consciousness dependent not on any sort of inexplicable psychic or telepathic communion, but on a "language" of high-frequency pulses precisely attuned to the thermal variations arising from the Ur'sadi's private spectral displays. Perhaps the huri had once been the pets, or the blind gyrfalcons, or the totemic court animals of Ur'sadi masters. If they had, the huri had gradually appropriated the language of their masters—albeit in the medium of sound rather than light—so that ultimately they were able to unite as a single consciousness and enslave the very species that had first either enslaved or domesticated them. A turnabout of no mean proportions, but one that seemed to be indicated by everything Elegy and I had experienced over the last several hours.

The breakdown in the ascendancy of the huri had come long after the migration to BoskVeld from a home world still unknown to us. Their power was first crippled when they permitted the Ur'sadi to engineer genetic changes in their eyes and bloodstreams to combat the quirkish solar activity of Denebola. The huri permitted these changes in order to insure the survival of their hosts, their instruments—but once the Ur'sadi had altered their blood, ostensibly to regulate the production of lymph cells as a defense against radiation-induced diseases, the huri found themselves sickening and occasionally even dying. They fed not only on the thallophytes imported from their home world (a planet long since engulfed by a solar catastrophe of its own), but also—periodically—on Ur'sadi blood; the change in its composition, although not technically of a basic chemically nature, was enough to incapacitate large numbers of the huri who fed upon it.

When the Ur'sadi whose eyes were newly capable of photosynthesis began fleeing into BoskVeld's jungles, as much to escape the bemused and wounded huri as to separate themselves from their progenitors, the breakdown in huri control reached a critical point of no return: The enslaver/enslaved relationship that had existed for ages between the two species finally began to move toward total collapse.

. The huri depended a great deal on the centralization of the host population to maintain their control; and the Ur'sadi dispersal, which in their weakness the huri were unable to prevent, threatened to sabotage the principal unifying element of their transcendent consciousness. The huri themselves had to disperse. Most of them went after the fleeing renegades, into the jungles, where they were eventually able to regain a measure of control and so influence the construction of huge temple-memorials. These they had built against the day when the Ur'sadi inevitably found the means to abandon them. They foresaw their abandonment even as they struggled to prevent it. The grandeur of the wilderness pagodas, in fact, was a concession to the Ur'sadi spirit they had bridled for so long with ultrasonic reins. The huri kept control just long enough to get three or four of these structures built, whereupon the photosynthesizing Ur'sadi, rekindling the fires of their own extinguished wills, broke free and set themselves on a devolutionary course none of them could have predicted.

Meanwhile, the Ur'sadi in their original veldt settlement prepared to pull up stakes and leave. They had cast off the huri yoke by means of the self-protective alteration of their blood and the creation of a photosynthesizing subspecies of themselves. The huri superorganism, believing its future must lie with those Ur'sadi altered to manufacture food from Denebolan sunlight, opted to follow the defectors. That decision both freed the original Ur'sadi and tormented them, for they feared a reimposition of the huri yoke and deplored the continued captivity of their altered children. They couldn't leave BoskVeld until they had taken care of these matters. Relying on sporadic spy reports about the monumental building projects in the Wild, exercising an inhuman patience, and in several instances even lending their physical and technological aid, they awaited the completion of the temples. After the huri took up residence in the completed pagodas, the Ur'sadi's photosynthesizing offspring dispersed again, this time into the jungles.

Only then did the Ur'sadi act. They razed their own settlement on the veldt—a *single* settlement, not many as Elegy had once conjectured—and mounted separate attacks on the wilderness pagodas. These forays were swift, comprehensive, and pretty much effective. Their purpose was to destroy the huri for all time, eradicate any vestige of their memory, and bequeath the planet in perpetuity to the neo-Ur'sadi tribes that had diffused through the Wild in quest of solitary fulfillments of their own.

But the huri had had their neo-Ur'sadi slaves equip the largest of these temples with light- and perception-polarizing minerals quarried from areas near the shores of Calyptra and then toted inland by small groups of porters ultrasonically programmed to resist detection. These materials came to only one site in the Wild (the one beneath which Elegy and I were huddled beside the transfigured form of her father), but they accumulated so slowly that several decades passed before the great amethystlike windows were precision ground, hoisted into their moorings, and activated so that the excavation and furnishing of the catacombs beneath the pagoda could proceed undetected, too. Thus, the largest of the wilderness temples disappeared one twilight midway through the huri's century-long building program. Although the temple was then conspicuous by its absence—once the Ur'sadi had *perceived* its absence—they eventually came to believe the huri had dismantled it for purposes of their own, perhaps because it was too damn *big* to be realized according to plan. In reality, then, the Ur'sadi attacks on the other huri pagodas in the Wild were little more than the demolition of enormous architectural decoys erected, adorned, and furnished for the sole purpose of focusing and thereby diffusing the Ur'sadi wrath.

After which, reasonably well pleased with themselves, the Ur'sadi fled to the stars. The huri remained underground, and the neo-Ur'sadi, at last almost completely free of their host role, began their melancholy decline toward the ritualized cannibalism and photoperiodically dictated life-style of the maned Asadi beasts they were to become. . . .

\*

Waiting for Chaney to come around again, crouched beside Elegy in the dark, I recited for her the complex chain of reasoning and deductive historiography you have just read. My purpose was at least as much to keep Elegy's mind off her father's unknowable agony as to sort out and illuminate the mysteries of an unknowable past.

"It makes a good story," Elegy said when I was finished. In the prison of iridescent cables raying out from Chaney's cocoon, she smiled at me. "Do you believe it, Ben?"

Telling it, I had almost come to. "The facts—"

"The facts are diverse and open to multiple interpretations," Elegy broke in. "Not only that, Ben, in many instances they're not facts at all, but suppositions arising from our bewilderment. They're seductive because we'd rather concoct an explanation than admit or live with our ignorance."

"Goddamn it, Elegy, who's getting analytical and superrational now? All I really wanted to do was—"

"It's enough for me that I've found my father."

Understanding that, I shut down the nagging little homunculus within me who wanted Elegy's gratitude. Nevertheless, I began to wonder what—exactly—we had found. Had Chaney really spoken to us already? Would he speak to us again? I was ready to leave.

Then, as if from the cavernous basement of his soul,

Chaney repeated, "Nor are any of us. Being what we are." He was surfacing at the place in his free-associational monologue where earlier he had chosen to go under.

Elegy and I stood up, silk cables taut across our arms and torsos where we leaned into them. The caul covering Chaney's head shimmered wetly, a thing both fascinating and painful to see.

A strange sound escaped Chaney. Then it came again, confounding us. We exchanged glances.

"He's laughing," I said.

"Laughing," Chaney acknowledged. "I'm laughing." His laughter was a metallic-sounding ratcheting that reminded me of a chain being dragged across a surface of tin or aluminum.

"Why are you laughing?" Elegy asked him.

"Eyebooks," Chaney said.

"The eyebooks," Elegy prompted. "I've got several with me. We took them from the great wall in the pagoda."

The torn membrane at Chaney's mouth fluttered. "The huri have told me. That most of them are garbage. The Ur'sadi programmed them. With epithets and fear. They knew for what. Those eyebooks were intended. And they released. To huri posterity. Only the hatred they felt. For their—" the final word was awhile in coming—"enslavers."

"If the Ur'sadi deprived their enslavers of knowledge," I reminded Chaney, "they also deprived their Asadi children of knowledge they might have recovered one day."

"Not so long as the huri themselves exist," Chaney responded with some fluency. "And they still exist. Don't they, Ben."

I looked to the top of the amethyst wall and saw The Bachelor's huri roosting there. It attended our colloquy without appearing to take any genuine interest in what we did or said.

"They continue to exert," Chaney was saying, "a kind of vampiric power. Over mute and feeble Asadi. Like The Bachelor. Like Eisen Zwei. Like how many previous chieftains. Since the Asadi began."

Chaney stopped, almost breathless, and his pause lengthened until it seemed I would again have a chance to fabricate and recite several chapters of Asadi history.

At last, though, Chaney picked up the dropped stitch himself: "The chieftain's huri terrifies his people. It recalls for them their cannibalism. Stirs memories of a nobler but

more troubled past. The huri brings the Asadi. At unpredict-
able intervals. To look at the standing remains of that past."
Chaney's tongue probed the membrane rimming his upper lip.
"Which is finally. Inescapable."

I touched the man's shoulder. "Are you saying the Asadi's
case is hopeless so long as there are huri alive on BoskVeld?"

"The Ur'sadi devolved. At least in part. To survive as an
independent species. The threat of future enslavement hangs
over them. Like a sword. And partially enslaves them. Now."

"And they did this to you," Elegy asked, "in hopes of en-
slaving you as they had once enslaved the ancient Ur'sadi?"

Chaney ignored his daughter's question. "Ben," he said. "I
want you. To uncover my eyes."

I hesitated, and Chaney, encysted and bound as he was,
registered my hesitation. His breathing altered subtly.

"I'll do it," Elegy said. She ducked beneath the several
silken lines between her and Chaney and popped up beside his
head. She had no knife now, only her hands and fingernails,
but she grasped the shelf of caul above her father's upper lip
and began peeling it carefully backward. This time, contrary
to her experience with the film over Chaney's hand, her effort
proved startlingly successful.

The skin beneath the caul was as smooth as volcanic glass,
blue-grey in the shifting light. Chaney's moustache and beard,
as if they had been sprayed with an ultramarine dye and
lacquered, revealed the same blue-grey glassiness.

"Does this hurt?" Elegy whispered.

"I. Don't. Feel. Anything."

As deliberately as the defusing of a bomb, the unveiling
continued, and when Elegy at last eased the caul backward
over Chaney's forehead, twisting it once and letting it dangle
down behind his bandaged skull, we saw a pair of opalescent
and nearly opaque lenses sunken into his face where his eyes
should have been. Insofar as they were visible, the human eyes
beneath these carapaces resembled tiny mouths whose lips
have been sewn together. Chaney was right: His transforma-
tion had not taken. The vivid botching of his eyes synopsized
and condemned the folly of the entire procedure. I blinked
and looked away.

"Father—"

"You can see," he managed, "how it didn't take."

Elegy was as distraught as I had ever seen her. Her cheeks
were wet. Her body trembled. She seemed to be discovering

unrecognized villainies in herself as well as fresh horrors in the manipulative genius of the huri.

"Father," she said, weeping.

And Chaney heartlessly inquired, "Who."

"Your daughter," I told him angrily. "A woman who has striven for eleven years to accomplish what we've accomplished today."

And with a clipped and brutal clarity Chaney said, "I. Have. No. Daughter."

Elegy didn't recoil from this emphatic disavowal. She kissed her father on his altered lips. "I love you," she murmured defiantly. "I've loved you for as long as it's been possible for me to love you. Since the beginning. I never stopped, not even when you didn't deserve it and apparently no longer wanted it. That's why I've put such implicit faith in you, even going so far as to manipulate others—like Ben here—to find you again. All this, Father, I've done out of love and a desire to redeem myself in your eyes."

"In my eyes," Chaney echoed her.

"You know exactly what I mean, even in this pitiable and distant state! Don't you! Don't you, Father?" Elegy pushed herself away from Chaney and grabbed a handful of the lines fanning out past us toward the limestone wall at our backs. These she bunched in her fists and yanked as she spoke: "You loved me once. You loved my mother once. You loved the Ituri pygmies whom none of us had any power to save. So you know. What I'm saying. Don't you. *Don't you?*"

"Elegy!" I grabbed her hands. "Stop it! You sound like you're mocking him!"

"He knows I'm here," Elegy declared, releasing the runners of bunched silk and wiping her face with the back of her hand.

"I. Know. You're. Here." The vibration of the chrysalis imparted a weird tremelo to Chaney's words.

Elegy knelt again beside the pit.

"I have no daughter," Chaney said. "Unless." The qualifier hung in the air like a scimitar, poised.

"Unless what?" she asked him.

"Unless she redeems herself." The pottery glaze over Chaney's features appeared to crack, the oddly human expression beneath it warping to betray a sense of unspeakable loss. "My eyes—blind or sighted—are of no consequence anymore." His tone was now almost conversational. "The

Japurá business broke me. And the Asadi. The Asadi put me under."

"What do you want me to do?"

"I want you to kill me, Elegy." A breath so deep it was almost a moan. "That's why they led you down here."

"To have us kill you?" Elegy exclaimed incredulously.

"The huri superorganism doesn't want. My death. On its conscience. Or on the debit side of its ledger. Of interspecies relationships." Chaney's face was beginning to look human, despite the eyes. "Maybe it's a karmic reluctance on their part. But I'm dying. And they don't want to hasten my death. For fear of having to shoulder." Deep breath. "The blame."

"We'll get you out of here," Elegy said.

"No use. You can see I'm unredeemable. Unless."

"Unless I redeem you?"

"By redeeming yourself." Deep breath. "With your love."

Elegy twisted toward me in the cables and put her hands on my chest. "I want you to get out of here." She was pallid. In the same way your knuckles whiten when you clench something firmly, her pallor arose from resolution.

"He's trying to blackmail you," I told her. "You can't let yourself be swayed by anything he tells you know. Look at him."

"He's forgiving me. And himself, too. For the way he screwed up our lives after the Japurá Episode."

"By letting you kill him?"

Elegy put her cold hands on my face and thrust my head back so that her eyes could laser mine with her resolve. "Are you capable of understanding what's happening here, Ben? Maybe you are. If you are, you'll let me do what I've come all this way to do. If you aren't . . . well, you're going to have to kill me to keep me from this."

"Maybe we *could* get him out," I protested. "That's what you yourself had in mind until he started this insidious love-me, kill-me business."

"Just how are we going to get him out? I wasn't considering how, or what for, and neither are you. Look back that way, Ben." Elegy pointed over the forward wall of the compound into the eerie gloom of the catacombs, at the immense central column by which we had descended from the pagoda. "Do you really think we can carry my father back up that thing, Ben? Just the two of us?"

That central column-cum-stairway was a landmark of

towering prominence, visible despite the gloom shrouding its highest reaches. It climbed upward better than half a kilometer through the dark. We would never get Chaney up its switchbacking scaffolds and into the light of the day. If we did get him up, and if the Komm-galens in Frasierville somehow managed to prolong his life, he would be something less than either a human being or an Asadi.

Still, with help, Elegy and I might be able to manage that otherwise unlikely mission.

And the white-blue beam of an emergency torch, probing the catacombs from a set of scaffolds halfway up the column, suggested that help was reasonably close to hand. Jaafar had entered the pagoda and descended into the pit comprising the huri sanctuary.

"Jaafar's coming," I said, "and that gives us a chance."

Elegy shook her head. "That isn't the point, Ben. Maybe the three of us could lick the *how* of getting my father out, but the *what for*—Ben, you haven't even addressed that!" She struck me in the chest hard enough to make my breastbone sting. "It's *my* grant, Ben. It's *my* father. And it's *my* decision. Leave me alone with him for five minutes. Go. Right now. Or don't ever expect to own a jot of my regard again."

"That's blackmail, too, Elegy—virtually the same kind your daddy's working on you."

"Interpret it however you like. If you really think you're right, you'll be able to live with my contempt. But if you're interfering with me now to establish a sense of your own authority, or to worry aloud some abstract notion of higher morality, well, you'll deserve what you get. Worse yet, Ben, you'll know it."

I swore at her. "Get out of here," Elegy said evenly. "Wait for Jaafar at the base of the column. I'll join you there as soon as I'm finished."

I swore again, ritually. Then, obeying her, I duckwalked beneath the chrysalis's support lines and headed for the opening at the front of the compound. When I glanced back, Elegy was crouched beside her father's head like a worshiper in the tomb of some Egyptian or Mesoamerican god-king, her deity's face masked in tarnished bronze and lapis lazuli, the mummy itself winged in silk like an angel.

Curiously vivid and affecting, the scene stayed in my vision even as I negotiated my way past the subterranean lagoon, the huri dovecotes, the walls festooned with molds, the guano compounds, and all the oozing amethyst dividers of the labyrinth. The memory clung like a burr. I couldn't shake it. By the time I reached the base of the column I was trembling uncontrollably. Half in awe of the tears streaming down my face and beading in my eyelashes, I eased myself cross-legged to the floor and waited.

It felt astonishingly good to cry—even if, astonishingly, it hurt like nothing else I had ever known.

# CHAPTER TWENTY ≡≡≡

# Transfigured Lives

"*Dr. Benedict,*" droned a voice in my ear. "*Dr. Benedict, sir.*"

It was Jaafar, on his throat radio, perched on a platform high above me, for our connection was reestablished now that we inhabited the same volume of space. I hadn't thought to call him before, nor, apparently, had he remembered the radio until better than halfway down the chamber's central tower. Elegy, I assumed, was too busy, too preoccupied, to respond, and I knew that the only decent thing to do was to tell Jaafar to stay put until she and I could join him aloft. Otherwise, he would make the trip down for nothing. It took me a few moments to compose myself, but I finally activated my radio and did the decent thing.

"*Please, Dr. Benedict, what business is Civ Cather about?*"

"I'm not sure, Jaafar. We'll have to wait until she gets ready to come back and tell us. Just sit tight for a while."

"*There's an Asadi ahead of me, sir. It led me down here.*"

"You mean Kretzoi, don't you? Surely you're able to tell the difference between Kretzoi and a real Asadi by now."

Jaafar waited three or four beats before responding. "*Yes, sir. By now I'm capable in that way. This is not Kretzoi who leads me. It's an Asadi, with empty eyes and a —how do you call it?—a ratty mane.*"

"The Bachelor!" I radioed in surprise. "Where's Kretzoi, then? You saw him, didn't you?"

"*Oh, yes, sir. He's with the helicraft. I used him to point me to my landing in front of the pagoda.*"

"You were able to see it then? The pagoda, I mean?"

*"As large as a hammered thumb it showed from the air, sir. Larger, I guess one should acknowledge. It's very large indeed."*

"What's the Bachelor doing now, Jaafar?"

*"Who?"*

"The Asadi. What's he doing? How did you happen to pick him up as a guide? And what in Allah's name made you want to follow him?"

*"He wanted me to come. He emerged from the pagoda only a short time ago, indicating by movements that I should follow. Kretzoi told me—with his hands, you know—that Elegy and you had gone down beneath the floor. Civ Cather, I mean."*

"Go ahead and say 'Elegy,' Jaafar. She's not military, you realize—you can call her anything you and she mutually approve."

Jaafar's voice was dubious: *"Yes, sir."*

"What's the Asadi doing now?"

*"Listening to me talk on the radio. He's two platforms down, almost directly below me. It makes me dizzy to survey such bigness."*

"Didn't it scare you, following him into a cavern this size?"

*"Oh, very much."*

"Then what made you do it?"

Jaafar was silent.

"Was it Elegy?" I asked him.

*"It was Elegy more than it was you, sir,"* said Jaafar forthrightly.

"Touché. You have a decidedly medieval concept of chivalry, Jaafar. You know that, don't you?"

*"I would call it Persian rather than medieval. Even if the naming makes little objective difference in the description."*

"Your prerogative, Jaafar. Be my guest."

Then we both shut up and waited. Elegy was not long in coming. She greeted me with a touch, her hand cold. Neither of us said anything. She preceded me to the first platform and began to climb. It was much harder than coming down: We had to belly our way to each new scaffold and then lift ourselves onto it with our arms. Wearying and time-consuming. It was mortifying to think The Bachelor had bounded up these steps so quickly and easily. But Jaafar—in a clear, chaste tenor—sang ancient Persian ballads to us as we climbed.

*

It was already late afternoon when we got back outside. The Bachelor had accompanied us for a good portion of the ascent, always several platforms above us, until the huri—*his* huri, we supposed—intercepted him near the catacombs' ceiling and apparently directed him by tunnels or passageways unknown to us through the thick central column and out of our lives. There arrived on the surface of the planet, then, only Elegy, Jaafar, and I.

Kretzoi greeted us. As I retrieved my holocamera from the pagoda's stone bier, his glee was such that he spun about in the clearing like a top. Then he ran up the steps and nearly knocked me over attempting to embrace me. Elegy he held against him for a long, quiet time. Finally the four of us retired to the shade of the Wild to recuperate from our ordeal. None of us slept. We were too haunted by events to close our eyes.

It was growing dark by the time we decided to leave. I insisted on piloting, despite my weariness. Beneath the invisible halo of our rotors, we lifted off with gratifying swiftness. I circled the pagoda several times, marveling at the magnificence of the structure. I kept waiting for it to cant its amethyst windows and blink out of existence—but it remained solid and distinct below us.

"You think you could find this place again?" I asked Jaafar.

"As it is now, sir, anyone could find it."

"If the temple does its disappearing act again, I mean?"

"Even then, I'd certainly think. We have the coordinates, you see, and the rain forest here has a most distinctive feel."

"That may be true, Jaafar, but I'd swear I've flown over this very region two dozen times in the last six years without ever having suspected the pagoda's presence. It's preposterous, undoubtedly, but I'm afraid we'll lose it again."

"Governor Eisen, I believe, thinks it too bad we can't lose our probeship hangar in such an effortless way."

Dog-tired, I took us out over the jungle, rechecked my instruments, and put us on a course for Frasierville.

Jaafar said, "I will never forget this place, Dr. Benedict. No one needs to worry that I will forget."

After a while I looked into the passenger compartment and saw Elegy grooming Kretzoi with languid, almost dreamy pensiveness. Kretzoi, to accommodate this methodical combing, kept his head down. I felt pretty sure he was half asleep. The look in Elegy's eyes was blank and unreadable. I wanted to shoot questions at her, dozens of questions, but knew the futility of trying even to gain her attention.

Forty minutes later I looked into the passenger section again.

Her head against the wall, her hands folded in her lap, Elegy was asleep. Kretzoi lay sprawled in front of her like a throw rug.

Jaafar turned to me sympathetically. "Wouldn't you yield the piloting to me, sir? You, too, could—" He gestured.

"No," I said, "thanks. This trip is mine."

"But—"

"It's the last one out of here I ever intend to make."

*

Back in Frasierville, Elegy and Kretzoi safely installed in their original first-floor guest suite in the hospital, and Jaafar God only knows where, I slept for twenty-two straight hours. If I dreamed, I don't remember any of my dreams. Those twenty-two hours, though they may have purged the poisons of sleep deprivation from my system, were otherwise a period in which not a scintilla of my consciousness had an existence anywhere in the universe. For those twenty-two hours I was totally excised from Creation.

Nonexistence, I learned, holds few terrors.

When I awoke, I felt that it had been only two or three minutes since the BenDragon Prime had set down on the polymac of Rain Forest Port. It was dark again, and I was lonely. Nightmares didn't assail me until my eyes were wide open and a melancholy animal hunger was grumbling in my gut. I chose not to feed it. It was impossible to eat with images of both Egan Chaney and the huri catacombs flashing against my mind's eye. For a while I slammed aimlessly about the homey squalor of my living quarters.

Then I put through a telecom to Moses Eisen and asked him if it was too late to visit him. He told me it wasn't.

The walk to his house—past the lamps bordering the rain forest and the silent quonsets arrayed against the fuzzy lights of town—lifted the nightmares from my immediate vision, without letting me forget the reality that had provoked them.

I tried to fix Elegy in my mind's eye: Elegy as she had been in the catacombs, ordering me out of her presence and then kneeling in fierce devotion beside the ungodly thing her father had become. I wanted a strength like that, a strength like Elegy's.

When I arrived at the little peninsula of land from whose tip the Governor's mansion jutted up like a lighthouse beside an ocean of trees, I found the place a conflagration of candles, torches, spots, deck-mounted fluorescents, and ground lamps. Moses had lit up his house like a bonfire. The gallery at the front gleamed amid the intersecting arcs of several colored ground lamps, and the whole place shimmered. This, for Moses, was a fantastic display of opulence and courtesy. He usually let late-night visitors stumble to his door in the dark.

Moses was waiting for me. He looked spic and span in white coveralls and a pale-blue neck scarf. A pair of deck chairs sat in the middle of the verandah facing Frasierville, as if a conference of major import were soon to be held between their occupants. My step faltered. Moses beckoned me forward, and in a moment I climbed to the deck and suspiciously shook his hand.

"How are you, Ben?"

"Good," I mumbled. "Pretty good."

Only when he invited me to sit, and waited for me to compose myself comfortably in the chair, did I understand that he had arranged this entire scene—the lights, the chairs, even the immaculate tastefulness of his attire—out of genuine respect for me. Respect and friendship. My discomfort increased. This was going to be harder than I expected.

"Young Civ Cather was here earlier this afternoon," he said, finally allowing himself to sit.

"How is she?"

"Fine, I'd suppose. Quite subdued and intermittently very grave. She told me about your . . . your *adventure*." The way he spoke the word indicated he meant to imply that Elegy had told him the whole story.

"Kretzoi?" I asked.

"She didn't bring him. I think she feared he wouldn't be welcome here. That isn't the case, but I'm afraid that's what she feared."

"Quarantine," I said reminiscently. Then I laughed a little.

Moses shifted in his chair. "I congratulated her, you understand. I have to congratulate you, too. I *want* to, that is. You've succeeded in something very important, and I'm glad you're back. Very glad."

"Me, too, Moses. Jubilant, in fact."

At that Moses laughed, surprising me. "You hardly sound it. I've never really encountered a jubilation in such a minor key before."

"Call it a realist's jubilation."

Nodding once, Moses granted me my point. Then he put his hands on his knees and gazed toward Frasierville. "You're the only one of the remaining members of the Third Denebolan Expedition, Ben, with whom I was ever able to establish any degree of rapport." He stopped, embarrassed.

"I know that. It served us reasonably well, didn't it?"

"Yes, it did. It does. That's why I wanted to explain to you Glaktik Komm's decision in regard to—"

I cut him off. "Before you explain anything, Moses—owing me no explanations at all, you understand—I have a request to make. A very simple one. A very important one."

Moses waited.

"I'd like to go home," I said.

"Earth?"

"East Africa. Kenya. Nairobi. The National University." The names of these places squeezed my heart, and the ache spread through my chest. "I know some people there, Moses, and if God and Glaktik Komm approve my wishes, they'll still be alive when I get home."

"*People?*" The Governor's face betrayed a touching puzzlement, as if he'd never really considered the possibility that Earth might any longer harbor such an animal.

"Human beings," I said, laughing again. "Latter-day representatives of *Homo sapiens sapiens*. Man the Wise the Wise." I had a sudden vision of Elegy in the catacombs. "I'm speaking generically, you understand."

Moses smiled. "Oh, *those*. Yes, people."

"I've been here a long time, I'm close to deserving a little special consideration, and I'd like you to initiate the personnel procedures approving my early release and my passage home. I ask you to do this out of your friendship for me, Moses, and out of my own awareness that I've nothing else to offer BoskVeld."

Moses's silence was a key to his agitation. Finally, he got up and strolled along the deck to the hooded doorway leading downward into the main living area of his house. He opened the massive door and pushed it inward. I saw some elegant wallpaper, some hardwood wainscoting, and a gleaming brass stair rail descending into light and coziness.

"Come in, Ben. David and little Reba are in bed. Come have a drink with Rebecca and me."

The gesture was almost unprecedented. I gaped at Moses and the open doorway. What would it mean to refuse his hospitality? Not a negation of our friendship, surely. We had survived as friends for many years without ever once attempting to rake through the coals at the bottoms of each other's hearts. Moses—in his quiet, reclusive way—had made commitments much deeper than I ever had. I wasn't one of them, and, in truth, he owed me nothing.

"Moses, I haven't eaten. A drink would undo me. Let's stay on the verandah. This is a very comfortable chair."

The words sounded makeshift, false—but it was a matter of absolute necessity that I say them, afterward fervently hoping that Moses didn't take offense. They were not, after all, a rejection of him, but an affirmation of the remaining possibilities of my life.

"We could get you something to eat, Ben."

"Please, no. I'm going to fast for the next few days, purge my system. Hot water and citric acid." I suddenly realized that this was the truth, not a spur-of-the-moment apologia for my refusal to enter Moses's house. "After that, well—I'll probably ease back into shameless carnivory."

Moses, bless him, laughed. He pulled his door to and rejoined me at the center of the verandah. Standing with his hands in his pockets, he rocked a little on the soles of his feet and stared at the moist, melon-green lights of Frasierville.

"Consider your request approved," he said. "There's a probeship arriving within the week. Young Civ Cather and her primate friend will be aboard. No reason you shouldn't be one of the passengers, too."

I got to my feet, murmuring thanks. My hands went into my pockets in imitation of my friend and superior.

Then I began talking desultorily about the need for an archaeological expedition to the Asadi pagoda. I mentioned that Chiyoko Yoshiba of the Museum of Indigenous Artifacts was probably the most likely person to head up such an expedition. Chiyoko was middle-aged and rather stout, that was all very true, but she had impeccable credentials, surprising stamina, and a skill at reconstruction and classification bordering on wizardry. Middle-aged, had I said? Shoot, she was only a year or two older than I. There was no reason Robards de Feo couldn't find a substitute for her at the Museum and Chiyoko herself immediately undertake the mounting of—

"Wait a minute," Moses put in, touching me. "The huri in the pagoda—beneath it, rather—constitute a possible obstacle to these plans. After Elegy left here this afternoon, I had Farber in Communications send a light-probe message to Kommthor. The message detailed what the two of you encountered in the Wild. It also outlined some of your speculations about the huri/Asadi relationship and its history."

"You've received a reply?" I asked, my heart thudding.

"Farber relayed it to me about an hour before you called."

"What?" I demanded. "What did it say?"

Moses stopped rocking and removed his hand from his right pocket; he still didn't look at me. "That if the huri did indeed once enslave and control the Asadi's intelligent Ur'sadi forebears—" He put his hands on the railing in front of him and grimaced as if trying to dislodge the tie in his left cheek.

"Go on," I urged him impatiently.

"It's obvious, isn't it? Kommthor's afraid the huri may pose a similar threat to humanity. They want the wilderness temple cordoned off and the entrance to the catacombs sealed. There won't be any archaeological expeditions into the Wild. Moreover, Kommthor's considering the desirability and the feasibility of depositing a nuclear device in the huri labyrinth."

I stared at Moses in disbelief. "You're kidding."

"No, I'm not."

"Has Elegy heard about this—this grandiose executive madness?"

"No, she hasn't. And, Ben, it's no more mad than was the quarantining of the astronauts upon their return from extraterrestrial worlds. In the early days of the American space program, that was an eminently sane precautionary measure. Kommthor's decree against archaeological expeditions is precautionary in the same way."

I clomped off three or four meters, then clomped back.

"That's possible, that's very possible—but Kommthor's decision to nuke the huri would be a preemptive measure of the highest, humanity-first arrogance. Preemptive, not precautionary! God, Moses, it's the diction and vocabulary of the Big Lie. Elegy and I don't even know if our reconstructions of huri/Asadi evolution are in *any* way on target. Can we ever know? We're talking about twelve million years of evolution, and we're doing so as finite beings with a limited if occasionally rather breathtaking mental capacity and clairvoyance. I'd kill myself, Moses, if I thought Kommthor had actually annihilated an entire alien species solely on the basis of Elegy's and my unverified speculations. I'd literally kill myself."

"I hope," said Moses wryly, "you're not speaking for Civ Cather, too."

"She does that very well for herself, as you already know. And she wouldn't kill herself—she'd mount a retaliatory strike on Kommthor headquarters, even if she had to muster her own goddamn Martial Arm to do it!"

Moses finally looked at me, spreading his hands in a gesture that clearly meant, *So there you are*.

"She told you about her father?" I asked, changing tacks.

"Yes, she told me about Chaney."

"Everything?"

"I believe so. It wasn't easy for her, but she told me everything."

"Chaney's failed metamorphosis is evidence we're *not* susceptible to the motivational control of the huri, Moses. We're simply not very likely victims of their peculiar brand of parasitism. Chaney himself kept saying we weren't huri 'saviors.' "

"I understand that, Ben. I think even Kommthor understands that. But it may not always be so. Besides, Elegy told me that the huri immobilized you for a period, actually reached into your brain and jammed your own psychomotor equipment. That's *control*, Ben, and it's a frightening thing to contemplate on a planet-wide basis."

"They simply wanted to find out what I was. They cast my statue in order to get a grip on my identity."

"In order to see if you might not serve their purposes better than Chaney did, perhaps. But you were clearly the same sort of creature as Chaney and therefore of no current use to them as a host."

I threw up my hands. "That's exactly what I'm arguing, Moses. The huri pose no danger to us because we're exactly the sort of creature Chaney was. Their experiment with him was a pathetic failure."

"The key word is 'current.' They may not pose any danger to us now, but ultimately—tomorrow or a few thousand years in the future—they may. They may be able to adapt their role of psychic parasitism—or whatever it is—to us, to humanity, even if they still haven't managed to resubjugate the Asadi."

"Is that really what you think, Moses?"

"I don't see how you can rule out the possibility. But all I'm really trying to do is give you a basis for understanding Kommthor's position. What *I* think is immaterial." He looked at me with a strange mixture of sympathy and disapproval. "Do you still want to leave BoskVeld, Ben?"

"Yes—but I may stick around longer than a week."

Moses smiled. "You do that. It would please me—it would really please me—if you did that." He sounded disarmingly sincere.

*

"Where's Kretzoi?" I asked. It had taken me only a few minutes to walk to the hospital from Moses's gaudily spotlit mansion, and Elegy met me at the door to her suite with an affectionate hug but no passion.

"In surgery," she said. She wore loose khaki trousers and a lightweight grey pullover. The room was reproachfully neat, except for the notes, microfiche cards, and other assorted research materials scattered across the top of her dressing table. An expression of scholarly concentration was fading from her face, in just the way that a thumbprint on sunburned flesh invariably fades.

"In surgery?" I echoed her.

"Well, not exactly in surgery. They moved him to preop facilities in the other ground-floor wing. He'll be operated on in the morning."

"What for? I didn't realize anything was wrong with him. Is he suffering from some weird sort of hypoglycemia again?"

"Worse than that."

"What, then, Elegy? What's happening?"

"From the same thing my father was suffering from before

I . . . before I stopped his suffering.'' She motioned me to a chair. "Oh, hell, Ben, we can't undo everything we did to Kretzoi—not without killing him, anyway—but in the morning they're going to take the plastic carapaces off his eyes and remove the alien protozoa from his gut. This last isn't really a surgical procedure; they're going to give him an emulsion that ought to do the trick, but it's a necessary part of the rehabilitative process, I think. Kretzoi's and mine, too.''

"A Komm-galen's going to operate on Kretzoi?"

"Yes, to give him back to himself."

"How did this come about?"

"I made the request of Governor Eisen earlier this afternoon. He put through the papers authorizing the surgery and assigning a Komm-galen to do the work. Everyone assures me she's very good. I've talked to her. She's not appalled to have a 'monkey' under her hands. I trust her.''

"What about Kretzoi?"

"I asked him if he wanted this done, and he signaled, *Yes, of course*—as if he'd been patiently enduring his bondage until the day I came around and recognized it for what it was. We wept, Ben. Both of us together, even though he hasn't any tears to punctuate his emotions.''

I nodded, struck by the rightness of the thing. "What about Jaafar? Do you know what he's doing?"

"Governor Eisen okayed a transfer to another GK colony world—to get him out from under the gun of harassment in the barracks."

"Jaafar wants to go?"

"I believe so. What would keep him here?"

"You," I said carefully.

Elegy laughed. "I'm leaving when the next probeship comes in. With Kretzoi. Dar es Salaam, and then back to the Gombe Stream Reserve."

I told her the details of the conversation I had just had with Moses. Then we talked a good long time. Just talked. We were no longer lovers. That was the way we both wanted it, and that was the way it was.

\*

Elegy, Kretzoi, and I remained in Frasierville another month. We spent our time—at least Elegy and I did—drafting, manuscribing, and preparing for light-probe transmission lengthy rebuttals to Kommthor's tentative proposal to set off a nuclear device in the catacombs beneath the Asadi pagoda. We urged continued protection for the Asadi and advised the creation of an official instrumentality to preserve the pagoda itself. Our efforts didn't lift the military cordon that had been thrown about that building, but they played a large part in scuttling Glaktik Komm's plans to bomb the huri back to the stone age. They also gave us a degree of peace of mind.

*Your descendants may live to curse your name*, people have said.

That's a possibility I'm able to live with. Kommthor's agents have had the same chances to draft, manuscribe, and transmit their arguments as Elegy and I have, and opting to annihilate the huri remains within humanity's power until such time as we recognize their essential harmlessness or find ourselves performing their ultrasonic commands utterly without resistance. In my view, it's sanity versus melodrama—but the fact that I could be wrong is what keeps the music so sprightly and the dance so hazardously sweet.

Here in Nairobi, where I've lived since returning to Earth, I've just married a woman whose name, age, and description I don't intend to set down here. Elegy has met her, and approves. Next week the three of us, along with a mixed contingent from the National University and the Goodall-Fossey College of Primate Ethology, are going to Lake Turkana on a three-day fossil hunt. The lake shore, especially the narrow spit called Koobi Fora, has been worked to death over the last century or so, but sunset on the lake still has the power to translate a human witness better than four million years into the past of the species, and the sunset is one of the reasons we're going. I relish the prospect of staring into it with my new wife's hand in mine.

And, in the strange, doubtful hour before dawn, she and I will lie together anticipating sunrise. It's not so spectacular an event as sunset, perhaps, but it's just as dependable, and I've come to appreciate that quality in nature as well as in my fellows.